Thunder & Flare
Cat Porter ©2023
Wildflower Ink, LLC

Editor
Jennifer Roberts-Hall

Developmental Editor
Christina Trevaskis
BookMatchmaker

Cover Designer
Najla Qamber
Qamber Designs & Media

Very special thanks to Alison, Larri, Nancy, Natalie, and Rachel

All rights reserved.

No part of this book may be used, reproduced or transmitted in any form or by any means, electronic or mechanical, including photocopying, recording, or by any information storage and retrieval system without the written permission of the author, except for the use of brief quotations in critical articles or a book review.

This book is a work of fiction. Names, nicknames, logos, and symbols of motorcycle clubs, gangs, and rock bands are not to be mistaken for real motorcycle clubs, gangs, and rock bands. Names, characters, places, and incidents either are products of the author's imagination or are used fictitiously. Any resemblance to actual persons, living or dead, events, or locales is entirely coincidental. The author acknowledges the trademarked status and trademark owners of various products and locales referenced in this work of fiction. The use of these trademarks is not authorized, associated with, or sponsored by the trademark owners.

THUNDER & FLARE

THE LOCK&KEY MC ROMANCE SERIES
BOOK 10

CAT PORTER

CONTENTS

CHAPTER 1
TRICK

SOUTH DAKOTA WINTERS can feel like forever; they are long, dense. Often mercurial.

These first warm days of spring, the sun comes out strong and blares over us, daring us to ditch our hats and scarves and sweaters and find our short-sleeved T-shirts, drive with the windows open, and ride our sweet bikes again. A blessing, a sign, a feeling of good things to come. New beginnings, and hell yeah, resurrection.

Maybe. Maybe for me.

But this morning was something totally different.

Wind and a spark in a darkened, churning morning sky. I should have been on the road for Kansas City already, but I needed to wait and see how this storm would play itself out. Would it linger, gather strength slowly, and burst on us here in Meager? Or would it lumber off to another corner of the Black Hills?

Maybe this was another kind of sign.

This run would be my first business trip on my own for Eagle Wings Repair and Custom Detailing. Lock had put his trust in me to go take a look at two vintage muscle cars we'd gotten a lead on in Kansas City and grab them if I thought they were a solid buy and if I thought they had potential.

I grinned to myself as I checked the straps on my pack for the tenth time. This was a big step for me. A big deal because my input was not only being valued but trusted. I wasn't the fix-it guy anymore; the boy who'd started out at Wreck's Repair what felt like a century ago. I'd got to work side by side with Wreck and all the men from the time I was sixteen when I'd lost everything. A brutal time, but with the club I'd gained so much.

Yet those raw wounds hadn't healed. I'd sealed them over.

A while back, it'd been hard giving up on one of my dreams, and even though it wasn't like me to quit, I did it, I had to. I forced myself to ignore the ache that was still there spiraling in that hollow inside my chest. For the past two years, my days had been chock full of working on cars, working for the good of the club, partying when I was up for it, but nothing more. Not really.

No matter. Everything I'd learned from my years under Wreck, all the discipline he'd taught me, all the freedom he'd given me, as well as my Uncle Willy's love and support, and my own will to survive, had brought me here to this moment.

This new road.

And there I'd thought yesterday's warmth and sunshine was a good omen for today's long run. I blew out a huff of air. The sky seemed to darken all over again. Fucking mercurial as ever.

"You ready?" A hand clapped on my back. Boner, my Sergeant at Arms.

"I'm ready." I met his heavy gaze. "And I know what you're going to say."

His green eyes narrowed. "Oh yeah, what's that?"

"You're going to be in Smoking Guns territory…"

He slanted his head. "That's right, Trick. I got to say it. I know it's a big city, but you and Dawes got to be careful. You're going to be alone out there. Avoid their part of town, avoid their bars, their playgrounds, whatever the hell it is. Of course, no matter where you are, you never know who you could run into."

"We'll be careful. It's two days. We'll be fine."

He pressed his lips together. One of the most fearless men I'd ever known was worried. "Yeah. You'll be fine."

Thunder grumbled in the distance, interrupting our conversation. Three long, thin bolts of lightning crackled north of us and Boner and I took in the sight. We'd probably witnessed this sort of sky show a thousand times or more, but still, it was arresting.

The sounds and visuals of a storm didn't make me anxious, not like they used to make my sister. Brie would shout, *"Oh my gosh! Oh my gosh!"* and run to whoever was closest to her, mostly to Ma, sometimes to me, and we'd hug her and say, "It's okay, B. Mother Nature is giving us a show. Enjoy the dazzle."

Sure was dazzling. More lightning bolts charged and danced in the distance on a pulse. Light synced to music but only the sky gods could comprehend their rhythm. Even so, I could feel their mysterious beat inside me. A force greater than us, beyond mere humans. This kept you humble, didn't it? Curious. Gave you that nudge of *wow*?

The thick clouds now drifted northwest, taking the darkness with them. Thunder boomed once more, but this time farther away. Things turn on a dime out here.

Boner put a hand on my saddle. "You should be able to take off soon, huh?"

"Think so."

"Stay in touch." Boner clapped me on the back and stalked back into the clubhouse.

Maybe all this dazzle from the heavens was a good sign. A rumble of aggressive energy ready to unleash itself like these clouds twisting and unfurling in the distance. But would they unleash devilish twisters? I'd find out soon enough.

My skin prickled with an odd sensation as I took in the dynamism working itself out beyond Meager. Puffs of bleary white, grayish blues and yellows, seeped over the sky. Movement that blustered and battled. My spine straightened. Something powerful just beyond. Was it something new?

I zipped up my leather jacket and got my gloves out. Dawes came up alongside me. "Ready, bro?"

My lips tipped up. "Hell yeah."

CHAPTER 2
NICOLE

AS THE WHISKEY rolled down my throat at ten thirty in the morning, I had no idea that in less than an hour my life as I knew it would be over in a shower of glass, threats, and diamonds.

Taking in a breath, I held my gaze in the mirror behind the bar in my parents' living room. No more tears. Not one more for that man. I poured myself another. Not one more for myself either. The time was now for action.

"Honey, you're back so soon?" My mother stood at the entrance to the living room. "Did you find what you were looking for?"

"No, and yes." I raised my glass and drank.

I'd found what I'd been ignoring and denying and pushing away for so long. Ugly reality. The truth behind the curtain. This morning, I'd looked it square in the face.

I'd lied and told Mom I'd gone shopping, but I'd gone to see my estranged husband at our house first thing this morning before he left for the office. On purpose, because he hated being late, so the conversation would be quick and to the point, and I would then turn around and leave.

I wanted to tell him to stop. Stop sending me flowers, stop

making promises. But when I got there, the taxi waiting for me at the curb, he wasn't on a phone call, sipping coffee as he expertly tied his tie in the big living room mirror, admiring himself as he often did.

No.

I found Logan with two women in what had once been our bed. I'd heard them first. The moans, the grunts. I'd made the choice to track stealthily down that hallway and see it with my own eyes. I needed to see it myself. A spectacle. Undeniable truth, wasn't it? I needed that shock to my system. I did. I saw it and then I turned around and left as quietly as I'd come in.

Logan hadn't once sent me flowers in the whole year we'd been separated and living apart. But yesterday he had, along with a note full of earnest promises. Why now? Judging from what I witnessed at our house, he obviously wasn't pining for me.

Pouring another glass, my gaze went to the reflection in the mirror of the large framed family photo that hung over the fireplace. I was eleven at the time, and Jackson and I were dressed in our Sunday best, me on Daddy's side and him on Mom's, perfectly staged by the photographer. The four of us with huge say-cheese grins on our faces. Mom in a baby blue Chanel suit wearing pumps, her long legs perfectly pressed together, pearls at her neck and diamonds in her ears, a gracious smile on her face. Jackie O who?

Daddy, the successful gentleman in a business suit and tie. The fine upstanding citizen, husband, and father. Not the constantly irritated man of the last few years. The one who drank too much at every meal, who made demands, who snapped at you, insisted, who had to always be in charge, always have the last word. Who grabbed the wheel—

I gulped at the liquor.

"Isn't it a little early for whiskey?" Frowning at me, my mother crossed her arms, and the Tiffany diamond necklace she wore, which dad had given her years ago for their anniversary, glinted in the morning sun.

"Not today." I wiped at my lips.

"What's wrong?"

"I'm finally seeing things very clearly, so that's worth a drink of Dad's favorite five hundred-dollar whiskey." I knocked back more booze and it slid down my throat with greater ease. I'd never been interested in drinking it before. Dad kept it for special occasions only. For him and Jackson. Warmth zipped through my insides as I ran my tongue along my teeth. It was good; it was perfection.

"Is this about Logan? Nicole, you need to—"

I always "needed" to do things, and I always did them. But what did I need? What did I want?

"Isn't it a little early for all those diamonds?" I cut her off as I poured myself a bit more. "What's going on?"

"I'm trying to pack for Palm Springs."

"You always leave packing to the last minute. Isn't your plane first thing in the morning?"

"I can't decide what to bring."

"Mmm." I swished the liquor in the crystal tumbler engraved with Daddy's initials. "Palm Springs with Mr. McLeod. Very romantic."

She sent me a cold look. Had my tone been sarcastic? *Oops.*

"Buttercup, Daddy died a year ago. There's nothing wrong with me meeting a new man. I like companionship. I don't want to be alone. Never have, never will."

"Okay." I sipped at my liquor.

"Don't you want me to be happy?"

"Of course I do."

"Just like I want you to be happy, too. You should patch things up with Logan."

I let out a short laugh and whiskey spewed from my lips. "I got that separation for a reason."

"I realize that, but maybe it's time to forgive and let that go?

He offered to go to counseling, didn't he? Did you make the appointment?" Smiling, she moved to the corner table where her housekeeper had placed that poisonous vase of red roses Logan had sent me yesterday along with a note dripping with (facetious) yearning and hope and promises. "Come on, honey. He's trying. Don't be so stubborn."

I gripped the crystal glass tighter. "Was the counseling your idea? Because it sure isn't his style."

"What does it matter?" She moved the roses to the coffee table in the center of the room. "He's a good man, and good men are so hard to find. Go back to him, go back to your home. If you get pregnant, everything will turn around. I know it will."

"Wow. Are you really using *that* to push me back to him?" I drained my glass.

"Push you? What a thing to say. I'm only pointing out the obvious. We're a family. You and Logan are a family."

"Ah. And we should behave like one, look like one to the outside world, right?" The glass slipped out of my hand and thudded on the counter. "Especially to the board. Is that what all this is about? The board meeting? The vote? Are you all in on this together?"

"Honey. Think about it. We can't lose control of the company. Your father and Logan's father founded it, made it the powerhouse it is today, and now that they're gone, Logan and Jackson deserve to carry on. We need to show a united front. A harmonious united front. Can't you understand that?"

My back shot up. "I understand very well. If Logan and I are still on the road to divorce, that would look very unharmonious. That would mean our family was at odds, that I am now a wild card, that I could possibly vote differently from him, from Jackson, and you. But mostly it signals that Logan, the current CFO, can't be trusted because the whole town and the whole company know why we split up, and they've certainly heard rumors of Jackson's naughty self-indulgent behavior. No, not good for Dumont Jameson Oilfield Technologies."

Mom let out a tiny exhale of exasperation. "Are you going to let all that go up in smoke on a whim?"

"A whim? You mean my whim? What about Jackson's numerous whims and sour reputation? What about Logan's whims?" I brought the glass to my lips once more.

Last year I'd left Logan because I found out that he'd been sleeping with a woman he'd met at a strip club. *"Come on, she's just a stripper!"* he'd declared. As if professional strippers didn't count as ordinary women—they existed for one reason only. Were they a different species of human?

Then I opened my eyes a little wider and realized that my husband had been sleeping with *a lot* of other women. That was when I took action. I'd hired a lawyer and filed for a separation, opened a separate bank account, and left the house. A move that was met with uproar by him and my family.

Mom took the glass out of my hand. "This is so unlike you."

It was, wasn't it? I was always the good girl, the quiet girl, agreeable to everything. No one ever had to worry about Nicole, worry about her jumping the lines, hopping over the boundaries, or overdoing…anything.

Mom rearranged my messy locks of blonde hair, the color I'd inherited from her, smoothing my hair away from my face like she'd always done since I was a little girl. "We've known Logan and his family for years and years." Her tone had defrosted, mellowed like a marshmallow melting over a flame. She was pulling out all the stops. "You two are perfect together, Butter-cup. Yes, he made a mistake. What man doesn't at some point?"

"Did Daddy make a mistake too?"

Stiffening, she ignored me. "Your husband deserves a second chance from you, and now is the time for you to give him that. Don't drag this separation out anymore. You made your point. Now, it's time to get on with your life."

"Get on with my life?" A dry laugh sputtered from my lips. Getting on with my life meant going back to a husband I didn't love and who didn't love me? A relationship that wasn't much of anything but a contract on paper? Had I ever loved Logan? Had he loved me? I doubted it.

There had to be more to life for me, so how would I "get on with it?" No, there had to be more, something else. Or maybe *someone* completely different. Wow, there was a thought. Sure, why not?

Glancing at the ornate antique Italian mirror over the bar, Mom adjusted the large diamond solitaire earring on her earlobe. "Nicole, it's time for you to make a move with Logan."

"Is that a Cindy strategy?"

"Don't talk to me like that." Her suddenly sharp voice had me flinching. "You need to rethink the attitude."

"I need to rethink everything."

"Oh Lord, you have such a great life. Unlike some of us, you were born and raised with a silver spoon in your mouth."

"You put it there."

Her eyes gleamed, a harsh gleam, cold and hard. "Damn right, I did. Don't you dare be ungrateful. You have no idea what it's like out there without that silver spoon."

"You're right, I don't."

"Oh, sweetie." A slight smile pushed at her lips as she touched my arm. "Come help me figure out what I should take on my trip. I'm so excited about finally seeing Palm Springs. You know how I've always wanted to go."

Cindy strategy had certainly worked wonders on Larry McLeod. After weeks of turning him down, she'd finally agreed to a second dinner and now, barely a month later, they were taking off on a lavish getaway vacation together.

Cindy's still got it. Do I? Wait—did I ever?

Leaving the empty tumbler on the marble bar, I followed Mom through the house and up the stairs to her bedroom suite. The room looked like robbers had rifled through her closets. Dresses and blouses and trousers littered the bed, sandals and slingbacks were tossed on the floor in a corner.

She cleared her throat as she swiped through a pile of brand-new bathing suits, their tags still attached, on the bed. "You know, your brother has a lot riding on this board re-election. I wish that housing project he got himself tangled up in would finally get off the ground. It's been a long haul, and he deserves some good news for all the effort and money he's put in."

"You mean my money too, don't you?"

"I know you helped him, baby, and that was wonderful. Daddy was proud of you." She shot me a grin as she opened her large, polished wood jewelry box on her dresser.

"Would Daddy also be proud of me for paying off Jackson's mistress so she could go to California and have an abortion and keep her mouth shut about it all?"

"Thank God that's over."

"It's not over. She never went to California. She's decided to have the baby."

"What?"

"He didn't tell you? She demanded a mighty big hunk of cash from him to keep quiet and stay comfy."

"Oh no…"

"And did he tell you she only just turned eighteen last week?"

A hand flew to her face. "Oh my Lord. If that ever gets out!"

"I don't think that would play very well with the company's conservative board members, do you? If they find out by the vote next month, Jackson will be out as CEO and he knows it. Not to mention, he could get arrested. And then there's Melissa and the kids, of course." I peered into the full jewelry box and fingered a thick gold chain. "Melissa must know something, don't you think? Last Christmas, Jackson went on that trip to Vegas, supposedly alone on business. Come on. I'm sure he had Jolene with him if not—"

"Melissa knows what side her bread is buttered on, and she certainly enjoys her butter." Mom plucked rings from her jewelry box. "As for your brother, we all make mistakes. Part of being in a family is being supportive of each other in the ups and the downs, not critical." She shot me a pointed glance as she tried on a sapphire ring.

Jackson certainly had her support. Mine and Logan's, too. It was the one thing I felt I didn't have from anyone. I only got patted on the head and told to smile and keep on walking or do as I was told. And if I dared not toe the party line, like now with my wanting a divorce? I was incessantly criticized.

The liquor sloshed in my stomach. "Just a note, my inheritance is being drained in its support of Jackson and all his many ups and downs."

"You have to help your brother. His money is tied up in that damned housing project. So many expenses he didn't expect. But dammit, I didn't realize this girl was so young."

"It's been going on for over a year, so…"

"Oh, stop." She raised her hands in the air.

"He's being played. What teenage girl would want to keep her older married lover's baby? Wouldn't she just want to move on to her next sugar daddy?"

"Nicole! You have to pay her the money or we'll all be dragged through the mud and Jackson will lose the board's confidence. That can't happen. Everything your father left me is tied up in the company and this house. I just have my dividends every month."

Daddy had been well aware of Mom's spendy ways, and he'd provided for her in an economical fashion in his will, to her outrage.

"Don't worry, the money for Jolene is in the works. I already set the funds in motion at the bank."

"Wonderful. What a relief." She turned to her jewelry box and put back the sapphire ring. "Why can't I find that ring?"

"Which ring?"

"The amethyst with the gold filigree? I haven't worn it in such a long time. I took it out the other day, and I put it right here next to my perfume so I could clean it. Where did my glasses go…." Her gaze darted around the room.

"I'll take a look." I went through the jewelry box, lifting the small square compartments. I slid my fingers into the small pouches and slits lining the sides of the box. In one pouch, my fingers curled around the tiny heart locket which had been mine as a young girl, as well as small gold baby bracelets engraved with flowers that had also been mine. In the next pouch, my fingers grazed a rough surface, not smooth gold. Leather? Beads? I grabbed it and took it out.

Another baby bracelet, but this one wasn't gold. Tiny red beads on a worn piece of leather. I'd seen this before a very long time ago, and I'd asked Mom about it. All she'd said was that it was a childhood souvenir from South Dakota where she grew up. A South Dakota she never talked about.

I knew my mother had been married before. She'd married as a teenager and had a son, Richie, who she'd left behind in Rapid City when she came out to Oklahoma to marry Dad. Richie had just gotten home from Vietnam back then. Could this baby bracelet have been his?

She never talked about Richie, and we'd never met him. I'd always been fascinated by him, and I fantasized about meeting my eldest brother one day. I'd always hoped that Mom would take me to South Dakota to show me where she grew up, and then I'd finally meet him, meet her family if there was anyone left out there, but she never had. She never spoke about her parents or anyone back in South Dakota. And then, when I was ten years old, we'd found out Richie had been killed in a bar fight, and I'd had to let go of that dream forever. Something had crumpled inside me.

Dipping my finger in a wider satin pocket, a stiff paper's edge scraped my fingertip. An old photograph, a square one in black and white. My lips tipped up. I loved this photo. I hadn't seen it in a long time.

A handsome and very serious young Richie in a combat uniform stared at me. *1971* was printed along the edge. Richie looked like Mom. Did I look like him? I glanced up at the mirror in front of me. Mom had once told me that I had the same dark blue eyes Richie had, her eyes. I'd liked knowing that. It felt important. Significant. It was a connection.

Behind me, Mom yanked off the dress she wore and slid on another one in a busy floral pattern, adjusting it over her slim frame. "What do you think? Is all this green too much?"

"It looks good on you." My mother knew how to shop. She was a pro at it, and she always looked her best. This weekend away with the new man? She had to be on the top of her game.

"You didn't find the ring?"

"Not yet." I continued my jewelry box exploration, fingering that wide slot again, and found a yellowed newspaper clipping. Carefully unfolding it, I scanned the headline. The murder of a brother and sister from Meager, South Dakota. I read the article.

"Law enforcement officials believe that the local motorcycle club, the One-Eyed Jacks, may have been involved in drug deals with underworld crime figures that led to this horrible tragedy for a beloved local family. The motorcycle club is under suspicion for involvement in criminal activity that may have led to the killings of local siblings, Isadora Dillon and Leo Dillon, an alleged methamphetamines dealer."

A large photo bordered the bottom—a group of angry young bearded bikers on their motorcycles arguing with cops. The biker in the front had been circled with a blue pen. He faced the photographer, dark hair long and wild, his lips a snarl, his hand a fist. My heart skipped a beat. It was Richie.

The subtitle to the photo read: *"The Road Captain of the One-Eyed Jacks, "Wreck" Tallin, after being interviewed by law enforcement at the Meager PD.*

Richie had become a biker outlaw? My pulse raced. Mom had never *ever* mentioned that, but obviously, she knew. Had a friend of hers back in South Dakota sent this to her? I skimmed the article. Meth making, rival drug dealers, underworld crime lords…*holy shit.* I folded up the article as Mom went into her bathroom, closing the door.

Were there other things she'd hidden in here? I quickly went through the other wide pocket in the jewelry box. My fingers brushed over the glossy surface of another photograph and I took it out. A faded square of Kodachrome. My mother, a young, glamorous beauty, smiled confidently at the camera as she leaned against a magnificent horse. In her arms she held a little boy, who was somewhere between a baby and a toddler. A handsome, rugged Native American man, wearing a rodeo outfit and a cowboy hat, had his arm tightly around her. My mouth dried.

They looked like…a family. My heart thudded loudly in my chest. The little beaded bracelet was around the baby boy's wrist.

"Did you find the ring?" Mom's voice came up behind me.

"I found this." I held up the photograph, and her face blanched, she stilled. Had the whiskey emboldened me? *How refreshing.* Confrontations were not my strong suit, but something roared in my soul, propelling me forward. "Who is this?"

Her mouth tensed, and an eyebrow lifted. "It's me."

"You in another life, another world. Who are they? Who's this man? This little boy can't be Richie. Richie wasn't Native American, and the—"

Her hand swatted at the photo, but I pulled it away. Her eyes flashed at me. "You have no right going through my private things."

"Did you have another family back in South Dakota?"

She took in a tight breath. "I had another baby when Richie was in Vietnam. With him." She pointed at the cowboy in the old photo. "He was a rodeo star, and I had a huge crush on him."

"You cheated on Richie's dad?"

"Obviously, you've never been swept away by a passion greater than yourself." Her voice positively seethed, washing over me like ice cold searing acid.

"No. No, I haven't."

"After it happens to you, then come talk to me." Clenching her jaw, she shuffled through a pile of blouses, throwing them to the side of the bed.

I glanced at the photo again. All these years along with the beaded bracelet it had laid forgotten and unseen, dormant for decades in its jewelry box tomb alongside gold, pearls, gemstones, and diamonds.

"Is that all you have to say about them?"

"What are you asking me, Nicole?" she snapped.

"What about this little boy? Your little boy? Where is he? Is he still alive?"

"We didn't stay in touch." She went back to her pile of clothing.

"Mom?"

"Don't you go pointing fingers at me, young lady. You have no idea what it was like for me back then in that town. When I met your dad it was like a whole new world opened up for me." She moved closer, her voice a simmering whisper. "I couldn't tell him I had an illegitimate child with an Indian. He would have run the other way." She went to the jewelry box, flicking at bracelets and gold chains.

"But the boy…"

"His daddy took him to live with their family on their reservation, which was the best thing for everyone." A slight smile broke over her lips. "And I came here to marry your daddy."

"Were you already pregnant with Jackson when you married Daddy?"

"Enough!" She slammed the jewelry box closed. "Your father and I were very much in love, and I was thrilled I'd finally met the man of my dreams." She loosened her shoulders. "Honey, your daddy and I had a wonderful life together, and I miss him very much." *She declares as she packs for a romantic getaway with her latest boyfriend.* Her face tightened as if she'd read my mind. "And he'd still be here if only you had—"

My blood simmered, my fingers curling around the photo and the newspaper clipping. "What about your baby boy, Mother? Do you miss him too?"

She charged toward me. "You listen here. When I come back from Palm Springs, I do not want to see you in this house."

"You're kicking me out?"

"You've had enough time to lick your wounds. You need to go back to your husband, where you belong."

"I don't belong with Logan. I don't belong anywhere!" My pulse pounded in my neck, in my gut, in my soul. "What was his name, Mom? The little boy, your other son? What's his name?"

Her chin lifted. Her eyes seemed to darken, and in them I saw—*How dare you ask? How dare you refer to him? How dare you rip open the secret I'd buried so successfully years ago?*

Jackson burst into the room like a superhero on a mission, a desperate one. "There you are!"

Thunder boomed in the distance and rolled in closer and closer. Louder and louder. An unusual foreign symphony of metallic rumbling and roar. I rushed to the window.

"Get away from there, dammit!" shouted Jackson. "Don't let them see you!"

I blinked at the sight of tens of men on motorcycles approaching our property like ants swarming. "What are all these bikers doing here?"

"Honey, what's going on? What's wrong?" Mom gripped Jackson's arm.

He pointed at her throat. "I need that diamond necklace."

CHAPTER 3

NICOLE

MY BROTHER FISTED the diamond necklace, his face reddening. Was triumph coursing through him or good ol' panic?

"Mom, you're just giving it to him?"

"He needs our help. Obviously, it's serious."

"It's always serious, and we're always helping him."

Jackson ignored us, his rabid attention on the jewelry box. "Aren't there matching earrings? Where are they? Isn't there something else? Where's that cocktail ring with the—"

"Jackson, honey, are you in trouble again?" Mom's voice had considerably softened.

"Where are the earrings?" he demanded. "And those pearls with the—"

"Jackson, please. What's wrong? What happened?" Mom touched his arm.

"There's no time for chit-chat!" He grabbed the jewelry box, lifting it high like some pirate having snatched a treasure chest, and emptied its contents onto the king-sized bed. A heap of glittering baubles.

"Jackson!" Mom yelped as he stuffed rings and earrings and bracelets and necklaces into his pockets.

"How much do you owe this time?" I said.

"Fuck! This isn't enough!"

"My necklace alone is worth over fifty thousand!" Mom exclaimed.

"How much do you owe Mr. Rooney this time?" I asked.

"It's not Rooney. That asshole went and hired a biker gang to bounty hunt me, would you believe it?"

"I'd believe anything after what you've put us through."

"What are you talking about?" Mom's face was absolutely pale and stricken.

"Your son has owed money—gambling debts—to this Mr. Rooney, a big player in our parts. Last year I bailed him out of a serious debt—around eighty thousand dollars. And he promised he'd mend his ways. Obviously, he didn't."

"I thought it was just that woman who was blackmailing you," said Mom.

"Keep up, Mom. She's a *girl*, not a woman," I volleyed.

She ignored me. "There's gambling too? Oh, honey…"

Jackson clenched his jaw. "Mom, I—"

"Daddy knew how to play a good hand of poker," I said. "But he also knew when to walk away from the table. You never learned how to do either."

"I need you both now more than ever," he said. "I need those earrings and the cash you keep in the safe. You always keep cash here at home. If I can offer them this for now at least…"

"You're going to give Mom's jewelry to a gang? Won't they want only cash?"

"This is all I've got right now!"

"It's not even yours!" I shot back.

His hand flew at me, and a sting exploded across my cheek. Gasping, I stumbled back.

The roar of bike engines swarmed around the house. Louder, harsher. Taunting. "Jackson! Where are you? Come out, come out wherever you are! Come on, Jackson, come out and play!" A snide, deep male voice rose from the front lawn, and I froze. We all froze.

"I have cash in the safe I can give you," said Mom.

"How much is it this time, Jackson?" I rubbed at my sore cheek.

"About two hundred thousand give or take."

"Oh, Lord!" Mom's hands flew to her mouth.

He adjusted his shoulders and leveled his hard gaze at us. "I am taking steps. I'm selling my house and moving in here."

"What are you talking about?" Mom's eyes flared.

"You're a widow. You don't need all this space now."

Mom's mouth fell open. Fury. "This is my house."

Ignoring her, he shoved a finger in my face. "And you're going back to your husband."

Crack crack boom crack

The windows exploded. A scream left my throat as I threw myself on the floor, tucking my head to my chest, my hands protecting my head. A storm of cut glass rained over us. A shower of diamonds.

Glass and plaster and bullets popped and cracked in the air. Dust and acrid smoke. My mother's muffled cries rose in the distance. A thick gold bracelet splattered onto the carpet by my face, nesting in glass shards.

My lungs constricted. A sudden *woosh* of air from the broken windows slapped my skin.

"Was that some kind of drive-by shooting?" Mom screeched.

"They've come for him, Mom!" I gritted out. "For the money."

"Jackson Dumont, where are you?" A husky male voice rose from inside our house. "You missed our meeting, so we've come to you." Clomping steps drew closer and closer as my heart pounded harder and harder.

I raised myself up to see four big, burly, bearded men wearing jeans and leather chaps filling the doorway of my parents' bedroom.

The older one, his dark hair streaked with gray, glanced at me, licking his full bottom lip. A small grinning skeleton holding two smoking guns was stitched on the front of his leather jacket with the word PRESIDENT above it.

"What the hell are you doing here?" said Jackson, wiping at his shirt front.

"Rooney told us you were a slippery dick—his words. I decided to come to you."

"Rooney had no right to sell you my debt."

"Pay the fuck up and shut it or we're going to shut your trap for you." The president biker with the most patches on his leather jacket approached me. The name "Dog" was also on the patch.

"You the wifey?"

My head shook. My lips parted. No words came out.

"She's not my wife. She's…"

"The bitch on the side, huh? All right. Fucking long ride to get here. I'm aching for some entertainment, and you are a pretty thing," he said on a chuckle. A thick hand went to my waist and squeezed. "For all my troubles you owe me some extra, Dumont."

"How about gas money?" slid out of my lips.

Dog's eyes flared at me and he let out a loud laugh. "Your girlfriend's funny, huh?"

"She's my sister."

Dog grinned. A wolf savoring a new flavor. "All in the family then. Even sweeter." He licked the side of my face, and my body jolted in his grip. His men watched without any reaction. He shoved me back on the bed and eyed my brother. "You lied to me, fucker. Had to come out here myself to make you under-stand how important this is."

"I get how important this is. That's why I'm here. To get you—"

The biker spread my legs with his knee, and my heart stut-tered. Leaning over me, he planted his two hands into the mattress on either side of my head. The smell of leather and gasoline, coffee infiltrated my senses. His face met mine and he kissed me, his taste sour, his tongue driving through my mouth. My stomach twisted as nausea flew up my throat.

I pushed against his broad chest but it was no use. Laughing, he released me, a hand trailing down my torso to between my legs where his fingers groped me. I froze. Everything froze. He turned his gaze to Jackson. "You feeling me now, Mr. Dumont?" He spit out the final T.

"Yeah. Yeah, I feel you," Jackson replied.

Dog pushed up off me. "So—what you got for me?" His fierce gaze ate up the jewelry strewn on the bed. "Uh-uh. Cash only, Mr. D. There a safe in this palace? That why you came here, to Mommy's?"

"No, no safe."

"Don't waste my fucking time."

"I have a safe no one knows about," Mom declared, and all eyes shot to her. "There's cash in there."

"Lead the way, darlin'. Let's see how much you got." The president tilted his head at one of his men, who grabbed Mom by the arm and shuffled her out of the room. The safe was in the dining room behind a sterile landscape painting of oil wells on a dusty plain.

"Just please don't hurt us," my mother's voice echoed down the hallway.

Jackson raised a finger and pointed it at me. "She has cash, too."

Everyone's gaze shot to me, and I blinked. My face heated, my breath cut. I gripped the bedding, and the familiar thin edge of the square Kodachrome photo scraped my hand as I sat up.

"What a piece of shit you are. You came crawling to your women to bail you out, didn't you?" The president got in Jackson's face, and my brother flinched. "You didn't think we'd come for you? You were wrong, asshole. Way the fuck wrong." He raised his chin at one of his compadres, and the overweight one who sported a very long black beard grabbed Jackson and dragged him into the bathroom.

"No! You can't do this to me! Stop! Get off me!" yelled Jackson.

As everyone's attention was trained on the bathroom, I slid the photo into my back jeans pocket. Glancing around me quickly at the debris on the beige bedspread, I spotted the little beaded bracelet on a pile of gold chains and the photo of Richie, and on the other side of me, the yellowed newspaper article. Chewing on my lip, I grabbed them all like a starving squirrel having found precious acorns at long last and shoved them in my pockets.

Digging a hand in my hair, Dog jerked my head back to face him. "I don't know how you put up with his shit, baby. Where I come from, you care about family. You're loyal."

"Huh. Must be nice."

He stared at me wide-eyed and burst into laughter again.

Jackson was only ever loyal to himself. Our mother was the same way, only she was much better at finessing.

"Please, no!" my mother cried out from another part of the house. "Please, not my boy!"

I shoved at Dog's chest. "I have money in the bank. I've paid his debts before."

His head jerked back. "Oh yeah? You got two hundred fifty K handy?"

I had the cash ready to pay off Jackson's pregnant girlfriend, Jolene. She was expecting it today. But this debt was far more important to pay and far more dangerous to leave unpaid. Still, Jackson would be in the hole, but that was his fault, his problem.

I swallowed hard. "He said it was two hundred."

"Interest is a bitch, huh? Especially when you gotta make house calls across state lines." Dog gripped my jaw. "I am owed big time."

"Fine," I said. "Two hundred fifty it is. I can get it for you."

"Oh yeah? If you're lying to me, your pretty momma is gonna pay the price. One finger at a time."

"I'm not lying."

"Huh." He let go of me and rubbed his hands together. "This seems like a real nice house. Me and my crew could make ourselves real comfy here. Take whatever we need. Whenever we want. You and your momma know how to cook? 'Cause we get real hungry."

I held his leering gaze and forced myself to speak. "I want this over with just like you do."

"I don't know, I kinda like this idea of the plush life for a while." His finger went to the edge of my blouse and pulled on the fabric until my bra was visible. "Yeah, you know, take a load off…" He let out a sickening laugh.

"I'll give you the money today and you leave my mother and her house out of it. Promise me."

He made a face. He was about to break out into a laugh. "Are we pinky swearing?"

"You rode all the way out here for that cash. You want it or not?"

"Bitch, it's owed to me."

"Then I'm all you got. You aren't going to get anything out of Jackson. He doesn't have the money to pay you, and I think you know that. And my mother doesn't have that much cash in the house. But I have the money. I'll have to go to the bank and place the order, and—"

He blew out a huff of air, his upper lip curling. "You're boring me, babe."

"I'm relaying facts here. You probably don't know much about how banks work. I thought I'd explain it to you."

"I know plenty. You probably have the money in some fancy brokerage account, so you're going to have to place an order to cash the amount and it's gonna take forever?"

My pulse thrummed. "Actually, I have it ready in cash, so…"

"Well, isn't this my lucky damned day, huh?" His face

twisted into something between greed and zeal and plain ol' crazy.

"Sure is."

White trash, Daddy would have said if he could see them now stomping through his house, rifling through his precious collections of memorabilia and antique knick-knacks, his liquor bottles, his golf clubs. His safe. I shifted my weight on the bed. Stuffed in my pockets, the photos and the bracelet pressed against my flesh.

A scream howled from the bathroom, and a shudder radiated through me. They were torturing my brother.

"Get the fuck up." Dog grabbed my arm and dragged me into the bathroom.

CHAPTER 4
TRICK

I HAD to make the phone call that I didn't want to make.

"Hey," Boner answered.

"Hey. Wanted you to know that we're heading to the Smoking Guns MC."

"Say again?" Boner's voice razored over the phone.

I shifted my weight. "Dawes and I ran into a couple of them, and I ended up helping them with an engine problem. And then they invited us to their clubhouse for this big party they're having tonight and to stay over if we wanted."

Dawes caught my grim gaze and twisted his lips.

"How the hell do you manage to do the exact thing I said not to do?" Boner's voice simmered over the line. "What the fuck, Trick? I said stay away from them. From any sign of them."

"We did. We even kept to the other side of town. We're at this nice barbecue joint in this fancy-ish neighborhood, and we managed to bump into a couple of them on the way out. We gave each other grim looks and parted ways in the parking lot. Fuck, I should have ignored the one trying to start his bike and—"

"But you couldn't."

"I couldn't." Me, always helping out those in need. A girl. An elderly lady. A struggling engine. What an idiot.

A grumbling sound filled the line. "Can't say no to an invite," said Boner.

"Which is why we agreed to go to their party but we're not staying over, no fucking way. We got a motel lined up."

"Glad you checked in and told me." Boner let out a huff of air. "Keep your eyes and ears open and be cool. Do not get drunk, no confrontations, no fights, and for fuck's sake make sure you stay away from their women. In fact, stay away from ALL the women there."

"What?"

I looked forward to runs out of state for this very reason—hook up and enjoy and then get back on your bike and head home to South Dakota. Far, far away never to be seen again.

We lived in a small town, and I'd been through most of the women—the local town girls as well as the hanger-ons who came from all over the Black Hills for the parties. I rarely dipped in a second time, and I was never interested in "more" than what it was—getting laid.

By now, many of them didn't think much of me for my commitment to once and done, but to hell with it, I was always straight up with them. That's what kept me free of dreaded complications, and it wasn't going to change any time soon.

Having experienced a relationship gone south in a small town like ours was more than enough to keep me from going through any kind of messy connection or mixed signals bullshit to a local woman ever again. The strategy worked for me. I'd kept things clean and simple for a change, and I'd finally gotten used to it. Didn't mean I liked it so much, but whatever. It worked.

"Trick, think about it. This invite might be a nice gesture and it could also be a setup. With the smallest incident—they don't like the way you talk, the way you looked at them, that you were ahead of 'em in line for beer—it all goes south with lightning speed."

"True."

"Put me on speaker so Dawes, the chick magnet, can hear. He's the one I'm worried about."

"All right." I eyed Dawes as I put my phone on speaker.

"Dawes you listening?"

"Yeah, go ahead, Boner."

"I do not care if a hundred hot babes stick their tits in your face, lick you, grab your dick, you do not touch. You do not breathe in their direction. You do not pass any kind of go. Do you understand me?"

Shaking my head, I rolled my eyes as Dawes mouthed, "Fuck!"

"Do you understand me?" Boner raised his voice as if he could see us pouting.

"Yes, we understand. We get it."

"Some girl might tell you she's not attached, and that may be the truth. However, one of them might consider her his and she doesn't know it yet or keeps rejecting him. And if he sees her with a Jack from South Dakota, he will go apeshit and sound the alarm. Or they'll use your flirting or looking as an excuse to pop you in the face and then chaos will reign. You see how this goes?"

"Chaos will reign," repeated Dawes.

"I know you two know the drill, but I need to spell this out for you. You are tourists over there, very polite tourists."

"Got it."

"And since you're going to be there, keep your eyes and ears open without being obvious. Bottom line, stay clear and stay clean. That is an order."

"We will. No worries."

Famous last words.

CHAPTER 5
NICOLE

"HE'S CRYING, PREZ," laughed the heavyset biker who held a long blade streaked with red. He wiped at his face and the blood swiped through his long black beard. A chill snaked through my veins at the sight.

Jackson's blood.

Jackson, shaking and moaning, was zip-tied to the fancy water knobs on the pink-tiled wall of our mother's shower, his pressed white shirt ripped, his bare chest cut, and blood dripping down his torso, dripping on the shower floor. My legs flopped like noodles at the sight, but Dog held me up, his fingers digging into my upper arm, the pain stinging, the pain telling me—*Toto, we're not in Kansas anymore.* Clenching my jaw, I fought the dizziness, I fought to stay upright.

"Take a look at your sister, fucker. She's got more balls than you do."

Jackson's watery eyes widened at the sight of me. His bloodied jaw hung open.

"I got your attention now, huh? This will be the last time you see her until you make that payment. She's coming with us."

My back snapped straight, my heart thundered in my chest.

Was he making this look like a kidnapping to twist my brother's arm some more?

"But she's got the money!" warbled Jackson.

"What a son of a bitch."

A gunshot exploded, and I jumped back, my hands over my ears. The glass wall of the shower shattered to the floor in a thousand bits and pieces. Jackson howled like a lone injured animal in a dark forest.

The biker who held the gun whooped loudly, and the others laughed and cheered. Hooting, the black-bearded one held up his bloodied knife. Raiding vikings celebrated their victory in my mother's fancy pink bathroom where the scent of her candy-sweet orange blossom perfume did battle with the dank stench of sweat and blood.

Dog dragged me back into the bedroom, throwing me on the mattress. "Don't fucking move." He turned away, issuing orders to his crew.

A pile of Mom's bathing suits fell on me, and I swatted at them like they were bugs, flinging them off me as I sat up. The diamond necklace slid off the bedspread and slumped onto the carpet at my feet. No longer an elegant trophy. No longer a glittering prize. Or was it? I slid it into my pocket.

A couple of the men grabbed at the jewelry on the other side of the bed. "Hey! Don't even think about it, you fuckers," Dog growled at them. "That shit can get traced real easy. Ain't worth it." Grumbling, the two men tossed the jewelry back on the bed and stalked out of the room.

Jackson's howling and muttering rose from the bathroom. More laughter. The bearded biker with the knife came out of the bathroom, wiping his wet hands on his pants, his now holstered knife hanging from his side. "She coming with us, Prez?"

"Yep."

"Tasty." Winking at me, the guy followed the rest of the bikers out of the room. Dog grabbed my arm and hoisted me up. "Listen up, sugar lips—if you don't get me that money like you said, if you're lying to me, I'm going to have to punish you." He pulled me in close, his humid coffee breath fanning my face. "And I'm gonna enjoy it something fierce."

I jerked my face away from his. "I said I'd pay you. But you have to leave my mother and her house alone. She's got nothing to do with this."

He rolled his eyes. "Yeah, yeah."

"Can we go to the bank and get this done now?"

On a snarl he shoved me ahead of him, and we marched out of the bedroom, down the stairs, and through the house. Stopping at the front door, I grabbed my small leather backpack which I'd left on the sideboard earlier, and moving out of view, I stuffed it with all the treasures I had hidden in my pockets.

Outside, my eyes squinted at the chrome army glinting in the sun. Massive metal motorcycles stood side by side in the circular driveway surrounding my mother's white Mercedes convertible. Bizarre. Freakish. The end of the world.

An idea flickered through me, stopping me in my tracks.

Dog shoved me toward a vintage red and gold Harley with long handlebars. I swiveled around and faced him. "Wait— inside you told my brother you were taking me with you until he paid you, but I'm the one paying you and we both know it, so what did you mean?"

"I wanted to scare him, I ain't joking around. He strikes me as the kind of guy who thinks he can wiggle out of anything. Slippery dick."

"You would be right." Jackson wiggled. Logan wiggled. My mother did too. Very slippery. I cleared my throat. "I have a deal for you."

"Get on the goddamn bike. I don't got all day."

"Like we said, I'll give you the money he owes you, and you'll leave my mother and her house alone, but I also want—"

"I don't give a fuck about what you want."

"You should since you want my fucking money." My insides shuddered under his harsh glare. I'd never spoken like that to anyone, ever, let alone an outlaw biker club president. "This can be clean and simple."

Dog let out a grunt. "Clean and simple? Wake up, princess. Nothing in this life is clean and simple."

I took in a breath. "Now you're boring me. Here's my deal: if you already threatened my brother by telling him you're taking me until he pays, let's let him and my mother think you did take me."

His eyes narrowed as his hands went to his waist. "You want to run away from home, darlin'? Aren't you a little old for that?"

"That's my business. I have my reasons."

Dog dragged his fingers through his short gray beard. "All right. Here's my deal for you: I'm gonna need you to help me get that money back to my club in Kansas City."

I blinked. "You need me?"

"Yeah. We can't carry all that cash on our bikes on the road."

"Why not?"

"The police stop us all the time, always suspecting the worst."

"I can't imagine why," I remarked.

"You want me to lie for you so you can kiss this town's fat ass goodbye, I'm offering you a way to do it. Making that brother of yours squirm some more will be loads of fucking fun. And, like you said, no momma, no house. How's that for you?"

My heart thudded in my chest. Crazy is how it was.

And a way out.

Out from under my husband's and my brother's unrelenting commands. Out from under my mother's manipulations. Out from the ticking clock of the board vote. Out from living a lie. Stopping the noise. Stopping my asphyxiation.

I didn't want my mother, Jackson, and Logan to know where I was, and that *where* was the one place I wanted to be right now. The only place I could try and find the brother I had no idea existed until now. The only bright light in this chaos.

Making a deal with a bunch of dangerous, petty criminals,

not-to-be-trusted outlaws, who rode the asphalt on loud, brawny motorcycles certainly wasn't ideal, but it would immediately give me the time and the freedom I needed.

My palms were laced with sweat. *Quick, before you regret it.* "Okay. I agree."

"Give me your phone."

"Why?"

"Why do you think?"

I gave it to him and he smashed it with his boot. "Get on." He got on his bike, the massive machine fitting somehow between his legs as he ignited the engine. "You been on a bike before?"

My legs shook, my fingers tightening over the straps of my backpack. "No, never."

He hooted. "I get to pop that juicy cherry, huh?" Grinning, he held out a helmet. "Follow directions and hold on tight. Now get on. We gotta roll." He put on a pair of goggles.

I managed to put on the helmet and climbed onto his huge bike, adjusting myself behind his leather-clad body. The motorcycle exploded underneath us, reverberating through my every cell. A metal storm. Gnashing my teeth, my insides screwing tight, I put my hands on his thick middle.

With a roar we blasted off, and everything blurred.

CHAPTER 6
NICOLE

I FINALLY GOT the cash out of the bank in town. I went outside and waited at the corner as instructed, lugging the duffel bag one of the bikers had given me.

The one called Lex pulled up in a dusty orange old Honda Civic. "Get in."

I got in, shoving the bag in the backseat.

"What's with this car?"

Lex only shot me a dark glare that had me shrinking against the door. He pulled up in the back of an old strip mall where a couple of the Smoking Guns were parked. "Rooney & Associates," said the dingy nameplate on the brick facade. "Stay here." Lex got out of the car without the duffle bag.

"Wait! Don't you need the—"

"Shut up," he growled at me over his shoulder. Prowling over to his buddies, he high-fived them.

Dog and another guy burst out of the back door. His pale face was flushed, tense. He ripped off a pair of stained gloves from his hands. Stained with red.

My heart knocked against my ribs.

"We're done here," declared Dog, and everyone immediately got on their bikes and roared off. Lex and Dog had a man-to-man. Dog handed him the stained gloves as he caught my eye and winked at me. I averted my gaze.

Lex got back in the car and tossed the gloves in the back seat. I glanced at them. "Did he hurt Mr. Rooney?"

"Hurt?" He guffawed loudly.

My insides iced over. Dog had killed Mr. Rooney. Of course, why not? In a shocking twist, Dog had managed to get the entire amount Jackson owed Mr. Rooney in cash. Not just a couple thousand, a few diamonds, and a wad of empty promises. No, the whole enchilada all for himself. He'd won the bounty hunter mega lottery.

Sour acid rose in my throat. My head ached. All that whiskey was doing a tango with the adrenaline coursing through my system.

Ten minutes later, we stopped again at some abandoned gas station outside of town where the rest of the Smoking Guns waited. I stood in the hot sun, freezing, my skin crawling, my legs shaking. They split open the lining of the Honda and the doors and stuffed the cash in there along with the drugs and extra weapons they were carrying. They burned the bloodied gloves.

Dog planted his feet in front of me and I blinked. He held the car keys in his hand. "You'll be driving the car to Kansas City."

"Me? But I—"

"That was our deal, sweetheart. You're going to play the carefree, innocent all-American girl next door on the road. Keep within the speed limit and stay ahead of us."

My throat squeezed. There was only one problem with that plan.

"I can't drive," I said.

His brow furrowed. "What? What the fuck are you talking about?"

"I don't…"

"You don't have a license? Are you shitting me?"

"I have a license, I just—"

Dog grabbed me by the chin, his fingers digging into my flesh. "Get in the fucking car."

I twisted out of his hold. "I can't!"

"Why the hell not?" he shouted.

"I was in a bad car accident recently, and ever since I can't drive…"

"You killed somebody?"

"Yes. My dad and…and…" My mouth went completely dry. I couldn't say the words. I could not say them out loud to him. To all of them staring at me.

"You killed two people? Jesus." He smashed his lips together. "Lex! Get your bike in the van."

"What? Why?"

"You're going to drive the car with her in it. Like a happy fucking couple. Take off your colors, and get your hair in a cute man bun. Do something to look as clean as she does."

Lex swore under his breath and stomped away.

"You do whatever Lex tells you to do. You try anything funny, know that I will kill your mother myself," spit out Dog. "You hearing me?"

"I hear you."

It was a relief to no longer be on his bike with him, but now I'd be with Lex, who obviously hated me, and who hated even more that he had to give up his motorcycle to drive this car with me in it.

Once we took off, I didn't attempt to make small talk or any kind of talk. Lex kept his eyes on the road, his jaw set the entire time as he kept flicking at the radio station buttons. Hours later, in the darkness of night, we hit the Kansas City city limits. Suddenly, Lex veered off from the direction the bike club took and brought us to a seedy motel. My pulse banged in my neck. "W-why are we here?"

He ignored me. In the gloomy parking lot, three other bikers waited for us in the shadows.

"Get out," said Lex.

I got out, and the other bikers immediately took the car and drove off, leaving a motorcycle behind.

I blew out a heavy breath as Lex got on the bike. "Let's go," he barked at me.

"Where are we going?"

"We got to get out here. Move." He handed me the helmet and started the engine. Its explosive rumble made my pulse hammer. "Now!"

I got the helmet on, climbed on the bike, and we drove through the outskirts of the city in the grim darkness, past abandoned houses, past a strip mall with a tired fast-food restaurant, a laundromat, and a liquor store. All deadly quiet. We shot over small roads, turned left, turned right. Lex finally slowed down toward the end of the road where bright lights buzzed. We were in a cul de sac. Noise filled the air–a jarring, ominous furor of commotion, music, shouting, dogs barking.

Ahead of us loomed an old sprawling ranch house with a warehouse attached to it with no windows. Surrounded by a high metal fence topped with barbed wire, the bleak property was lit with blazing lights with smoke wafting overhead. The closer we got, the more intense the noise, laughter, and music became.

I'd never seen so many motorcycles in all my life.

A chill razored over me. I was about to enter a motorcycle club's clubhouse. An underground universe. Once we passed through that gate, would I ever get out?

What the hell had I gotten myself into?

CHAPTER 7
NICOLE

A LONG GATE SAWED OPENED, and Lex guided the bike through the crowded lot and parked. My muscles were painfully stiff, my palms sweaty.

"Stay close to me," Lex muttered as we made our way to where the crowd was gathered.

There was a party in full swing here at the Smoking Guns MC of Kansas City. And it wasn't only Smoking Guns—there were a bunch of different clubs here judging from the patches on their jackets.

"Where did they pick you up from?" asked a grim-faced woman, her dark eyes glinting at me, her long black hair highlighted with silver.

I shifted my weight. "Oklahoma."

"Whose are you?"

"I'm not anyone's."

She shot a hard look at Lex.

"I got to get her inside, Carrie." Cuffing my arm, Lex pushed me past Carrie and brought me through their courtyard, our boots scrunching over the gravel.

"Who was she?" I asked him.

"That's Prez's old lady. His wife."

Terrific.

Lex let go of me as men greeted him. They high-fived and hugged, slapped each other on the back.

"Good to see you, brother!"

"Yo, Lex! It's been a while, man."

A hand slid over my rear, and I jumped. It was Dog.

"Welcome to my MC, sweetheart."

"Thanks. I get y'all are having a party and celebrating, but I need to leave."

"Leave? And go where?"

"I need to get to South Dakota."

"Tomorrow is another day, honey."

"Tomorrow?"

"Yeah." He chuckled. "And so's the next day and the next… lots of tomorrows." He slid his arm around me and planted his lips against my ear. "And before tomorrow gets here, you and me got lots of celebrating to do."

That icy cold chill I knew so well slithered up my spine, rendering me numb. My mouth went dry.

"You're gonna hang with Lex for a while, and later on tonight, I'll come for you."

I pushed at his side. "No, no, no. That wasn't part of our deal."

"Deal's done, sweetheart. Now you're here with me on my turf. And you're mine."

"I'm not yours! By the way, I just met your wife. Carrie?"

"Oh yeah?" He was not impressed, not fazed. Maybe amused.

"She wasn't happy to see me. She asked whose I was."

"Don't worry about her." He planted his fat lips on mine, his tongue pushing to get in. I twisted away, shoving against his chest. "You-you can't keep me here. You can't!"

"Calm down. You did right by us and—"

"That's right, I did. So now you need to do right by me. That was the deal."

He laughed again. He was enjoying this. "Tonight, baby. Tonight, my cock's gonna do right by you. I'm going to fuck you on that pile of cash, sweetheart. I've had a hard-on for hours just thinking about it. I'm gonna rub those bills all over your tits, in your cunt. We're gonna do all the blow we want with 'em, then I'm gonna bang you so damn hard you're going to forget your own name and I'm going to forget mine." He let me go, letting out a deep breath, panting. "Until then, with Lex, you got that? He'll keep you safe." He gestured to my left where Lex stood, arms crossed, a scowl etched on his face.

"Safe?"

"Until I can catch up with you." He squeezed my ass cheek, and I jumped. "That fucking ass…shit. Can't wait to get in there."

I pulled back from him. "You can't do this. I'm married."

"He ain't here, is he?" He let out a laugh.

Say something, Anything. "He's in South Dakota, and he's waiting for me."

"Oh yeah? Well, he'll just have to wait a little longer."

"I…I need to get to him. He'll know something's wrong. He'll come looking for me. He probably already is."

"Sure he is, darling, but I can't let you go now." He stalked off, leaving me shaking, dazed.

Lex came up alongside me, running a hand through his hair. "Just keep close to me, all right?"

"He can't do this."

"He can do whatever the hell he wants. Chill the fuck out. Have a beer." He handed me a plastic cup. A red plastic cup. A tall, red, plastic cup with those three ridges on it. Just like that red plastic cup I was given at that party a zillion years ago that changed my life forever.

"No."

"Jesus, take the fucking beer."

I took it. I dumped it.

"Whatever, bitch. Stay close and keep your mouth shut."

We strode around the party. A carnival of fighting, betting, laughter, dancing, bellowing. Barbecued meat was being sliced up and served to a hungry mob as a group of girls stripped to an enthusiastic audience. Loads of different drugs were being done, but what the hell did I know? Couples screwed on picnic tables, against walls. Men got blow jobs. People danced, sang.

My legs grew weary, and my shoulders slumped. My heart had stopped pounding a while back. The thick acrid scent of cigarette and pot smoke burned through my nose.

"You stand here and don't fucking move."

"Huh?" I wiped at my eyes.

Lex took out a very long zip tie and wrapped it around my one wrist and attached it to the fence.

"What are you doing? You can't—"

"Fucking pain in my ass. Shut the fuck up and do as your told."

I gnashed my teeth. *Do as your told? I've been doing that all my life, asshole.* I stared at the zip tie tying me to the fence, keeping me prisoner. My whole life had come down to this little strip of plastic.

Lex gestured to a woman in high-heeled boots, who sported a red vinyl miniskirt and a string bikini top. "Hey, you." His tone had changed considerably to something slick, warm, and inviting.

"Heyyyy," she said as she latched on to him, giving him the deepest kiss I'd ever seen. It was hot, crude. It was dirty. It had intention—sex.

They bantered and a few more kisses, laughs, and gropes later, she dropped to her knees. They both undid his leather pants and she took out his already hard dick and licked at it like a massive popsicle. *Well, all righty, then.* I pressed my legs together, my teeth scraping my lip. He fondled her boobs, his hips thrusting, her head bobbing furiously.

She seemed to be getting him there quickly; she was efficient. Her lips sucked on him firmly as she slid his dick in and out of her mouth, her hand on one of his balls. This was a technique I'd never mastered.

I was more slow and steady, delicate. A few licks here and there. A rub up and down. I never liked having to do it; it seemed subservient to me. But this woman was all in—and in a *big* way. Lex's head knocked back against the wall, a groan escaping him. He liked what she was doing. He was at her mercy now, wasn't he?

Lex muttered something to her, his fingers tightening at her jaw, and she went even faster, saliva dripping from her mouth. His other hand dug into her scalp and held her head fast. I tilted my head. He was literally fucking her mouth. His hips jerked against her face as he grunted, and she kept on sucking, drawing it all in. How was she breathing?

Lex helped her rise to her feet and squeezed her tits some more as they spoke and kissed, and she tucked his spent cock back in his pants. He sank his hands under her skirt, revealing her naked rear. More dirty kisses and she hitched herself up on his thigh, grinding her pelvis on him, her jaw slackening. Was it finally her turn to get some?

Suddenly her hard gaze fell on me and my chest caved in, my back pressed against the fence. "Who the hell is she, and why is she staring at us? Has she been following you around all night? You want me to get rid of her for you, baby?"

Rolling my eyes, my body slumped against the fence. The adrenaline had faded from my system and exhaustion had claimed every cell of my being. "He's making me stand here, how's that for you?" I shouted out to her.

Lex slapped the girl's ass, and she returned her attention to him. "She's nobody. Just a cold bitch that I gotta keep an eye on tonight for the Prez."

Nobody.

Cold bitch.

I closed my eyes as the sting of his words whipped through me. How many times had I heard that? Too many to count.

Was I a cold bitch?

"She's probably watching us 'cause she don't know how to fuck a man right," said Lex on a laugh. "Ain't that right, cold bitch?"

"Got nothing better to do." I lifted my restrained arm. "Might as well learn a thing or two while I'm standing here."

Lex let out a hard laugh. He bent his head and said something to the woman in a low voice. Was it something dirty? The girl's face broke out into a grin as her hand went into his pants and drew out his dick again, roughly stroking it up and down. "Love your cock, Lex."

With his heavy gaze pinned on me, Lex grunted, his hips rocking, a wicked smirk slicing over his face. She throttled his dick firmly, and his attention jerked back to her.

"Smart girl," I muttered to myself.

"Watch and learn, cold bitch," she announced as she hooked her legs around Lex and lowered herself on his curved stiff blade. Sheer acrobatics. Were her loud moans and groans for my benefit or for Lex? Probably both—to make me jealous and to impress hin with how stellar he was doing her. I blew out a huff of air. You've always got to impress the man with how amazing he is or you're not a real woman worthy of his masterful performance and the gift of his cock.

"You waiting your turn with him? Does the line form here?" said a deep, warm voice behind me. I twisted around, tingles rushing over my skin.

Big velvety brown eyes met mine, and warmth swept through my body. Thick, wavy, brown hair streaked with dark blond fell in his face, which was all sharp lines and cut angles shadowed with stubble. Under his black leather jacket, he wore a white V-neck T-shirt that fit tightly over the contours of his long torso. A maze of wild tattoos were visible over the low hanging V of his tee. Silver necklaces lay on the impressive curve of his pecs and a couple of bulky silver rings were on his long fingers, a small silver hoop in one ear.

My breath cut. Boy-next-door handsome but with an edge; a dark edge of been-there-done-that-and-just-don't-give-a-fuck.

I stumbled back against the fence. "E-excuse me?"

His lips tipped up into a sharp but sensual grin and something inside me ignited like a tiki torch, heat flaring over my flesh. His tongue shot out and darted over his generous bottom lip, and my body tightened in a new, strange almost painful way, somewhere between excited and stinging.

Hot, dark edge, and dangerous too.

CHAPTER 8
TRICK

I FIRST NOTICED her messy long blond hair, as if it were windblown or she'd just gotten out of bed. I liked that. Carefree and a little careless. Long legs in tight white jeans, a curved waist. A pretty, feminine blouse. There was something graceful about her. Something that did not fit in this insane rumble of a party at the Smoking Guns MC in a dark corner of Kansas City.

I made a snide comment just to see her face; see what kind of reaction I'd get. She turned around and knocked the breath out of me. Those dark blue eyes hit me straight in the gut. On watch. Curious, maybe scared, and…fucking beautiful. A mouth that looked like it was pouting, but no, those lips were round and full and inviting.

She squared her shoulders. "Hell no, I'm not waiting my turn."

"Uh-huh." My eyes roved over every inch of her, and she shifted her weight under my attention, her long-sleeved blouse sliding off one shoulder. A thin strap over pale bare skin gleamed soft and smooth under the dim lights over us. My dick hitched in my leathers. "You're not dressed for this party are you?"

"I had no idea I was coming to this party, so shucks, I didn't get a chance to get dressed up properly, like her." She gestured at the club girl who was being nailed by the Smoking Gun she'd been staring at earlier, only a few yards away from us. "Is that what you mean? Is that what every female should be dressed like around here?"

I let out a laugh as I gripped the fence next to her. "You don't like her outfit much, huh?"

"I didn't say that." She met my gaze, those full lips pressing together.

I leaned in closer to her. "Makes it real easy to fuck, though, doesn't it? See how he's gripping her ass cheeks just right, keeping her steady. Can't do that if she's wearing jeans."

"Excellent point. So there's a strategy at work here?"

"Oh yeah. And her bikini top, those teeny tiny triangles—I mean, she's wearing *something*, but he can still touch her tits."

"And kiss them?"

My gaze fell to her parted lips. The couple's grunting and groaning was a live porn soundtrack in my suddenly blurred background. Only this woman remained clear. Only her. "Uh…yeah."

"Yeah," she mimicked me.

"What's that supposed to mean?"

"It's always about the guy's convenience, that's what that means."

"No, no. Think about it—easy access makes things hotter and easier for both of them. Trust me, he's gone commando under those leather pants to give her easy access to his cock."

"Well, yahoo. That's something, I guess." Her gaze returned to the duo as if she were studying a lab experiment. "She wants it just as bad as he does, doesn't she?"

"Yep, she sure does."

"So you're naked under there for easy access?" She glanced down at my crotch, and my cock jumped and shifted under her sharp gaze. She bit her lip as if she'd regretted saying it, which somehow only lured me in more.

I shot her a grin. "Want to find out?" *What the hell am I doing? I shouldn't be talking to her, let alone flirting with her.*

Her face reddened. "Gee, babe, I'd love to, but I'm not wearing a miniskirt, and there's *this* cramping my style." She raised her left arm. She was zip-tied to the fence. "Or maybe not, depending on your mood."

"Fuck, that's an accessory I wasn't expecting." My back stiffened. "Hang on—are you his property, and he's fucking that girl to punish you or some shit?"

"Property?" Her neck stiffened, her eyes bulged out of their sockets. "What the hell are you talking about?"

This woman was definitely not club material. I lowered my voice. "What I meant was are you with that Smoking Gun, or did you come here with friends to get your dirty wild on?"

Her jaw jutted. "They brought me here."

"They?"

"Dog. I did a favor for him and—"

I tilted my head, my pulse thrumming in my neck. "You did a favor for Dog?"

"That's right, I did."

My eyes narrowed at her. "What kind of favor?"

"Paid off my brother's debt to him. All of it, cash, in one go."

"A lot of money?"

"A whole damned lot."

"That's damned impressive."

"Dog thought so too, and he suddenly decided to keep me here instead of—"

My chest tightened. "Keep you?"

"He made Lex my bodyguard until he can have a private party with me later tonight." She sucked in a small breath. "I don't think he's going to let me leave anytime soon."

"So you don't want to be here?"

She leaned into me as far as the zip tie would allow. "I want to get the hell out of here. Does it look like I'm having fun?"

"No. No, it doesn't." My eyes darted around us. The party

was in full blast, and everyone's attention was now on a band playing on a raised platform in the center of the yard or they were huddling together getting high, having a laugh. No one was paying us any attention here on the periphery of the party where there were only random acts of sex happening.

Her gaze flicked down my chest. She was pretty in a delicate way, like a doll made of porcelain. A doll you never touched for fear you might ruin her perfection, dirty her, break her. You didn't play with her. You admired her quality and beauty from afar.

The sudden need to see her dirtied, to do it myself, jammed at my insides, and I blew out a breath and wiped at my damp upper lip. This woman zip-tied to a fence with this wild carnival going on around her was an insane visual. She had to be in her late twenties at least, but for all her sass and smarts there was a core of innocence in her that was unmistakeable and—dammit—fucking irresistible.

"Hey—" Her deep blue gaze snagged on mine, and my insides tightened. "Could you help me get out of here?" That rough whisper, that genuine plea, sent my pulse ticking wildly. Ah fuck. She was a time bomb on a ticking clock.

I was supposed to be keeping a low profile here until I could leave—OR ELSE. Yet, of course, somehow, I ended up finding the ONE woman I shouldn't even be looking at let alone talking to and wanting to dip into. Dog's shiny new pet. I grit my teeth. I had a special talent for self-fuckery, didn't I?

Boner's voice from earlier shouted at me: *Chaos will reign!* Clearing my throat, my gaze fell to my boots. "I…uh…"

"Oh—do you need to screw me first? See if I'm worth it? Is that it, *baby*?" Her facetious tone laced with some kind of southern twang had my gaze shooting up to meet hers. She was angry. She was desperate.

And I didn't blame her one bit.

I shifted my weight. "I didn't say that."

"No, you didn't." She moved in closer and I could feel the

heat from her body. "I'm not hot enough for you? Not biker chick enough for you? You can tell me, go ahead. Is there something wrong with me? Am I a cold, hard bitch?"

"Whoa, woman. You're definitely…"

"Definitely what?"

"Fucking hot, dammit!"

Her head jerked back at my emphatic declaration. Her cheeks streaked with pink. "Thanks. Huge compliment coming from a guy like you."

My back straightened. "A guy like me?"

"A guy who obviously only goes for biker chicks."

"Why would you say that?"

"You're here, aren't you? You're a biker, right?"

"Yeah, and?"

She chewed on her lip. "And you're…"

"Spit it out, Zip."

Her eyes flashed at me. "You're rough around the edges with, I imagine, lots and lots of experience down there under your commando leather pants." She moved to face me straight on, as much as the zip tie would allow. "You are a guy who has certain expectations that he needs met in a woman, no tolerance for anything less. A woman like her." She gestured at the girl again.

"She's not my kind of woman."

She rolled her eyes. "Sure." Her lips tipped up into a caustic smile, but her incredible blue eyes told another story. She was sad, miserable. Sapped. And it drilled a hole right through me.

I leaned in closer to her, and her breath quickened. I could smell her skin, something warm and sweet. In any other circumstance I would have had this woman in my arms, taking that mouth, tasting her tongue. BUT NO. Gritting my teeth, I shook my head. "I wish I could help you, but…"

"But it would go against your bro code, right? That's it, isn't it? That's the deal around here. God, I'm so screwed." She let out a brittle laugh. "All I did was help out my family and what did I get for it?"

"You got zip-tied."

"Exactly." Her eyes filled with water, and she hiccuped a breath. "I'm such a royal fuck-up. I trusted a man like Dog to follow up on his word. I mean, I followed up on my end of the deal, why couldn't he? Fuck-up."

My insides dropped. "You're not a fuck-up."

"Trick! Come on, man!" Dawes called out to me from the crowd, his hand raised.

"Trick? That's your name?"

"Yeah."

"It's your bro nickname, right? Would mine be Zip?" She slumped back against the fence. "Perfect. A name to commemorate my all-time low in life."

My jaw stiffened as I whipped out my Swiss Army knife and clipped the damned zip tie from her wrist. "I can do this much for you. The rest is up to you."

"Thank you," she breathed, rubbing her wrist. "I mean it, thank you." The genuine emotion in her voice wrapped around my chest and squeezed.

I quickly put away my knife. "What's your name?"

"Nicole."

I stepped back from her as if the knowledge had shoved at me. It was pretty, elegant but simple. Fucking perfect. "I got to get over there."

"Right. Dandy to meet you, Trick. Enjoy the party."

"Trust me, I'm not enjoying this party. I'm from another club, another state, and I've got to go pay my respects to Dog and his officers."

"Well then, don't tell him you met me. He might get pissed off."

"Damn right he would. The Smoking Guns don't like my club much as it is. I only came here tonight because I had to."

"You better go. Shouldn't be late for your big meeting with His Highness." Her back straightened. "And thanks again."

"I—"

"Trick!"

Stepping backward, I retreated as her lower lip trembled, my gut heavy as my boots pushed me in the opposite direction. Away from her. *Dammit.*

I headed into the frenzy.

CHAPTER 9
NICOLE

TRICK TURNED AROUND and took off, and as he passed under an overhead light, my breath jammed in my chest. ONE-EYED JACKS MC - SOUTH DAKOTA was emblazoned in red on the back of his leather jacket.

My heart flew out of my chest. "Oh my God!" I darted forward but stopped myself. I couldn't follow him. His friend was shaking hands with Dog and his inner crew. "Shit!"

"Whoa, what's got you in a tizzy?"

I swiveled back at that voice. Carrie, Dog's wife. My insides pitched, my heart sank.

"Huh." She caught sight of Lex and the girl screwing a few feet away. "Aww, did Lex dump you already? Typical asshole, huh? Why aren't you over there, beating her off your man?"

I rubbed at my wrist where the zip tie used to be. "He..uh… made me wait for him here."

"Seriously? What a fuck." Carrie gently squeezed my arm. Was she trying to be reassuring? Lex and the girl panted wildly, both of them groaning and carrying on as he buried his face in her breasts, the party brewing on around us.

"You should be enjoying Smoking Guns hospitality. Not this bullshit."

"The truth is, I want to leave here. I need to get to South Dakota."

"Oh, yeah?" She shot me a warm grin. "I could help you."

"Really? You would? Oh Carrie, thank you!"

"We girls have to stick together, look out for ourselves, don't we?"

I grinned. "Yes, we do." *Let's hear it for the sister code!*

"Come on." Carrie took my hand in her cold one like we were besties in grade school off to have fun in the playground. "Come with me."

With her hand gripping mine, I kept up with her fast pace, stumbling through the crowd. The pandemonium of the party-goers was thick and rowdy. People shouting, laughing, carousing, the music deafening. We weaved our way through the mayhem, Carrie greeting friends as we kept moving. My gaze darted everywhere for Trick and his blond buddy, but no luck. And no sign of Dog, either.

We reached the other side of the massive courtyard, at the perimeter, close to the end of the parking lot. Carrie's posture visibly perked up as her focus zoomed on a mountain of a macho man who had a zillion silver earrings along his ears along with bulky rings on his tattooed fingers. His patches seemed different from the others. His said "Nomad."

"Hey, baby! Good to see you." Letting go of my hand, Carrie stood on her tiptoes and planted a quick kiss on the guy's mouth. His tattooed bald head tilted at her, a slow sly smile slicing his features. My stomach curled at the sight of it.

"Lady Carrie. Good to see you." His deep baritone voice sent a warning bell through my veins and sent Carrie into a fit of warm giggles. He turned his heavy gaze on me, and my breath cut. At the base of his throat and down his upper chest was an enormous tattoo of a dinosaur's head, his jaw hanging open, vicious fangs and teeth ready to chomp on whatever was in its way. On you.

On me.

He dipped a finger under my chin, and I flinched at his presumptuous touch. "Who's this?"

"Someone new," said Carrie. "Someone I thought you might be looking for."

"What?" My voice squeaked. "Carrie?" She ignored me, focusing on Dinosaur Man.

His brow furrowed as his gaze scraped over every inch of me, making my skin crawl. He touched my hair, and I stepped away from him, bumping into Carrie. She laughed and pushed me back toward him. "She's shy."

Her shove, the taunt in her voice, sent a cold slime slithering in my veins, tightening around my heart. The biker slid a beefy arm around my waist, pulling me close, sniffing me. "How old are you?" A hand dug into my rear.

I twisted in his iron hold. "Let go of me!"

"She's twenty-three," replied Carrie swiftly.

"Come on, babe, she's older." His lips curled as his hand grabbed a breast and squeezed. "Hmm."

I jerked in his hold, panic rising in my chest, burning in my throat. "Stop it!"

Releasing me on a huff, he grabbed at my backpack, easily snatching it from me. He fished out my wallet. My driver's license. "She's thirty-three, Carrie, what the fuck?" He took all my cash from my wallet and shoved it in his pocket.

"What are you doing? Hey!"

Carrie grabbed my arm, her fingernails digging into my skin. "Shut up. You wanted out of here, honey, you got it." Her voice was as sharp as a dagger, and my body shuddered.

"What's this?" his sharp tone had us both turning to face him again.

My mother's diamond necklace hung from the biker's thick, tattooed, ringed fingers. "Now this I fucking like. A lot."

"Wow, that's nice." Carrie's voice had gone warm and syrupy as she took in the diamond necklace, her lips falling open. She shoved me at him again. "So, what do you think, hon? She good?"

He ignored us as he fingered the diamond necklace. My mother's necklace that I'd managed to scoop up from the floor before we'd left the house. I knew it might be useful as a bartering token, but I hadn't counted on it being stolen from me. Seeing it now in his hands…worlds colliding.

"Where did you get this?" he asked me, his voice firm and business-like.

"It's my mother's. It's all I took from home when Carrie's old man brought me here."

Taking out his cell phone, he trained the light over the clasp and turned it over. "Huh. Tiffany. We got us a rich girly girl, huh?" The biker's thick eyebrows jumped, a deep laugh rolling from his chest as he tucked the necklace in his inside jacket pocket.

"Hey, that'd be a nice finder's fee for me, don't you think?" Carrie said.

Ignoring her comment, ignoring her, he pulled down the front of my blouse, tugged down my bra, and I yelped as he inspected my chest. He lifted my shirt and twisted me around, his hands sliding down my hips, my rear. "Body's banging. And, hell, a blonde American with that scared deer in the headlights look gets' em in the *cojones* every time." He let out a loud laugh, and my teeth chattered. My soul chattered. The world swirled around me. "Am I right, Kling?"

A younger guy with a tattooed face and a black bandana around his head, wearing a black tank top and jeans appeared from the shadows. Inspecting me, his lips curled like some animal. "Yeah, she's good." He dragged out the heavily accented words. He came closer. "How old?"

"Twenty-three," the biker replied smoothly with a grin, winking at Carrie.

"She's good," said Kling, his hand stroking a sheathed knife hanging from his side as his gaze crawled up and down my body. He approached the biker and they talked in hushed tones.

"Carrie, please. What's going on?"

Grabbing me by the wrist and twisting it, her fingernails digging into my skin, Carrie snarled at me. "This is your ticket out." She peeled her fingers off my wrist and her gaze widened at my diamond tennis bracelet which I always wore, a birthday gift my parents had given me. "What's this?" She quickly undid the clasp and shoved it in her pocket. "You won't need that anymore."

"Carrie, please!" I begged. "Please—"

"You done right by me, babe," the biker's voice boomed behind us.

Carrie stood at full attention, her grip on me tightening, keeping me at her side. A seductive smile slashed her mouth. "Great. Let's celebrate." Her voice practically purred.

"No time." The biker turned to Kling. "Go get the happy wipes. We gotta get her in the van."

"Maybe I give her a test drive, yeah?" murmured Kling.

"Maybe we both will," said the biker.

Van? Test drive? My heart pounded in my chest, the blood drained from my head.

"Babe—" Carrie's tone had turned steely and insistent, still gripping me with one hand as her other creeped up his muscular arm. "Let him take her, and you and me could have our own party."

Grabbing Carrie, he smashed his mouth on hers, and my stomach sickened with sour. A deep, tongue-filled kiss that had her moaning and pressing against him. The kiss dragged on, and her grip on me went lax. Footsteps approached. Kling reappeared. Something white was in his hand. Wadded-up fabric?

Every cell in my being stood at attention. *No. No. No.*

I bolted. I ran.

Ran.

Ran.

My heart flew out of my chest. My lungs burned. Everything a blur. *Keep going, keep going, don't stop. Don't stop.*

Faster.

Faster.

Shouting.

Yelling.

A wall stopped me. A wall of muscle held me.

"Zip!"

His voice broke through the blur. It was him. He'd seen me. He caught me. He held onto me. I struggled for air, struggled for words. "Trick?"

"I got you." His hand dug into my hair, our gazes locked, and his mouth crashed onto mine, our bodies surging together.

Was this hello? Goodbye? Fuck the world?

A world where everyone was out for themselves. A quick buck, a selfish thrill. Cold revenge. Plain ol' spite. I didn't care. All I knew was this—this was *something* I needed right now, and I seized it for myself, joining him in this pact. This insanity in the insanity.

His kiss, his bear hug of a hold on me, ignited something new inside me. Something bold and shameless and fiery.

"What the hell?" screeched Carrie from behind us. She grabbed at my arm, yanking.

Trick pulled me to his side, away from her. "Do not touch my woman!" his voice seethed, his embrace a vice around me. His declaration vibrated in my veins as I wrapped myself around him, my face pressed against the back of his leather jacket, Something rough scratched my cheek. My fingertips grazed over the big patch of the One-Eyed Jack skull with the gleaming eye on the back of his jacket, and my heart squeezed.

Sanctuary.

"Who the hell are you?" asked Carrie.

"You don't get to ask me questions," he spit out, his body stiffening, towering. I slid my arms around him. Yep, I would play his woman to the hilt.

"What the fuck is going on?" Lex swooped in alongside Carrie, joining her in shooting laser death rays at me, at Trick.

"You got busy and she took off, asshole. That's what the fuck is going on!" Carrie hissed. "Wait till your Prez finds out that your dick was more important than his order. I can't wait to tell him all about your colossal fuckup."

"No!" Lex exploded, launching at me.

Trick's hand shot out, grabbing Lex's throat, shoving him back. "My old lady is leaving with me, dick for brains."

A strange hush settled on the crowd around us.

"Your old lady?" Lex said.

I took in a gulp of air. "I told you, Lex, like I told Dog, that I needed to get to South Dakota to get to my—"

"Yeah, but—"

"No, no buts! I'm Trick's property." My spine straightened, and my heart beat so fast in my chest that my lungs couldn't keep up. "My family hates him, and we'd broken up for a while. My brother made my life hell. When y'all showed up at my house, I took the opportunity to take off and get back to him." I swallowed hard. Trick squeezed my waist in response to my explanation. Once I got going, I wasn't half bad.

"Are you shitting me? A fucking One-Eyed Jack?" Lex threw his arms in the air.

Trick tucked me behind his body once more, and a new surge of adrenaline pumped through me, my fingers digging into his waist.

"How did you know she was here?" said Lex. "She's had no access to a phone since we left Oklahoma. I've been with her the whole time."

"Obviously, not the whole time, dipshit," said Carrie. "Aw, you two…so romantic." Her voice dripped with amused bitterness sending ice through my veins. She knew we were most probably lying but she wanted to get rid of me, didn't she? She would shift gears. "You lovebirds better get the fuck out of here before my old man notices his precious catch of the day is gone."

"No!" Lex raged. "She's not going anywhere!"

"Shut the fuck up." Carrie sniffed in air as she met Trick's hard gaze. "I'll give you ten seconds before I let Dog know you took her—just for shits and giggles."

Trick tightened his big, warm hand over mine, and we took off.

CHAPTER 10
NICOLE

TRICK and his friend Dawes argued as we darted through the parking lot.

"Are you fucking kidding me, man? What the hell are you doing with this girl? I heard all about Dog's adventure in Oklahoma at the party. They're all waiting to get their taste when he's done with her."

"She doesn't belong here, Dawes. He lied to her. She followed through on their deal, and he's keeping her here against her will. She's just a civilian."

"Not our problem. Jesus, we were supposed to lay the fuck low tonight. Get through it and leave."

"Now we're leaving, how's that?"

"Boner and Kick are gonna have your ass and mine. Not to mention Finger."

"Can we get out of here first, and discuss and debate later?"

"Fuck, we're locked in…" Trick scanned the rows and rows of bikes, his chest heaving under his leather jacket.

"We got to get out of here now." Muttering a thousand and one curses, Dawes scrambled in between motorcycles of all shapes and sizes. I held my breath. If one toppled over, it would be like a massive domino slap down, and I was sure all those bikers at the party wouldn't like it one bit.

"Follow me. Very fucking carefully." Trick slid into the maze and I followed close behind. We zigzagged around motorcycle after motorcycle.

He finally stopped alongside Dawes at a blue and silver bike with a skull with a gleaming star in one eye painted over the gas tank. The heavy metal music seemed to grow louder from the party, the thick billows of smoke rising from the fires in the courtyard casting an eerie glow over the world.

"No matter what Dog's old lady says, Lex isn't going to just let us leave. His ass is on the line with his Prez for this," muttered Dawes as he put his key in his bike. He put her in neutral and wheeled her in reverse and then down a narrow pathway. Trick did the same with me right behind him.

We finally got clear of the mass of bikes, and we all let out heavy breaths.

Something whizzed past us in the air, and Trick's arm flung around me pulling me close, shoving me down. "They're shooting at us?" I crouched behind him.

"Speak of the fucking devil," Dawes spit out.

"Leave the girl!" shouted Lex stalking toward us, gun in the air.

My fingernails dug into Trick's arm.

"She's my old lady, asshole!"

Pushing me away, Trick flew at Lex, fists flying, landing a punch in Lex's stomach, the side of his face. Lex howled. Punches flew, curses and grunts filled the air. Lex landed on the ground, and Trick staggered over him, kicking him in the ribs. A metal object spun across the asphalt and landed next to me. It gleamed in the dim light, beckoning me.

A gun. Lex's gun.

Lex grabbed onto Trick, the two of them rolling over, grunting, yelling. Lex was bulkier than Trick, angrier. Adrenaline blew through my veins. Dawes cursed loudly in the dark. A man had wrestled him to the ground, and punches flew. There was only one thing to do, and I was going to do it. I grabbed the gun. The safety had already been released.

Lex stood up, and his ringed fist flew down over Trick. Taking aim at Lex's thigh, I waited for the moment when Trick was clear. Tightening my insides, I fired. Howling, Lex collapsed on the ground in a thud, and my lungs surged with oxygen once more.

"What the fuck? I've been shot! Goddammit!"

Trick groaned as he heaved himself upright. Dawes punched at his assailant, but the guy got him in a chokehold. I approached with my gun ready. "Get off him now, or I'll shoot you too. Now!" Cursing, he shoved at Dawes and darted back into the darkness.

"Jesus! Where did you learn to shoot like that?" said Dawes.

"My daddy."

"Well, fuck." Dawes took the gun from me and tossed it under the bikes next to us. "Thanks."

We grabbed Trick, pulling him up as Lex sputtered. "You motherfucking cunts, We're coming after you. You hear?"

"Get my lid on." Groaning, Trick shoved a helmet at me and got on his bike and ignited her in one move. Shaking, I put it on, latching it under my chin as I got onto the saddle behind him. Ahead of us, Dawes aimed his gun at the biker at the gate, spewing threats. The gate opened and we roared out of the property. My arms tightened around Trick's taut waist as we shot down the road and into the dark night.

Within moments, the thunder of motorcycles rose up behind us as we zoomed through the grim, ramshackle, inner-city neighborhood. Trick's gaze darted to his rearview mirror as he hit the throttle, and we rocketed forward.

I was on a rollercoaster fueled with dynamite that would never stop. My stomach flew up into my throat and jammed there, my heart hammering wildly. I kept my eyes on the road over Trick's shoulder. I wanted to see. I wanted to know, not hide. If this was the end, I wanted to be awake for it.

Here, we weren't on Oklahoma country roads. We were in the big, sprawling city on the run for our lives. Suddenly, we were in the flow of traffic on a boulevard heading onto the freeway judging from all the road signs and arrows. Trick and Dawes effortlessly weaved in between all the cars, trucks, and buses on the road, and we finally got on the main highway out of Kansas City.

We kept on, and on. My cold, numb body became a part of Trick's body, part of the roaring metal machine between our legs.

"Nebraska...the Good Life." The big green road sign whipped past us.

Show it to me, Nebraska.

The two men communicated over a wireless comm once we got further over the border. They agreed on stopping in Lincoln because someone they knew was there. I held on, bracing myself on the bike. My back ached, my butt was sore, my head hurt, but we were alive, and I was so damn grateful.

We rode through the city and, finally came to a stop in front of a restaurant, a biker hangout by the looks of the parking lot we entered. More bikes than vehicles.

Dawes tore off his helmet and wiped at his face. "You sure about this, man?"

"This is all we've got and it's our best shot."

"You could call Butler, have him pave the way?"

"No. I got to do this."

"Dude, we're talking about Finger. You and Finger."

"It's all water under the fucking bridge now. We've all been working together this whole past year without a hitch."

"All of us except for you. You stay a thousand miles away from him."

"Do you blame me?"

"No, I don't."

Did Trick have a tainted history with this Finger guy at this other club? A guy whose help we desperately needed. Nothing like personal drama to screw with everything.

Trick brushed a hand down his face. "We're in Flames territory now. We're being respectful by saying hello, and we're being smart by letting them know we had an altercation with their enemy."

Enemy? Oh boy. Factions and rivalries seemed to abound in the biker world.

"Did you just say altercation? What a sophisticated pretty word for this clusterfuck." fumed Dawes. "Their enemy, who is now on our tail."

Trick and Dawes muttered back and forth about the risks of what may lay ahead. I stopped trying to translate it, make sense of it. I stopped listening. My neck, my back, and every muscle in my legs screamed at me. My stomach cramped. And by their heated exchange and tense body language, it was obvious Trick and Dawes were real dang uptight about having to deal with this Finger and his Flames of Hell club.

And it was all my fault. *Once again, Nicole. Way to go.*

"If you don't mind my asking, why are we here?" I said, hoping to cut the tension between the two men.

"We've been on the road for three hours," Trick said. "We got six more to go, and I'd bet anything that Dog has sent out a search team for us. We need to get home, but we need to do it under the radar and with backup."

"Makes sense."

"And the best way to do that is with the help of a Nebraska club we're in an alliance with. A very powerful club."

"A club that's Dog's enemy?"

"Exactly," Trick replied.

"Oh."

"Exactly," quipped Dawes as he pulled a thick hoodie jacket out of his bike and put it on over his leather club jacket.

Trick did the same.

"What are y'all doing?"

"This isn't our neck of the woods if you know what I mean. A lot of these joints on the main highways don't allow club colors —the club patches on our jackets—so that petty fights don't break out. But since this is Flames territory, we're covering up our colors to play it safe and be respectful. But the good news is they know us so things should be cool."

"Should be?" My weight shifted under the weight of all this information, of all the what-ifs. This would probably blow up in my face like everything else had so far.

Everything except for Trick.

Trick dragged a hand through his hair, his forehead rippling, that scar visible. He was used to this sort of thing, wasn't he? "You doing okay, Zip?"

I took in a breath. "Fine. Glad to be off the bike for a break."

"Thanks for having my back and shooting Lex."

"You're welcome." My pulse ticked up as I held his warm gaze, heat filling my chest. "I had to help you. I couldn't let him beat you down."

His eyebrows jumped at my words, and his chin lifted. "Good to know you know how to use a gun."

"My dad had a massive gun collection. He was the president of our local gun club. I've known how to use a firearm since I was a little kid."

"Well, thanks, Dad." He let out a soft laugh and touched my arm gently. One minute Trick was on the razor's edge of dangerous, and the next the cozy hot guy next door, who you wanted to wrap his arms around you to keep you warm; make you feel safe. I swallowed hard. Which was it? He couldn't be both, could he?

"Let's do this." Dawes stalked toward the front door and pulled it open. A jangle of music seeped out into the night. Trick held out his hand to me. An invitation…to a new hell? Or safety? I wrapped my arms around my middle. "I can just stay out here." My left foot shuffled back stiffly. My right. "Y'all go on in and find whoever you need to talk to, and I'll stay out of your way…"

"You gonna run off?" Dawes's eyes narrowed. "Where the hell you think you're gonna go? We're in the middle of nowheresville!"

"Hang on, man. Chill—" Trick patted his buddy on the chest and leaned into me. "We want to go home too, Nicole. And in one piece. Getting their help is gonna be huge and will get us back to South Dakota safely." His voice was even and smooth. He was trying to convince me with logic. He put a hand on the side of my face. Gentle. Warm. "Zip, I took you. You shot Lex. They're coming for us." That was logic, all right.

"You're just going to pass me off to one of them because you'll owe them, or they'll demand it for helping you, right? Just like everybody's been doing. I was an idiot to trust Dog, an idiot." My insides clenched tight as my back went rigid. My throat burned with the words, clogged with emotion.

"No, Zip. Not us. I promise you. We've come this far. You've come even farther. Don't give in to the panic now." His hands slid down to my upper arms. He was being patient. Kind. "You trusted me to get you out of there, and I did. We made a good team. I'm real sorry you're suffering, I am. You don't deserve any of this. But right now the three of us are going in there together to get help from good people that we know. You got to believe me. Please. This is all we got and it's damn good. You saved my life, you saved Dawes, and I'm not going to let anything happen to you." He held out his hand to me again.

My chest heaved for air. There was nowhere to go, nowhere to run. Only this. Only Trick and Dawes and whatever and whoever lay behind that bar door. I slid my trembling hand into his, and he took it and squeezed. Warm, firm. We headed for the entrance of the bar. Dawes shoved the front door open wide.

Chaos spilled forth, and we dove in.

CHAPTER 11
TRICK

THIS WAS the last thing I wanted to have to do.

My hand tightened over Nicole's as I scanned the vast, dark bar through the thick haze of smoke. Packed wall-to-wall with bikers and women. Mostly Flames of Hell bikers.

As we'd entered Lincoln, Dawes had called a Flames biker who we worked with, Catch, who was also our VP's brother-in-law. Catch said they were on their way home from a run south to Lincoln and they'd be staying the night and we were welcome to join them. Big relief.

But I had to face Finger, the Flames president, who had once beat me down on the living room floor of my then-girlfriend's house. Force of habit calling her that. Was Lenore ever my *girl-friend*? No, and that had been the point. She'd only been interested in a booty-call relationship, which I'd agreed to, which had been great until I fell hard for her and wanted way more.

Until I'd wanted her to want more.

But she never did. She'd made it perfectly clear from the very beginning, but I was so infatuated with her and thought we were so good together, that I was sure I could convince her. No girl had ever said no to me before. How could it possibly happen when I was so invested; when I'd been giving her everything?

Ha.

I'd kept pushing unable to believe that she couldn't see it, couldn't feel it, couldn't want it. Little did I know she was yearning for the lost love of her life, who was none other than Finger.

Then I'd fucked it all up when I'd lost my temper with her that night. She'd blown me off from an invite to a club party, and I'd gotten so angry that I'd showed up at her house kind of drunk and way the hell pissed off, which led to me insisting, accusing, and then strong-arming her. Lowest moment of my life. How could I have been such an asshole? How could I have let it get that ugly?

Denial, that's how.

Then came the surprise beat down by the almighty Finger who showed up at her house out of nowhere and right on time. On my knees, arms twisted behind me, face smashed into the carpet of her living room floor. In that very moment of rejection and utter humiliation, I'd gotten the message from the universe loud and fucking clear: How dare I?

I would never have what I wanted—my own woman, a woman I wanted more than anything. I was good for one thing only: a good time between the sheets.

Yep, I was done with hopes and plans. *My girl, my old lady, my woman*—none of that was in the cards for me. For the past two years, I'd steered clear of anything remotely resembling an attachment to a female.

I loved my bike club family. Hell, I'd come from one. My Uncle Willy, my mom's older brother, was a founding member of our chapter of the One-Eyed Jacks. Even my dad had been a prospect in the early days, but he had given it up when he was offered a good job opportunity he wanted to take on for his family. Even so, my parents' social life revolved around the Jacks.

I'd known MC family life from the time I was in my mother's womb and then later, at sixteen, I worked and lived around the club when I moved in with Uncle Willy. I loved club life, and my place in it. I had a great job at the club's custom detailing business, and I was fucking Road Captain now and so proud to serve my brothers as an officer. The club was family, a sure thing. My good thing. The club never let me down.

And whenever I wanted to get laid, I didn't have to work hard to find very willing and sexy women to play with. The high fucking life of Trick. Who could ask for anything more? Only an idiot.

"Whoa," Nicole murmured, her voice tense, a sound that had me snapping out my skip down shit memory lane. Her lips parted as she took in the thick, raucous crowd in the dimly lit old bar. Her cool, long fingers pressed into my flesh. Somehow that eased the tension in my own veins.

"Hey, dudes, what's up? Good to see you." Catch greeted us with handshakes and slaps on the shoulder.

"Yo, look who's here." Pick, another Flame we knew well, stretched out his massive hand to Dawes and they shook and bumped fists. "Trick, what's up?" Pick and I greeted each other. "Welcome to Nebraska."

"Thanks, man. This is Nicole. Nicole this is Pick, and this is Catch."

Nicole's eyes opened wide at the giant that was Pick. "Hi. Nice to meet you." She nodded her head at Catch.

"You too, hon." Pick dipped his chin, his lips curving slightly at her. "Need a beer, y'all?"

"Hell yes," said Dawes.

Catch held up three fingers at the bartender and was quickly rewarded with three bottles of brew, which he handed to us.

I gave one to Nicole and took a long swig of mine. The cold liquid flooded down my hot throat like an icy waterfall on an August afternoon. "Thanks, man. Thanks for letting us know where you are. We got us a situation."

"We could use your help," added Dawes.

"Spill, what's going on?" Catch's forehead wrinkled as he

listened to our story, his gaze darting to Pick. "That is a situation, and I kinda like it."

"I thought you would," I replied with a tight grin.

"Riding home to Meager on your own would sure as shit be unwise," said Pick. "You gotta stay with us tonight, and tomorrow we roll to our clubhouse. From there your boys can come get you."

"Thanks, man," said Dawes.

The Flames and the Smoking Guns had been mortal enemies from decades ago, and that hostility had reached its peak when, almost thirty years ago, they'd kidnapped a young Finger and tortured him. I swallowed hard as my gaze landed on Finger, their President, on the other side of the bar, a glass of liquor in his mutilated hand, a slash of a dark grin on his scarred face.

I cleared my throat. "I realize this will be putting the Flames in a tough spot.

Pick chuckled. "Fuck off, man. You think we can't handle it?"

"Of course you can handle it. What I meant was making your sticky relationship with the Smoking Guns even stickier."

"Dude, we've been playing pat-a-cake with them way too fucking long." Catch's head slanted. "Of course, this needs to be cleared with the Prez first."

"Of course," said Dawes, shooting me his buckle-up-here-we-go look.

I sucked down the last of my beer, as did Dawes, and we plonked the empty bottles on the bar top.

"This way." Catch led us through the crowd, toward Finger.

At my side, Nicole's body trembled. Taking from her the beer bottle she hadn't touched, I put it on the bar and took her hand in mine once more. The three of us followed Pick and Catch, weaving through all the bikers and their women who glared at us.

"It's okay, don't worry. We're good," I whispered in Nicole's ear. On top of being exhausted, nervous, and strung out, she probably needed something to eat and drink. Hopefully, we'd get to that soon.

"Prez, they're here." Pick stepped aside, and my heart bonged in my chest like a gong as Finger's cold stone-like gaze met mine, his scarred features revealing only a thin veil of contempt as he took me in from where he sat on a barstool. There was movement next to him. A figure turned around.

My muscles tightened. Lenore stood next to Finger, a hand sliding over her old man's massive thigh, that familiar blue-green gaze of hers gleaming its icy coolness at Nicole. At me.

Fuck, fuck, FUUUCCCKKK.

CHAPTER 12
NICOLE

I'D THOUGHT Dog was scary. I'd thought Dinosaur Tattoo Man was loathsome. I'd thought Pick was menacing, Catch threatening.

But this incredibly tall and muscular older tattooed man with a deeply scarred face, severe metal-like eyes, and chopped-off middle fingers on both hands?

Spine-chilling epitome of merciless. Ruthless. Sheer brutality.

My insides shuddered as we came to a stop before him. A beautiful woman in a tight black leather outfit, blue hair, and stiletto boots stood next to him, a hand on his leg. There was an air of seriousness about her the moment she locked eyes on us. Finger's hand closed over hers. They both wore matching wedding bands. She gave Trick and Dawes a slight smile, her gaze lingering on me. We were introduced.

She seemed so unlike Dog's wife, Carrie. Carrie was brittle, highly strung, with a boulder on her shoulder. Finger's woman had nothing to prove and bore the confidence you earned over a troubled road. She seemed to be a sea of steady calm, but who knew what lurked under the surface of those waters?

Trick's hand tightened even more around mine as he cleared

his throat. "Our apologies for interrupting your evening, but it's real important."

"I would think it is for you to be here." Finger's raspy voice and tight gaze made my lungs constrict.

"Dawes and I were on a run for Eagle Wings to Kansas City—"

An eyebrow on his scarred face twitched ever so slightly at the mention of the city we'd taken off from. He knew what was coming.

"— and I ended up helping a stranded Smoking Gun with a bike repair, and he invited us to their clubhouse for a party. I felt we couldn't turn down the invite, so we went, and I met Nicole there. She was zip-tied to a fence." Lenore's head tilted slightly as Trick went on. "They'd kidnapped her from her home in Oklahoma after she'd paid off her brother's debt to Dog."

"Kidnapped?" said Finger, his voice so deep, so scratchy, that my insides twisted at the unusual sound. "Took her across state lines?"

"Yeah. Dog was planning on keeping her for himself."

That eyebrow twitched once more. "And you took her?"

"It wasn't like that. At first, she asked me to help her, but I turned her down for the sake of the greater peace. Felt like shit about it, but I knew our visit there had to be free of complications."

"And you were right."

The tension in Trick's arm sent a flare of pain through my own. Trick standing here before a great outlaw judge and jury in one was because of me.

I had to step in.

"Trick cut the zip tie, he cut me free, but that was it." I shifted my weight. "At first..."They all stared at me. A slight smile flickered over Lenore's face, and I continued. "But Carrie, Dog's old lady, found me and..." My stomach heaved with the memory of Carrie and what could have happened.

Finger's brow wrinkled. "And?"

"And she had other plans for me…" I pushed myself to not crumple, not puke. "To make a long story short, she got distracted, and that's when I ran back into the crowd—which, now that I think about it, was a dumb thing to do—but it wasn't, because I ended up crashing right into Trick, and that's when he helped me get out of there." My gaze lifted, locking on Trick's molten one, and a zing shot through my sapped veins. Light and heat. Hope.

"So you didn't take her to have yourself a good time?" said Finger.

"No," Trick replied.

"Then Carrie caught up with us," I added. "That's when Trick told her that he and I were … together. That I was his old lady." Dizziness buzzed through my head. Was it anxiety and exhaustion? Embarrassment before these people? Or was it saying *his old lady* out loud?

This is real life, Nic. Their real life. And now it's yours. You got yourself into this. Deal with it.

"And Carrie let us go," Trick finished for me as my weary gaze fell to my once polished and now very scuffed boots. "But the guy who Dog had body-guarding Nicole, Lex, the one who'd zip-tied her to the fence so he could party, got pissed off and came after us. He shot at us, we got into a fight in their parking lot, his gun went flying, and Nicole grabbed it and shot him in the leg."

"Uh-huh." Finger pressed his lips together.

"Some of his guys chased us on their bikes until we got out of the city. We got this far, but I knew that it'd be real stupid to carry on through Nebraska for six more hours on our own with Lex shot and Dog knowing that Nicole's gone. I'm sure his old lady tried to stop him, but now with Lex down, he has reason to come after us."

"He does."

Straightening his back, Trick met Finger's grim gaze. "So I'm asking you for help to get us back to Meager."

A silence crackled between us. Even in the corner of this loud, loud bar. I could sense it, and it numbed me. Stilled my pulse. My head hung.

A cool hand pressed against my cheek and I let out a small gasp. Lenore. "Dog lied to you? Kidnapped you?" Her voice was very gentle yet charged with emotion. "He tied you up like a stray dog to use you when he was good and ready?"

"Y-yes," I breathed, drowning in her soft gaze.

She wrapped her arms around me. Firm and resolute. Warmth oozed through me, and my free arm went around her back as she held me close. A soft yet spicy perfume invaded my senses and invited ease into my lungs, into my heart.

"It's over, Nicole. You're safe now," she whispered in my ear. "We won't let them take you. No way in hell."

My head sank against her shoulder. My body slumped against her. The room spun. I spun.

And the dark world got darker.

CHAPTER 13
TRICK

"NICOLE!"

She'd fainted in Lenore's embrace. I took her in my arms, cradling her limp body tight. "I got her. I got her." Her beautiful blonde hair tumbled over my shoulders, her pale face ghostly in the dim light of the bar as Lenore pushed everyone back from us.

"Move!" Finger bellowed at a group of bikers sitting on a banquette to his side and they jumped out of his way. "Over here, lay her down. Get her feet up."

"Shit!" spit out Dawes, throwing chairs out of the way.

"Get me a water, quick!" Lenore shouted behind me.

I laid Nicole down on the banquette, and Dawes took off his hoodie and tucked it under her calves.

"Nicole! Nicole...motherfuck..." I slid my hand over her eerily cold forehead.

Lenore cracked open a small water bottle, taking water in her hands and patting Nicole's face and throat, dabbing her pale lips. "She's been through the wringer, huh?"

"Yeah, she has. And I don't think she's had anything to eat in a while either."

Nicole's head moved, and her pale lips parted.

"There she is," murmured Lenore. "Hey, Nicole. Hey. You're okay. You're safe."

I slid my arm under her upper body and got her sitting up, while Lenore put the bottle of water to her lips. So vulnerable. Her features tightened and relaxed. She focused on Lenore as she drank.

She raised her eyes to me. Was I a blur? "Trick," she breathed, and my heart beat again.

I cupped her cheek with my palm. "Yeah, Zip, it's me. Welcome back." Her cool fingers wrapped around my wrist, and I smiled at her. "I got you."

A shaky smile wavered on her lips in return.

"Trick." Finger gestured at me to join him, Dawes, Pick, and his VP, Drac.

"Go on, I've got her," said Lenore. "We'll be right here."

I gave Nicole's arm a squeeze and then joined the men.

"She okay?" asked Finger.

"Yeah."

"Stay with us here tonight, and first thing in the morning we'll get you out of here in our van. Call Butler now and let him know to send a Jacks van to our clubhouse tomorrow to get you home."

Dawes got on his phone.

"I appreciate this, Finger. Thank you."

"You did a good thing, Trick. The risky thing. The right thing." Finger lifted his chin at me. "History has a way of repeating itself with that club. You took his pirate booty out from under him, and he's probably all sore about it. And even though she doesn't amount to a hill of beans for him, he'll use this and his boy being shot to go after you and the Jacks."

"I'm sure he will."

"Of course, you understand that the smart thing to do here is to continue the lie that she's your old lady. The two of you get your story straight and stick to it. The whole club."

I froze. He was right. *Jesus, what the fuck? I have an old lady now? An old lady verified by Finger of all people? Karma is way more than a bitch.* I let out a tight breath. "Right."

"You sure all Dog wants from her is her snatch and more of her cash? He took her across state lines after she paid off her brother's debt, and I'm betting it was a lot of money."

"I think it was a hell of a lot of cash."

"You sure there isn't anything else he's got on her brother, or maybe she's useful to him in another way?"

"I don't know any details yet."

"You need to find out. She was with them for a couple days, right? With Dog. Get her to tell you everything and anything she saw, heard, the people she came into contact with, what they said, how they acted. She's new to the life, so she may think it's all strange and random, but you'll know."

"I'll do that. The more we know the better for us and for her."

"Do it when you get to Meager, when she's feeling better. Not tonight." His jaw tightened. "Tonight, she needs to feel safe."

I blinked. Had he been on this carousel ride before? "You're right. She does, yeah."

"Dog's been president for over two years since our bust up. He's gotten fat and happy and real bored. Part of our truce was that there be no retaliation of any kind for his predecessor's death, which we explained nicely, but he knows it was us. And now if he's pissed at us over anything, even for this crumb flying off his tablecloth—" he gestured at Nicole—"he'll take it and build on it. Build a three-ring circus around that pole."

"Good times," laughed Drac, his super long canine teeth showing.

"Since the Smoking Guns lost bringing in the Broken Blades to the Flames, they've been scrambling to beef up in other ways," said Pick. "Word is they've started working with some outsiders in Kansas City and are making bank."

"Not just this bounty hunter gig?" I asked.

"Nah, he's always done that shit," said Finger. "This is something else, something bigger, and I want to know who it is they're working with and what they're moving. Not only did we take away the Blades, but we broke the Guns' pathway to a cartel back then. Dog laid low since we agreed to a truce and he became President, but no way was he ever going to let all that drop. He's still eyeing our territory for a channel south and west. He was in on that plan before we destroyed it."

Lenore came up next to Finger. "Sorry to interrupt. Nicole's doing better. And I ordered food for you guys." I glanced back and there was Nicole seated at a table, staring at a tall burger and fries that had been set before her. "Whenever you're ready."

"Thanks, Lenore," said Dawes. "Much appreciated."

"Thank you," I said.

"Of course."

Finger's arm slid over his old lady's shoulder. "Go, eat. Relax," he said. "We'll be here another three, four hours at least before we head to the motel. Give Pick your keys so we can get your bikes dealt with in the parking lot."

Dawes and I gave Pick our keys and joined Nicole at the table. "Looks real good," I sat down next to her and downed the icy cold beer from the bottle before my dish.

"So good," said Nicole between bites, wiping at her mouth.

I let out a laugh. "Feel better, huh?"

"Hmm."

I wiped at the ketchup smudge on her cheek. "You look better." She stilled under my touch. Why the hell was I touching her? I took back my hand.

Dawes let out a groan as he shoved the burger in his mouth. "Just what the doctor ordered."

Nicole took a napkin and rubbed at her cheek, her lips. "Did everything work out?"

"Sure did."

"That's a relief. Lenore is very nice."

"She's good people," I said. "We're going to spend the night with them at a motel and then leave in the morning in one of their vans."

Her eyes tensed. "A van?"

She was freaked out. What the hell had they done to her?

"We're hiding. We can't be seen on the road." Dawes stuffed fries in his mouth.

Nicole put her burger down.

"Hey." Swallowing hard, she met my gaze. "The three of us will be together in the van along with our bikes. That cool?"

"And along with a thousand tools and cables and engine parts…" Dawes lifted his bottle of beer and drank.

"On a long run, clubs have a van that follows the bikes on the road," I explained. "So in case someone has engine trouble or whatever, they can stop and fix it right there and then."

"Oh. That makes sense." She dipped a thick steak fry into a puddle of ketchup and chewed on it.

"The thought of being in a van for that long is giving you claustrophobia, huh?" I asked. "I get it. Any kind of closed-in vehicle doesn't feel normal to me after riding my bike for so long."

"Riding a motorcycle is definitely not a claustrophobic experience." A smile tugged on her lips as she picked up her burger again.

"Bro, what did Butler say?" I asked Dawes. "He must have been pissed, huh?"

"Pissed? Meh. I'd say flabbergasted, furious, flipping out, and yet somewhere underneath all that was pride that we'd gotten here safe and hooked up with the Flames."

"That's something, I guess." I finished the bacon cheeseburger. I wouldn't think about what waited for us once we got back to Meager. Now I would only enjoy my food, my beer, and relax with Dawes and Nicole.

"Who's Butler?" asked Nicole.

"Our Vice President," replied Dawes.

"Y'all are in trouble because of me, right?"

"I had to help you," I said. "There was no decision to make. I mean, I know I said no to you when you first asked me for help—"

"Trick, I get it. You were following orders. Being responsible. Believe me, I get it. But you cut the dang zip tie, and I'm grateful for that."

"I was on the lookout for you the whole time I was with Dog, and I extricated myself from that bullshit chit-chat as soon as I could. And that's when I saw you, running, and that woman coming after you. There was no question in my mind. No debate." I held her gaze, and it was as if an electric current coursed between us on my words. An electric current we both needed, both craved.

Stop it, Trick, Stop it now.

I tore my gaze away from her and let out a short laugh. "Shit, what was it you said to them—"*I'm his property*"? Damn, woman, you're a quick study."

She let out a laugh. It was good to hear it mixed with mine. A flush crept over her cheeks, and her eyes lit up. The most beautiful deep blue I'd ever seen.

Dawes let out a satisfied groan, pushing his empty dish aside. "I'm wiped. I'll go pay the bartender and then find Pick to see where exactly we're going to crash tonight."

I handed him a wad of cash, and he took off from the table, leaving me and Nicole alone.

"Trick, I want you to know, that I really appreciate everything y'all have done for me. And I'm sorry that I put you in a terrible position with your club, that you're going to get in trouble on my account."

"Won't be the first time, won't be the last." I drained my glass. The beer was lukewarm, but I swallowed it down anyhow. Now would be a good time to tell her about having to be my old lady for a spell. *"No good deed goes unpunished,"* my mother used to say. My mother was a hell of a wise woman.

Nicole's hand brushed my arm. "Thank you for everything."

That jolt of heat flared through my flesh again. Who knew, maybe this punishment would be a sweet and sizzling kind of torture?

Trick, for fuck's sake! I wiped a hand across my mouth. Me? An old lady? I'd done nothing but fight against that ever happening for two years now. My fucking luck astounded me.

Biting on her lip, Nicole scanned the bar like she was in the center of a ghoulish fish tank and all of us piranhas circling her. Best leave telling her for tomorrow once we got on the road or, maybe when we finally got to Meager.

"Where in South Dakota do you live?" she asked.

"Meager. A small town in the Black Hills." Her eyes widened like double full moons. "It's about an hour plus southeast of Rapid."

She relaxed against her chair, a slight smile lighting up her face. "Meager?"

"Funny name, huh?"

Dawes and Pick arrived. Dawes held up a card key for a room at the motel next door. We'd go over there with Pick.

"Nicole?" Lenore came over. "Could I ask you a quick question?" She tilted her head.

"Sure." Nicole's face immediately brightened and she shot up from the table and went over to her, and the two women talked.

"What's that about?" Dawes asked.

"No idea. But I get the feeling Lenore's reassuring her about everything."

"That's good. Nicole seems cool 'cause, let's face it, she could have been way the fuck hysterical from the get-go and all the way up to now, and that would have been a fuck of a problem."

"Truth." Dawes was right. Nicole could have been pitching a fit the whole time—and I wouldn't have blamed her—but instead, this woman was cooperative, grateful, and practical. Fatigue and panic notwithstanding.

The women hugged, and Lenore lifted a hand in goodbye to

us. Nicole returned. "Everything okay?" I asked as Dawes and I got up from the table.

"She asked me if I'd be more comfortable spending the night with her instead of you."

"And you said…"

"I said I wanted to stay with you."

CHAPTER 14
TRICK

SHE WANTS *to stay with me.*

She wants to stay with me.

Those words kept drumming through my head as Pick led us to our motel room in the dark.

So what? So the fuck what? Don't read anything into it. It just means you saved her ass and she feels safe with you. End of.

But I liked that Nicole felt safe with me. A hell of a lot.

Blowing out a breath, I allowed my ego to enjoy the brief stroking, but I commanded my twitching dick to stand down.

Dawes swiped the room key card in the slot and the motel room door clicked open. "Thanks, Pick."

"You bet. See you in the morning. We'll roll by nine."

Dawes pushed the door in. The room had two single beds and a small sofa.

"Yesssss!" Dawes flung himself on a bed.

"I'll take the sofa," I said.

"No, I'll take the sofa," said Nicole. "You don't have to do that."

"I want to."

Dawes let out a groan as he kicked off his boots. "Figure it out kids and lights out, eh?"

"Take the bed, or I'm going to tie you to it, Zip."

"Fine," she murmured, her face reddening. Jesus, her blushing over the littlest thing did something to me, something kinky. The shy, innocent girl. The modest lady with a body to die for. I dragged my fingers through my hair. This was going to be a long night.

I found an extra pillow and blanket in the closet and tossed them on the sofa.

"I'm going to use the bathroom." She stepped around me, her hips brushing mine, and she jerked back and darted into the bathroom. I scowled at the rush of testosterone surging through me at the contact.

"What is it?" Dawes shoved down his pants, ripped off his T, and got under the covers.

"Nothing."

"You like her."

"No."

"It's okay if you like her, man."

It was not okay. Nicole was a super civilian who had no idea about the life. A woman who looked and sounded like she came from the other side of the tracks from me, a different world, and she did. Money, education. The finer things. There was no fucking way.

"I don't like her."

"Do I need to put on my earplugs?" Dawes sat up. "Let me grab 'em—"

"Go to sleep, asshole."

On a lazy laugh, he flopped back on the mattress. "Sweet dreams, bro." With one arm under his neck and the other on his chest, Dawes fell asleep right away. He always did. Me, I got monkey mind the second I hit the pillow. But tonight, after everything we'd been through and then some, the adrenaline finally draining from me, I was hoping to be a goner the minute I got horizontal.

Nicole came out of the bathroom and busied herself taking off her boots. I took in a deep breath. Then again, maybe I wouldn't be able to fall asleep with Nicole in a bed a few feet away from me. I headed into the bathroom, took a piss, splashed water on my face, and brushed my teeth. My weary gaze settled on my bruised and haggard reflection in the mirror. What a night. *It ain't over yet!* Again, I rubbed my face with icy cold water.

Back in the room, the lights were off, and in the dark, I peeled off my leathers and settled onto the sofa, relief chasing away the tension in my muscles. The sound of Dawes's shallow breathing filled the room.

"Good night, Trick," came Nicole's small voice in the dark.

I got under the thick blanket. "Hey, Zip—if you need anything, let me know, okay? Don't hesitate."

"Okay. Thanks…" her voice had softened, her breaths. She'd drifted off already too.

I willed my brain to stop thinking and my every muscle to sink into the too-soft cushions. We were safe. We weren't alone. Tomorrow we would be home…and tomorrow I would get the shit kicked out of me by my Prez and every officer…and take on an old lady for the first time in my life. A woman I didn't know at all. A woman I found so damn hard to resist. Enticing, sweet, so damn hot…

On a groan I buried my face in the pillow and drifted on that sweet and hot. Hot and sweet. Drifted.

"I'm not. I'm not…let go…let go of me….stop, please, don't…" A tortured, desperate voice pierced my brain.

"Nicole?"

Shuddering moans and small cries filled the room. I darted over to her. "Hey, Nicole. Wake up, you're having a bad dream is all. Nicole!" Sitting on the edge of her bed, I wiped back the hair from her damp forehead.

Her eyes blinked open and she flinched and relaxed her shoulders in the same breath. "Trick?"

"Yeah, it's me. You okay? It was just a dream, a bad dream. That's all. You're okay. You're with me. With me and Dawes."

Her head fell back, and she let out a heavy breath, a hand clasping my arm. "Thank God. It was Dog, he was laughing and chasing me, and then his wife came after me, and then Lex and…."

"They're not here, they're far away. And we're safe."

She sat up. "We're safe." She hugged me.

My veins combusted with heat as her body pressed into mine. My arms wrapped around her tightly and I hugged her back. We stayed that way in the loaded silence, her heart beating hard against my bare chest. Her silky hair sliding against my skin.

I hadn't been this close to a woman in this sort of way in forever and it was doing something to my head, not to mention to my body. "You need some water maybe?" I whispered.

"No." She nestled in closer to my chest. "I need this hug."

My lungs squeezed. No woman had ever said that to me before. I'd heard, "I need your mouth," "I need your tongue," "I need your cock." "I need a drink." But a request for a hug? For comfort, understanding, support?

"You got it, Zip." My voice came out raspy as I held her tighter and inhaled the scent of her warm skin, her flowery shampoo, my hand stroking her back.

She let out a soft sigh. Relief and pleasure swirled in one. A combination that made my heart tick up. I felt it too. "Thank you," she whispered, her lips brushing my cheek, sending that electric current through my veins again.

I could have held her like that for hours, but I slowly released her and she laid back down on the bed, a hand still wrapped around my bare arm. "Hmm." She let out a soft moan, turning toward me. The dim glow from the parking lot lights through the cracks in the heavy curtains allowed me to see her relaxed face. So fucking beautiful. My hand trailed up and down her back like it didn't want to let go of her.

"I like your tattoos," she murmured.

"Thanks."

"Is that an eagle wing?" Her finger traced the long wing wrapped around my arm and shoulder just to my chest. A thousand sparks raced over my skin.

"Something like that."

Her eyes focused on my chest.

"May 24..." she said softly, referring to the date tattooed on my chest in the wing. "What's that about?"

My insides tightened. "Just...a big day in my life."

"Hmm." She drifted off. My fingers traced the side of her cheek. She sighed once more.

Fuck, that sound was going to kill me. Innocent and sensual all at once. It filled my veins with molten heat and jackhammered at my heart muscle. No matter, I was glad she felt comfortable with us, with me. Trusted me.

At least for now.

How was she going to feel when she found out she was going to have to live with me as my old lady?

CHAPTER 15
NICOLE

A WALL of warmth cradled my body and I sank against it once more. My lips found smooth, taut, warm skin and I nestled deeper. My eyes unstuck. Light seeping through the curtains glowed over a naked muscular male form alongside me, his arm around me, my face against his incredibly chiseled and very tattooed chest.

Trick. How did? Did we?

My muscles tightened, and then it all came rushing back through the haze. He'd sat with me in bed last night after I'd had a nightmare. He'd held me, said such soothing things to me, and I'd fallen back asleep, clutching his arm. He must have fallen asleep on the bed soon after.

His face riddled with black and blue marks from his fight with Lex was peaceful in sleep, the soft rush of his breathing fanning my chest. His tattoos up close were very impressive. My fingertips brushed over his tanned skin, over that inked date with the blood drops, and a small sound escaped his lips, making my heart beat skip. His eyes blinked open, narrowed, focused on me. His fingers pressed into my skin, and my pulse jangled.

"Nicole..." he breathed.

"Morning," I whispered tightly.

We remained still. His skin radiated heat, the current of his breath picking up as his lips parted. "Shit, I must have…"

Dawes stretched out and groaned on the other bed, behind me. "Oh man," came his voice. "Did you two—"

"No!" Trick and I both said.

"Geez. All right. All right." He got up and shuffled into the bathroom.

Trick released me from his hold and sprang off the bed. A chill swept over my skin, and I brought the sheet close to me. The sheet was warm with him, and my toes curled, my legs pressed together.

"Sorry, I must have fallen asleep here after your nightmare."

"I figured. It's fine. It's…"

"We were talking one minute and then…I must have crashed." He grabbed his pants and pulled them on. His legs were all lean muscle. His rear was perfectly sculpted.

"We were both exhausted." I forced myself to look away, my fingers digging into the nubby white sheet as I sat up in the bed. "Thank you for waking me up from that nightmare."

"Didn't sound fun. Glad I could help." He unzipped a small duffel bag and pulled out a black T-shirt and tugged it on. The fabric wrapped around his corded muscles. "I've got an extra T-shirt. You want it or you good as is?"

"Could I?"

"Sure." He tossed another black tee on the bed by my legs.

"Thanks."

Dawes came out of the bathroom. "Peck just called me and gave us ten minutes to be ready to roll. They'll come get us."

"Cool," Trick said. "Nicole, you want to use the bathroom?"

"You go on ahead first."

He ducked inside.

"I had a nightmare and Trick woke me up," I said to Dawes.

"You've been through a lot. Anyhow, not my business. You guys do what you want." He dragged a hand through his thick blond curls as he checked himself out in the mirror. "But hey, you two are playing old man/old lady now, so going at it keeps it real, right?" He chuckled.

"What?"

Dawes dragged his teeth over his lower lip. "Uh…you and Trick, you told the Guns that you're together, right? That you were coming to South Dakota to be with him?"

"Um…yeah."

"So to keep off Dog's radar you got to…uh…" He cleared his throat. "Play the part now."

"Oh." Heat flooded my face, enflamed my skin. "I thought once we got to South Dakota I would just…"

"Yeah, no. No. It's not safe for either of you. Me either. You and Trick got to play house for a little while until things settle down with the Smoking Guns. 'Cause you two just tripped a wire and lit a few sticks of dynamite that are probably lighting up a few more right about now."

"Makes sense, I guess."

"In our world, it does. Now you're officially spoken for, making you hands off to every man, especially Dog."

Spoken for. By Trick. Playing house. With Trick. This biker who was the complete opposite of my husband, Logan, in every way. I felt like I had landed in Eleven's upside down. Stranger things, indeed.

"Don't sweat it, Nicole. Won't be forever."

"I can't seem to stop flinging myself from one frying pan to the next."

Dawes sat on the one chair in the room and pulled on his thick boots. "Trust me, you got yourself a good man in Tricky. I've known him for years and years. He brought me into the club. I trust him with my life."

"Good to know." And on that good side, I'd be in Meager and at the very same motorcycle club that Richie had been a member of. That was why I'd wanted to get to South Dakota in the first place. I was on the right path.

But to be a member of a bike gang? No, rather, the girlfriend of a member? I was being forced to play a board game without knowing the rules.

Dawes adjusted the belt at his waist. "I'm sorry for laying that on you now, I should've waited for Trick to…"

"No, no, I appreciate your honesty, Dawes. I do. Just like I appreciate all the trouble y'all have gone to for me. Like you said, all this is new to me, and I don't quite know…"

The bathroom door flew open, and Trick filled the doorway, his gaze ping-ponging between me and Dawes. "Everything good?"

"Uh…yeah…" Dawes glanced at me to make sure we were cool.

"Everything's good," I affirmed shooting both men a grin and getting out of the bed. Everything had to be good. I'd gotten us all into this mess, and now I had to see it through.

I straightened out my crumpled blouse. Of course I'd slept in my clothes with a bare-chested Trick around me. "Do I have time for a quick shower?"

Dawes glanced at his watch. "You've got four minutes."

"Okay." I grabbed Trick's T-shirt from the bed and darted into the bathroom. I stripped off and took the fastest shower of my life, dried off, and got dressed. My body tingled and was so happy to be clean and refreshed, even if I had to wear the same underwear and jeans and socks. I was super grateful for the clean T-shirt. Trick's fabric softener smelled like my favorite rain fresh-scented one. I rejoined the guys.

"And super quick she is." Dawes grinned at me.

"Why, thank you." I sat on the edge of the bed and got my boots on, and a knock came at our door, making me stiffen in attention.

Pick glowered at the three of us. Or was that his regular, normal, everyday face? Guess I'd be figuring that out soon enough.

"Hey," said Dawes.

"Wanted y'all to know, Dog and a couple of his men were spotted an hour ago crossing into Nebraska."

Trick's hand slid up my back. Warm, firm. Steadying. "You ready?" he said, his voice rough.

Ready for what exactly?

Running away from Dog and his crew under the radar? A six-hour ride with two bikers I barely know in a van belonging to yet another motorcycle club? Finally going to South Dakota to find my (secret) other family? Or being fake "married" to you for however long and whatever that entails while hopefully Logan and Jackson would not find me?

The look in Trick's eyes was steady, and I took it in, swallowing past the tightness threatening to close my throat. We were in this together, and so far, we'd looked out for each other. So far, so good.

I stood up next to him. "I'm ready."

CHAPTER 16
NICOLE

RIDING in the van with Trick and Dawes and the driver, a nice guy called Hook, wasn't too bad. The van was no ordinary van, but a brand new, extra-long, cargo van. There was plenty of room for us to sit along with the bikes and all the bike parts and tools, and the air conditioning worked like a dream.

We sat in the back with the bikes, not in the passenger seats. There were no windows, and the only view we had was from the windshield. I kept my water drinking to the bare minimum because I didn't want to be stuck having to pee. There would be no hope in hell of *all* the bikers stopping so I could relieve myself. I was sure they must have some sort of schedule when they rode long distances. I would find out today.

"What exactly does a Road Captain do?" I asked Trick.

His lips twitched. "Look at you, trying to learn biker-speak." He chuckled.

"You're a Road Captain, right?" I gestured at his patch. "I came across the term once in a newspaper article about a bike club. Wondered what it meant." My fingers fiddled with the straps of my small backpack. That newspaper article that had mentioned Richie or "Wreck" as the One-Eyed Jacks Road

Captain was in there along with the old photographs and the beaded baby bracelet, all of them burning a hole in the leather.

"The Road Captain plans out all the club runs, our road trips, which roads we're going to take, that sort of thing. He rides behind the club members on the road, making sure everyone's all good, and if a brother has a problem, he stops and gets the bike fixed or pulls it in the van. And if the President and Vice-President aren't present, he'll lead the club formation on the ride."

"Oh." I leaned back on the cushions Trick had put together for me and imagined Richie being the final rider in the men's formation like the guy ahead of us on the road. Being the fix-it guy. The one everybody depended on.

A smile tugged at my lips as the Flames Road Captain riding in front of us on the road transformed into my lost half-brother, his long eighties hair, his engine roaring underneath him. Would that scowl be on his face? Maybe, but I imagined on the inside he'd probably be so high and at ease as he flew over the asphalt, knowing he was taking care of his club.

Trick's feet tapped mine from across the van. "Where did you go? What are you thinking about?"

"Just trying to imagine being a Road Captain. Lots of responsibility for one guy. Sounds like you'd have to be able to think super quick on your feet to get that job done. Be incredibly attentive and focused."

"He is," said Dawes.

"You do got to be a quick thinker, problem solver, see the bigger picture, make snap decisions," said Trick. "Two men I admire were amazing road captains for the Jacks. I aspire to be half the officers they were."

"Are they still with the club?"

"One is yeah. The older one got killed a while back. He was something." He crossed his arms around his chest, his muscles bulging. "His road name was Wreck because he never, not once, got into any kind of car or bike accident."

My insides pitched. Had Trick known Richie? "Never ever? Not even a little scrape?" I leaned forward, hugging my knees. I didn't want to miss a word.

"Nope." A smile creased Trick's face. A genuine deep one, one that said this memory felt good through and through and he wanted to savor it. "But if you got into a wreck—he'd fix you right up."

The three of us laughed together, and a tickle twisted through my insides. I'd forgotten what it was like to simply hang out and enjoy a conversation with other human beings. And learning about Richie? The best. "Did you know Wreck, or he was way before your time?"

"You bet I knew him. I was lucky I got to work in his repair shop when I first started at the club as a teenager. Everything I learned about cars and bikes is because of him. Just a few months and then…then we lost him."

"I'm so sorry," I breathed.

"Me too." Trick held my gaze. His brown eyes gleamed in the light flooding the van. "He was the one who gave me my road name."

"He named you Trick?"

"He did."

"I was curious about that, but I wasn't sure how to ask."

Leaning back against the wall of the van, the lines of his face relaxed. "It was my first road trip with the club. We were with the Jacks from Colorado, a much big chapter than ours. One of their guys was having engine problems. Wreck offered to help, and I tagged along.

"It was a vintage Harley, from the late 50s and the mousetrap was corroded, it had snapped. A mousetrap is a clutch booster, a spring attachment used on these bikes back in the day. Anyhow, I could tell Wreck was frustrated 'cause we were on our way to meet up with another club on this big charity run and he hated being late, but more irritated with the guy who should've been keeping his bike clean and not let it go to shit. And it was shit.

"In the end, I scrounged up some wire and a nail I found on the side of the road and together Wreck and I figured out a way to keep the mechanism attached and functioning, at least for the time being. We tested it, it held."

"Wire and a nail?"

"My dad was a wrench too, and he always used to talk about being resourceful with what you got. That brother got on his bike and he made it to the next town, where he got the replacement part he needed. Wreck turned to me and said, "That was some trick you pulled off there, son." After that he kept calling me "Trick" and it stuck." His smile deepened. A memory he truly cherished. A memory he had with Richie, whom he obviously felt a connection to, had a relationship with. Mentor, friend, brother…

My heart thudded in my chest. I wanted to tell him, to share that I was Richie's sister. But how would he take it? Would he be willing to help me find my other brother? Did they even know about him?

Trick kept his gaze on the road ahead. "A lot of the guys call me Tricky to be cute," he murmured, his slight smile fading, his jaw tightening. He had a lot on his plate now thanks to me. Things were insane for both of us and, now for the club too. Maybe once we weren't on the run, once things cooled and settled down I would—

Settled down?

I shoved *that* out of my mind as I adjusted myself on the cushions for the zillionth time, my butt aching.

Trick cleared his throat. "I guess all this biker-speak is new to you, huh?"

"Like a different country kind of new."

He let out a short laugh. "You'll catch on quick. You already have."

"I hope you don't mind me asking questions here and there."

"Of course not." He shot me that look again. Gentle yet blazing, making my skin prickle with an unusual stinging heat. I crossed my legs the other way, diverting my gaze to the road ahead, even though there was nothing much to see but a long, long ribbon of highway slicing through flat grasslands.

My body was telling me I was attracted to Trick in a way I'd never felt before. A visceral, all-over sensation from head to toe, not just a prickle of delight, a swoosh of warmth, or those cliché butterflies fluttering in your tummy. Nope.

I knew allowing myself to feel that attraction to him would only allow it to grow, and that would get me into trouble. All men wanted was one thing, to swoop in and conquer, to enjoy you until the bubbles stop fizzling in the glass. Everyone knew that yesterday's Champagne was a flat, tasteless bore.

My fingers went to the tie in my hair, pulling it tighter. I was done giving in. I was done doing as I was told, as I was expected. I was done not questioning I was done not putting myself first. And I was going to stick to that. I hadn't come this far, tossing everything I knew in the air, for nothing. Risked my own life only to…no. Getting involved with a man on any level only meant giving in, didn't it?

Of course, I was grateful Trick had saved my life, but I didn't have to marry him to thank him for it, did I? My teeth scraped my lip. I guess I kind of did, but it would be a fake biker-type marriage, not legal, no official paperwork filed with the state.

"You don't have to marry him, silly!" That's what Mom used to say to calm me down whenever we had a Sadie Hawkins dance at middle school and the girls would have to invite the boys. How I dreaded it every year. *"Relax, honey, you're just asking him to go to a dance. You're not asking him to get married."* How she'd laugh and laugh. But it never made me feel better or made asking any easier.

Well, Mom, now I do have to marry him. What do you think of that?

I leaned my head back against a cushion. I'd made the deal with Dog because I'd wanted to be free of Logan and his pressure to reunite for the board vote, and my family, who were equal parts unrelenting and unresponsive. I took off because I could no longer breathe.

But most of all, that desire to find my heretofore unknown brother, the knowledge of his existence, was the flare that had signaled the crazy idea to take off immediately and do it any way possible.

Road signs flew past us. In only a few more hours I would finally get to South Dakota. Everything would be better then, wouldn't it? I had to believe that. I had to.

"Aw fuck..." Hook's voice broke my reverie. "Smoking Guns at five o'clock."

CHAPTER 17
TRICK

CROUCHING FORWARD IN THE VAN, I spotted five Smoking Guns catching up to the head of the Flames formation.

"Jesus," muttered Dawes, sliding further back next to me. "Is he going to try and stop Finger? Holy—"

Of course, being President, Finger had been riding at the head of the Flames formation with Lenore on the back of his bike.

"Not good, not good…" Dawes tugged on his baseball cap.

Suddenly every Flame of Hell hit the brakes and began to pull over on this long stretch of flatland Nebraska interstate.

"They're stopping us?" Nicole's eyes grew wide as she leaned forward to get a look through the windshield.

"It's okay." I crouched next to her. "Finger knows what he's doing,"

"Lay low, people," said Hook as he pulled the van up on the side of the road behind the riders, rolling his window down barely a couple of inches.

Nicole let out a breath, pressing her body against mine, her hand sliding around my arm. She was scared. My arm went around her, and I held her close.

Dog dismounted from his chopper and stalked toward the

head of the Flames formation. Finger and Lenore got off their bike. She remained by his chopper, her face unreadable, while Drac came up beside her.

Dog got in Finger's face. "I know you're hiding them! They shot one of my men on my own club property after having been invited to party with us."

"I don't know what you're talking about, and what the fuck has that mess got to do with me?"

"Something happens to us, it always has to do with you."

"I could say the same, Dog." Finger took in a long, slow breath, his chest expanding. "We've been on a family run for days and now you blocked my club on the open road." He gestured with a hand to his club, and Dog's gaze raked over the Flames. Each biker had his old lady on the back of his bike. "We're on our way home, and I'll remind you, this is my territory you're in."

"You and the Jacks are good buddies now. Don't tell me you wouldn't—"

"A lot of clubs have working relationships nowadays, Dog. Don't tell me the Guns don't work with other clubs. Other groups." In a whirlwind, Finger whipped out a gun and nuzzled it into the side of Dog's face, his one hand cuffed around his neck, a leg shoving at his, kicking him off balance. "Move and he dies." Finger barked to the Guns who'd darted forward.

The Guns froze. Drac shoved Lenore behind him. My fingertips dug into Nicole's arm.

Finger's face was a wild snarl, his raspy voice full of venom, full of menace. "You do not stop me on the road with my family, ever. You do not get in my way, ever. You do not challenge me, ever. Repeat after me: Not ever."

"Not ever," gritted out Dog. "Fucker."

"Leave and don't come back." He released Dog, and Dog stumbled forward.

"You got what's mine. I know you do!" he shouted at Finger, pointing at the van.

My arm tightened around Nicole as her body trembled, her face burrowing into my chest. The soft, flowery scent of her hair filled my nose, and I pressed my lips against her head.

Finger's body language betrayed no stress, no annoyance, no fucking nothing. "I don't have your gun, or your old lady, or your bike, or one of your brothers. That covers the word *mine* for me. How about you?"

Dog planted his hands on his waist as he took in a deep breath that made his chest heave. "Ever since you took the Broken Blades from us, you think you're the shit."

"I stay in my lane, Dog. Keep my house clean, and get business done for my club and my brothers. That's what I care about. That's what I do."

Dog rubbed a hand across his face, then gestured at his men and got on his bike. His brothers quickly did the same. They all roared off, making a fat U-turn on the road, and blazed away back to Kansas.

Dawes turned to me and we bumped fists.

"They're gone, Zip," I whispered to Nicole. "Dog's gone."

A muffled cry left her lips as her fingers curled into my T-shirt, and I stroked her back. A flare of heat filled me in a new place inside, a forgotten place, and a rush of adrenaline pumped through my veins like a goddamn drug. An irresistible, addictive drug.

I liked being able to give this to her, the safety she'd asked me for, the safety that she deserved. Just like I'd promised her. My fingers smoothed down her silky hair and a sense of ease flooded me. Going to Finger had been worth it. It'd been the right thing to do.

My gaze went out the windshield once more. Lenore went to her man, and his big hand gripped the side of her face. She reached up and planted a deep, long kiss on him. Their gazes met for a beat, and then they both got on his bike. Intimacy and trust on the grand scale if ever there was.

A breath dragged out of me, and I peeled my arm off of

Nicole, letting go of her. I was glad to help her, but that's where it had to end for me. We'd do what we had to do to keep her safe, keep the club safe, and then it would be over. And she'd be gone. And I'd get back to my life and she'd get back to hers. Yep. Terrific.

Engines roared to life. Nicole sat up, pushing her hair back from her face, her cheeks flushed, and she turned away from me, adjusting the cushions and the folded blankets around her.

We got back on the road and took off toward home. But now with an old lady, a woman I barely knew, home would be a mighty different place for me, wouldn't it?

CHAPTER 18
NICOLE

"CHANGE OF PLAN," Hook's voice came loud and strong, jarring me from sleep.

The van stopped, and my eyes opened, something heavy weighing down my chest, my shoulders. Trick's leather club jacket.

"We're here," said Trick.

"Where exactly?" I asked.

"Outside of Chadron, Nebraska, where the Flames live. Our brothers are waiting for us in the back of this restaurant parking lot."

I sat up and peered out the windshield. We'd pulled into an empty parking lot alongside a loading dock where another van was parked. The Flames of Hell bikers were no longer with us.

I put on the beanie hat that Pick had given me when we'd left the motel this morning, tucking my hair inside it.

"Put on my jacket too." Trick held up his leather club jacket for me.

"Okay." Sliding my arms through the warm, thick sleeves of his jacket, a little thrill spiraled inside me as the heavy leather pressed down on my limbs and shoulders, enveloping my upper body. I was the envied high school girl wearing her quarterback boyfriend's varsity jacket. *Sure.*

I slid on my sunglasses as the door of the van jerked open. Fresh, cool air rushed over us, and it was a relief to my senses. We had arrived. Sort of.

"Jesus," said an insanely handsome man with long black hair and flashing green eyes. The name "Boner" was on his One-Eyed Jacks patch along with "Sergeant at Arms."

"Dude," said Dawes as he scrambled out of the van and slapped Boner's shoulder, giving him a hug.

"I'm never going to say don't get in trouble to you again. Obviously, you two go and do the opposite of what I tell you."

"Or maybe by saying all that you only manifested it for us, huh?" laughed Dawes.

"Shut up," said Boner.

Trick got out of the van. "I'm sorry, Boner. This is all on me."

Boner said nothing, only scowled at him, and an icy prickle raced up my spine. Trick was definitely in trouble. I was definitely in trouble.

I got out of the van, and Trick immediately guided me into the parked van next to us, where Dawes waited inside along with the driver, a One-Eyed Jack named Bear. Finger stepped through the back door of the restaurant. He and Boner clasped hands and shook as they talked, slapping each other on the shoulders. Finger caught Trick's gaze, and the two of them raised their chins at each other. Was that the biker *thank you* and *you're welcome?*

Trick and Dawes's bikes were loaded up in the back of the van, and Trick climbed in and slid the door shut. Boner got in, and we took off.

One more road trip. I didn't want to see the back of a van again for a very, very long time, if ever.

Boner kept his eyes on the road. "Church is scheduled. Everyone's waiting on us."

"Church?" I whispered to Dawes.

"Business meeting," he whispered back.

More biker-speak for the mental list I'd been keeping.

Trick clasped his hands together, his jaw flexing. Was he anxious about the meeting? I put a hand on his thigh, and his tight gaze darted to me. His hand covered mine on his leg and his features relaxed.

———

After roughly a silent forty-five minutes except for the loud hard rock music, we were on a road cutting through granite hills and a massive rolling sea of evergreen trees. Suddenly the road dipped, the trees towered above, and a small town opened up before us.

Meager, South Dakota.

Finally, Meager.

I sat up straight as we got on the main road, Clay Street. We stopped at a red traffic light in town. "That's Lenore's store," said Dawes, tapping at the window. The shop had a gothic-style purple sign hanging out front—*Lenore's Lace*. "It's a fancy lingerie shop." Dawes grinned.

"You go there a lot?"

Bear laughed uproariously.

"Shut up, asshole!" said Dawes. "I have been known to go. It's pricey, so..."

"For special gifts only, and only for special girls, right?" I asked.

"That's it, yeah." He stretched out his legs, a grin on his face. Dawes was very cute with his boyish features and blond hair and not so innocent body. Undoubtedly he had lots of special girls to pick from all the time.

Bear had slowed down the van's speed, and I returned my attention to the town storefronts. Since I was going to be staying on here, I'd need to find a job fast, and there wasn't much I was qualified for. There were lots of interesting shops in this small town quietly nestled in these grand forested hills. An Italian restaurant, a trendy-looking coffee shop, a pottery shop, a bank, an old-style bar on one corner, an antique store, what seemed to be a fitness studio, and—oh my God—a boot shop.

Some of the buildings had a vintage frontier aesthetic in the lines of their stone and brick design. Two beautiful lampposts stood at two different corners. Had there been more of them at one point? Pick-up trucks, SUVs, and lots of motorcycles were parked all along the road and the side streets. Meager was busy.

We braked at a stop sign, where a group of schoolchildren holding hands were crossing the street with two adults. A historical landmark sign caught my eye, and I scanned it quickly. Meager had been founded in 1874 after gold had been discovered in the Black Hills. The Dakota gold rush had made Meager a boom town back then along with the Homestead Act. The promise of a new life, a prosperous life. For some at least.

Yes, please.

We moved again down Clay Street and picked up speed, past an old-fashioned gas station from another age. Leaving the town behind us, we sped along the curvy road, ascending through tree-carpeted hills, and ten minutes later turned off onto a road that led us to a private graveled road that had an electrified fence and signs for Eagle Wings Repair & Custom Detailing and the One-Eyed Jacks MC.

I took in a breath, my heart fisting in my chest as the van barreled down the road. Another motorcycle club headquarters. What would this one be like? But this was Richie's motorcycle club, I reminded myself. This was where Richie worked and spent most of his days, most of his time.

Another gate opened for us, and we entered a twisting asphalt road that finally brought us to what seemed to be a former factory or warehouse from another era although fully renovated. The club logo of the skull with the gleaming eye hung over the main door, and over another new building on the right of the clubhouse hung a sign with a red and black eagle logo that read "Eagle Wings Repair & Custom Detailing" with its own driveway and courtyard that led to a storefront and a wide garage. This had to be the shop that Richie used to run for the club.

My heartbeat ticked up as the van came to a stop before the clubhouse entryway. I was here. I was finally here. All the mayhem that had come before had been worth it, hadn't it?

Trick shoved the door open and hopped out, holding out his hand to me, making my insides flare with that flash of heat. This rough-and-tumble guy was a gentleman in all the little ways, the ways I'd never been treated to before by a man, the ways that made me melt inside. Even now that he was in trouble he was still thoughtful to me.

I put my hand in his and my feet landed on the ground as the heat of the sun poured over me. Taking in a deep breath, a distant sweet, resiny scent made my lips curve and my muscles ease.

A group of men stalked toward us. Tall, towering, muscular, tattooed, and I held my breath.

"He's finally got himself an old lady! See, I knew it'd happen for you one day, man."

"I'd take off with her too. Hot." A whistle ensued.

"Enough!" said Boner, a hand in the air. "Church in fifteen minutes."

Dawes brushed past me and high-fived his brothers as they all entered the building. Boner turned around and took me in for the first time. Every inch of me. A cold, cold substance slunk through my veins, chilling my heart. "Inside. Now."

Here we go. Welcome to your brand spanking new reality.

Trick put a hand on my back, which eased my tense muscles. We followed Boner into the clubhouse, our boots tapping a hollow rhythm on the cement floor of the long dim hallway. Through a large central living area, where two women who stared at us sat at a bar smoking cigarettes and drinking coffee, down another hall to an office that said "President" on the door in old-fashioned lettering.

Boner knocked, and we entered. A mustachioed older man sat behind the desk, his eyes narrowing at me. Another man, with longish wavy blond hair and piercing light blue eyes, sat on the corner of his desk. "Vice President" was stitched on a patch on his vest. "Have a seat," the VP said. "My name's Butler and this is our President, Kicker."

"Hello," I murmured as Trick and I took the two seats opposite the desk. Boner leaned back against the wall on Trick's side. I swallowed hard as I took off the beanie and sunglasses, my hair falling to my shoulders. The president leaned back in his chair.

"Well, well, well. I can understand why you felt you had to have her, bro…"

"It wasn't like that, Prez," said Trick.

"Oh yeah? What was it like?" Boner's voice was tight and unamused.

Trick explained, and the officers relaxed just a bit after hearing that Trick had not taken me because he was being self-indulgent.

Butler let out a huff of air. "You're so fucking lucky that the Flames were in Lincoln. So fucking lucky."

"We were," said Trick. "Finger and his men were amazing to us. They didn't have to help us, but they did."

"Lenore too. She was very kind to me," I said. They all stared at me, the interloper. My face stung with heat. Perhaps I shouldn't speak until spoken to here in the inner sanctum?

"So what's your story, Nicole?" asked Kicker. "Your family going to come looking for you?"

"Dog turned this into a kidnapping kind of thing to twist my brother's arm into paying up his debt to him, but I already paid Dog all the money my brother owed him, so there is no debt anymore, but my brother doesn't know that."

"Technically there's no debt anymore," said Kicker. "But by

playing it like a kidnapping, he's trying to squeeze your brother for as much cash as he can."

"And I think he liked what he saw in our house."

"He paid you a visit at home?" asked Butler.

"More like shot out the windows and raided the place, cut up my brother, that sort of thing."

Boner slanted his head. "Ah, shit."

"Dog was hired as a bounty hunter by the loan shark my brother owed money to. There is something else you should know."

"What's that?" asked Kicker.

"I think Dog might have killed the loan shark guy."

"You think?"

"It was after I got the cash out of the bank. We stopped at Mr. Rooney's office. I assumed it was so Dog could give him the money and get his cut, but Dog didn't take the money into the office. When he came back out he had blood on his gloves and he was real excited. All of them were. I assume he killed him to pocket all the cash himself."

"Sounds about right," Butler muttered.

"Extortion, breaking in, robbery, battery, murder, kidnapping. We have a full menu today, ladies and gentlemen." Kicker twisted his lips as he rolled his chair back from his desk.

"You were there, you saw. You know," said Trick, his eyes wide. "Not good."

"You're going to have to contact your brother and let him know you're okay, not with Dog, and that you paid the debt in full," said Butler. "Because the last thing we all need is the FBI breathing down our necks."

"Although, seeing Dog get busted for kidnapping and murder would make my day, if not my year…" said Boner.

"The thing is—" I cleared my throat. "I don't want my family to know where I am right now."

All four men stared at me, and my mouth dried.

"Why not?" asked Boner.

"I have a husband who doesn't want to give me a divorce—"

"You have a WHAT?" Trick's voice boomed in the office, his chair jerking back, scraping over the floor.

My heart thudded in my chest. "We've been legally separated for a year, but he's trying to manipulate me, and I—"

"How come you never mentioned this before?" Trick's nostrils flared. Why was he so annoyed?

The men all narrowed their eyes at me. At Trick.

My chest caved in. "There was a lot going on, wasn't there?"

Trick blew out a huff of air.

"And the other thing is my brother continually wants my money to solve all his many problems."

"You got money?" asked Kicker.

"I do, yes. My dad founded a very successful oil parts company. He passed away last year, and my brother and husband run it now, and I inherited stocks and cash and a seat on the board."

Trick crossed his arms, that muscle along his jaw flexing, his entire body stiffening. "Uh-huh."

"Over the last couple of years, I've helped my brother with many big debts and now this one."

"How much did you give Dog on his behalf?"

"Two hundred and fifty thousand."

Butler let out a whistle, Boner remained motionless, and Trick only stared at me, his brow a firm ridge, that muscle along his jaw even tighter than before.

"Well, shit, woman." Kicker sat up straighter.

"Are you all going to want money from me too?"

Kicker scoffed. "No, we don't want your money. But I'm sure as hell Dog wants more of it."

I squirmed in my chair. "I didn't think Dog would try to keep me. He promised me he'd stay away from my mother and her house and would keep up the pretense that he'd kidnapped me. It was very stupid of me to believe him, but I needed to—"

"Jump ship?" said Boner as he pushed the sleeves of his long-sleeved plaid shirt up his arms.

"Exactly…" I blinked, my pulse drumming in my neck as I stared at the ink writhing around Boner's arm.

"Problem is you shot one of Dog's men on his property," said Kicker.

"Technically it was self-defense because I was being attacked, and so was Dawes," Trick said. "She saved our lives by shooting him."

"What you staring at?" said Boner.

"Nicole? What is it?" said Trick.

I pointed at Boner's tattooed arm. "That design."

Boner twisted his arm around. "What about it?"

"I saw it on this guy at the Smoking Gun's party."

"You sure?" asked Boner. "A scythe and a long axe are popular tattoo designs. A lot of people have them."

"It was this exact one—with the two eyeballs sitting on the blade, and the skeleton fingers around the handle. Same one." I swallowed hard at the harsh memory.

"Was this guy a Smoking Gun or a guest?" Boner's voice had gotten tense.

"I don't think he was one of them. He didn't have a jacket or a vest with the club logo on it like everyone else. I was running away from him when Trick found me." That fiery panic burned up my throat once more. "He was going to put me in a van and take me away."

"Take you away?" Trick raised his voice. "From their clubhouse?"

"Dog's wife wanted to get rid of me, and I told her I wanted to get out of there, and she said she'd help me. She brought me over to him and this other guy."

"When the hell did she do that?" Trick's forehead buckled.

"She found me right after you cut my zip tie."

His head jerked back. "Jesus."

"She brought me to this other man who was with the guy

with that tattoo. They weren't at the party with everyone but on their own at the edge of the parking lot. She offered me to the other man, and he wanted to know old I was, inspected me like I was prospective goods."

A wave of fierce hot rage filled the room, and I glanced at Trick. He took in a long, strained breath, his lips curling. Boner rubbed a hand over his mouth. "This other man, was he a Smoking Gun?"

"He wore a patch, but his was different. It said "Nomad" on it. Carrie seemed to know him real well. She was very flirty with him."

"Describe him."

"Very tall. Big, muscular. Bald. Lots of earrings. Lots of tattoos everywhere. He had this awful tattoo going down his throat to his chest of a dinosaur's head, his bloodied fangs showing. It was awful."

"Raptor," said Boner. "You met Raptor. She met Raptor."

"Holy shit," said Butler.

"Who is Raptor?"

"He's an underground renegade of sorts from another club, a club Finger put an end to. Finger's been after him for a while now, but he's been fucking hard to find." Butler eyed Kicker.

"Sounds like Raptor and Dog got themselves a side hustle." Kicker cleared his throat as his back straightened. "Let's finish this up. We got to get to Church."

Boner's harsh gaze darted from me to Trick. "So, Nicole, what's it gonna be?"

"How do you mean?" I asked.

"You need to stay here with us, under the radar to stay safe."

"Dog's out there waiting to grab you and punish you and Trick and Dawes," Butler added.

Boner crossed his arms. "You got two choices: Club girl—"

"Club girl? What are you talking about?"

"For fuck's sake," muttered Trick.

"We've got two women who live here and take care of shit and take care of the men," said Kicker.

My lungs pinched together. "Like, do their laundry?"

They laughed. *I knew it. Back to this crap again. The was no escaping it.* I pressed the heels of my boots into the floor. The walls of the office pressed in on me. "But I thought…"

"You thought what? That 'cause you're outta Kansas City, you're home free?" Boner said. "Dog took you across state lines to keep you as his personal bank account and to keep his ego and his dick happy. On top of that, you shot one of his men. You think he's gonna let this go? Think. Again."

Butler moved in front of the desk. "Nicole, to give you the big picture here—this whole situation is even worse because the Guns and the Flames have never gotten along. Not since day one. I'm talking decades and decades of legendary hate."

"I got that somewhere along the way." I bit my lip.

"You met Finger, right?"

"Yes."

"The scars on his face, the missing middle fingers? The Smoking Guns did that to him a long time ago. In fact, Dog's former President, Scrib, is the one who used the knife on Finger."

"Oh my God," escaped my lips.

"You don't know the half of it, darlin'," Kicker remarked.

Butler planted his feet wide before us. "So, Trick takes off with you, and you shoot down a Smoking Gun on the way out—"

"They were holding me there like a prisoner. And I wasn't trying to kill Lex. I shot his leg on purpose. I didn't want him dead. I only wanted him to stop hurting Trick."

Trick took in a sharp breath at my words.

"Believe me, we're glad you did it," Butler said. "But as we're affiliated with Finger and the Flames of Hell, we're now a part of their legendary hate. And now with what you two did at their clubhouse, you've kicked that sleeping beast awake."

I struggled for air. "I'm very sorry about all this, I…"

"That's real nice, appreciate it, but it doesn't solve much right now." Boner towered over me. "You owe Trick, and you owe the Jacks and the Flames."

"The three of you are on lockdown until further notice," said Kicker.

They'd passed sentence on us. "Lockdown?" I jumped up from the chair, my legs shaking. "I am no club girl!"

"You want to stay alive and keep Trick alive? You're one of us now," said Boner. "End of story."

Trick stood up next to me and took my hand in his. "And that story is that she's my old lady."

CHAPTER 19
TRICK

NICOLE SAT at the foot of my bed in my club room. This woman from another world. A rich woman, a married woman, was now stuck here with me. "I'm your old lady now?"

"Yeah. Not a club girl."

She wiped a hand across her flushed cheeks. "Is that who those two women are out there?"

"Yeah." The need to reassure her had me sitting down next to her. "This won't be forever. If we play this right, Dog will back off because he had no right to try to keep you for himself. You said you'd already told him you had a husband in South Dakota, right?"

"Mmm."

I cleared my throat. "But you got yourself a real husband in Oklahoma, huh?"

She let out a scoff. "He's real all right, but not a real husband."

"What happened?"

"Last year I caught him with another woman. One of my girl-friends."

"Shit."

"They even asked me to join them, would you believe?"

"I'm guessing you said no."

"I said no then I ran off." Nicole went to the window and looked outside, her back to me. Was she embarrassed? Her shoulders tensed. "But she was just one in a long, long line of other women. He'd cheated on me before, but told me it wasn't a big deal, a mistake, and wouldn't happen again. But it was seeing him with my friend that night that made me finally wake up to what was happening around me. I couldn't live with it any longer." She let out a heavy breath. "Our fathers were business partners, and he's my brother's best friend. He was my first everything. I was always told what a great couple we were. Everyone around me always encouraged it. My parents, my brother, our friends. It was easy, it felt good, and I never questioned it which was stupid."

"Not stupid. Lesson learned."

"My dad had just died at the time. I guess that made it easier for me to go against the grain and get the separation. I'd thought my mom and my brother would be outraged on my behalf, that they'd be on my side. Instead, they were upset with me for doing it." She chewed on her lip. "And recently, they started pressuring me to go back to him. Even my friends. They all said I'd punished him enough. That I'd done my thing, made my point, but it was time to go back to my home. Time to claim my man because I was damn lucky I had him.

"The day Dog showed up, that morning, I'd gone to our house to talk to him. He'd sent me flowers the day before and told me he would even go to counseling with me because our marriage was so important to him. I went over to tell him to stop, that I wasn't interested, and I saw him with two women in our bed. Nothing had changed." She let out a dry laugh. "Maybe that's not supposed to mean anything, but it does to me. Am I being an old-fashioned bore? I guess it must seem like that to you, right?"

"I don't think cheating is okay. Ever."

She leaned back against the wall by the window. "Do y'all do a free love thing around here?"

I burst out into laughter.

"Trick? Trick!"

"No, Zip. I mean, yeah, there's a lot of free everything around here, but when you commit to someone, you commit. That's taken seriously."

"Old man and old lady status?"

"Right."

She held my gaze, and I got sucked into a blue vortex of emotion. "Do you think I'm a fool for bailing on my life when Dog showed up? How crazy was that to make a deal with him *and* believe him?"

"For a girl like you? Way fucking crazy. But it's a good kind of crazy. You were standing at the edge of a cliff with no way out, and I think you wanted a way out real bad. So bad you could taste it."

"Yes," she whispered.

"Dog shows up, you saw the possibility, and you took the risk. In my book, you're brave as fuck."

Her eyes widened, her lips parted. Had she never heard that before? Someone admiring her? Respecting her? Telling her she was brave? That was fucking wrong. "There's only one problem."

Her eyebrows scrunched together as she pushed off the wall. "What's that?"

"You need to believe it. I saw it in you, I believed it, but you don't, do you? Unless you believe it, Zip, you aren't going to get anywhere in life. Get to that place you want, whatever it is. I think you wanted change so bad that you were willing to go as far as getting on the back of that motherfucker's bike to get the hell out of Oklahoma come what may."

Her body wavered, and I darted to her, catching her at the waist. "Come on, sit down." I led her back to the bed. "Get your boots off already."

She kicked at her cowboy boots, but I intervened and yanked them off her legs. "Now we have to live together," she murmured.

"Got to make it look real."

"Who knows? Maybe this fake relationship will be more real than my 'real' marriage." She let out a soft laugh, and my pulse thudded at the seductive sound. "We're going to live here while we're on this lockdown?"

I put her fancy cowboy boots next to my cracked and scuffed work boots. "Yeah. I know it's nothing like what you're used to."

"How do you know what I'm used to?"

I rubbed my hands together. "I don't. But it sounds like you come from a real rich family. This here is real simple, no frills."

She shrugged her shoulders. "This is where you live, so—"

"No, I don't. This is just my room here at the club where I crash sometimes."

"Oh." Her teeth dragged against her bottom lip as her back straightened, her gaze scraping over my bed. Was she imagining all the ways I "crashed" on this bed?

I cleared my throat. "I also have my own apartment in town."

"Ah. Nice."

"I know this is all a whole other world for you, but the main thing, the most important thing, is that you're now safe from Dog and his men."

"And his wife." Her face broke into a dark grin.

"Her too." My lips twitched. "And your husband, and your brother."

"Yeah, them too." She swept her blonde mane off her shoulders, a casual but somehow elegant move, and my insides lurched. We stared at each other, the temperature in my small room getting warmer, hotter. The visual of this beauty sitting on my bed like a gorgeous mermaid who'd just washed up on shore, lost, unsure of her new surroundings…

Fuck. How the hell was this gonna go?

Her eyes widened. "I just realized something."

"Yeah?"

"I don't have any clothes or…anything."

"You sure don't. I'll see what I can do about that."

"You will?"

"I'll take care of it. Why don't you get some rest? Take a nap. You've been non-stop for days." I went to my small fridge, grabbed a bottle of water, and put it on the table by her side of the bed. "You're not a prisoner anymore."

"Isn't this lockdown just another in a long line of prisons?"

Was she including her home in Oklahoma in that line of prisons? I sat down next to her. The need to touch her, reassure her, was overwhelming, and I put a hand on her thigh, her leg tensing under my touch. "Nobody here is going to force you to do anything. I promise you that. Especially not me." I took my hand off her.

"Okay." Her mouth lifted in a slight smile. "You're right, I could definitely use a nap."

"Go for it. I got to get to that meeting." I got up from the bed.

"Mmm. Church…" Laying down, she let out a long sigh.

The sight of the lost mermaid relaxing on my bed had me twisting inside. I had to get the fuck out of here. "We'll have something to eat after, how's that sound?"

"Sounds good."

"Great." I backed away from the bed, from her lying in my bed, and opened the door to leave. "Nicole?"

"Yeah?"

"So you know, this whole thing is new to me. I've never lived with someone before or had an old lady."

She turned over on the bed and faced me as I stood in the doorway. "Never?"

"Never. This should be real interesting for both of us."

CHAPTER 20
TRICK

"WITH ALL DUE RESPECT, what the fuck was that? Telling her she'd have to be a club girl?" I said to Boner inside our club meeting room as everyone gathered and took their seats.

He only threw back his head and laughed.

"What the hell is so funny?"

"I got a reaction out of her and you, and it was the right one. She owes you, and you owe her. Doing this is the honorable thing to do."

"Did you think I wouldn't do the honorable thing by her?"

"You're nothing but honorable, Trick. And you give a shit about her. That was the other reaction I was looking for. But I already knew that."

My jaw stiffened. "Why the hell do you think that?"

"I know these things. And I knew what you did for her wasn't some dumbass move 'cause you wanted to get laid." He slapped the side of my arm. "You did a good thing, man. The right thing. I'm proud of you."

"You freaked me out."

"That's my job."

"Now I got a job for you."

"Say again?" His brow furrowed.

"Could you call Jill and get her to round up all the other old ladies? Nicole doesn't have any clothes or…anything. Plus, this is all new to her. I think it'd be good for her to meet them all sooner rather than later and see for herself that they're good women who she can talk to, be friends with."

Grinning, he whipped out his phone and hit a button to, I presumed, call his wife.

"Now what's so funny?"

"Ah, Trick. There you are, already doing your job as an old man looking out for his old lady."

"Yeah, yeah." I stalked over to my seat at the long, wood slab table.

As soon as Boner got off his phone, Kicker called the meeting to order. "We got us some action going on. Trick, explain."

I told them everything from A to Z.

"Dawes?"

"The thing I want to emphasize is that Nicole saved Trick's life. She grabbed Lex's gun right when it got tossed next to her and used it, no hesitation, no fear. I'd gotten jumped from behind. I don't want to think about what might have happened to all of us if she hadn't."

"Me neither," I muttered.

"She did good," said Kicker, and all the others agreed.

"Nicole was at their club for a handful of hours. At their party she recognized my gang tattoo on a guy who wasn't a Smoking Gun," said Boner.

As a kid in Denver, Boner had been a member of a now-extinct El Salvadoran gang. In the years since Boner had escaped Denver in his late teens, the gang had transformed itself into a grown-up sophisticated crime organization called the Calderas Group.

"She said he was there at their clubhouse with a Smoking Gun nomad. Guess who—Raptor."

"Raptor?" said Bear. "That Blades officer who took off when we took them down?"

"Yep. Refused to join the Flames of Hell, and he disappeared before they could get him down," said Kicker. "He was the only one who took off. Looks like Dog pulled him into the Smoking Guns as a nomad. Hate and revenge sure make for cozy alliances."

"If Raptor is hanging with this Calderas guy, sounds like he and Dog could be trying to revive Scrib's great idea to pull in a cartel through our parts," I said.

"I have no doubt," muttered Boner.

"Didn't the Feds dismantle Calderas?" Dready asked.

"They did," said Butler. "But there are probably a few young guns still out there who are looking to raise the Calderas flag once more and are doing it by working with Raptor and Dog."

"From what Nicole said, sounds like they might be running a new business together," I said.

"What kind of business?"

"Slaves," replied Boner.

Grumbles and groans shot around the table. "Fanfuckingtastic, huh?" said Kicker. "I'll call Finger, let him know. He's gonna love this. In the meantime, Trick, Dawes, and Nicole are on lockdown until further notice. Be on watch for any Smoking Guns in our area. Oh yeah—and Nicole is Trick's old lady." He banged the gavel, signaling the end of the session.

"Ooooo, Tricky's finally got himself an old lady, yo!" Bear hooted, and I rolled my eyes at him. Applause and whistles broke out as everyone got up from the table.

"Trick, how did Nicole take lockdown?" asked Butler. "She's a civilian. Is this going to be a problem for her?"

"She gets it. Won't be a problem."

"Keep her happy, bro." Dawes winked at me.

A roar of laughter and more hoots exploded.

"Show your old lady what your tongue can do, man!" laughed Bear, his chest shaking. "Remember, lot of tongue first, then cock. You gotta warm up bitches right, that's key."

"Great advice coming from the guy whose old lady dumped his ass."

Bear's old lady of many years, Suzi, had taken their son and taken off after years of putting up with his blatant cheating. It had bothered Bear's ego, but not his emotions.

"It was too much for her." Bear waggled his grotesquely long tongue at me as he slung an arm around my shoulders. "If your old lady doesn't like yours, I'm here, bro." Patting his massive chest, he roared with laughter.

"Fuck off."

CHAPTER 21
NICOLE

KNOCKING SOUNDED AT THE DOOR, and my body jerked itself out of sleep, my pulse kicking up. The knocking came again.

"Nicole?" A woman's voice.

I unlocked the door and standing in the hall were four women with big smiles on their faces and overflowing shopping bags filling their arms. All at once they burst into Trick's room.

"Hi, Nicole!" their voices rang out in unison.

A beautiful woman with coppery brown hair came forward. "I'm Grace, and this is Tania, Jill, Mary Lynn. Our husbands told us you arrived today, and we wanted to introduce ourselves and welcome you to Meager and the club."

"That's so nice of you, thank you."

"Did we wake you up? We can come back—"

"No, no. It's fine. Please."

"My husband said you don't have anything, so we thought we'd bring you what you might need to get started." Jill tipped over a full shopping bag on the bed, its contents spilling forth. A small pink toiletry bag and a larger purple one, a hairbrush, toothbrush, toothpaste, tampons and pads, shampoo and conditioner, deodorant, coconut scented body wash and matching body cream, baby powder. "A girl's got to have her goodies, right?"

"Yes she does. Oh my gosh, thank you."

"I grabbed whatever I thought you might need, but of course, you tell me if you'd like something else and I'll get it for you pronto."

I scanned the wealth of products on the bed. "This is amazing. Thank you, Jill. Which One-Eyed Jack is your husband?"

"Boner."

I blinked. Jill seemed so delicate and effervescent, and Boner so…grim and harsh. "Boner is your husband?"

"The one and only." She laughed softly.

"I got you some makeup and skincare…." Mary Lynn dumped the contents of her shopping bag alongside Jill's toiletries. Moisturizer, face wash, lip gloss, lip balm, mascara, a neutral eyeshadow palette along with a bronzer and blush combo palette, an assortment of makeup brushes and eye pencils, and a small mirror. "Like Jill said, these are basics, but you let me know what else you'd like, another color, another brand, and I'll bring it over. I'm a beauty junkie. I know my stuff."

"Thank you, Mary Lynn."

Tania took out two pillows and folded pillow cases from her bag as well as a selection of blue towels. "These are all freshly washed. I thought you should have fresh clean pillows of your own and towels." She plumped them on the bed.

"And we got you pajamas, a robe. Underwear, a couple bralettes, socks, sweatpants, yoga pants, leggings, T-shirts, a couple sweatshirts, all washed." Grace stacked the clothes on the bed. "It's a start."

"It's fantastic! How did you know my size or…"

"My man's a data man," said Jill. "He can suss out a person and a situation immediately. It's a gift."

They all laughed warmly, and a grin pushed up my lips. These women's energy was palpable, warm and inviting, and I wanted to trust it, to bathe in it. Tears filled my weary eyes. "This is so kind and generous. I can't tell you how much I appreciate this. No one's ever done something like this for me. You don't even know me."

"We'll get to know each other," said Jill.

"From what we heard, we're glad you're here and that you and Tricky and Dawes are safe." Grace squeezed my arm.

"Trick saved my life," I said. "They both did."

"Oooh, Tricky to the rescue…tell us more." Mary Lynn sat on the edge of the bed, a wide grin on her dimpled face.

They all waited.

I told them the story.

"Wow," said Mary Lynn. "He just took you in his arms and said, 'She's my woman.' I told you guys, that man is full of hidden depths."

"I never doubted it," said Jill. "Remember how he was after —" She clamped her lips shut, and a sudden silence filled the room.

"After what?"

Jill pushed her thick strawberry blonde hair back behind her ears. "He went through a bad breakup a while back and took it real hard. He's been a dedicated bachelor ever since."

Grace eyed Jill. "Until now."

"Until now," Jill agreed with a grin.

"He told me he'd never had an old lady before."

"That's right. She wasn't his old lady." Tania folded the last towel on her pile.

"I wanted to ask y'all. I met Lenore in Nebraska."

"You did?" Jill's eyes widened.

"She was with Finger and the rest of their club. She was so kind to me. The minute she heard what I'd been through, she reassured me. She was very empathetic and supportive. It meant a lot to me."

"She's the best," said Grace. "She's a good friend of ours."

"Is she? I wanted to ask if y'all knew her. Dawes showed me her store in town."

"She lives here in Meager. We hang out a lot," said Tania.

"Great. I'd love to see her again."

"I'll let her know," said Tania.

Grace stood up. "You must be starving, and you and Trick and Dawes certainly deserve a huge homemade meal. Tonight we're going to cook up a ton of food so we can all eat dinner together, and you can meet everyone."

"Is there anything you don't like or are allergic to?" asked Jill. "Are you vegetarian or vegan?"

"No, not allergic to anything. Not vegetarian or vegan."

"We're going to get things cracking in the kitchen.," Tania said. "Take your time. Come join us when you're ready. There will be lots of wine."

"We always have wine." Mary Lynn laughed.

"And whiskey, too. Really good whiskey," said Grace.

"I'd like that. I think I'll take a shower and enjoy all the wonderful treats y'all brought over and then I'll come meet you in the kitchen."

"Great. We'll leave you to it. Let's go, ladies." Everyone filed out the door as they said their goodbyes. "See you in a bit, Nicole." Tania closed the door behind her.

I sucked in a deep breath as I took in the heap of treasures on the bed. I was so grateful for them. I organized everything on one end of the dresser and, filling the larger toiletry bag with the goodies I'd need for a shower, headed to the bathroom with a grin on my face.

The water was very hot and very strong, and I thoroughly enjoyed scrubbing up and washing my hair. I rubbed my body dry and hung the towel up over the small rod of the shower. Moisturizing my skin, I grinned at my reflection in the small steamy mirror. I so looked forward to wearing clean clothes again.

Pulling open the door, I headed to the bed. Someone was on the bed. A blur of sudden movement.

Screeching, I covered my naked body with my hands.

"Shit! Sorry, Nicole…" Trick stood by the bed with only black boxer briefs hugging his sculpted form.

Darting back into the bathroom, I grabbed my damp towel and wrapped it around me. I hadn't even let my husband see me naked in over two years. Securing the towel, I took in a breath and re-entered the bedroom, my face burning with heat.

"Sorry, I—"

"No, it's all right. I didn't think. I should have used the robe the girls got me, but I was so excited to get in the shower…"

"I wasn't thinking either." He held my gaze with his own, his hand absently brushing down his sculpted chest. "This is going to take some getting used to, huh?"

"Mmm." Stinging heat raced over my skin as we both stood there, staring at each other. "It was such a great shower." My voice came out small.

"Uh-huh." The edges of his lips flickered with movement.

He didn't make a move, and neither did I. The sight of his bare skin covered with tattoos held me spellbound. Wings wrapped around his right arm and on his bicep was a skull with a sparkling star for an eye, the club logo. A large bird's wing was tattooed on his chest, and on its edge was a date inked in a vintage style with drops of blood dripping down that I remembered from that night at the motel in Nebraska. The combination of all this dynamic artwork on his tanned skin along with the fresh bruises from Lex on his face gave him the appearance of a devastatingly handsome and rugged underworld warlord.

My mouth dried, and I licked my lips. His thigh muscles seemed to tighten, and another muscle too. The one between his legs. *Damn, he's big.*

He let out a chuckle. "You're staring."

"Sorry." I immediately averted my gaze as I clutched at my towel. "I've never seen…so many tattoos before."

"I've been getting them since I was around fifteen. Each one tells a story." Even though I now had my back to him, heat radiated from his body warming mine. "The old ladies brought you an amazing stash, huh?"

"They sure did. I'm so blown away by their generosity and thoughtfulness. How did they know to…"

"I asked."

I turned around and faced him. "Trick—" My heart squeezed. "Thank you."

"You're welcome. I'm going to take that shower…"

"Right. Yes. You do that. And I'm going to get dressed."

He moved by me to get to the bathroom, and the warm smell of him filled my senses. All man. I blinked at the sight of a huge tattoo of the One-Eyed Jacks star-eyed skull engraved on his broad back. Yep, underground warlord.

The door closed behind him, the shower water turned on, and I finally let go of my breath and the towel. I quickly moisturized and threw on underwear, the bralette, the yoga pants, a T-shirt, and a cropped black sweatshirt with the Eagle Wings Repair logo. Smoothing my hand down the soft fabric, I grinned to myself. Everything fit and felt so comfortable. I brushed on the face powder, used the dark blue eye pencil, the mascara, swiped on lip gloss and instantly felt better as I checked myself out in the mirror.

A different me. A fresh me. Back in Oklahoma, I wouldn't dare leave the house without a full face on and my hair blown out. My fingers flicked at the waves in my hair. None of that mattered to me at this moment.

I knocked on the bathroom door and opened it a crack. "Trick?"

"Yeah?" His rough voice rose from the steamy coconut scented depths.

"I'm going to go find the ladies. Where's the kitchen?"

"Right off the lounge, can't miss it."

"Okay. See you later." I left the room but stopped myself in the hallway. I needed to make sure the photo, the newspaper clipping, and the tiny beaded bracelet were safe. They were still loose in my backpack and I didn't want them crumpled or tattered anymore than they already were. I went back down the hallway to Trick's room.

I meant to put them in the new smaller toiletry bag to stay safe and clean after I got dressed, but … Trick. Those items were precious to me, even more than Mom's diamond necklace or any of my own jewelry had ever been to me. If they got damaged or lost I'd be devastated.

I quietly opened the door to Trick's room, went to my bag and got the pieces out. I put them in the small pink cosmetics bag and stuffed that in my backpack. Guttural moans rose from the bathroom over the spray of the shower. Trick was moaning? My spine straightened. Was he all right?

I froze to the spot.

Was he…? He was. Trick's moans were a symphony of deep need and raw desire. My mouth dried as I imagined his large hand stroking his cock which had hardened before my eyes moments earlier. Water streaming down his taut flesh, sliding over those wild tattoos, his long leg muscles clenching as he got more and more excited, his hips rocking…

A small moan escaped my lips as heat prickled my skin like a thousand tiny flames and stoked a fire between my legs.

"Aww fuck…" he groaned loudly.

My heart stopped at the crude, guttural sound of his voice raking against my flesh. He was coming. My clit throbbed, sending shock waves of sensation and pulses of heat all through me. I hadn't felt anything remotely like this in…I couldn't remember when. Had I ever?

Had he been too long without or maybe…maybe seeing me naked had sent him into this self-soothing session?

I darted out of the room before I could entertain that possibility.

CHAPTER 22
NICOLE

I FOLLOWED the din of voices down the hallway to the center of the building which was the club's lounge. Music played, the television was on, and men were seated at the bar drinking and talking. On an armchair, Dawes had one of the club girls in his lap and they were fooling around, kissing and grinding on each other. His hands roamed under her tiny T-shirt, groping her breasts underneath.

I was in a new country now—Bikerland, where anything went at any time.

Which way was the kitchen? There were a number of rooms and hallways that radiated from the central lounge.

"You lost, baby?" A black-haired young guy with a mustache and the beginnings of a beard grinned at me, a beer bottle in his hand. A patch with the word "Prospect" was stitched on his leather vest.

"Could you tell me where the kitchen is? I don't know my way around yet."

"Oh, you're a newbie, huh?" He came close and leaned over me, his eyes gleaming. "Give me a kiss and I'll show you exactly where to go." His hand went to my middle and squeezed, making its way up my side. "On your knees would be a start."

I shoved his hand off me. "I don't think so, buddy."

"You don't think so?" A thick eyebrow arched up his forehead.

"Get the fuck off her or I chop your hand off myself," Trick's voice gritted out from behind me.

"She yours already? First time I've laid eyes on her."

"She's my old lady, asshole! I just brought her home a few hours ago."

"Fuck!" The Prospect jumped away from me as if I were suddenly red hot off the grill and he'd gotten burned.

Trick's arm went around my waist, pulling me close to his warm body and my pulse pounded. "Now apologize, you fuck."

"Trick, he doesn't—"

"Yes, he does." Trick's forehead wrinkled as his grip on me tightened. The woody fresh scent of his skin filled my senses.

"I'm real sorry, ma'am. So sorry. Won't ever happen again. Welcome to the One-Eyed Jacks. If there's ever anything I can do for you around here, anything at all, please, please let me know."

"Now walk away."

The prospect scurried off. Quickly.

"He's a member in training. Got to keep 'em in line. You okay?"

"I'm fine. He just thought—"

"I know what he thought." His lips smashed together. "We got to get this over with and be done with it."

Taking my hand firmly in his, he charged into the center of the lounge. "Everybody—I have an announcement." Everyone turned toward us, and my face heated. "For those of you who don't already know—this here is Nicole and she's my old lady. You got that? Good."

"Way to go, Trick!" someone shouted out.

"Yeah, yeah." He scowled, letting go of my hand. Was he as uptight about all this as I was or just grumpy? Well, he'd never had an old lady before and now he had a fake one.

"Hey, Nicole, I'm Dready."

"Hi." I shook Dready's huge hand. Trick introduced me to the other men that I hadn't met before and the two club women, Shannon and Lucy.

He put a warm hand on my back. "Come meet my Uncle Willy."

We went over to the oldest man in the room with thick white hair and a trim body, who sat at the end of the bar nursing what I assumed was a whiskey, maybe a bourbon. He took us in, a smile warming his face."Uncle Willy, this is Nicole."

"Welcome, Nicole," he said, holding out a hand to me. "Good to meet you."

"Good to meet you too." I shook his hand.

"You two staying here for a while, right?" he asked.

"Yep. Hopefully lockdown won't last too long and then we'll go to my place, I guess. Depending on how things play out," replied Trick shooting me a bleak look. How would things play out? How long would we have to stay together?

A smirk cracked Willy's features. "Your place? You kidding me, son? You better start looking for another apartment or a house. You can't bring Nicole there. No woman would want to live there."

"I didn't think of that. You're right."

"That bad?" I asked Willy.

"Even though my nephew here is a very tidy animal, that place is a small dark man cave, and I'm being generous." He laughed loudly.

"I'll get to looking online."

"You better. I'll ask around. Let you know."

"Appreciate it."

"So Nicole, I hear you're from Oklahoma?" Willy asked.

"I am, yes."

"I've ridden through that state so many times, but the last time I stopped there was over ten years ago, I think." He chuckled. "Whereabouts you from?"

"Guymon. In the panhandle."

For an instant, his smile vanished and his eyes tensed. "Guymon, huh?"

"Have you been there on your travels?"

"Nope, but I've heard of it." He averted his gaze back to his liquor, twisting the glass in his hand. "A good friend of mine went there once. Long, long time ago." He cleared his throat. "I hear you saved my nephew's life."

"He saved my life, too."

"Let's get you a drink, darlin'. What would you like?"

"A shot of whiskey would be good, thanks."

"Same," murmured Trick.

"Hey, Lucy, get us two shots of whiskey for Trick and his old lady, would you?" he said to the girl behind the bar.

"Coming right up!"

Lucy put two fresh glasses on the bar and poured out whiskey in each from a bottle of Jameson's. Willy handed Trick and me the glasses and raised his toward us. "Here's to the mutual save. And Nicole, welcome to Meager."

"Thank you." We clinked glasses and drank. "I'm going to join the ladies in the kitchen. They're expecting me."

"Nicole! Over here!" Jill stood at another open archway across the lounge from us.

"See you in a bit," said Trick.

"Nice to meet you, Willy."

"You too."

Crossing the lounge, I went to Jill. "Trick introduced me to his uncle. And to the whole club."

"Ah, that's what that was about." She let out a short laugh. "We're in here."

"There she is!" said Tania. "You ready for wine?"

"Definitely."

Tania filled a tall wine glass with a Merlot and handed it to me.

I sipped. "Wow, that's good."

"Our local winery knows their stuff," said Grace.

"They certainly do."

"They have monthly wine tastings we always go to," Tania said.

"Count me in." I laughed.

"The chicken cacciatore is now in the oven," said Grace. "And we're making mashed potatoes to go with it, as well as a big green salad."

"Where would you like me?"

"Give the girl a knife!" exclaimed Tania, and a large chef's knife was given to me. Suddenly, I was in front of a chopping block with loads of freshly washed romaine lettuce and scallions and a big bunch of dill. I got to work.

Jill brought over two enormous bowls and we filled them with the thinly cut greens. "We realize this is your first time living with a motorcycle club, and we wanted you to know that if you have any questions or whatever that you can ask us anything anytime."

"Thank you. I appreciate that."

"Trick's a good guy. You're lucky to have him…on your side." She grinned.

"He is a good guy, and yes, I am lucky."

Mary Lynn brought over the salt and pepper shakers. "Do you like Trick? In that way?"

"Might be a little early for that conversation," said Jill.

"Well, I have to say…" I sipped at my wine, and all eyes landed on me. "He's very good looking."

"He's a hottie." Jill giggled. "Don't tell my old man I said that."

I giggled. "He is a hottie. But you know what else? I feel I can talk to him about anything."

"So important." Tania sliced a long baguette.

"It is." I leaned against the counter next to Tania. I liked being able to have a genuine conversation with these women. They had terrific senses of humor and seemed levelheaded, seasoned, responsible—so unlike my friends back in Oklahoma. "Trick's a great listener and very supportive. Even though I've only known him a couple of days, he's already helped me figure a few things out. I've never had that before in my one relationship." I drank more wine, savoring its robust flavor and steadying warmth seeping through me. "He's been good to me."

"How good?" Mary Lynn burst out in a singsong voice, and we all laughed.

My face heated, and I put down my wine glass. "At the moment, I have a husband back in Oklahoma who I'm trying to divorce, but he's refusing to sign off on it."

"Been there, done that," piped in Tania as she shook a glass mason jar with the mustard and balsamic vinaigrette dressing she'd put together.

"Oh yeah?"

"Yep. And now here I am back in my little hometown happy as fuck with the man of my dreams and living my dream career. You have to look out for yourself, Nicole. The time is now for what feels right and what makes you feel good."

"Absolutely," said Grace, tucking a thick wad of napkins into a holder. "Your instincts won't steer you wrong."

Mary Lynn refilled my wine glass, and I sipped. "You're right. Our whole separation, almost a year now, I've just been thinking about everybody else's feelings, how they're handling things, what they're going through."

"And how did that make you feel?" Grace passed two sticks of butter to Mary Lynn.

"That's just it…I wasn't feeling. I was existing, shuffling through every day. God, I don't want that for me anymore."

"Good for you." Tania raised her glass at me. "It doesn't have to be that way anymore."

"No, it doesn't."

"One more thing, if I may be so bold?" Tania leaned into me as she poured the vinaigrette over the salad.

"Sure, go ahead."

"If being with Trick feels good, there's nothing wrong about going with that feeling, exploring it. There is no shame in enjoying yourself now, not on any level."

"Enjoying myself, huh?" I tossed the salad with the big serving fork and spoon.

"New concept?"

"Yes, and I'm embarrassed to admit it."

"Don't be. Again, been there, done that." Tania gave me a hug. "I think more often than not, we women have to remind ourselves to do it. That it's important, because it is so very important."

I nodded, my vision getting blurry, and I sucked in a breath against the tears.

"And, of course, if you find a man who wants you to enjoy yourself and makes it his mission in life to assist in that…well, that's amazing." Grace handed me a towel.

"Wow. I have to meet your husband, you lucky woman." Laughing, I wiped my hands on the towel.

"Oh, I'm blessed. Extremely blessed." Grace grinned. "My husband's out of town on business right now, but he'll be back later next week. You'll meet him then."

"Everything y'all are describing sounds amazing, but to me, right now, it's more like a fantasy."

"I get that, trust me," said Tania. "But it all starts with you wanting it and believing it. You have to make that decision. Your life is up to you, Nicole."

"Well, except for the being on lockdown part," quipped Jill.

My spine straightened. "Trick said the same thing, that I need to believe it." They were right. Trick was right. Now, I was living a whole new life because I'd believed there had to be a better way for me. I'd wanted it that bad that I'd made a deal with the devil that was Dog. I'd taken that first step already and landed in the very place I'd wanted to be, Meager, South Dakota, with Richie's other family. That was the best sign that I was on the right path.

"All right then. Here I go. Ladies—" I raised my wine glass. "I believe."

"You rock it, girl."

"There you go."

"Yass!" Mary Lynn clapped.

"I'll drink to that."

I wiped at the corner of my mouth. "By the way, Tania, which of the men is your old man?"

"Butler is my husband."

"The VP? We met in the office earlier. Hottie, if I may be so bold."

"You may, and he is." Tania laughed. "I realize you and Trick have been thrown together by crazy circumstances, but no matter what, I hope the two of you are able to get along and become friends."

"Me too."

"Did you say 'thrown together?'" Jill laughed. "That's how Boner and I happened. He stepped in and claimed me as his old lady to keep my mean-at-the-time ex-boyfriend away from me."

"Who happens to be my baby brother, incidentally," said Tania as she arranged the bread in napkin-lined basket.

"No kidding?" I brought over the other salad bowl and the sliced bread.

"He's reformed now. Well, kind of," said Tania. "He's a member of Finger's club. His name is Catch." She handed a salad bowl to Mary Lynn who brought it out to the table.

"Catch is your brother?" I said. "I met him in Nebraska."

"Back to my story—" Jill grated parmesan over the mashed potatoes. "Being thrown together like that, Boner and I got close and kept getting closer."

"There already was a high-octane attraction there," said Tania.

"Yes, but neither of us had ever made a move."

"High-octane?" I giggled. "I like the sound of that."

"It was and it is," said Mary Lynn, her eyebrows waggling, and everyone laughed.

I had a feeling all these women and their men kept their high-octane passions alive.

The chicken was ready and we brought the rest of the food to the long table the men had set up in the central lounge, and everyone gathered and took a seat. Trick signaled me, pulling out the chair next to him, and I went over.

"Hi." I put my wine glass next to his beer bottle as I eased into the chair, my face flaring with heat. Why did I still feel this mixture of shy and excited whenever I was close to him?

Maybe it was a high-octane kind of thing?

Maybe I'd had too much wine.

"Everything good?" Trick asked.

"Real good."

Platters and bowls were passed around the table. Plates filled. Beer cans and bottles snapped open. Soda frothed into cups, and wine poured into glasses. Butler stood, and silence fell. Everyone raised their drinks. "To the defiant who came before. To the bold who ride on today. All of us. Together. Burning hearts, bleeding road. Fierce wind. Forever."

"Forever!" everyone exclaimed and drank.

Trick leaned into me. "That's a club oath of sorts we say when it's just us on special occasions."

"Like a family."

"We are a family." His velvet brown gaze met mine and something swirled in my chest.

"You are, yes."

They truly were a family, and all of these people and this place were Trick's whole world. He belonged here.

"Nicole, you ever been to South Dakota before?" Butler asked from across the table breaking my and Trick's moment.

"No." All eyes were on me. I cleared my throat. "No, I haven't. I always wanted to, though. My mother was born in Rapid City."

"Really?" said Trick.

"Mmm." *Dang wine. Maybe I should keep my mouth shut.*

"She never brought you for a visit, huh?" said Dready, scooping more mashed potatoes into his dish.

"No."

"Do you still have family here?" asked Jill.

My stomach knotted. "I don't know." My fork grazed through the chunky tomato sauce with pieces of garlic and red bell pepper in my dish. I hadn't outright lied, but I'd cloaked the truth. How would they react if they found out I was their Wreck's sister? I wasn't sure. I still didn't understand their culture, their traditions, what I'd wake up to tomorrow, and for now, it was safer this way. I swallowed down another mouthful of wine. Or maybe not saying anything about Richie was easier for me?

"Once our lockdown is over, I'll take you to Rapid, and we can ride through the Black Hills," said Trick. "We got beautiful country."

A tour of this magnificent country on the back of his bike? "I'd like that."

From across the table, Boner's dark, heavy gaze drilled through me as he slowly chewed his food. He didn't trust me, did he? Next to him, Willy studied me as he drank his beer. I averted my attention to my dish heaping with chicken in a rich tomato sauce along with the creamy mashed potatoes and green salad. I ate as Butler told everyone a story and laughter ensued.

"How'd it go in the kitchen?" Trick wiped at his mouth with a napkin. "You and the ladies got along okay?"

My shoulders eased. "We had fun talking and getting everything ready together. I like them a lot."

Over the next hour, the clubhouse was filled with laughter and off-color humor. Stories from the road, stories about the local townsfolk, and as I ate I listened in rapt attention, learning about Meager, about the One-Eyed Jacks.

The men and women spoke in a forthright kind of way I

wasn't used to. Around our daily family dinner table, Jackson and I had to constantly watch how we opened a conversation, if our elbows were on the table, and how we used a napkin. If we spoke out of turn or took too much food without asking others if they wanted more too. How we asked a question, and what we implied. Even as adults.

There was none of that here. No self-consciousness. No proper or conventional anything about this dinner.

Now the platters and bowls were empty, and the tablecloth stained. An army of empty beer bottles stood in clusters over the table. Bear had one of the club girls, Lucy, on his lap and they were flirting and laughing. Boner and Jill spoke intimately as she fed him a piece of Mary Lynn's toffee nut brownie. Those two had a special kind of electricity between them. He smoothed back a coil of her hair and nuzzled her cheek as she turned to Grace and asked her a question. Butler and Tania were in a debate with Kicker and Mary Lynn over a store in town and its eccentric owner.

Trick's arm slid around my chair. "You good? Was this too much for you?"

A tickle raced over my flesh with his arm around me, his body close to mine, his checking in on how I felt. "It was fun."

Slowly but surely everyone pitched in, stacking the dishes and bringing everything into the kitchen. I helped rinse and pile the dishes into the big commercial dishwasher. The men settled back at the bar while a few others left. Grace and I went around the lounge and picked up leftover cups and glasses and beer bottles, cleared out ash trays.

Holding the plastic bag, I bent over to pick up an empty cigarette box by the main entrance to the lounge, and as I stood up, my gaze snagged on the framed photographs on the wall. Mostly black and white pics, a few color images placed in odd frames, a number of them were small squares, some were faded or yellowed with age. Here was history.

I studied them one by one, my pulse ticking up. Was Richie

here? Yes, there he was, with Willy who sported a huge 70s style mustache, the two of them with their arms slung around one another, chests bare, sporting their One-Eyed Jacks leather vests, their bikes behind them, beers in their hand, growling playfully at the camera. My finger grazed the simple black frame. Trick's uncle and Richie had been good buddies, maybe best friends?

My heart thudded in my chest. Yes, this was where I needed to be. By insane hook and crazy crook, but I got here.

All roads lead to you, Richie.

And in my rearview mirror, I could see Dad, Mom, Jackson, and Logan—only now they weren't as imposing as I'd always thought they were.

Underneath Richie and Willy, hung another small photograph, this one in color but slightly faded. A grinning young woman in a black bikini held onto by a handsome, bare-chested, hot guy in cutoff jeans who was fiercely kissing her cheek. And there was Richie to their side, holding a beer bottle in the air. The three of them full of energy and joy. Celebration.

Why did she look familiar?

"Hey, I think we got everything," Grace's voice broke my reverie.

I pointed to the pic. "Is this you?"

A small smile lit up her face. "That's me."

"And this is your husband?"

"My first husband. Dig."

"Oh. He's very handsome."

"He was, yes." She took in a tiny breath, emotion flickering over her face, and something pinched inside me. "He got killed about four months after this photo was taken."

My hand flew to my mouth. "Grace, I'm so sorry. I didn't mean to—"

"No, no. It's okay." Her gaze returned to the photograph, her smile deepening. "Those are good memories. The best. This clubhouse is full of them."

CHAPTER 23
TRICK

"SO GOOD TO BE BACK IN my own bed," I groaned as my back eased onto the familiar firm mattress.

From the other side of the queen-sized bed, Nicole glanced at me as she rubbed moisturizer into her hands. This was her bed now too for however long. I shut off the lamp on my side. Was she nervous? On edge? I didn't want her to be. I sure didn't want to be.

Of course, a woman I'd just met being in my bed with me was nothing new, but this was different. A whole lot of different. I was sharing a bed with my "old lady." The mattress dipped as Nicole got under the covers.

When I'd left here for Kansas last week, I'd had no idea what the hell was in store for me. This wasn't for real, but it was for real. For the time being at least.

"Trick?" Nicole turned on her side to face me, her head leaning on her hand, the outdoor lights from the window glowing dimly over us. "Could you tell me what happened to Grace's first husband? I saw a photo of them when I was cleaning up in the lounge. She told me he got killed."

I turned to face her. "It was a rough time. I was living with Willy by then. Dig was a good guy. Did a lot for the club. Became

Vice President too. Dig and Boner had met in juvie in Denver, broke out together, and had been living on the road for a couple years when Wreck met them. They were stealing something at the time. He brought them to Meager, into the club. At some point, Dig met Grace around town. Her older sister, Ruby, used to hang out with the club. Long story short, they fell for each other, got married, and a few years later Dig got caught in the crossfire for a good deed—he saved Jill, actually."

"Jill? What happened to Jill?"

"She'd been kidnapped by this fuckhead drug addict. She was a teenager. Dig found them by accident, killed the guy, got her out. But the guy's brother came after Dig and shot him. Almost got Grace too, but she survived and ended up killing the guy." I let out a breath. "She was pregnant at the time and lost the baby."

"Oh no. That's awful."

"Yeah. It was a fucking mess. She left South Dakota after that, but then she came back a few years ago when her sister Ruby got sick and ended up getting together with another brother. My boss, Lock."

"She said he was out of town this week."

"Yep. We invested in these two muscle cars, a Plymouth Road Runner and a Pontiac GTO, rebuilt them completely, new paint, mod looks. They are so fine. He took them to an auction in Minnesota where there are some very interested collectors we've hooked up with before. So we're hoping to get new eyes on our work, make bank, and get our name out there more. Each car is a new opportunity."

"You worked on those cars?"

"I'm in charge of the rebuilds at the shop—the engine, the insides mostly, but I get a say in the overall design. We all do."

"You like your work a lot, don't you?"

"It's obvious, huh?"

"It is." She smiled softly. "That's the best."

Loud moans and grunts rose from Dawes's room next door.

His bed banged against the other wall. Nicole's eyes widened, and her teeth scraped her lip. "Is that…"

"Yeah."

The woman's moans grew quicker, deeper, louder.

"That's Lucy coming," I told her.

"Oh."

Raw grunting and the loud jerking of the metal bed fought with Lucy's cries. Nicole's eyes widened even more.

"And that's Bear fucking Lucy," I added.

"Yeah, Luce, yeah…" A deep groan followed.

"And that's Dawes probably getting a blow job from Lucy…"

Nicole burst into laughter.

"What's so funny, Zip?" I whispered, moving in closer to her, her warm genuine laughter drawing me in like a goddamn magic spell.

"You know whose moans are whose and who's doing what to who?" Her head knocking back against the mattress, she burst out into more laughter, laughter that had this sexy, easygoing quality. I hadn't seen her laugh like that before. Let go. Not like this.

"I've lived here a long, long time and been on the road with these guys for just as long. There are things you get real familiar with, real quick."

"Of course." She rolled over to face me again. "You've slept with Shannon and Lucy too, right?"

"You want me to lie?"

"No, I don't. Please don't ever lie to me." She'd gotten serious all of a sudden. I didn't want lies between us either.

"Yeah, I've slept with both of them. We all know what it is. It's straightforward, easy. That's how this works, and it works for everybody. We all get something out of it."

"Without any complications."

"And no expectations."

"Clean and convenient."

"It is." My gaze clung to hers as she studied me, her teeth

gnawing on her lip. A lip I wanted to bite, a lip I wanted to feel against mine. "Spit it out, Zip."

"So no relationships for you?" she asked.

"Nah. I've been burned one too many times. The last one was when I called it quits."

"A tragic ex."

"Tragic?" I made a face.

"The one that stung the deepest."

"It stung all right."

She stacked both her pillows under her head. "Did she cheat on you?"

"No. She just didn't want what I wanted, and I ignored that for a long while. I got to pushing, which got ugly. It turned out she was still in love with her ex, and they got back together right after."

"I'm sorry."

"Don't be. I'm happy she's happy and real happy to be free of all that."

"Of messy complications and expectations?"

"Exactly. I'm done."

A high-pitched cry rose from the other side of my room.

"Is that Lucy?" Nicole whispered.

"No. That's Shannon. She gets squeaky when she's close to coming."

A long guttural grunt followed with "Fuck, fuck, fuck..." interspersed with thudding got louder and louder.

"Who's that?"

"That's Dready. His bed always knocks into his dresser, and..."

Nicole exploded into laughter again, her gorgeous hair splayed all over the pillow. She turned back to me, pushing her hair from her face and my chest squeezed.

She could have been bitching about how she needed to get to sleep, that this place was a nightmare, but she wasn't. She wasn't uptight or pissed off. She was laughing. "Is it like this every night?"

"Pretty much. A hell of a lot more when we have parties."

"I can only imagine." She sat up, crossing her legs. "I didn't think of this before, but…"

"But what?"

"I don't want to hold you back from what you usually do. I've messed up your life enough as it is."

"There's nothing to mess up."

"Oh, come on. I don't want to interrupt your usual lifestyle."

"My lifestyle?"

"You're used to having sex with Shannon and Lucy and whoever else whenever you wanted, and you shouldn't not do that because of me."

"I'm not going to cheat on you, Nicole."

"But it wouldn't be cheating because this whole thing is fake, right?"

My jaw tightened. Why did this annoy me? I sat up. "It's fake but we're still doing it. And we're doing it because it has to look real. So we should stick to it and be clean about it. Less complications that way."

"True. I agree."

"Don't get me wrong. I appreciate the thought, I do, but you're my old lady now for however long, and I'm not going to fuck anybody else. Okay?" My voice had gotten louder, sharper, and her body stiffened.

Shannon's moans suddenly became long and drawn out, and we both laid down again, listening. "Tell me, you get loud when you …"

"Me?"

"Yeah, you."

"Um…" She twisted her lips. She was thinking about it. She had to think about it? "Not really, no."

Why was I asking? Because I couldn't help myself. Because I

wanted to know. Because I wanted to picture her coming, imagine her moaning, twisting, bucking.

I fingered a lock of her impossibly soft hair. "So you're naturally quiet all around, or maybe…"

Somehow we'd gotten closer on the bed. Somehow her breaths had gotten deeper. "Maybe what?" She pressed her legs together, her body stilling alongside mine.

"Maybe you haven't had it real good yet?" I whispered.

"Yes, oh shit. YES! YES!" Lucy shouted out as Dawes and Bear muttered and groaned. The three of them grunting, moaning, cursing.

"Like Lucy?" Nicole breathed.

"Like Lucy. Like Shannon."

She blinked. "No, not like that."

Why the fuck not?

She was gorgeous, beautiful in every classical way. Startling dark blue eyes, wavy and long pale blonde hair. Long legs, curves…this girl was unbelievable. Pin up material. "Did you and your husband…fuck, forget it, none of my business." I let go of her hair.

She steadied her head on her arm, her gaze firmly meeting mine. "My husband was the first guy and the only guy I've ever slept with. It happened, and I hardly realized it."

"What the hell does that mean?"

"I was nineteen. We were at a house party, drinking, talking, and laughing with a bunch of our friends. He and I were flirting, kissing. And then the next thing I remember I woke up on a bed in a dark room and my panties were gone and my body ached."

My pulse jolted. "What the fuck?"

"I didn't know what to do or how to feel, what to think. I got out of the room, found him at the party, and he acted like nothing bad or unusual had happened. Nothing wrong. And eventually, so did I."

"Nicole, he raped you. You realize that, don't you?"

"I do," she whispered roughly.

"He must have put something in your drink and then the fucker raped you. Your first time and he…" I swallowed hard, tamping down my blood-red rage. I didn't want her to freak out.

"I know," she said. "I know."

Had she never put that into words, into *that* word, identified it for what it was? "Did you ever tell anyone? Confront him about it?"

"No. He's my brother's best friend, and we've known each other since forever. Our dads were business partners. My brother liked us together. Our parents loved us together. All my friends were envious. I couldn't…"

"It's okay." I stroked her arm, and her body relaxed again.

"We got engaged, we got married. Everything seemed perfect, the way it should be."

"Should be, huh? But it wasn't perfect. It was abusive on so many levels."

"It took me a long time to figure that out. But I finally did."

" And the sex?" I asked.

"The sex was always about him. When he was in the mood, how he wanted it. I went along with it, and he…handled every-thing, so I let him. It seemed easier that way." She let out a tight breath. "God, I feel so stupid."

I wanted to pull her into my arms, hold her tight, but I knew that would be a bad idea. "You're not stupid. Listen to me, Zip—he took that away from you. That part of you."

Her chest heaved and her hands covered her face. "He did take that away, but I let him. I let it happen, and I let it go on."

"Hey." Sitting up, I took her hands away from her face. "Look at me." She finally lifted her watery eyes. "You left him. You said no more. You stood up for yourself."

"I did."

Heat flared through me at the sight of the lines on her face that told of hurt and pain and confusion. *That motherfucker.* This beautiful, gentle woman had been taken advantage of in the worst possible way. The fucking worst.

Lucy's soft laughter and murmurs of satisfaction rolled through Dawes's room on the other side of the wall. Her sighs quickly transformed into drawn-out moans. Were they licking her now?

Nicole chewed on her lip again. Had she ever even come before?

"Lucy and Shannon just took what they wanted. They got what they needed. Just like Dawes and Bear and Dready did. You get what I mean?"

"I know what you mean."

"You can do that too."

"Yeah. But…"

"But what?"

"I don't know what I want or need. I always figured I didn't need much of anything."

"Is that what he told you? 'Cause that's bullshit." I grit my jaw as my knuckles grazed her cheek. I had to touch her. Had to. "He took that away from you like a fucking thief. The worst kind of thief because you trusted him, and he fucking knew it."

Her forehead scrunched. Had she never seen it that way before? Probably not. She'd probably only been blaming herself for her hell all along. She'd locked all her needs and desires down and thrown away the key because the man in her life had hurt her and made her feel like shit over and over again.

"Trick, I've never told anyone any of this," she whispered. "Not ever. Not my mother, not my girlfriends, nobody ever."

My heart thudded against my ribs. What had started out earlier as a laugh between us had turned into something completely different. My chest swelled. She'd felt compelled to share all that with me, but most of all, she'd felt safe enough to do it.

"Come here." I opened my arms and she pressed herself against me with a sigh that seeped over my skin like a warm mist, her soft body melting into mine. "Thank you for trusting me with it." My mouth brushed the top of her head as I stroked her hair. "I hope I didn't upset you with anything I said. I didn't mean to."

"You didn't." Her lips moved against my chest. "You helped me see it differently. You helped me face the truth."

"Good. Because it's fucking wrong." Her body settled against mine and I reveled in her scent, in the feel of her curves, and the weight of her body against mine.

"When I left him, my friends told me to go have my own affairs, to not be his victim, and have my own fun. I honestly didn't know what to say to that. Power games and revenge, showing off, were not the point for me. Never have been." She let out a heavy breath. "Lately, my mother and brother started pressuring me to go back to him, to stop making a big deal out of it."

"But it was a big deal."

She snuggled closer to me, and my hold on her tightened. "But the funny thing is, that made everyone around me uncomfortable, my family, even my girlfriends. As if I was the one who'd ruined everything. I guess it's easier to slither around the house of cards, as long as you look good doing it and don't knock anything over."

"Fuck should. Why should you? 'Cause that's what society wants? Your parents, your friends? Fuck that, you didn't want to."

"No, I didn't want to." Her fingertips dug into my flesh.

"I'm going to say it again, because I think you need to hear it. You're brave for getting your separation and for getting yourself out of there. You're here with us now, and you don't have to do anything you don't want to do ever again. That's a promise."

"A promise from my old man, huh?"

I let out a soft laugh. "That's right, Zip. We look out for each other." My hand skimmed the top of her ass, but I immediately brought it back up to the slope her waist. Safer territory.

"I like the sound of that." Her warm fingertips traced a trail along my jawline that had my insides warm and my lungs jam.

She felt good. So fucking good. Holding her body, talking honestly, whispers in the dark, all of it. This could oh so easily lead to sex, hell, I was already visualizing it, tasting it, but I would control myself. I would not jump into that right now. It would just confuse the situation.

I cleared my throat, forcing my muscles to relax. "Let's get some sleep, huh? We deserve it."

"We do," she whispered against my chest, sighing, tickling my skin. "We do…." Her voice drifted off, and my lips brushed the top of her forehead, but I didn't take my arms away. Not just yet.

She let out a low hum as the curves of her body relaxed fully into mine.

And mine into hers.

CHAPTER 24
NICOLE

"HEY, Nicole. What are you doing over there?" Lucy poured herself a mug of coffee and sat on a stool at the bar in the club lounge.

"Washing out a couple of coffee mugs I found sitting here."

"You could've put them in the dishwasher. We just installed one back there to make life easier."

"I didn't see it. Good to know." I wiped my hands on a dishcloth.

"Did we keep you awake last night? We heard you guys laughing." She let out a short laugh as she lit a cigarette.

"The rooms are definitely not soundproof, huh?"

We both laughed out loud.

"Can I ask you a question?" I came around the bar and sat on the stool next to her.

"Sure. Anything."

"You live here at the MC, right?"

"Going on two years now. I have my own room. It's great."

I nodded, not sure how to—

"Go ahead, ask, it's okay. I know this is all new to you."

"I was just wondering how you decided on being here. If you decided…"

"I did decide, yeah. I was going from job to job, and making ends meet was getting hard. I'd gotten to know the guys from parties I'd come to here, and I liked them and they liked me. Then I had this weirdo stalking me, which got pretty scary, and the guys dealt with him for me."

"Wow, thank goodness."

"Oh yeah. One thing led to another, and I got invited to stay. It's a huge relief to have a safe, clean place to live without having to worry about rent and utilities and food. "

"Sure." My mother's remark about how I didn't know how good I had it flashed through my brain.

Lucy sipped on her coffee. "I knew Shannon from a bar I'd worked at once in Rapid, and she had just quit because her boss was coming on to her and being a real asshole, then her long distance boyfriend cheated on her and they broke up. She was at a crossroads, and this appealed to her so she came over too.

"This won't be forever, but it's been a great place to land, to take a moment and regroup. Shannon and I take care of general clean up around here, food shopping and cooking, bartending, and we get a small salary which is nice, and I'm able to save money for the first time in my life, which is awesome. And we keep the guys happy." She lifted her eyebrows as she sipped on her coffee.

"Any time they want, right?"

"Any time, anywhere. Having sex with hot men day and night is not a hardship in my book. Yeah sure, sometimes I'm not in the mood, but it is what it is, and by now we all know each other real well, so it's good."

"Even with the men who are married?" I whispered. "Don't the old ladies—"

"No, no. Never with them. Those men are the most loyal beasts you'll ever meet. They don't even get tempted, not even by all the women who show up at the parties. Not them." She blew out a huff of smoke.

"Such men exist?"

"Here they do. I swear, something must be in the water in this building." She let out a laugh. "I want a man like that one day."

"That'd be nice."

"Girl, you're lucky—you got Trick."

"We're not…not um…you know…"

"Uh-huh." Eyeing me, she exhaled a long plume of smoke. "Nicole, you're together. Why the hell wouldn't you make the most of it?"

My throat burned as I gulped down more coffee.

"Hey, you guys, what's up?" Shannon sat down next to Lucy.

Lucy put out her cigarette in the ashtray. "I was just filling in Nicole on how stuff works around here."

"Ah." Shannon poured herself a coffee.

"Do y'all work outside the club too or is this …"

"I don't," Lucy replied. I've started taking classes in auto detailing a couple days a week. I like it. I helped out cleaning the shop when I first came here and I liked the work they did, so I thought I'd give it a shot."

"That's great."

"She's hoping to get an internship at Eagle Wings this summer," said Shannon.

"I don't know, you might need real insider connections for that," I quipped, and the three of us laughed.

"I work outside the club every other week or so," said Shannon. "I dance at The Tingle as a substitute if one of the girls can't make it. Gives me a sweet amount of extra cash, which is great."

"You're a dancer?"

"I am."

"I am too."

"You are?"

"I am. And I need a job."

"Well, I could get you an audition with the manager if you want." Shannon and Lucy exchanged a quick look.

"That would be great. I've kept up with all sorts of classes for years now."

Lucy poured herself more coffee. "Would Trick let you, though? Have you discussed it with him at all? Not all men are—"

"Into their woman working? Trust me, I know. Since Trick is my old man, would he have to approve what kind of job I get? Is that a thing here? I would've thought bikers were a little more progressive than that."

Lucy slanted her head as if I'd just spoken a foreign language she couldn't understand. "Hang on, Nic. You do realize we're talking about dancing at a strip club, right?"

"A *what*?" I sputtered.

"A strip club. The Tingle is the club-owned strip club at the edge of town."

"The One-Eyed Jacks own a strip club?"

"Yep," laughed Shannon. "A good old-fashioned legal money-making business with some flash and tits and ass."

"Ohhhhh."

"Ohhhhh." Shannon grinned. "You're not that kind of dancer, are you?"

"No. I'm more your ballet and modern kind of dancer with a college degree to show for it."

We all burst into laughter again.

"If you wanted to branch out into stripping, you'd do amazing. I could teach you some hot moves if you like," said Shannon.

"I have always been curious about the pole."

"Best workout there is," Lucy said. "Look at her fucking legs. Don't get me started on her abs."

"Would you teach me, Shannon?"

"Seriously?"

"Seriously."

"You're on. Once you're off lockdown, we can go to The Tingle one morning."

"Great. Now, how can I help around here? Y'all must have a routine in place, so tell me how I could fit in."

"You sure?"

"Of course. I'm here every day and every night. I want to help out and be useful."

The three of us went over how the two women kept the club in top shape. I volunteered to sweep and dust the common areas early every morning for starters, since I had no problem waking up before seven a.m., and I knew the girls were often up very late every night. Then I'd help with the meal prep and cooking.

Lucy's phone beeped and she glanced at her screen. "Got to dash, girls. Bear's morning wood needs my special attention."

"Go get it, girl," said Shannon.

"Always do, babe." Lucy headed down the hallway for more orgasm giving and receiving. A part of me envied her. No rules hemmed her in. No burdens of right or wrong weighed her down. No one to disappoint, and no one to disapprove.

Freedom.

Shannon went to get the day's laundry started, and I tackled sweeping and organizing the central lounge and all the hallways. As me and my broom reached the long hallway that led to the mens' rooms, I recognized Bear's raw grunts and Lucy's loud, drawn-out moans.

"Go get it, girl," I murmured to myself.

CHAPTER 25
NICOLE

"WHAT ARE YOU DOING IN HERE?"

I jumped at the deep voice. Trick stood in the kitchen entryway, arms crossed, white T-shirt full of dirt smudges and grease stains.

My breath cut. He filled the space, the room, and my heart thudded in my chest. "Oh hey. I thought I'd make lunch for you and the Eagle Wings crew. I helped Shannon and Lucy clean up and organize stuff earlier, and then I thought why not do something nice for you...and everyone."

He grinned a lopsided grin. He was pleased. "So, what are you making?"

"Club sandwiches. Found this applewood smoked bacon in the fridge and ...."

"That's a lot of sandwiches." He scanned the large cutting board where I'd laid out stacks of sandwiches.

"It is." I spread my mustard and mayo sauce on the last slice of toasted bread and pressed it gently on the double-decker sandwich.

"You seem to know what you're doing." He tore off a piece of paper towel and handed it to me.

I took it and wiped my fingers. "My grandfather loved a

good sandwich. He used to make these triple-deckers, and he'd call them his "Dagwood" sandwiches. You know, from that old-time comic strip—"

"'Blondie'?"

"Yes, Blondie. That was his favorite."

"Willy and my dad loved that one, too. I liked 'Hagar the Horrible.'"

I let out a laugh. "And Peanuts?"

"Snoopy? Of course. So, how we going to bring these next door?"

"I was going to wrap them up in foil. I have a pile of napkins here and baggies."

"Let's do this." He washed his hands, and we got to work wrapping up the sandwiches. I put them in two bags and along with napkins and a selection of sodas, we brought them next door to Eagle Wings.

"What's all this?" a tall, good-looking guy with a Southern accent greeted us as he took off his spray painting goggles.

"Travis, this is my old lady, Nicole."

"Hi, Travis."

He grinned. "Hey, Nicole, what's all this?"

"Nicole made club sandwiches for everybody for lunch. Gather 'round, assholes."

One guy after the other grabbed a sandwich I held out to them from the bag.

"Thanks," said Boner as he took his.

"You're very welcome," I replied.

"These are really good," said Travis through a mouthful of grilled chicken, bacon, cheese, tomato, pickle, and lettuce.

"Glad you like it."

"Mmm. Real good," said Trick munching.

"So what is it you do exactly around here, Mr. Trick?" I asked.

"Want to see?" He wiped at his mouth.

"I do."

"This way."

I followed him around a freshly painted car and a massive motorcycle on a platform that was being put together like an oversized puzzle by Boner. We entered a large area that had three cars lifted up on elevated poles. Trick put his sandwich on a long wide table in the center of the room that seemed to be the base of operations and designs. Sketches and papers and magazines stood in piles on one end of the metal table.

"We're a customization and restoration shop. People bring us their beloved junk, and we breathe new life into it, making it not only gorgeous but a one-of-a-kind piece of work that runs on the road like a devil." He grinned.

My gaze darted all over the vast interior of the space. Framed artwork of eagles and American Flags covered the upper walls. "This used to be Wreck's, right?"

"Back then it was a straight-up repair shop. But Lock made some amazing changes. This whole section is a new building added on to the original shed that was the old Wreck's Repair. Now we do custom painting, which is Lock's specialty, upgrading interiors, new upholstery—rebuilds and restoration."

"Is that a Monte Carlo back there?" I gestured to the mustard-colored car with a black top.

"It is. Good for you."

"My grandad's favorite car."

"That was one hunk of junk when it came in. Rust, old paint. We had to soda blast the shell to get it to clean bare steel. Finished the bodywork, primed her. Painted the shell this color, and now she's waiting for Lock to do his custom detailing and then we'll give her the high gloss magic. I rebuilt the 402 big block with custom domed pistons and....well...anyhow." He rubbed his hands together. "She's going to get outfitted with bolstered and stitched bench seats, and a new audio system. We're waiting on her custom set of wheels, but as is she hums, she roars. She jets." Enthusiasm glimmered in his eyes. He truly loved his job. His work was satisfying to him.

His grin was infectious, and my lips tipped up. "Vintage cars are the house speciality?"

"We love 'em, that's for sure, but we do all sorts of projects. From basic upgrades to this kind of custom detailing. Depending on the client's budget, we can come up with all sorts of bells and whistles to fit their personality, their vibe, which means a lot of cool stuff inside and out and under the hood. It's a real team effort. We all have input on each project."

"Fantastic."

"It is." He smoothed a hand down the spotless stainless steel counter. "Once it's all done, my favorite part is taking them for a test drive on our track out back."

"There's a track here?"

"This used to be a go-kart factory back in the day. It's a small track, nothing massive, but we've fixed it up over the years, and it's a hell of a lot of fun. It'd be nice if it were bigger, but, maybe one day, that'll happen."

"You live for speed, don't you?"

"It cures whatever ails you. At least for me."

A thrill rippled through me at the sudden deep timbre in his voice. I tore my gaze away from his, and clearing my throat, focused on the car before us. "You test the engine and all the insides, making sure everything's running the way it should?"

"Yep. And when a client comes to pick it up and we roll it out…nothing better. They get emotional. Not just excited, but down deep emotions to see their old car restored to a new glory. Or a dream car that they'd found and were finally able to afford to restore it."

"Making dreams come true. Eagle Wings is building a good reputation."

"We are. Grace has been doing some solid marketing, and Lock and Travis are out there going to shows and auctions, shaking hands. And the motorcycle end of the shop is doing real well."

I let out a laugh. "It'd sure be a humiliation if it wasn't."

Trick grinned. "That it would."

The club had built on what Richie had created. A solid business that was growing and gleaming brightly. They were building on what they had inherited from previous club members, building on Wreck's legacy.

Images of my husband and brother and their two-hour-long liquid lunches with friends and clients surged through my memory. They disliked being in their fancy offices. Logan was a lawyer who'd hated law school with a passion, but knew it was the only gateway to our fathers' oil company. Just as my brother had hated business school but did it as our father had stipulated graduation to gain entry to the company he would ostensibly rule one day. It was all because they were told to do it. They had to get the keys to the kingdom.

Had they ever given any thought to what they wanted to do with their lives? Furthermore, were they truly interested in building on the legacy they had inherited or only bent on enjoying the cash flow? Had they ever created anything?

Had I?

"I'm happy for you, Trick. That's rare that someone loves their job because they love the work. That it's meaningful and satisfying to them, not just a way to pay the bills."

His grin grew wider, deeper. "That's exactly how I feel. I love that we're building something good here, doing it together, it's the best. Keeps my hands real dirty, though." He fluttered his fingers. Hands that were callused, rough, stained. Experienced.

"I like your hands." My face heated, and he let out a low chuckle. I had no verbal control around this man.

"I heard you were here," Grace's voice came up behind me, snapping me out of my Trick reverie.

"Hey, Grace. I made lunch for the guys. Could I get you something to eat? There's plenty more."

"No, thanks, Nicole, I'm good. You watch out, these wild creatures around here aren't used to fine dining and friendly service. Careful you don't spoil them."

"Yeah, yeah…" laughed Trick. "Grace runs the joint, by the way."

"That's right." Grace laughed. "Would you like a tour of my executive suite?"

"Yes, ma'am, I sure would."

Trick lightly touched my arm, his hand dropping to mine, squeezing my fingers. "I got to get back to work. Thanks for lunch, Zip. It was real good."

"You're welcome." I smiled and he held my smile with his. Heat burst through me.

Oh, that felt real good.

CHAPTER 26
NICOLE

GRACED USHERED me through the door to her office, and as we entered the sun-filled space, the front door opened, and in stepped Lenore wearing oversized cat eye sunglasses and bearing a cardboard holder filled with three iced coffees.

"A visitor!" said Grace going to Lenore and kissing her on the cheek. "What delights did you bring us, madame?"

"Iced caramel lattes."

"And this, Nicole, is why Lenore is always my favorite visitor. Don't tell anyone. Sit down. I was just giving Nicole the tour."

I gave her a hug. "Good to see you again, Lenore."

"You too, honey. I wanted to come by and see how you were doing, settling in and all. I've been thinking about you." Lenore set the coffees down on Grace's desk and removed the colorfully embroidered thin leather jacket she wore. She handed me a coffee. "I spoke with Tania and she assured me that the old ladies were taking good care of you."

"Everyone's been terrific. They brought me new clothes, towels and pillows, makeup, the works."

"I have no doubt." She crossed her legs and sipped on her coffee. "You settling in okay with Trick?"

"We filled Lenore in." Grace tucked a straw in her coffee cup.

"Everything's good."

"Good, I'm glad."

"I saw your shop in town when we first drove through. It looks beautiful."

"Wait until you go inside. Pure magic," said Grace.

"Once you can leave here, come right over, and I'll give you the tour of the store and the town," said Lenore.

"I look forward to it. I wanted to ask you, I was hoping I could find a job in town once I can leave the clubhouse. Would you know of anything?"

"I'm sure we could find something. What kind of work experience do you have?"

"Not much. I got married young and my husband didn't want me working. But I have a background in dance. That's what I studied at school and I've taught a few classes here and there."

"Dance?" Grace sipped her coffee.

I told them about the earlier misunderstanding with Lucy, and they laughed.

"I have an idea," said Lenore. "We have a small fitness studio in town, down the block from my store. The guy who owns it is a good friend of mine."

"Craig is her good friend because only Lenore can keep up with his military-style cardio workouts. Ugh." She groaned on a laugh as she sat back in her office chair.

"And that right there is my point—Craig only offers those types of high-intensity aerobic and calisthenic workouts. He's a classic. They get the job done, but that's not up everyone's alley."

"Definitely not mine." Grace made a face.

"But if you're a trained dancer, maybe you could..."

"I've taught dance to children at my local dance studio. And dance cardio and barre and Pilates floor work at a health club."

"I love Pilates, and I've always wanted to try barre," murmured Grace.

"Excellent." Lenore grinned. "I'll stop by Craig's today and talk to him."

"Be persuasive in that special Lenore way." Grace sipped her coffee. "The way that makes ordinary men shiver in their boots."

"You can count on it." Lenore winked at us.

"In the meantime, Nicole, if you're up for it, I could use some help around here," said Grace. "Bear's old lady used to work for me part-time doing simple admin, but she left a couple of months ago and things have piled up on me. I even had to put my framed photos away because the paperwork just piled up on my desk and is still growing as you can see." She smacked a hand on a tower of folders. "I've been so backlogged since Suzi left, it's been making me nutty."

"I'd love to help."

"Terrific. Ah! Also—Meager's Ruby Red Festival is literally around the corner and I would love your help there too. That gig is volunteer."

"What kind of festival?"

"The club runs it every year as a fundraiser for local cancer patient families. We also raise awareness for testing for bone marrow transplants. A good match is hard to find, most especially for non-white ethnicities and races. Raising awareness and getting people to be tested and register for donating is so vital for our community."

"Grace started the donor drive a few years back and it's blown up since," said Lenore.

"That's wonderful. Good for you."

"It's good for all of us," murmured Grace. "My sister Ruby had gotten sick, and with the club's help, I put together a drive to attract potential donors. It's since transformed into an annual street festival that kicks off spring in our parts. I'd love for you to participate if you're able to."

"I'd love to."

"It's fun," said Lenore. "All us storeowners have booths to showcase our goodies, as well as other interesting vendors from all over the Black Hills. It's become a real thing for Meager."

"It has, hasn't it?" Grace had that emotional faraway look on her face again. Ruby hadn't survived, had she?

"Count me in." I grinned at this strong woman, this survivor of so much heartbreak. "Put me anywhere you need me. I've worked on a few charity events in my time, and I'd love to help."

"I would love an eleventh-hour liaison to all the vendors, checking in with them to make sure they've got what we asked them to have and that they have everything they need from us before opening day. It's been a lot to keep up with."

"I'm your girl."

Lenore let out a dry laugh. "You better put me at the top of your to-do list, Nicole, because I'm pretty sure I've left a few things to the very last minute."

"Terrific! I'll send out an email to everyone introducing you," said Grace. "I'll let them know you'll be calling to touch base with them. Once your lockdown is over, you can visit each store-owner at their shops in Meager. I'm sure one of the guys could go with you if need be."

"Sounds good." My chest swelled with warmth. Helping out with this important festival and working here at the place that my brother Richie had founded, the place where Trick worked and the company he loved so much, were gifts. Slowly but surely I was being woven into the fabric of this club, this town, these people by a force greater than me. Was it my desire to make it happen? Was it simply the goodness of those around me?

And if I could get that job at the fitness studio?

The year before I'd taken a job teaching dance cardio two mornings per week, but Logan had found out, was furious, and made me quit. *"My wife does not work at a fucking health club!"*

Whatever it was, be it the air or the water or all the woo, that growing, deepening connection with these people here in Meager was vibrant and genuine to me, and I loved it. Sipping my iced coffee here in Grace's office with her and Lenore as they talked excitedly about the festival, I not only savored the flavor of the sweet roasted brew that filled my mouth but this connection, this opportunity to belong over and over and over again.

And even though this was the previously foreign-to-me unconventional world of a motorcycle club, it was here in this most unlikely of places, that I was beginning to feel like I fit.

CHAPTER 27
NICOLE

TRICK SLAMMED the metal drawer of his tool chest shut.

"Closing time?" I handed him a clean cloth for his hands. The one hanging from his work pants was way too dirty.

"Thanks." He grabbed it, his face lighting up. "We got a lot more done today than we expected, and everyone cut out early."

"Can I help you clean up?"

"You don't have to do that. You've been doing so much around the club, cooking, cleaning, you don't have to clean in here too."

"I want to help you."

"Ahhh."

"What?"

"She knows what she wants."

I let out a laugh.

He grabbed the big broom to his right against the wall and handed it to me. "I won't ever deny you what you want, Zip." He got in close to me, and I could smell the minty gum he liked to chew when he worked.

A grin tweaked my lips as I took the broom from him. "That's what I like to hear from my old man."

He chuckled. "So, I thought we'd order in dinner tonight. It's just us and Bear and the girls. Everyone left for Pete's. And you've been in that kitchen a lot. You deserve a break."

"I don't mind. It's my way of giving back after what you guys have done for me."

"You don't have to feel obligated."

"It feels good to contribute around here. And I have to say after years of not being so busy, it's been a good change of pace. Anyhow, I want to do these things. I want to do them for you."

My grip tightened around the broom handle. I'd meant to say "for everybody."

His gleaming eyes held mine, and my insides melted like a chocolate bar in the summer heat. I opened my mouth to say something, but under that heavy, loaded look of his on me, no words came out. I got busy sweeping the dirt into the dustpan and sliding it in the trash as Trick locked up the main bay doors. We shut off all the lights and locked the office door behind us.

"I'm going to jump in the shower before we eat," he said. "You good?"

"Are you saying I'm a dirty, smelly mess and need a shower?"

"Are you kidding me, Zip? In the week I've known you, no matter the disaster hanging over us or if you're knee-deep in cleaning and cooking—not once have you been any kind of mess."

"Oh come on, that's not true."

"It is true." He ran a hand down his smudged T-shirt, the contours and curves of his chest clearly visible. "I'm the one who's a dirty mess."

"You don't look so bad to me." *There I go again!*

He did a double take, letting out a sharp laugh. "Oh yeah?" He opened the door to our room, and I ducked past him and darted inside.

Trick ripped off his T-shirt, balling it up and tossing it into the dirty laundry basket in the corner, his arm and back muscles flexing. My pulse kicked up as he prowled through the room, opened drawers, rubbing a hand across his stubbly jaw as he chose a fresh T-shirt, underwear, socks, and jeans.

As he stalked to the bathroom, Trick shot me a cheeky grin that made my insides twist. I loved watching him get dressed. I loved watching him get undressed. He knew it. He liked it. And I'd stopped trying to hide it.

I flopped back on the bed and let out a sigh. Compared to Logan, Trick was a rough-and-tumble kind of guy. The kind of rugged guy I'd never imagined myself with. The irony, of course, was that Logan, for his clean-cut looks, tailored, designer suits and imported leather shoes, sophisticated accessories and silk ties, was incredibly messy and careless. Always flinging dry cleaner packaging on the floor, leaving socks and underwear and worn shirts around the room. Jackets were sloppily tossed on hangers, shoes thrown in his closet.

Not Trick, nope.

Sitting up on the bed, my gaze went to the open closet door where Trick kept his clothes and shoes. He did not own one piece of formal designer clothing, only Ts and jeans, athletic clothes, and professional riding gear, and he kept each piece squarely and smoothly folded or evenly hung, and all his boots and sneakers lined up.

Changing out of my thin sweatshirt, I put on a pale pink blouse. I freshened up my face with powder and added mascara and a smudge of smoky gray eye pencil around my eyes for a bit of oomph, and for a grand finale, dabbed pink lipgloss on my lips.

Friday night in the clubhouse, y'all!

I knew what all my friends back home were doing about now. Putting on a new pricey outfit and high heels, lavishing themselves with luxury make-up and expensive perfume to go out for twenty-dollar cocktails they didn't like all that much but they were pretty and made for good Instagram pics. Friday night was our girls' night out. What would the three of them think if they could see me now?

Cringe, cringe, and cringe.

The bathroom door flew open, and a waft of hot steam blew past Trick. The fresh scent of his shampoo and his deodorant mingled in the air as he stretched a black T-shirt over his head, his back muscles flexing in the process. I grinned to myself. The girls sure wouldn't be cringing at the sight of Trick right now, that's for sure. They'd be panting. But this show was all mine.

"I'm ready." He glanced at me as he dug his fingers through his thick hair. "You look pretty."

"Oh. Thanks." My skin flared with heat.

"My compliments make you uncomfortable, Zip?"

Shrugging my shoulders, I averted my gaze from those velvety brown eyes that didn't miss a thing. "A little. But I like them."

"I'm no bullshitter." He opened the door.

"That's a fact. You're no bullshitter." I gave him a small smile as I walked through the doorway.

We headed down the hallway. Standing in the center of the lounge, Shannon, all made up, her long brown hair pulled back into a sleek ponytail and wearing a white T-shirt and jeans with a long waiter's apron around her middle, held a tray with two glasses of red wine like a servant girl out of Downton Abbey. "Good evening, Mr. Trick. Miss Nicole. Dinner for two?" she said loudly with a serious face.

"That's right," said Trick, equally serious and unsurprised as he took both glasses and offered me one.

I let out a nervous laugh. "What's going on?"

"Right this way, please..." Shannon extended her hand in a dramatically grand gesture toward a door between the lounge and the kitchen.

Trick tilted his head, a gentle hand on my back. "Let's go."

Through the door, we followed Shannon up a dimly lit stairwell, climbing up the metal staircase until we got to the top where a rush of cool air greeted us. The door of the roof was open.

"This way, please." Shannon gestured again, and we followed.

We got to the top, and my heart stopped. "Oh, my God."

CHAPTER 28
NICOLE

TWINKLING LIGHTS in the shapes of stars were strung
around the roof. Candles tall and short burned in lanterns, in
glass pots of all sizes, and on their own, creating a soft other-
worldly feel. We were in a secret lair. A square table in the center
was set for two with a small bouquet of an assortment of wild-
flowers standing in its center.

"Welcome!" said Lucy, dressed the same way Shannon was.
"Please have a seat and dinner will begin."

"Y'all are incredible!" I sputtered. "This is so beautiful!" I
darted around the rooftop.

"You like it?" Trick pulled a chair out for me, his lips tipping
up. Shannon and Lucy giggled.

"It's beautiful." I took my seat.

"I wanted to surprise you. You've been through a hell of a lot
and your life has changed completely in more ways than one.
And I wanted to treat you to something nice. Something
special." Fiddling with his fork and knife, he cleared his throat,
his jaw stiffening for a moment. "You deserve it."

I reached out and touched his arm, my fingers clasping his
muscles. "Thank you. And thank you Shannon and Lucy."

"I asked the girls to help me, and they were all in...and, here we are. I know you've been stuck in here all week with me, watching everyone else come and go. You've been pitching in everywhere, no complaints. I wanted to do something nice for you."

Trick became a blur. My eyes filled with tears.

"Hey," he whispered. He moved his chair next to mine, his arm sliding over my shoulders, holding me close.

His touch eased my every muscle and made me more emotional all at once. "No one's ever done something like this for me."

"Enjoy it." He cupped my chin, lifting my face. Leaning down he brushed my lips with his. My whole being took on the energy, the pleasure, the goodness of that grin, of his wishes in that simple yet sensual kiss.

Lucy brought over an opened bottle of red wine. She refilled our glasses, left the bottle on the table, and darted off. Trick raised his glass. "To…tonight."

"To tonight." I sipped on my wine. Its mellow warmth filled my mouth and aroused my senses. "Mmm."

"Man, the stars are incredible tonight. What a view."

"You're incredible." I let out a laugh.

He let out a small breath, smoothing a hand down his chest.

"Our first course." Shannon laid down a massive platter of antipasti. "Bruschetta with roasted tomatoes, grilled red peppers and eggplant and zucchini, mozzarella balls in olive oil and fresh oregano, and artichoke hearts in a vinaigrette."

Lucy fit a small basket of small breads in between our dishes. "There you go. Um, Trick?"

"What?"

She rolled her eyes. "Your phone?"

"What about my phone?"

"For God's sake, dude, the—"

"Oh, right." Trick opened his phone and tapped on the screen as Lucy and Shannon retreated into the darkness laughing. "I forgot." Light jazz wafted in the air.

"You thought of everything."

"I tried."

"I love Italian food," I murmured, crunching into a bruschetta. "Hmm. So good."

"This is all from the Italian restaurant in town, The Bay Leaf. I love their food. Tasty, fresh, and you get plenty of it." He heaped a serving of roasted eggplant and zucchini in his dish and the mozzarella balls and their vinaigrette on top. "I figured you must miss going out and eating at nice restaurants."

My stomach fluttered and it wasn't from the tasty appetizers in my otherwise empty belly. Trick's thoughtfulness hit me in my chest like a missile and radiated its explosive energy all through me. I dabbed my napkin at my mouth. "Believe me, going out to eat all the time can get tedious real quick. But this, this is so special."

He cleared his throat. "More wine?"

"Yes, please."

We demolished the appetizers as we talked. Lucy and Shannon reappeared, clearing the dishes and serving us the main courses.

"Wow!"

Manicotti, penne with vodka sauce, porterhouse steak pizzaiola, and veal scallopini with lemon filled the table.

"I figured I'd get a bunch of different stuff for us."

"Family style. Love it."

"Me too." He picked up a platter. "Manicotti?"

"Yes, please." I held out my dish and he filled my plate with the luscious pasta. "Penne?" I served him from the platter of pasta next to me, as he cut into the ginormous steak, giving me several slices of the medium rare porterhouse with the aromatic sauce poured over.

"Gosh, Trick. This is heaven." I savored the mouthful of tasty food.

He cut into his steak, his eyes flashing at me. "Yeah, it is."

We ate and ate. Shannon and Lucy brought us a tiramisu for two to share. We laughed and ate until we couldn't eat anymore.

"We could stay up here a little while longer unless you're cold?" he asked, crumpling his napkin into a ball.

"Let's stay."

"Come over here." We got up from the table, and he led me to two lawn chairs with cushions and a big throw blanket. "I set this up, thinking you might enjoy checking out the stars. It's nothing fancy, but—"

"It's perfect." We sat down and stretched out our legs, and I took the light blanket and flung it over the both of us. "You've thought of everything. It's so nice to just sit back and stare up at the sky. And breathe."

The sky was so clear tonight, the stars were a million tiny diamonds hovering over us, shimmering just for us. The moon was a sliver of a crescent, and the fragrance of the evergreens surrounding the clubhouse was the finest perfume.

"What are you thinking?" Trick asked.

"That I've never felt so at ease. So relaxed."

"Speaking of, you contacted your family yet to tell them you're okay?"

I blew out a breath. "Don't ruin it now."

"I'm taking that as a no?"

"Not yet." Trick had given me a burner phone to use the other day. "I know, I know I should, but I don't want to deal with it. This week has been an escape from all that. It's been my time, and I've been grateful for every minute of it."

"Jesus. You're on lockdown at a biker clubhouse and you're not pissed off or freaking out. Just grateful."

"Sure, I'm still scared on the inside, but—"

"You're not scared of me are you?" His gaze suddenly serious, he rubbed a hand along the line of his jaw.

"No, I'm not." I swallowed hard. "I've made a choice to focus on the good feelings. And right now, being here like this with you …feels good." Once again, I'd said too much without realizing. But this time, I was glad I did. I wanted him to know that what he'd done was special to me.

He shook his head, licked his lips. "Sitting on a roof in the middle of the woods in South Dakota on a rickety old lawn chair, huh?"

"That's right. And you gave this to me."

"You're welcome," his voice had softened, sending a hum though my veins. "I wanted you to see our patch of Meager like this, without walls and wide open."

"I like it. A lot."

He leaned back in his chair, stretching his legs out, his gaze on the night sky above us. "I've traveled with the club, I've seen California, the Pacific Ocean, the Rockies, Florida's beaches, and a hell of a lot in between, but this right here, for me, is always the most beautiful, the most peaceful. I love it here."

"It's always been your home."

"And always will be." His voice was full of emotion, his Adam's apple bobbing in his throat.

Under the blanket, I touched his hand that rested on his thigh, curling my fingers around his. "Thank you for sharing it with me like this."

He squeezed my hand, his lips tipping up. It wasn't that sly grin this time, no, this time his pleased grin was almost shy. He tucked the blanket around me. "Have you traveled a lot?"

"We would go on a family vacation every year. Aruba, Cancun. And Logan loves Tulum, so we'd do that every winter."

His forehead crinkled. "Where's Tulum?"

"Mexico."

"Uh-huh. Winter beach vacations to me are the height of luxury. The club has been known to hit Florida every other winter which is a good time."

"I'll bet, when it's super snowy and cold here, right?"

"Crazy cold and very snowy."

"Oh, I have good news. Lenore called me today and she set

up an appointment for me to talk with Craig, who runs the fitness studio in town."

"You want to take classes there?"

"I was hoping to teach classes there. Dance cardio, Piltaes, that sort of thing."

"Really? Cool. Craig's a good guy."

"I hope it works out."

"You ever taught that stuff before?"

"A bunch of times. And I studied dance in college."

"Oh, college grad, huh?"

"My parents weren't thrilled with my choice of major, but that's what I loved." I told him about the misunderstanding with Lucy and Shannon, and he laughed. "Shannon's going to teach me how to use a stripper pole."

An eyebrow hitched on his forehead. "Oh she is, is she?"

"Is that a problem?"

"Hey, do what you want. You want to dance at The Tingle? Go for it."

"Do you mean that?"

His eyes narrowed, his neck tensed. "You want to dance at The Tingle?"

"No."

"Oh." He settled back against the chair again. "Okay."

"Okay."

"You'd sure make a hell of a lot of money, a good-looking woman like you. I mean, if that's what you wanted, money. But you have money, right? Of course, I don't know what your plans are once this is over…"

"You mean lockdown or—"

"Me and you."

"Right."

"You going to stay in Meager, move on, go back to Oklahoma?"

"I don't want to go back. I'm not going back."

"What about your husband?"

"I'm determined to get that divorce."

"If that's what you want."

"It's definitely what I want. He just needs to agree to it. In Oklahoma, an uncontested divorce can be finalized within ten days. I didn't even have to file that separation, but I wanted him to know I meant business. My lawyer told me it was a good idea so that we severed our finances and any legal obligations between us ahead of time. I don't care about the house or alimony. I want out."

"Gotcha."

"You probably can't wait to get rid of me, right? An old lady forced on you out of the blue?"

"I don't think that, Zip. What I do think is how odd everything must be for you here. Whole new life, the opposite of everything you're used to, new people, new town. A town you haven't even seen yet because you've been stuck here in our clubhouse in the woods. Then there's Dog after you. And I'm sure the last thing you expected or wanted was another old man."

I shoved at his shoulder with my own. "Aw, you aren't so bad, Trick."

"Gee, thanks."

Laughing softly, I turned over, facing him. "This week definitely has been a change of pace, and, sure, yes, not being able to go into town has been a bummer. But I like everyone here a lot. And you've been great."

"I thought you said incredible?" His lips curled into a deep grin.

"I did, didn't I?"

"Can I ask you a question?" he breathed.

"Hmm."

"Can I kiss you?"

My pulse tumbled into overdrive. "That's very gentlemanly of you to ask first."

"My instinct is telling me to be gentlemanly with you." His heavy gaze fell to my lips. "Am I wrong?"

My lungs squeezed together. "Not wrong, no." I brushed the hair from his face. Soft and thick waves. Full, generous lips. My insides knotted and twisted, my heart pounded out of my chest. And for the first time in my life, I said the words: "Kiss me."

He dipped closer to me, his warmth heating my skin like wildfire. His lips touched mine, and sparks flared through my veins, igniting my pulse. This kiss was different. I didn't close my eyes as I opened my mouth to his. New sensations. Entering new territory.

On a soft groan, Trick's tongue danced and slid against mine, explored, tasted. The sweetness of our dessert lingered. He dove deeper. Trick took his time, and that tight knot unwound inside me. Unwound and twirled. My hand found his chest and stroked across his torso, down his side, his muscles flexing under my touch. His arm slid around my waist, pulling me closer to his tight, firm body, and a small sound escaped my lips. We fit.

His mouth released mine, and his fingers caressed my cheek. My heart beat hard and steady in my chest at his gentle touch. This man…He looked like he could devour me if he wanted in an explosion of moves, but with me, he was caring and kind. And so damned sensual. Trick's kiss took its time to relish and savor, a kiss that was all about getting to know you, about wanting you.

Was this what it felt like to be wanted? To be cherished?

"Trick?"

"Yeah?"

"That was the most exciting and erotic kiss of my entire life," I whispered. "So you know."

On a growl, he took my mouth again, and that heat inside me flared like a stick of dynamite finally exploding.

CHAPTER 29
TRICK

WE HEADED BACK to my room, me shutting off lights in the halls as I went. The girls had already cleaned up everything from our dinner by the time we came downstairs which was great. Otherwise, I knew Nicole would've pitched in, and I wanted this night to be a treat for her, not just any other night around the clubhouse.

And I think it had been.

That fucking kiss, Jesus. The heat, the sweetness, the desire rolling off her in waves had me rocking in her sea. I was drunk on it. That ages-old ache spiraled inside my chest lighting up all those dark tunnels I'd worked so hard to seal shut.

Wasn't this what I always wanted?

My phone dinged with a message, and I blinked. It was from Lock in Missouri, asking me to check on a part order. He liked double-confirming everything. I knew he'd had an important business dinner tonight with two collectors, something must have come up. "Nic, I got to check on something on the Eagle Wings computer. You go on in. I'll be back soon."

"All right."

Half an hour later, after confirming the order and texting with Lock, I opened my door softly so I wouldn't wake up

Nicole if she'd already fallen asleep. Her loud gasp filled the room, and she quickly turned over in the bed.

"Zip, you okay?" I leaned over the bed, over her. "Was it another nightmare?"

"No, no nightmare. I'm fine."

Bear's grunts thudded against the walls. Shannon's squeaks grew louder. Nicole licked her lips, pressing them together.

My eyes narrowed over her. "Were you....touching yourself?"

"No! I ..." She let out a groan, shutting her eyes, gripping the sheet. "Yes."

"It's okay," I whispered roughly, my hand rubbing her middle over the sheet. "How did it go?"

"Um. Not great," she gritted out as she threw her arms over her face. "This is so embarrassing."

"You don't have to be embarrassed with me. Not ever." I got on the bed. "You touch yourself a lot?" I figured maybe she did since her husband hadn't provided much if any sexual pleasure.

"No." Her hands fell from her face and she met my gaze. "I've only done it a few times, but..." She shrugged.

Oh man, no.

My hand cupped her face, and her breath caught. "So Bear and Shannon inspired you?"

"Kind of."

"Kind of?"

"You inspired me a lot more."

"Ah." I stretched out on the bed, my veins pounding with heat. "How about I inspire you a whole lot more?" I took her working hand in mine and licked her fingers, the tang of her making my cock hard as iron. Her eyes widened as she watched. Her body squirmed, a sound escaping her throat.

"Was that a yes, keep going? I need to hear it."

"Yes. Keep going."

"We could explore whatever you want. What do you think about that?"

"We could?" she breathed.

"Yeah. Whatever you want."

What I wanted was for her to let go, get out of her head. She obviously did too. I also wanted her to destroy the stain that fuck of a husband of hers left behind on her body and her mind. Action was always a good remedy. And if she needed guidance, needed permission, I'd fucking give it to her. Me.

A sound escaped her lips. "Whatever I want?" she repeated.

"Mmm." I kept licking her fingers slowly.

The bedding fell from her hands. Her breathing kicked up. "Okay."

"Okay what?" I sucked on her index finger, taking it all the way in my mouth.

"Let's do more."

I kept going until her breaths came in hard and fast. Leaning over her, my tongue swiped at her lips, and they parted on a sigh. "Kiss me, Zip."

She pressed her lips against mine, her tongue sliding inside. Her body stirred against mine. Pushing the sheet aside, I slid my hand under her thin camisole top and across the warm skin of her tummy. I'd been wanting to do that since night one. Me on her hidden skin. She shuddered, and I hadn't even gotten to the soft curves of her tits yet.

"I want you to feel good, Zip." I found the curve of her heavy breast and stroked gently. My thumb brushed over her nipple, and it hardened immediately.

"I want to feel good." Her voice had thinned out.

Pushing the camisole top up, I licked along that swell of silky flesh, licked at that hard pebble. Her back arched. "I want to help you find that, Zip." My hand slid down her pelvis and sank into her pussy, and she stiffened. "Too much?" I said against her breast.

A nervous giggle escaped her mouth. "No. I'm just sensitive."

My fingers gently stroked. Wet and juicy. I sucked in air, my pulse pounding through me. "Help me learn what you like."

She only nodded, her breathing ragged.

"And you tell me to stop if you want me to stop, and I'll stop. I promise."

"Okay." Her voice was clearer now.

Her hips relaxed as my fingers stroked and swirled in her wet heat. "You feel so good, Zip," I whispered against her ear, and she sighed for me, her cheek pressing against my face. "Wet velvet, baby."

"Trick…" she brushed her lips over mine.

I stroked her core, swirled my fingers around her swollen clit, increased the pressure against her nub. Her pussy got slicker, and my cock got harder. Her breathing got shallow and clipped. "Hold onto me if you want." Her fingertips dug into my arm, her gorgeous tits in my face. I licked at her other breast and she shuddered.

"We're not racing to any finish line. This is about you feeling good. If you come or if you don't that doesn't matter. You hear?" Her gleaming eyes met mine, and I planted a quick kiss on her lips. "You want me to stop?"

"No, no, don't stop."

I suckled her breast again as my hand pressed harder against her clit.

"Oh God…Trick…Trick!" Her face smashed into the pillow at her side, her legs tightened, her body trembling.

"Babe. Feel it. Yeah."

She gulped for air as she came down off her high, her eyes blinking open, and her hands went to my face. "I felt it…it was like this small *pop* but it was definitely an orgasm." She grinned, exhaling. A victory.

I let out a soft chuckle. "That's good. So good." My hand trailed up her skin to her throat. "You ever had one before?"

Her shoulders tightened. "I've had a few almosts but never the *actual* thing."

"Everybody's different." I caressed her throat, a breast, and she relaxed again. "I'm guessing it'll take practice to tune into those feelings, to let your body feel them."

"Are we going to keep practicing?"

"You want that?"

"Yes. Do you?" Her voice was barely above a whisper.

"Yeah."

Another alliance, another agreement between us. My hands stroked up and down her soft as silk flesh. "You're real sexy, Zip."

"And you're crazy sexy, Trick." Meeting my gaze in the dim darkness, she surged up and took my mouth. My breath cut. Her tongue dove in, finding mine. My hands cuffed her neck as I gave her more and took the more she offered. My pulse pounded in my stiff cock.

She wanted it from me. She wanted me.

And I wanted her. So damn bad.

Her head fell back against the pillow. "I'd like to practice, to feel comfortable. And..." She pursed her lips.

"Yeah?"

"Have more orgasms. Could we do that?"

"We could do that." *Holy. Fuck.* Blood surged in my veins.

"I'll be your special project."

"Make your engine sing, huh?"

We both laughed as she traced a line across my pecs. "That is your specialty, isn't it?"

"Sure is. In the shop, I learned how to pay attention to an engine and trust that it would tell me what it needs, and they always do."

"Wow." Her body shifted as she giggled softly. "And no messy complications, right?"

Was she comparing this to club girl benefits? Maybe. So practical of her. So why did I have a sinking feeling in the pit of my stomach?

Her fingers pushed back the hair from my face and lingered

on my cheeks. "I like the way you describe those things, Trick. It's not just a…" She pressed her lips together.

"A what?"

"A cold fuck."

My knuckles brushed her soft skin. This girl deserved all the gentle in the world, and when she was ready, all the wild. She'd never been shown any of it by the one man in her life.

I wanted to be the one to give it to her. To show her what could be hers. Was that arrogant of me? I didn't give a fuck.

My tongue darted out to my bottom lip, and her gaze flicked to the movement. "Can I try more inspiration for you?" She nodded, and my fingers sank between her legs again, firmly squeezing her pussy lips, and her eyes flared. "I want to kiss you, right here." I tongued her lips.

Her eyes flared. "Trick…"

"You don't have to prove anything to me or even to yourself. Just enjoy it however it hits."

Her thighs relaxed under me, her legs parted. "But what about you?" Her hand rubbed alongside my hard shaft.

I let out a hiss. "Don't worry about me. Don't even go there in your head. Stay out of your head. This is about you. You feeling it."

"I want you to feel good too." Her delicate whisper in my ear sent an unusual shiver over my skin and filled that hollow tunnel in my chest. "We got time for that. Right now, I want to go down on you, Zip. Want to taste you." My voice came out rough. "You want me to lick you?"

Her breath deepened as she let out a small cry.

"Want to hear you say it, Zip."

"Lick me."

Pushing back the bedding, I got myself between her legs and slid my hands down her torso. Her back arched, her hips twisted. Spreading her legs out wider, I stroked her thighs. My lips brushed up and down her warm skin, and her gorgeous legs shuddered at my sides. My fingertips slid under the thin waistband of her damp panties, and I tugged them down her legs. Her scent filled the air and I took it in like some wild beast ready to mate.

"Trick." Her hand reached out for me, and I took it in mine, brushing it with my lips.

"I got you, Zip." My tongue slicked through her wet pussy, and she let out a sharp gasp. My intention was to lavish her with strokes and tongue, no fingers, not tonight. My gut was telling me I had to take things one step at a time with her.

She was a virgin in so many ways, wasn't she?

My virgin.

No, asshole. She's not your anything.

Nicole and I were from two different worlds, and our situation was a temporary arrangement. Expecting, hoping for anything more or anything else was entering the danger zone. Land mines everywhere.

Little moans and cries and hisses erupted from her. I grinned to myself. But we sure as fuck could enjoy each other during this temporariness. My lips nuzzled her swollen clit and I was rewarded with a groan. Her hips twisted, her pussy following my tongue. She wasn't fighting it. Gripping her legs, I steadied her body as I gave her clit all the attention it deserved. Gentle and steady. Flicks and steadily increasing pressure.

My tongue laid a trail up and down her slit, finally sliding into her cunt. "Trick…" Her fingers dug into my hair.

Banging on my jeans, my throbbing cock wanted out and wanted in. *I* wanted in. Damn if I wanted to know what it would be like to take her. *Focus.* My tongue went back to her clit.

"Oh, Trick, Oh, Trick…"

My chest squeezed at the sound of my name as her body writhed in my grip. I wanted her to come on my tongue so bad. I wanted her to feel her own high, and I wanted to be the one to give it to her. Her pussy angled up and met my mouth more fully than before, and my blood rushed through my veins. I kept going.

Her breathing got short and fast. Her body stiffened. "Trick!" she yelped. Her pussy tightened and throbbed, flowing with her sweet cum, and I lapped at it. Her clit pulsated against my tongue as she cried out. I kept stroking, holding her ass firmly in my grip, insisting on more, as her body twisted with sensation.

"Trick, oh, my God…" Her body shuddered and trembled.

Kissing her damp stomach, I lifted myself over her, my wet lips nuzzling her skin up to her throat, up behind her ear. Her arms flew around my middle pulling me close. "Trick…." She took my mouth in a hard kiss. "I came."

"Was it more than a pop?"

A gentle laugh. "Way, way the hell more than a pop." Her body pressed against mine. Yeah, I'd found a couple of her sweet spots. Now I wanted to find them all.

My hand dug into her hair, tugging hard. "Kiss me, Nic."

She kissed me, her mouth opening fully to me, tasting herself, her tongue sliding against mine, her legs wrapping around me. The sweet smell of her warm, sweaty skin rising up between us. "Mmm."

My hand trailed down her side. "You liked it?"

"I liked it."

A rumble rose in my throat. "What did it feel like?"

"Balls of heat expanding and exploding all over me. I did what you said. I got out of my head and let my body feel it happening."

"Did you try to stop it?"

"At one point, but I opened my eyes and saw you, and I felt better." Her fingers stroked along my damp jaw. "I got more excited watching you on me."

My heart thudded in my chest. She watched me eat her and she liked it. She trusted me, felt secure with me. My thumb brushed the edge of her swollen mouth. "That sure was a Lucy-worthy shout-out."

"Was I that loud?" We both laughed. The laughs dissolved into kisses.

Exhaustion claimed my every limb, my every muscle. Peeling myself off her, I kicked at my boots, and she helped me rip off my T-shirt, my jeans. I sank into the mattress next to her.

She turned over, to face me. "You've probably only been with women who know everything there is to know about sex and do all sorts of wild things. Women who aren't work for you."

I tugged on a long strand of her hair. "Baby, that wasn't 'work.' That was an incredible fucking turn-on unlike any other." I grinned like a fool.

It was also rewarding as fuck to my ego, and that little smirk slashing her lips told me she knew that already. "Zip, sex isn't about only doing A, B, and C to get off. Sure, basically it is. But the way you get there every time can be different. Plus everyone's got different needs, different likes." As my body sank into the mattress, my tongue lashed at my lower lip at the thought of exploring all that *different* with her.

"The more you do, the more you learn what you like, right?"

"Mmm."

"And what your partner likes too."

"That's it." A chuckle fell from my lips as my eyelids sank. "Partner…"

Her warm fingertips stroked my forehead. "Very, very sexy partner."

My lips curved at her whisper in the dark.

CHAPTER 30
NICOLE

THE ZOOM and vroom of engines on the club track filled the air. Having finished folding the day's laundry with Shannon, I grabbed a bottle of iced tea and wandered over to the Eagle Wings track. Boner's long dark hair flew behind him as he rode a vintage motorcycle with long extended handlebars, Easy Rider style. A couple of the other guys stood at the edge of the track watching him closely.

Striding down the hill, I took a seat on the grass, drank my iced tea, and watched as a sporty maroon car waited to pull out on the track, Trick behind the wheel. Boner brought the bike to a stop, and the men crowded around him and they all discussed. One of the prospects rolled the bike off the track as Trick guided the car onto the asphalt.

Over the past two weeks of being at the club, I'd watched Trick speed around the track a number of times. Usually I watched from the top of the hill, but this was the first time I'd come right down to the track. Today, I wanted to watch up close.

Today was our last day living here at the MC clubhouse. All the men had agreed that our lockdown would be over, as there had been no recourse from the Smoking Guns, no sightings of them around town, but that didn't mean that things were all clear. We had to continue the show for the outside world for maybe a month more at least.

This morning, Kicker had lectured me and Trick about not "breaking up" just yet. We'd both declared, "Of course not!" which made Kicker grin and Butler and Boner bust out into loud laughter while Trick clenched his jaw and I'd turned beet red.

Tonight we'd be moving into Trick's new apartment that his uncle helped him find. Tania had called me this morning and said she and the old ladies and the guys had already moved everything into the new place, and she hoped we liked it.

"Tania, y'all didn't have to do that."

"We wanted to."

They were such good people who did right by each other, and who only wanted the best for one another, and they showed it by their actions over and over again. They weren't dishing out lip service and empty promises, not at all. I was overwhelmed by gratitude.

Of course, I wasn't quite sure what setting up a "home" with my fake old man would be like out in the real world and not here in the closed-off life of the club where I'd gotten used to the routine of things. But the one thing I was sure about was that I liked being with Trick. And it wasn't just the sexual discovery sessions every night.

It was the talking and laughing and sharing stories. It was not feeling awkward anymore getting dressed in front of each other, even brushing our teeth at the same time. Having meals together regularly. Him saying things like, *"Thank you,"* and *"Could you please."* Me stopping by his work where I was always greeted with a beaming smile. All that filled my chest with heat and a hit of adrenaline each and every time.

Trick brought the car to a stop in front of me, his head tilting, an arm leaning on the steering wheel. "Hey, beautiful, need a ride?"

A giggle escaped my lips, heat surging through me at the

sight of him. Dark Ray Ban sunglasses, gleaming small silver hoop earrings, cut-off T-shirt, taut arm muscles swirling with colorful tattoos in the sunlight. And that grin, that come-hither-but-careful-I-bite-and-you're-gonna-love-it grin. I loved that grin. I loved that I knew what that grin meant, that my flesh knew and wanted more.

"What is it, Zip?"

"I suddenly feel like I'm in a scene from the movie *Grease* and Kenickie just drove up and asked me to go for a ride in his hot rod. What was the car called? Greased Lightning?"

His head fell back and he laughed loudly. "Hang on—I'm not John Travolta?"

"Nope. You're Kenickie. Edgier guy. I always liked him much better."

"Ohhh...." He slid his sunglasses down his nose. "Zip digs the bad boy." That grin got more fatal, and my insides clenched. I approached the car, whose dull maroon surface was full of scuffs, dents, chips, and pockmarks. His thumb tapped on the steering wheel. "Greased Lightning here got herself a new engine and I want to feel her out. You coming?"

"Can I?"

"Hop into my hot rod, baby, let's go!" He chuckled.

My pulse charged, and I got in, pulled the heavy door shut, and tugged on the worn seat belt. "I'm assuming the car's going to get a new paint job?

"Hell yes. The full treatment. It's on the top of Lock's to-do list when he gets back."

Untwisting the seat belt, I finally clicked it in place. "And what kind of paint job does the owner want?"

"Cobalt blue with silver accents."

"Nice."

"It will be. Ready?"

My back pressed against the ripped vinyl seat, my legs tensing. "Ready."

We took off around the track. My mouth dried as I pressed

the soles of my boots into the floor, my fingers curling around the side handle as our speed steadily increased. I glanced at him. His body was at ease, but his gaze, his jawline told a different story. Complete focus, complete concentration. He was listening, feeling, strategizing with his whole being.

His lips tensed as we rounded a third turn, and he shifted gears and the engine responded immediately, shooting us forward at an even faster pace. My lungs squashed together, dizziness erupted in my head. I trusted Trick's judgment, his driving experience, but those familiar icy sharp fingernails of fear sank into me anyhow. A cold sweat broke out over my forehead as my heart vaulted in my chest.

My father's twisted features flashed in my vision. *"Don't tell me how to drive, young lady! I know what I'm doing! Stop backseat driving me!"* I jammed my eyes shut. His grumbling, cursing, the skidding, the crunch of metal. My hands went to my ears. The heat flaring around us. The metal trapping me, the airbag smashed against me, shards of glass in my hair. Glass everywhere. The scream I'd been unable to scream.

A hand pressed against my middle and my body flinched, my eyes opened. Trick.

"Zip? Zip! You okay?" He brought the car to a stop on the side of the track. "Hey—" Swiftly, he lowered the windows, unbuckled his seat belt, unbuckled mine. "That was way too fast for you, it freaked you out? I should have let you know what I was planning. You okay? Nicole, dammit, talk to me. You're white as a ghost."

I blinked. I'd seen a ghost.

My pulse chugged in my body and I took in a breath. "I'm sorry, sorry. I thought I could do it. But I…I'm sorry."

He brushed the hair from my face. "Do what, Zip? What is it? What's wrong?"

I swallowed past the sour in my throat. "Since the car accident, I haven't been able to drive. Even being in the front seat is a challenge." I gulped in air. "I was able to drive with Lex when we left Oklahoma because he kept under the speed limit, so we wouldn't get stopped. Being in the back of the vans was tough but okay. But this, this brought it all back."

"Take a breath. That's it." He swiped the hair back from my face. "Can you tell me what happened?"

On a long exhale, I finally met his gaze, dizziness swirling through me. "I killed my dad and my baby."

Dawes appeared in Trick's window. "You guys okay? Car okay? You—"

Trick put his hand up to stop him and his other hand on my thigh. "Everything's fine, we just need a minute."

"Gotcha." Dawes jogged off.

Trick squeezed my thigh. "You want to get out of the car?"

I exhaled, inhaled, stretched out my legs. "I'm sorry I ruined your test drive."

"You didn't ruin anything. You want to talk about it?"

My head fell back against the headrest and I focused on the tingling warmth that the pressure of his hand exerted on my leg. "It was over a year ago. I picked my dad up from the country club. He'd been playing golf and had a big lunch with his friends, which I knew meant a lot of booze, so I made it a point to pick him up instead of him driving home. I got there and it was obvious he'd had a lot to drink. It didn't show, but I knew. He didn't get sloppy, he got mad, moody. He was ticked off about a comment someone had made at the club about Jackson's gambling.

"When the valet came over with my car, he hesitated to hand me my own keys, and instead he gave them to Daddy, the big man of the club. I said no, I'll drive, and he told me to fuck off. He yelled at me, cursed at me in front of the valet guy and other people we knew who were there waiting for their cars. It was horrible. I shut up, and let him get behind the wheel. And like an idiot, I got in the car with him. It was an eight-minute drive home on quiet roads. What could happen?

"We took off, and he grumbled about Jackson, complained

about me and Logan not having babies yet. All of a sudden everything was a problem. I tried to respond calmly, but he wasn't even listening, just kept going on and on. And the car kept going faster and faster. I asked him to slow down, he yelled at me again. We got to our road and he took the turn much too fast and too sharply. The car bumped into something on the edge of the road, and suddenly we were spinning, rolling over. We were in the air one minute and crashed to the ground the next."

"Nic." His grip on my leg tightened.

"Daddy died from a heart attack and his injuries. I had a broken rib and cuts and bruises. And later the doctor at the hospital told me I'd been pregnant and lost the baby."

"Shit, you didn't know?"

I shook my head. "I was seven weeks along, had no idea, and then it was gone. I didn't even know how to grieve for my baby. I sank into numbness. How could my larger-than-life father be gone, bloodied and mangled and broken because of me? If only I hadn't given in right away, insisted, fought him harder. But I hadn't. I'd given in to him like always."

"There was no way in hell you were going to convince him otherwise."

"My mom and Jackson never came out and said it outright, but I knew they blamed me. I knew they felt it was my fault. That I'd been weak and foolish. I'd even gotten my own baby killed."

"Oh, Zip, no."

"After all that, and seeing the wreckage of my car, I couldn't get behind a wheel again. It was then I got my separation, and that was part of the reason why no one fought me on it. But after a year, it was time for Nicole to get back in line."

"That's fucking bullshit."

I turned to face him. "I don't want to feel this anymore, Trick. It's this dead weight on my chest, and I can't breathe. I want it gone."

"Of course you do." He threaded our hands together. "You'll conquer this, one step at a time, Zip. You will, and I'll help you."

"I know I'll need to see a shrink again. I did go for a little bit."

He caressed the side of my face. "You were close to your dad, huh?"

"Daddy's little girl."

"His princess?"

"He used to call me his 'buttercup.'"

"That's sweet."

"Yeah." My shoulders dropped. "After he retired, he changed. I think he thought retirement was going to be the best thing ever. Go on trips, have all the time in the world for golfing, relaxing, but it didn't work out that way. Not working frustrated him. Not being in control, maybe more. And I think he was concerned about Logan and Jackson's handling of the company. He seemed ticked off all the time. You couldn't talk to him anymore, everything set him off. And he started drinking more than usual. He wasn't the daddy I knew anymore. Then he was gone in this sudden and horrible way."

"Maybe you're mad at him too?"

I hiccuped in a breath. "I am."

"It's okay, Zip. A lot of confusing emotions happen after a death. Especially after a sudden accident like that."

"I think so, too." I relaxed my head against the headrest again and squeezed his hand. Talking about this after so long made me feel better, and Trick was truly listening to me express myself. There were no wrongs or rights. There was simply how I felt.

"When I was a teenager I lost my family in a car accident," he said.

"You did? I'm so sorry."

"It was like my foundation had cracked. Load bearing walls were knocked out of place. Everything was suddenly crooked, hanging by a thread. But I held it together. I had to."

I covered his hand in mine, our gazes remained straight ahead on the track. "Does the grief ever go away?"

"Nah. It's always there, still pulsing, but over time you shift, you grow around it. I heard that once somewhere. I think it's true." Trick cleared his throat. "Let me ask you—being on the back of my bike wasn't a problem for you, was it?"

"No. I didn't get that claustrophobic caged-in feeling. I was just…"

"Free." His lips twitched.

"Yeah."

"That's how most of us feel about vehicles. They're cages. Riding our bikes is the ultimate freedom."

"I completely get that." My lips tipped up.

"That's good, Zip, you being my old lady and all." He winked at me.

"Right?"

"We'll do this together. You and me. Now's your time." Leaning in, he brushed my forehead with a kiss.

"Thank you for listening. Just spitting all that out to you has made me feel loads lighter. It helped."

He brushed the edge of my face with his fingers. "You want to get out of the car or you up for a ride? We could go slowly around the track a couple times so you can feel that? And if that's okay and you want to try more, we can go another round a little bit faster. But at any point, if it's too much for you, you tell me and I stop and you get out."

"I don't want to hold you back, interfere in your work."

"You're not. Not at all. I got enthusiastic back there. Always do. I need to do this at all speeds anyhow."

"Like a test pilot?"

"Yeah. When you ride you can hear and feel issues or non-issues. Most times, we take turns on them, 'cause each one of us feels and hears something different—how she handles, grips the road, takes a turn, that kind of thing, ranging from basics to fine details. We all like paying attention to the finer details."

"I trust your driving skills, so you know."

"Smart girl." He shot me a grin.

"I'm up for a few rounds." I sat up straighter. "Let's do this, Kenickie."

The car engine blared to life over the rich sound of Trick's laughter.

CHAPTER 31
TRICK

I UNLOCKED the door of our new apartment.

Our apartment.

This was nuts, but this was okay. Was me handling this without freaking out, a sign of my maturity? Sure. But still there were no expectations between us about "tomorrow" and that suited me to a T. That made this okay.

Being with Nicole was pretty smooth going so far. For all her white-collar and plenty-o'-money upbringing, she'd gotten comfortable at the club, and that impressed me. No pretentiousness, no snobbery. She was nothing but respectful and kind with everybody.

I pushed open the door to the apartment, and Nicole and I froze. "Holy shit!" I said.

Nicole's hand went to her mouth. "They did everything. They…it's beautiful!"

"Jesus, look at this."

The few pieces of furniture I'd had at my old place were still here but now co-existed with a new smaller sofa next to the big one, a round table with four chairs in the dining area. I'd never had a "dining area" before, let alone a real dining table. And on that table was a bouquet of different colored flowers as well as a bottle of champagne and two fluted glasses.

My thumb wiped at the edge of my mouth. The ladies were at it again. After things had gone south with Lenore, they would often attempt to set me up with "a good woman" as they'd put it, but these women were not for me, dating was not for me. Each time, I'd shut each of these women down. Had I been rude? Cold? Maybe. But I was exhausted, mentally and emotionally. Luckily my bros had intervened and the old ladies threw their hands in the air and gave up their (lost) cause.

Now, years later, here I was in a fake relationship with a woman they really liked? Oh, they were enjoying this to the hilt.

Nicole opened cabinets in the kitchen, and I followed her in there. On the counter was every appliance known to man—a blender, a food processor, and a brand new coffee machine replacing my old shitty one that had leaked water for months.

I opened a kitchen cabinet. "Damn, those are all new dishes. I mean, it's a fucking dish *set*. Guess, I'm adulting now." A new set of water glasses greeted me in another cabinet. Striped dish towels and shiny stainless steel cooking utensils and forks and knives and spoons I didn't recognize were in the drawers.

"I have to call Tania." Nicole got out her new burner phone and hit buttons. She got Tania on the line on speaker and the two of them talked excitedly about the new apartment. Nicole's face was animated as she described every detail that she appreciated and loved to Tania. Her blue eyes danced as she spoke, her voice bouncing with excitement. But it was more than that. It was genuine gratitude that good people had done such a good and generous deed for her.

For us.

I took in the really nice view of the house's lush front garden, a huge change from my former view of my landlord's ratty garage roof. I shifted my weight. Maybe we'd only be playing house for a little while more, but while it lasted, I was determined to make it good for her, for me.

For us.

My lips pressed together. I never thought I'd be thinking in that historically for me seductive and slippery term of "us" ever again.

Nicole handed me her phone and I took it. "Tania, it's amazing. You guys hit it out of the park. We're real grateful for all the work you did for us."

"I'm so glad you like it, Trick. We all wanted to make sure you were comfortable in this new space. You guys deserve it."

"Appreciate it, Tania."

"We should have everyone over to celebrate," Nicole said.

"Oh no! I mean, not yet, at least," quipped Tania with a laugh. "We're not going anywhere. You two enjoy your new space first, get settled."

I rolled my eyes. "We're not on a honeymoon here, Tania."

"Oh, shut up, Tricky," she retorted.

"We'll plan on it soon." Nicole glanced at me, and I nodded in agreement. I loved that she liked the old ladies and my brothers, that she wanted to show them her gratitude for all they'd done. We said our goodbyes and Nicole shut down the call. "Wow," she murmured.

"You could say that again."

A new apartment, a new everything for a new life with the new old lady who wasn't really my old lady. But…yeah, here we were. I tamped down that fidgety part of me that knew it could all blow up tomorrow and probably would.

"Since we don't have any unpacking to do, how about I get you to your appointment with Craig? And then after, we can hit the supermarket."

"Sounds great."

Nicole changed into a workout outfit, threw on a jean jacket, and we took my Jeep and hit Clay Street, the main drag of Meager. I found parking down the block from the studio. "You don't have to come in with me," she said.

"I want to."

We got out of the car, and she slid her hand around my bicep —she liked doing that. I liked it too. We walked together into Craig's FitSmash Studio. An elderly woman walked out the door, a headband on her gray hair, her face red.

"Mr. Trick, good day to you."

"Hi, Mrs. Camden."

Now it all begins. Mrs. Camden was the elderly social butterfly of Meager who'd lived next door to my mom's family years ago. Within the hour, the town locals would all know about me and Nic. This was what we wanted, wasn't it?

"And who is this?" Her bright gaze roved over Nicole from head to toe and back again.

"This is my old lady, Nicole. Nicole, this is Mrs. Camden."

"Old lady indeed. Ridiculous. Aren't you lovely, Nicole?"

"Thank you, Mrs. Camden. So nice to meet you."

"You two come to take a class together? But you are not dressed for it, young man."

"Nope, we're here to see Craig is all. Good day to you now." I gently pressed my hand into Nicole's back as she said goodbye to Mrs. Camden and we went inside.

"Is that why you wanted to come in with me?" Nicole asked. "So people could see us together?"

"No. I mean, yeah, it's good to spread the word." My hand dug into her waist. "But I wanted to be here for you. This is a big day, getting a job. Your first real job. I wanted to introduce you to Craig and …"

"And?"

"And be supportive."

Her lips parted, her eyes lit up, and she planted a kiss on the side of my face. "Thank you. It means a lot to me."

My chest filled with heat. This woman was easy to please and I loved the effect it had on her. I fucking liked the effect her gratitude had on me.

Inside the studio, more red-faced women of all ages and wearing all forms of lycra were sucking down juices and water and nattering on as they packed up their gear. I spotted Craig and gestured at him with two fingers. He held up his hand and began to cut short his conversation with a client.

"Hey, you." My head slanted toward the familiar voice. Linda.

Linda was a waitress at The Tingle who I'd hooked up with a few days before I'd gone to Kansas City with Dawes. She moved toward me, and I slid my arm around Nicole's shoulders and lifted my chin at Linda, a blank expression on my face. Her long pink fingernails swiped through her black hair as her face went from soft to sour in seconds flat. Stopping in her tracks, she shot me an ever more sour look, her lips twisting, eyes narrowing.

She wanted me to know she was ticked, but she'd gotten my message loud and clear. Linda was a frequent hanger-on at the club and she knew the score. She knew my score. Didn't all the women in town at this point?

Craig's massive body suddenly stood in front of us, blocking Linda's view of me. The guy had to be pushing fifty-something, but he was in incredible shape. In fact, he did a lot of athletic wear and sports gear modeling. What had Mary Lynn called him? Ah, A Silver Fox in the making.

"Hey, man." Craig shook my hand.

"Hey, Craig. Good to see you. This is my old lady, Nicole."

Nicole's eyes lit up as she offered him her hand. "Great to meet you, Craig. Lenore told me about you and the studio."

"Yep." His eyes narrowed at her like the military sergeant he once was. "What do you got for me?"

"Lenore mentioned you don't have dance cardio classes or barre, pilates, and that's what I do." Nicole explained her dance background to Craig, her training, the classes she'd taught before.

He lifted his chin. "Show me what you got."

That was Craig, no chit-chat, but let's get right to the action. Show him the money.

Once the remaining ladies left the studio, Craig put on loud music, a bopping dance tune that was currently on the charts. Nicole took off her jacket and handed it to me.

"Kill it, Zip." I winked at her, and she lifted her chin.

Tracking over to the mirror, Nicole met her own suddenly steely gaze, and started moving. A warm-up that got more and more intense and always in the beat. She segued into low-impact moves and then morphed into more energetic dance moves. She varied the tempo, the style, and the complexity, giving the session a high/low HIIT feel. She even signaled to her imaginary class, giving them the heads up on which direction she would move in, and how many reps on each side. I grinned. She was organized and giving Craig a full audition.

Nicole's body was fluid and strong all at the same time, and she made it all look so damned effortless. Her cheeks had turned pink, her skin shiny with sweat as she maintained eye contact with herself in the big mirrors against the long wall. She flew.

"Okay, I got it!" Craig clapped his hands together and shut off the music.

Nicole spun around, her chest heaving. "What did you think?"

"How many classes a week can you teach?"

Nicole grinned. "How many do you need?"

———

Nicole's grip on my bicep tightened as we walked back down Clay Street. "Could we pop in to Lenore's shop? I want to let her know and thank her. This wouldn't have happened if it wasn't for her."

"Uh…" The last thing I wanted to do was visit my ex-booty call in her erotic lingerie shop with Nicole. I dug a hand through my hair.

"Is that okay? Is—"

"Let's go." I sucked in air and gestured down the block. "Her shop is right down here."

We got to "Lenore's Lace," the gothic-style, purple and black sign hanging out front heralding the sexy daring world Nicole and I would now enter. I opened the door for her. Now entering the fuck-with-my-head zone.

A rich tobacco and rose fragrance from a bunch of red candles burning on a small table stuck in my throat as I stood there, shifting my weight. It wasn't every day I went into a store where lacy bras, teeny tiny panties, corsets that made my dick hard with just a glance, and see-through nighties, some with holes others with tassels, silky, shiny fabrics and so much lace that begged to be touched, begged to be ripped, hung every-where. All of it designed by Lenore.

"Hey, you guys. Great to see you."

Nicole rushed to Lenore and they hugged. *And my old lady's new best friend.*

The stained glass pieces hanging in the store window filled the space with a soft amber light. My gaze landed on that wrought iron bookcase against the back wall filled with sex toys. Next to it hung a see-through black teddy, and my tongue lashed at my lip. My brain suddenly pictured Nicole's perfect tits, her long torso encased inside its magical webbing.

"I'm so glad you came by," Lenore said. "Hey, Trick."

Blinking, I wiped a hand across my mouth. "Hey."

"I had to come and tell you first. Craig hired me."

"Yes!" The two of them hugged again.

"I'll be teaching two classes a week. Maybe more if they're popular."

"They'll be popular, don't you worry," said Lenore. "When do you start?"

"In three days. He's going to put the word out first, send the info in his newsletter, and post a sign-up at the studio."

A grin perked over my lips. Nicole's enthusiasm, her deep pleasure in having been hired, was unmistakable. "I can't thank you enough for this." A catch in Nicole's voice had my pulse pick up speed. Genuine heart on her sleeve, this woman.

"Honey, I'm glad I could help." Lenore's voice gentled as she took Nicole in her arms and they hugged once more.

"It means a lot to me," said Nicole.

"So how are you guys doing?" Lenore asked. "Good to be out of lockdown, I'll bet."

"Hell yeah," I muttered.

"It's so great to finally be able to check out Meager, to come here. Your store is incredible." Nicole's gaze swallowed up the boutique, a laugh escaping her. Was she nervous or excited? She fingered a lilac lace corset. "Such beautiful things. So delicate."

"Thank you. When you get your first paycheck from Craig, come back and we'll find you the perfect lingerie. We'll make a party of it."

"That'd be great." They both laughed like co-conspirators. *Terrific.*

All the bras and panties and corsets, so many erotic tempt and tease tantalizers hanging all over the store seemed to smother me. I cleared my throat. "We should get going, pick up some food."

"Okay," said Nicole.

Lenore shot me a look. *Relax.*

I lifted my chin. *I'm trying.*

"I'll let you know about the class," said Nicole.

"I'll be at your first one for sure," Lenore told Nicole. "I can't wait. And I'll let people know."

"You're the best."

"Hang on—" She went to her counter and wrapped two red candles up in tissue paper. She put them in a purple shopping bag and handed them to Nicole. "For your new place. I just came out with these, I hope you like them."

We said our goodbyes and left the shop.

"I like her a lot," said Nicole.

"Yep."

"You seemed a little uptight in there."

I shrugged. "All that lacy, frilly girly shit...."

"Oh sure, sure. But I bet if I wore one of those corsets and stringy thongs you wouldn't be uptight, you'd like it just fine, like any other red-blooded male."

I burst out into laughter, stopping on the sidewalk. "Damn straight I'd like it." I hooked an arm around her neck and pulled her in close as we walked down Clay. "But on you, Zip, I'd love it." I bit her earlobe, and she let out a sexy gasp.

She pointed across the street. "Oh, can we go to the Meager Grand? I've been wanting to go there ever since I tried my first and incredibly magnificent Grand iced coffee."

I took her to the Meager Grand Café, where we picked up iced coffees for the road and a small chocolate cake for two to have for dessert after dinner. Mrs. Camden was seated at a table at the Grand with a group of her friends. She saw us and waved, and Nicole waved back. Her entire table of cohorts turned around and inspected us and smiled. Approval.

Erica, the owner of the Grand, rang up our order. "How's it going, Trick?"

"Hey, Erica. This here's Nicole, my old lady."

Erica grinned. "Nice to meet you, Nicole. Are you new to Meager? I've never seen you before."

"I am new, yes."

"Welcome."

"Thank you."

"Nicole's going to be teaching a dance cardio class over at Craig's. You should check it out." I handed Erica the cash.

"As long as burpees are not involved, I will definitely give it a go."

Nicole laughed, her cheeks flushed again. "No burpees, promise. Can't stand them."

"Great to hear. When's your first class?"

"Wednesday morning at ten."

"I'll be there." She handed me the change and the paper bag with our cake box inside as Nicole grabbed the coffees. "I hope you guys enjoy the chocolate cake."

"It looks delicious," Nicole said.

Outside the Grand, Nicole slid her arm in mine once more. "That was sweet of you to mention my class to her. Thank you."

"That's how you get the ball rolling, Zip. It's a small town. If the right people know, word will travel fast. Anyhow, I'm proud of you." She squeezed my arm, her sweet smile brightening her face, and my chest swelled at the sight. "Are you proud of you?"

"I am."

"Awesome. You should be."

"You make it easy, Trick." She squeezed my arm, and for the hundredth time that day, my dick swelled in my pants.

CHAPTER 32

TRICK

WE STOPPED at the supermarket and got food, and Nicole insisted on more vegetables and fruit than I'd ever bought in my life. Once home, she cooked up pork filets with a teriyaki sauce as well as steamed broccoli smothered in olive oil and grated parmesan, and a side of buttery mashed sweet potatoes. Beyond.

Sitting at the new small dining table, we ate, and something about that felt different and upscale as well as traditional. Maybe because I always ate on the couch alone in front of the television and almost none of that food was homemade?

I cut into the broccoli and forced myself to put it in my mouth. *Not bad.* "Tell me, what is it about dancing that you like, because I got to tell you, you lit up in there. Your body moved in a way that was...expressive, free. It was beautiful, I don't know how else to describe it."

"From my first ballet class as an eight-year-old, dancing transported me somewhere else, a place that was all mine. It was about what I felt and me expressing that to the world, using a different kind of language."

"The language of the body."

"Right. And also communicating feelings and emotions that weren't mine, that told the story of the dance as to its specific choreography and its themes. It was a way to jump into another world, like an actor does when he takes on a role. It's athletic too, you use your entire body and your emotions. Every movement tells part of the story while you're creating new definitions of space." Her fork pushed a piece of broccoli into the teriyaki sauce on her dish. "I loved it from the very beginning. It was exciting. It was my high. Still is. Like speed is for you, I guess. And to be able to explore it now again, in a different way, by helping people achieve certain goals and feel good about themselves, especially other women, means so much to me."

"Things go well at Craig's, you could offer a range of different classes maybe, or hell, even start your own studio one day."

"Right now, I'd like to take some classes in Rapid City."

"Rapid, Zip. We call it Rapid."

She giggled. "Right, Rapid."

"What kind of classes?"

"I'd like to learn something completely new to me, outside my comfort zone. Like hip hop. I've been wanting to do that for a long time now but never got the chance. Then I could incorporate moves into the cardio choreography which would be a lot of fun."

"You should do it. I think Jill sends her daughter to a dance class in Rapid. Ask her."

"I will."

We finished eating, and I started cleaning up.

"You don't have to do that." She rose from the table.

"I want to. You cooked. It's only fair." I took her dish from her hands and she blushed, her lips parting. "What is it?"

"I like that you consider fairness in all things. It's a big change for me."

I let out a grunt as I rinsed off our dishes and got them in the dishwasher. That asshole of a husband of hers had done a real number on her. And I was fucking enjoying providing her with those "big changes" from the kitchen to the bedroom. I tackled the frying pan and the pot. "Why don't you grab the cake and some dishes and I'll meet you in the living room."

"Oooh, that cake." She opened the fridge and grabbed the small box from the Grand.

After I finished, I joined her in the living room with the bottle of champagne the girls had left us along with the two new glasses. Nicole opened the bakery box, and the gooey chocolate frosting of the miniature three-layer cake, had my mouth watering. "That looks so good. I love chocolate. There's nothing better than Erica's cakes."

She swiped the side with her finger and licked the frosting from it. "So good."

I blinked, my dick surging in my jeans. "You cut, and I'll pour the champagne."

"We're celebrating?"

"You bet we are." I poured the frothy liquor into the tall glasses and gave Nicole one.

She held her glass up, her cheeks rosy. She was literally tickled pink. "To new beginnings. That's what this is, isn't it?"

"That's right, Zip. We're out of lockdown and in a new place, you got yourself the job you wanted. Good stuff." I clinked her glass with mine.

We drank, our gazes locked, and my blood heated, Was it the booze or something else setting off molten explosions in my every nerve cell? We devoured our slices of cake, chocolate frosting remaining on our fingers, our lips. "I forgot napkins." She lifted up from the sofa.

I grabbed her hand. "Don't. I like being messy with you." My voice had lowered, and her eyes widened. She sank back down on the sofa. She knew what I was meant. "I want to suck it off your fingers, Zip."

Her teeth bit into her bottom lip and she unfurled her hand in mine. "Do it," she whispered.

My tongue lashed at her chocolate-laced index finger, and a small moan left her mouth. She moved closer to me, her lips brushing my cheek, her tongue finding the chocolate at the edge of my mouth. Taking her mouth, I groaned into her kiss.

She climbed onto my lap, making my heart pound in my chest and my cock pound in my jeans. Gripping her waist, I pulled her up close to me. Finally, friction where I wanted it. Where she wanted it. Her tongue drove into my mouth, her fantastic tits pressing into my chest. My hands slid under her shirt and stroked her warm bare skin.

We kissed. We tasted. Our tongues dancing, wanting more. I wanted her to take, and she did.

"Need your tits, Zip." She yanked up her shirt, tossed it, and I got her out of that tight athletic bra, and tossed that too. Swiping more frosting from the cake, I lashed the chocolate on her breasts, my tongue licking, lashing, my teeth gently nipping her flesh.

"Trick…" Her chest arched, her body grinding against mine. "I want you."

"Nic?" My tight grip on her hips loosened.

Her hands cradled my face, her forehead slid against mine. "I want that new beginning. That celebration. I want to have sex with you."

My pulse jammed in my throat, my cock tightened painfully. "You sure?"

Up until now, we'd been keeping it to fooling around, touching, licking, kissing. I was methodical in all things. I wanted her to get used to coming. I wanted her to get used to me. Most of all, I'd wanted her to give it the green light in full confidence. Her to tell me out loud that she wanted cock from me. My cock. That she wanted me inside her. Wanted me to fuck her. Her choice. Out loud and clear.

She took in a breath. "From the moment I met the Smoking Guns up until I took off with you on your bike, I had so many crazy life-flashing-before-my-eyes moments. Too many. But they taught me that I need to live my life the way I want, and I want to feel good." She found my lips and we kissed, gently, slowly, my heart thudding in my chest. Her forehead slid against mine. "I want your kind of good, Trick."

"You deserve all the good, Zip, and I want to give it to you." I pushed her hair back from her face. "I want to feel you on my cock so bad, feel you take me all the way."

She let out a moan, her fingers rubbing the back of my neck as her body surged and pressed against mine, desperate for pressure. "I want that too…"

My grip tightened around her neck. "Say it the way I did. Say it. You tell me."

An eyebrow arched, her lips tilted up. There was need in that look, and my heart stopped. "I want to feel you inside me, Trick. I want to take you all the way. I want to come on your cock."

I flew up off the couch, Nicole in my embrace, and she let out a yelp, her heels pressing into my ass, her hands clutching me. "This calls for the new bed."

Our new bed. I'd sprung for a new one. I didn't want Nicole on the old one that had seen plenty of traffic.

New beginnings.

Yeah, I wanted to believe in it too.

CHAPTER 33
NICOLE

"DON'T TOUCH," his voice warned in the dark, and a thrill raced up my spine. "I want to strip your clothes off." Trick licked at my throat, down my chest. He liked licking, and I loved him licking me. That tongue had magical powers.

He pushed me back on the bed and my lungs crushed together as his hands kneaded my breasts. A beast claiming me. His tongue slid over their curves, teasing my nipples. He peeled my leggings off me, and his tongue made a wet trail down my thighs. I shuddered, and his grip on me tightened. My veins filled with liquid heat.

The hard line of his nose nudged in between my legs. "You want me bad, don't you, Zip?" came his low, dark voice in the darkness, sending a shudder straight through my soul.

And I replied with all the steadiness in that soul. "Want you so bad."

"I'm going to give it to you." That expert tongue of his padded my clit through my damp panties, and a moan I'd never heard before escaped my lips.

My fingers dug into his scalp. "Such a tease…"

"I'm making promises, baby." My panties flew down my legs and his hands went to my rear, kneading my flesh and, jerking my hips up, brought my pussy straight to his mouth. No delicate strokes tonight, no gentle exploring. No, tonight was about finally, finally diving in and enjoying the feast of each other.

A feverish wicked feast.

That tongue darted and dove. Suckled and plucked and pulled and stroked. I struggled for air through the delirium. I would burst. "Trick!"

He sat up and lightly smacked my outer thigh then stroked over the stinging flesh. "Get on all fours for me, baby."

I scrambled onto my knees, my hair falling forward as the sounds of him unhooking his leather belt and unbuttoning his jeans made my clit throb, my nipples tingle. He grunted as he ripped off his tee. Finally, we were naked together. The anticipation burst through me.

His large warm hands stroked the round curves of my rear and my skin stung at his touch. Spreading my ass cheeks, his fingers flirted and lingered and teased. He spit and the liquid dripped between my ass.

"Oh God…" My whole body rocketed with electricity, all my senses were alive, on edge, and ready. One hand cupped a breast, stroking it roughly while his other fingers probed and rimmed my rear hole.

"I want to touch all of you, Nic. Lick every inch of you." I let out a cry at his raw tone, his words, his strokes. I was in his capable hands and I loved it. His rock-hard cock, velvet and stiff, slid against a thigh, the tip wet, leaving a trail on my skin. This was it.

"Trick…" I panted.

A drawer next to me flew open. A package ripped and there was movement at my rear. The snap of elastic. "Trick?"

He flipped me over. His jaw was sharp as a blade, his eyes fierce. "I want to watch you take me." His hips sank against mine, and with a low growl, he rocked into me, his cock sinking in all the way in one long steady move that drove the breath from my body and my heartbeat from my chest. My head fell back. Elsewhere, another dimension.

"Trick…" My mind stuttered with the incredible fullness of him inside me. I let out a loud gasp as my body exploded with sensation, and my brain couldn't keep up. He brushed my lips with his. "How's it feel, Nic?"

"So full. So good," I said against his lips. "You're so big, so damn big." A lazy grin lit up his lips and he pinched a nipple, and I gasped. "It's true, not just saying it…"

His hips ground into mine, a slow torturously sweet circle, and the initial sting subsided into waves of feeling. "Oh God…oh…"

"You want more of my so damn big cock?"

My fingernails raked his skin. "I want all of you."

On a growl, Trick pulled out slowly, and my breath hissed at the loss of him. But he drove back inside, quicker this time, and a moan ripped from me, my fingertips digging into his tight rear. I raised my hips to meet his and ground against him enjoying that union, him inside me, me tight around him.

He thrust faster, and I pulled my legs up around his hips. His breaths coming hard and fast, Trick pounded into me on a relentless rhythm, the sweat on our skin mingling. The intense sensation building and heating through me, through him. A furnace on high.

This was a far, far cry from Logan's stiff jackhammering as I grit my teeth and looked away. Yes, this was fast and harsh, but the way Trick held me, the hungry gleam in his eyes hanging on mine? Never. Before. This man wanted me and wanted me to know. And in Trick's rough, brutal passion, I didn't feel those familiar insecurities or that agitation, no, I was confident that he was caring for me, savoring me. And that thing that had been wound tight inside me for so very long, unfurled.

He switched our positions and suddenly I straddled him. My breath cut. My heart beat faster. I was under the spotlight.

A hand dug into my hips. "Don't think, Nic. Don't judge

yourself." He tapped on my clit. "Feel what we got. Find more. Maybe something different. Something for you."

"I've never…been on top before."

A crude grin flashed over his face. "I'm glad you're on top of me, you gorgeous girl." He palmed a breast. "I want you to take what you want." He fingered a nipple roughly. "Now do it."

"Take?"

"You're in control now. I'll follow you."

"I don't know. I—"

Dim light suddenly glowed in the room. He'd turned on the small lamp at the side of the bed. He pointed to my right. "Look in the mirror. Look at us."

My blurry gaze went to the long mirror the ladies had gotten us. My breathing deepened. There we were in full form on the bed.

"What do you see?"

My mouth dried. "Me on top of you."

He rocked his hips and his cock nestled deeper, as his warm, salty thumb slid into my mouth. He tasted of me. His other hand went back to my breast.

I put my hand over his on my chest. "What do you see?" I whispered.

"Us, needing. Wanting."

I sucked on his thumb and I started to move again. Two of his fingers brushed my clit, and something inside me ignited hot and wild. I rode him, and that something I'd locked away years ago began to breathe, to blaze, to beckon.

His hands dug into my hips. "I see a dancer letting her body tell a story."

"Trick…" I ground over him, my gaze meeting his in the mirror. The raw look in his eyes, the one that craved a rough satisfaction, ignited that craving in me. I wanted that too. I found more friction in new places. Changing pace, I rocked my hips against his in a wave-like motion, and intense heat rolled through me. Everything tightened. "Oh shit. Shit…"

"Oh yeah..." he murmured, fingers rubbing my nipples, tugging my breasts. Claiming them, enjoying them. "Don't close your eyes, Zip." He turned my face toward the mirror again. "Look at you coming, look at yourself riding my cock. You feel good?"

"So good," my voice was breathless.

My need had compounded with the impressive thickness of him inside me. His hooded gaze snagged on mine as I took him. As I took him with me.

His palm pressed against my clit in a tense rhythm. "See why this position can be real good?"

"Yeah, oh yeah...." My brain could no longer form words.

"You're a fucking goddess, and I'm gonna blow inside you, 'cause you make me so fucking wild, Zip. Watch what you do to me." A savage edge to his voice, that dark insistence kept me riveted on his body. "You're coming, baby. Your gorgeous pussy is coming on me."

I moved faster, his fingers dipping in my wet, working me, my flesh responding to his every stroke. "That clit is humming for me," his voice grunted out, sending my insides throbbing.

"Yes. For you."

I'd always thought that sex would be effortless, that coming was a natural thing that happened to you each and every time. All my girlfriends talked about that incessantly. All the positions they'd tried, all the multiple orgasms they'd had. I'd agreed with them, but I was lying. It had never been that way for me, never natural or easy. I'd never had any of that. Logan, too, would tell me that was the norm. *"You're a lot of work. Just a cold bitch. Nothing for it."*

I trained my gaze on the gorgeous man who was pulling music I'd never heard before from me. The man who was so damned attentive to *both* our needs. I wanted to be that attentive too. For him.

Trick groaned loudly, his thick muscles flexing and tightening around me. "Love watching you ride my cock, Zip. Your pussy feels so fucking good, taking me all the way in." His deep strong voice filled my ears, kicking out Logan, kicking out all the voices and insecurities of the past. I ground down on him, and his hands squeezed my ass, holding me firmly. Together we chased the tornado of pleasure building around us, lifting us.

It was happening. *Yes!*

I'd always assumed I had a problem. That *I* was the problem. That I would never experience something so frenzied, so intense as had been described to me. This, now?

Ferocious, raw.

Overfreakingwhelming.

My breath knotted in my throat. That towering whirling twister we'd set off broke through me, carried me high on its crest. "Trick!" I clung to his sweaty body as he flipped me down on the bed and drove inside me, hitting a place inside me that cut my breath. He grunted fiercely, chasing his own end as my orgasm kept coming and coming and coming, every cell in my body pulsating. I washed up on his shore.

Gripping his slick shoulders, I raised my hips to him, tightening over his cock, and his jaw dropped open, his eyes shut and he let out a long grunt as he hammered inside me. Sweat slicked between our bodies, down his chest, over my breasts.

Tucking my hand between us, my fingers found our wet and curled around the root of him, his cock thrusting relentlessly. Frenzied, violent, and all consuming. At my touch his beautiful eyes opened, a long groan dragging from his lips. "Nic!" his voice seethed. His body jerked, his cock throbbed inside me. My legs tightened around him, keeping him deep, keeping him close as he came.

But he didn't stop moving. On a low moan, his eyes hanging on mine, his hips rocked slower, and slower, and he took my breath away. His body finally settled over mine and I relished the weight of him against me.

Sliding my hands around his muscular arms, the tattoos were damp under my touch. My hands slid down to the hard curves of his rear, as I brushed my lips across the scar on his forehead. The musky scent of our sweat and sex was a heady perfume between us. "That was incredible. You're incredible. You pay attention to every detail."

Chuckling, he palmed my breast. "My ego used to think all a woman needed was my fantastic cock, but ma'am, that just ain't so. It's a little more complicated than that."

"It is, isn't it?" I let out a lazy laugh. "It is."

He nuzzled my throat. "You're perfect, Zip. Perfect in every fucking way."

I held him fast. I didn't want to let him go, let this go. His weight on me, this closeness with this remarkable man who was continually kind and good and thoughtful and powerful. So powerful. Even at his roughest, I didn't feel used or alone. Trick made me feel that I was embraced by his powerful, a necessary part of it, and that I, too, could be that powerful. I already was. I only had to reach out and claim it. Embrace it for myself.

Trick smoothed my damp hair from my face. He was in no rush to slide out of me, something Logan would do abruptly, and then fling himself back on the bed on his side, get up and pour himself a drink. Not Trick. Still inside me, my legs, firmly around his hips, keeping us together, we were a tumble of limbs and breaths and pounding hearts in the thick silence of the bedroom.

His head rested against my chest. "The date on my tattoo?" he said, his breath rough, his voice almost tentative. "The one you asked me about a while back?"

"The date with the blood drops?" My hand stroked the dense curve of his back.

"That's the date of the car crash I told you about."

"Your family."

"When I was sixteen, my parents and my little sister were driving home from the movies and got smashed into by a truck driver who'd fallen asleep behind the wheel and drifted into the opposite lane. Nothing but a ball of fire and crushed metal.

"The irony of that was that my dad had been an original member of the riding club Uncle Willy and Wreck had going, but when everyone had decided to join the Jacks, become an official chapter, my dad decided to walk away from the life because he thought it was too dangerous and he had a family to take care of.

"Around that time shit had gotten heavy all of a sudden. Drug dealers were chasing each other, guns, raids, shootings, police. And a friend of theirs had gotten killed. All of sudden the life was about way more than just riding your bike and having a good time. He realized then that he couldn't do it, be a One-Eyed Jack. He was the only one with a wife and kids, and he didn't want to take that chance."

"An honorable decision."

"It was. He'd gotten a job offer with real good benefits from the railroad, and he took it. He felt he was doing the right thing, the best thing for his family, keeping them safe from all that crazy. A fine future lay ahead. Yeah…There was barely anything left of the three of them to bury in a coffin. That's when I knew that nothing's safe in this fucked up world. All he did was take his wife and daughter to see a Disney movie and they got smashed to smithereens by some asshole who said he didn't mean to do it.

"I got that fucked up day tattooed on me so I'd remember that bittersweet fucking irony forever. That day…that fucking day." He took in a deep breath. "That's when Willy took me in. That's when the club took me in as family."

My heart skipped a beat. "They're not eagle wings. They're angel wings?"

"Yeah, angel wings." His suddenly fragile voice hung in the air over us.

Angel wings with the skull of the One-Eyed Jacks surrounded with flowers. Hope in despair. Death in life and life in death. So much fucking love.

I dug my hands through his hair, and kissed his forehead.

"I'm glad you had Willy and that he is the fine man that he is and stood by you. Thank you for sharing that with me."

Raising up, his lips smashed into mine, his tongue claiming. All I wanted at this very moment was to give to Trick, to share with Trick. And I did.

Our kiss deepened, roughened, and made my blood blaze. Emotions hot and true melded with molten desires.

But a new desire enflamed me, and I pushed him back against the mattress and laid kisses down his musky throat and over the smooth plains of his chest to where that inked date was branded on his skin. Sliding down his slick body, my mouth took his cock.

He let out a long hiss. "Aw, Zip….what are you…"

I swallowed him down my throat and sucked. *You're not alone, Trick. You're not alone. You're not alone.*

Moaning, he dug a hand in my hair, his hips rocking against my mouth. "Hell yeah…"

CHAPTER 34

NICOLE

ONE PHONE CALL DOWN. One more to go.

I sat on the bed in Trick's room at the clubhouse, my grip tightening over the new burner phone Trick had given me earlier before he went to work.

"You nervous?" he'd asked me when he handed it to me.

"It's more that I feel bad, that I should have called sooner. It's unlike me."

"Zip, I think you're doing a lot of things lately that are unlike the you you used to be." He chuckled, and with that sly grin sparking over his face, pressed his lips against mine.

"Dirty mind."

"You love it." His tongue flicked against my lip.

"I do." I opened my mouth to his and we indulged in a deeper kiss, our tongues sliding, dancing, our bodies pressing together.

His hand gripped my rear and smacked it. "Got to get to work. Let me know how it goes."

Now, I finally dialed my mother's cell phone number, and my heart thudded in my chest with every ring.

"Yes?" her voice had my spine straightening.

"Mom, it's Nicole."

"Oh my God, Nicole! Where the hell are you?"

My gut pinched. The fury in her voice seeped through the phone line. I was a misbehaving child all over again. "I'm fine." *No idiot, she didn't ask you if you were okay.* "I wanted to let you know that I'm okay."

"Obviously, you don't care if we're okay, though, do you? Do you have any idea what your brother and I have gone through? No, of course you don't, because you're not here." Her voice raged. "Those animals stampeded through my home, manhandled me and Jackson, and what did you do? You took off with them without a word! I still cannot believe it!"

"I didn't just take off with them. I offered to pay Jackson's debt to them in full so we'd all be clear of them. Didn't Jackson tell you?"

"Jackson told me—when he was able to talk after the hell he went through—I can't even step foot in my bathroom anymore. The blood, oh my Lord. Jackson said you offered to go with them. That you wanted to go with them. What kind of daughter does that? You abandoned your family, your husband, for a bunch of low-life thugs? Why on earth?"

"Mom, I made a deal with those bikers to keep y'all safe. I paid off Jackson's debt in return for them not hurting you or raiding the house again. Jackson no longer owes them any money. They won't come after him or bother you again. It's over."

"Over? Are you crazy? It's not over!"

"What do you mean it's not over?"

"That Mr. Rooney was found dead in his office. Those animals must have killed him!"

"Is that her? She finally called? Give me that phone!" My brother's sharp voice rose in the background. A fumbling noise filled the line. "Is that you, Nicole? What the fuck have you done?"

"What have I done? I paid off your Mr. Rooney debt to that

bike club, Jackson, that's what. Thank you very much and you're welcome."

"That's not what that Dog says. He says you offered to pay him but then you took off. He wants his money."

"He's lying!"

"And Jolene is waiting for her payout. You promised you'd take care of that. But you took off and left us high and dry. Where the fuck are you?"

I shot up off the bed. "I'm telling you, I paid Dog the money you owed him and with a hell of a lot of interest, and he was real happy about it. There isn't anything left for Jolene."

"What am I supposed to do? She's threatening me every day with a smile on her face. Melissa found out and she's furious. She kicked me out of the house."

"I'm sorry, Jackson, but you've got to figure it out."

"Where's the diamond necklace, huh? It's gone. At least if I had that…"

My stomach tensed. "They must have taken it."

"Are you shacked up with this Dog now? You're a married woman acting like some street whore. Logan is furious. Furious. You've ruined his reputation and our family name. The whole town is talking about how you took off with those lowlife criminals."

"Those criminals came to our house looking for you because you owed them money. They threatened our lives, and I did something to stop it."

"Are you in cahoots with them and trying to milk us for all its worth? Humiliate us? I never pegged you for being such a sneaky ungrateful bitch. What did we ever do to you?"

"Jackson, do you honestly believe that of me? My money has come to your rescue over and over again. I always helped you when I could, you know I did. I don't regret paying the money to Dog so you could be free of him and that debt, and I don't expect you to pay me back."

"Oh, Nicole," he groaned. "I appreciate how you've always

helped me, I do, but the shit has hit the fan here. Where are you? When are you coming home? We need you."

"There's no more I can do, Jackson. Now you do me a favor, and encourage Logan to sign the divorce papers."

"Logan is your husband. You have to stop acting like some cheap slut and come home."

"Where is she? Did she tell you?" my mother screeched in the background. The phone fumbled once again. "Where the hell are you?" my mother shouted into the line. "Are you with those bikers?"

"No, I'm not. In fact, I had to run off from them because Dog had not-so-nice plans for me. He took me to his clubhouse in Kansas City, but I managed to escape. And now I'm…somewhere else."

Mom's deep inhale and exhale filled the line. "Tell me you're not in South Dakota," she hissed.

My back straightened. "I'm in South Dakota." I hung up the phone and tore out the battery, my fingers shaking, my chest heaving.

Do not cry, do not cry.

I marched through the clubhouse, through the courtyard, into the Eagle Wings' bay, until those big brown eyes found mine. "Zip?"

I handed him the battery and the phone. He dumped them in a crate next to him and without a word, took me in his arms, fingers in my hair, hand digging into my lower waist. "What did they say?"

I only shook my head, a tiny moan escaping my throat as I buried my face in his warm neck, his musky leathery scent comforting, exciting, easing. His pulse beat under my lips.

Lifting me up, he steered us a few yards away into the large bathroom in the back, slamming the door shut, and propped me up on the counter. He smoothed the hair back from my hot face. "Tell me everything."

"They think I ran off with Dog and kept the money. And Dog

told them I never paid him, that I lied to him and took off. Or something…I can't even…"

"Dog's mad at you for running away, and he's taking it out on you and your brother. And he wants more money out of the rich folk."

"My brother barely believes me. My own mother…"

"It makes them feel better not to."

"I did a good thing, the right thing. Why can't it be over? Why? What else am I supposed to do?" My vision went blurry and I swallowed hard past the traffic jam of emotions clogging my throat. "I don't want to cry about this anymore. Or feel sad or confused. I'm fed up and so frustrated. Frustrated as all hell."

"Of course you are." His hands slid around my face. "You did good, Nic. They're all fucked-up playing their little games, lying to each other, and, most of all, to themselves. It's got nothing to do with you. You taking off, getting out from under each one of them, pissed them off. And you know why?"

I sniffed in air. "Why?"

"They need you in your place. But you pulled that plug."

Clarity shocked through my system, like a rollercoaster with no brakes. I blinked. "Screw that. Not anymore."

Trick's face broke into a smile. He was the only person in my life who never required me to fill a role or play a part to his advantage. He'd only been encouraging me to find my voice, to be the person I wanted to be, from the very beginning.

His smile grew sharper. "Yeah, Zip. Screw that."

I crushed my lips against his, and his breath audibly cut. My legs snaked around his waist, pulling him in closer. "I want you right now," I breathed, my hands going to his belt and unbuckling.

His eyes widened, his head slanted. An unusual request from Nicole.

Slapping open his belt and fumbling with the button of his work pants, I pressed my chest against his. "I want to feel you inside me, Trick. You're the only real thing to me. The only good thing. And I want to feel that right now. I want it. I want it from you."

A growl escaped his lips as he took my mouth and took over unbuttoning his pants as I undid mine. "Fuck, I don't have a rubber on me."

"I don't care. Pull out."

Right there in the bathroom of Eagle Wings, eyes locked, his cock thrusting inside me, Trick and I breathed together, groaned together. I rocked my hips against his to take him in as deep as possible as he muttered all sorts of filth about pounding my tight wet pussy, his grip on my flesh painful, his harsh driving thrusts taking away my breath.

The hard edge of the countertop dug into the backs of my thighs and I didn't give one damn. The bite of pain only added to this wild stolen pleasure between us.

Yes, stolen—I wanted it, I took it.

The scent and taste of his salty, warm skin mingled with metal seeped onto my tongue. Gripping him, my pulse jammed in my veins as my hips drove down on his. I slid my hand between my legs and rubbed my clit, crying out.

"That's my Zip right there, fuck yeah." His teeth sank into my shoulder, and I shuddered. I exploded. "You like riding my cock, don't you, baby?" he gritted out.

"Fuck yeah."

His teeth nipped at my lip, the side of my face. He pulled out and came against my thigh with a rough groan that had my pulse thundering. His glimmering eyes met mine, and I kissed him.

This was real. This was good. This was me and Trick.

Me and Trick.

CHAPTER 35
NICOLE

I'D COME BACK to the apartment after a practice session at FitSmash. A shopping bag, its top stapled, stood on the bed. Written on the bag were the words: CALL ME FIRST.

I called Trick. "What's in the shopping bag?"

"Open it."

I ripped open the bag and took out black leather clothes and a pair of heavy leather boots. "Oh my."

"Put on the clothes and the boots and meet me out front in ten minutes." He hung up.

Were we going driving? We'd had a session yesterday for a couple of hours here in the neighborhood and it had gone well. He'd been at ease in the passenger seat, and I was determined to be relaxed as I slowly took his Jeep out of the driveway and turned onto the street. Stopping at the stop sign then looking both ways and making a right turn had felt like a small victory. Every afternoon after work, we'd go out for a drive on the quiet streets of our neighborhood. Baby steps. When I felt ready, he'd take me on the track for a controlled environment in speed, and then Clay Street traffic.

But black leather and these boots? A motorcycle was in my near future.

I ripped off my sweaty workout clothes, took a quick shower, and got dressed. I tucked into the boots and got outside. Trick, dressed in his leathers stood at the end of the driveway next to a bright red Harley-Davidson. My breath cut. Every girl's dangerous bad boy dream come true was waiting for me.

"There she is in all her glory."

I giggled gesturing at him and the bike. "The glory is all yours."

He handed me a helmet. "For you. Need help getting it on?"

"I got it." I clipped on the lid as he got on the bike. I settled in behind him. "Where are we off to?"

"You'll see."

We zoomed off, taking the turn which led outside of Meager to who knew where. My heart thundered in my chest as we cut through the wind at top speed, the bike roaring under us. I liked this, not knowing. And I knew why. Because I'd started to trust Trick.

That sexy grin of his promised something more, and he delivered that more. He wanted to give to me, he enjoyed giving, surprising me, making me laugh. He considered me, which told me I was important to him. Now, I knew what that felt like to the core of my being, and I loved it.

My body curled around his. Trick held me on equal footing with himself. I wasn't his cute pet who bounced through hoops on his whim, or the pretty chick on his arm playing a role.

Signs for Sylvan Lake shot past us. A sign advertising Mount Rushmore. Then another that noted "Needles Highway." Needles?

The road got twisty and Trick guided the bike on an endless series of tight hairpin turns. Several bikes were ahead of us, others behind us. Not a car in sight on this winding highway which was more of a narrow loop that cut through the rugged evergreen-loaded granite hills. A bikers' paradise.

I'd never seen anything like it before. Where I'd grown up the land was flat. In the distance, you could see miles and miles of…

more miles and miles. Not here. This was a rugged forest kingdom.

Up ahead a group of odd granite spires poked at the sky. Dramatic prehistoric sculptures. We shot through tight incredibly narrow tunnels of rock, and my breath cut each time. A very narrow road made for touring on a motorcycle. And all along were these tall slim fingers—no, needles—of rock around every curve. I let out a gasp as we zoomed into another dark tunnel, and just as quickly, light and air showered over us as we zoomed out. A clearly visible sheer drop off one side of the road had me holding onto Trick even tighter.

The heady green and resinous sweet scent of the thick evergreen forest filled my senses as we sped along this magical road. The sun dappled over us as we cut through the cool wind. Intimate yet grand at the very same time.

Had my mom ridden on this road? Maybe. Had my brothers ridden on this road? Most definitely. Countless times. Had their hearts pounded, their souls filled with air and light like mine? A smile broke over my face, and my heart swelled.

I'm here, Richie. I'm finally here.

My pulse surged. I had to find our brother. Had Richie even known about Mom's other baby? Because she very well could have hidden that fact from him just as she'd done with us. Maybe Willy knew? I leaned my chin on Trick's back as he cut his speed and brought the Harley to a halt off the road.

We got off the bike, and I ripped off my helmet. "That was amazing!" I lunged at him.

He hugged me. "I've been wanting to take you out here from the beginning, but with us being stuck at the club, and lately we've both been busy. I figured after yesterday's phone call, you needed this right now more than ever."

"It was exactly what I needed." I lifted up and gently pressed my lips to his. "Thank you for sharing your South Dakota with me."

His eyes creased as his brilliant smile filled my vision.

"You're welcome. There's plenty more I'd love to take you to see. Every road has a completely different view. Reservoirs, waterfalls, meadows, mountains. There's plenty of hiking trails too if you're into that. Then there are the Badlands which are pretty shocking compared to all this."

"I'd love that. All of it. Are we going to go back to Meager through those tunnels again?"

He squinted at me in the glare of the sun and a warm laugh erupted from his lips. "Is that what my old lady wants?"

"That's what I want."

"You got it."

I shot him a grin. Trick always urged me to voice what I wanted in bed, and so every night I got more comfortable with guiding his hand on my body to the place I wanted his fingers, his lips, his tongue. And then he'd guide my hand on his body and show me what he wanted and how fast or slow, how hard or gentle. There was no impatience, no judgement, no annoyance, or rejection of any kind. Only sharing and discovery.

It was heaven.

And I finally began realizing that saying the words, "*I want*," was okay, was good. That enjoying my body's capacity for pleasure was a good thing, and I completely trusted that Trick would and could give me what I wanted, and I did the same for him. Together, we made it happen for each other.

He'd made that my new reality. My new comfort zone.

Even now, voicing that I wanted to ride again on the Needles Highway was another satisfying victory for me, and he knew it too.

Taking my hand in his, Trick led me to the edge of the landing where he'd parked the bike. From up here we had a wide view of the mountains, the densely packed forest that slanted every which way. And a piece of Mount Rushmore in the distance.

"I can't get over how the air smells here. It's so fresh. Green and earthy sweet at the same time....there's something unique about it. Guess I'm used to dry and dusty."

We sat down on a rock formation and took in the view. He rubbed his hands down his legs. "Have you thought about what you're going to do when this is done with?"

My face heated. "You want to get rid of me, huh?"

"I didn't say that. I meant, that you're here because you have to be." His tone had gotten serious.

"I like being here."

"Are you planning on going back to Oklahoma?"

"No, I want to stay in Meager."

"You do?"

I met his gaze, and something hot and thick stirred in my blood. "This is where I want to be, Trick. Before I called my mother, I called my lawyer to push for the divorce."

"Good for you."

"It's time." I cleared the rising thickness in my throat. "I'd told you, my mom was born in Rapid, but she left South Dakota a long time ago before she and my dad got married, and she never looked back."

"Escape from Rapid, huh?"

"To wild and crazy Guymon." I let out a short laugh. "She never talked about her life here, so I don't know much about her family, if there's anyone still around." I shrugged in an attempt to loosen the sudden awkward stiffness in my body, to slow down my now galloping heart. "But I'd like to find out."

"I could help you find out. If you want."

"I'd like that. Actually, there is—"

His phone rang out loudly, but this was a different ringtone than I'd ever heard before. "Hold on." Whipping it out, he frowned. "Something's wrong at the club." He tapped at the screen. "What's going on?" His eyes narrowed. "Are you shitting me? Ah fuck. Terrific. We were expecting something to happen, so here we go. Yeah. Okay. We're by the Needles Highway. We're leaving now. All right, bro." He tucked the phone back in his pocket.

"What happened?"

"A special delivery of ours got hijacked, our men beaten. Cargo stolen. Fucking Smoking Guns."

"Oh no."

"Finger pushed him back, and now he's showing us his teeth. That cargo is a combined effort with us and the Flames of Hell."

"Can I ask what the cargo was?"

"No."

"Right."

"We got to get back to the club."

My insides seeped with dread as I grabbed my helmet and secured it on my head. Vengeful tactics from Dog, disruption of club business, whatever that was; obviously, something under the radar of the law. Once again, the club and Finger's club were under fire because of me.

Trick ignited the engine and the bike roared underneath us. I put my arms around his waist and his gloved hand clasped my wrist for a moment before grabbing onto the handlebar.

My fingers curled into his leathers. Maybe there was a way I could help the Jacks fire back at the Smoking Guns.

CHAPTER 36
TRICK

"THEY'VE BEEN WATCHING us for a while, waiting. They ID'd the vehicle, tracked it, and jacked it," said Kicker at the head of the table in our meeting room, the mood grim as fuck.

This enterprise was a special project we'd worked out with Finger's Flames of Hell chapter a couple of years ago when all that shit had gone down with the Broken Blades and the Smoking Guns. We'd decided that it was a good thing to work together and strengthen our alliance in our territories against common enemies like the Guns who'd been trying to bring in a cartel through our parts.

This was our first and only combined project, and it was a damn good one. Not only profitable, but our two clubs had proven to be able to work together and trust each other, which was fucking priceless in the scheme of things.

We only made two drops a year delivering product to a Flame chapter in Idaho, who would then distribute to their network in the west. We all made good bank on it, and while keeping it to only twice a year was modest, it was wise. We'd been able to keep it under the radar.

Until now.

Until Dog decided that he would find a way to kick us where it hurt.

We calculated the loss of revenue. Kicker reported that Finger was in a rage and wanted to plan a revenge move, but it would have to be a special one. But again, it had to be something that didn't expose us or the Flames.

The meeting ended, and I went out to the lounge with Dawes. "What a clusterfuck."

"We got to be careful, bro," I said. "We can't think he's not still gunning for Nic if not you and me."

"Nah, he knows he can't do anything about you and Nic anymore, which is why he did this."

Nicole opened bottles of beer with Shannon and Lucy, who handed them out to the men. Spotting us, Nicole brought us two beers.

"Thanks, Nic." Dawes took a long gulp of his brew.

She shifted her weight. "Guys, I had an idea, if…I mean…I don't know…I thought it might be useful. If you think it could be…"

"What are you talking about, Zip?" I swallowed the icy beer.

"I imagine that y'all might want to strike back at the Smoking Guns?" she whispered. "Or is that not something one does in these cases?"

"Oh it's done, all right," I replied.

"I thought of something that might be interesting. At their clubhouse party, when I was with Carrie, Dog's old lady, she noticed this bracelet I was wearing, and she took it off my wrist and shoved it in her pocket."

"Of course she did," said Dawes.

"She really liked it, and I'm pretty sure she was going to keep it for herself, not try to sell it."

My eyes narrowed. "Uh-huh."

"So I was thinking, she must have it at her house or she's wearing it, right?"

Dawes scoffed. "Wanna bet she's wearing it to lord it over her old man that at least she got something out of his runaway piece of ass?"

Nicole's eyes lit up. "That's exactly what I think. That's so Carrie."

"Did you just call my old lady a piece of ass?" Trick's jaw jutted out.

"But that's what I was to them, wasn't I?" Nicole's gaze darted from me to Dawes to me again.

"She was, bro." Dawes shrugged, draining his bottle.

I blew out a huff of air. "Where you going with this, Zip? You want the bracelet back?"

"No, no, no. What if I went to the police and reported it stolen by Carrie? Which is the truth. Wouldn't the police have to bring her in to question her, search her and Dog's house, maybe even the clubhouse? I don't think Dog would like that, do you?"

Dawes and I exchanged glances.

"In Oklahoma, when they were getting ready to leave my mother's house, one of the Smoking Guns wanted to steal some of my mother's jewelry, but Dog told him not to, that it would be easy to trace, or just plain ol' get them into trouble because it was proof that they'd been there. That bracelet is proof. If the police find my bracelet in Carrie's possession, this could put a humiliating squeeze on him, right? Not to mention unfortunate exposure?"

Dawes crossed his arms. "And what kind of bracelet are we talking about here, Nic? Some kind of gold—"

"A tennis bracelet."

"A what?"

"Twenty-one diamonds on a platinum chain with my name inscribed on the clasp. It's worth over fifteen thousand dollars if not twenty. My parents gave it to me for my twenty-first birthday. It's from a famous jewelry store."

My arm lowered the beer bottle from its original trajectory toward my mouth. Dawes let out a hoot. "Yeehaw, ladies and gentlemen." Grinning, he slung an arm around my shoulders.

"Tricky, I do believe your old lady has gone full-on old lady on you."

Nicole beamed at the both of us.

"Jesus." Wiping at my mouth, I handed Dawes my beer bottle. "Let's bring this to Prez."

I brought Nicole to Kicker's office where he was smoking a cigar on his own. "Nicole may have something we can use." I told him Nicole's idea, and she gave him the details on the bracelet, which he wrote down.

He exhaled a plume of smoke. "Ah, there's this cheap thrill I get when we can make a sting happen without getting our hands dirty and have the law do it for us. Finger will need to hear the details from you, Nicole, all right?" He picked up one of his many cell phones.

"Sure." She met my gaze, her back straightening in the chair. Pride surged through me. This woman from another planet, who blasted out of nowhere into my life, and was forced into the MC, sat next to me in my Prez's office composed and calm if not eager as she delivered the necessary facts to get a job done to Finger of all people. A job that was her very own idea.

A wonder in my fucking world.

"This is good," Finger's voice raised over the line. "Nicole you're going to have to go to the local police station and make the claim. Do not go with a Jack or one of the old ladies. Let's keep this clean for now. I'll have my contacts pick up that paper-work, and they'll make it happen. I'll be in touch."

Kicker and Finger signed off, and the three of us had grins on our faces. "This is one of those, tap on the domino and watch the stack fall and fall and fall while we lean back in our easy chair, cigar in hand." Kicker lifted his chin at Nicole. "Thanks, Nic."

"I'm glad I could help somehow," she said.

"Why don't I take you into town now?" I said. "I'll wait for you at The Meager Grand while you go to the police station."

The two of us left Kicker's office, and slinging an arm around her shoulders, I brought her close and planted a kiss on her cheek.

"Question for you?" asked Nicole.

"Shoot."

"Is going 'full-on old lady' a good thing?"

I exploded with laughter.

CHAPTER 37
NICOLE

MY GAZE WENT to my new sneakers as my damp hands smoothed down my new athletic leggings. I straightened my back and relaxed my shoulders. My first class was in two minutes. My very own dance cardio class at Craig's FitSmash in Meager, South Dakota.

Stretching out my arms, I let out a tiny breath, a smile curving my lips. I had no dark cloud hanging over me that Logan might find out and be angry with me, that my mother would roll her eyes and shake her head once she heard. Nope. I was here doing the job of my choosing, and I would enjoy it to the max.

"Hey, Nicole."

"Jill, you're here!"

Of course, I'm here. I brought my daughter too. She loves dancing and wanted to come. She takes modern dance classes in Rapid and loves it so much. Becca, honey, this is Miss Nicole, our teacher today and Mommy's friend."

"Hi, Miss Nicole."

"Hi, Becca, so good to see you. You like to dance?"

Becca stood up on her tiptoes, her face beaming under my attention. She nodded rapidly.

"I can't wait to hear all about what class you're taking. Maybe I'll come with you one day."

Becca giggled.

'We'll go put our stuff up. I'm so excited for this." Jill grinned.

"Me too. Thank you for coming."

Would the class fill up? I hoped so. I needed at least ten people in a class to make it worth Craig's while. Of course, he knew that one class wouldn't make or break me. What would make or break me was the power of word of mouth in Meager.

My hand went to my tummy. I needed to pee yet again. Cueing up the intro music that I'd chosen last night to set the mood pre-class, I ran to the bathroom, did my business, washed my hands, high-fived myself in the mirror, and stepped into the studio once again. My lips fell open.

All the ladies and more were there. Along with Jill and her daughter were Tania and Grace, Lenore. Tania introduced me to Livie and Solange, who worked at the local hair salon, as well as Alicia, a thin platinum blonde who used to be the First Lady of the One-Eyed Jacks for years when her recently deceased husband had been president. Her new man had just opened a branch of his famous Deadwood tattoo parlor here in Meager which she managed.

"Great to meet you, Alicia."

"You too, honey. Can't wait to see what you dish out today. This is Tish and Cleo from the shop."

"Hey." Two younger women covered in tattoos and body piercings grinned at me.

"Thanks for coming, y'all."

"Hey, Nicole!" Erica, the owner of the Meager Grand waved at me. A young blond who resembled her stood with her. "This is my daughter, Jessa."

"Hi, Jessa."

"I'm so excited to take your class. I hate Craig's HIIT classes with a passion, but he's the only game in town. Even though it does wonders for my hips and my legs, I still hate it. I don't want to hate my workout."

"I understand, believe me. Thanks so much for coming, I hope you enjoy the class."

"Nicole, you ready to give us all you got?" shouted out Lenore.

"Watch out for her!" said Grace. "She's hardcore."

"Y'all are amazing," I said clapping my hands together. "Thank you so much for coming out today."

"Woot!" Tania shouted out.

"Let's do this!"

Everyone took a place on the studio floor, and I let out a breath as I stopped the atmosphere music, willing my insides to relax. I took my place in the front and faced my class.

"Welcome, everyone. I'm Nicole and I'm a trained dancer who loves dance cardio. To be clear, dance cardio doesn't mean high-impact aerobics to super fast-paced music. And there won't be any complicated choreography here either. If you need to go slower, go slower, if you need to modify a move, modify. If there's jumping you don't feel comfortable with, don't jump, step instead.

"I don't shout out directions a lot during a session, I feel that interrupts the mind-body connection. This is all about feeling the moves, getting inspired by the music, and managing your energy and your space. We're exploring, challenging ourselves, and building on that.

"We build strength and agility and endurance over time through consistent effort, not in one class. We're not here to race with each other or ourselves. I'll start slow with stretches, warming us up, and then we'll move through some light chore-ography, interchanged with some faster moves to bring up our heart rate. Then we'll slow it down with more stretches at the end. Sound good?"

"Yes!" Everyone clapped.

I hit the class music on the stereo system, and the first notes filled the studio. I took my place before the class, facing our reflection in the mirror. Everyone waited for my cue. Grinning, I moved.

Forty minutes later, sweaty, red-faced, and huffing for air, we all exploded into applause. "Y'all did so great! Great job!"

"That was so much fun."

"How often are these classes?"

"Are you doing any other type of class, Nicole?" asked Erica.

"I wanted to ask if y'all might be interested in barre or Pilates?"

"Yes! I've never tried barre, but I've been hearing about it for years. I want to try it."

"Me too."

"What? Barre? I tried it in L.A., and it was amazing." Lenore came up behind us.

"I love Pilates. It'd be great to have a class here in town."

"Sign-up sheets are up front, ladies!" Craig's loud voice filled the studio. "Let's keep it moving now, I got a class to teach in ten. Good job, Nicole."

"Thanks, Craig."

I could do this.

I was doing it.

"Nicole, I want you to meet my good friend, Cassandra," Lenore gestured to the tall, elegant black woman at her side.

I'd noticed Cassandra earlier. She had a dancer's body and had moved through the class effortlessly with terrific form. "Great to meet you, Cassandra. You're a dancer, aren't you?"

She grinned. "I used to be in the good ol' days of my teens and twenties. That was a while back."

"Cassandra manages The Tingle," Lenore said.

"I know Shannon. She's told me all about the nightclub."

"My girls work themselves hard, and everyone's so busy these days, rushing all over. I'd like to talk with you about you coming to The Tingle one day and doing a kind of warm-up/stretching class, like a workshop, for them. Every few months I bring in dancers and choreographers to keep our moves on trend and push the envelope, but we need this too. This is important."

"I'd love that. Thank you for asking."

"Good. I'll get your number from Lenore and give you a call."

Lenore winked at me, and the two women grabbed towels and their gym bags and headed toward the front door.

I twisted open my water bottle and drank, the cold liquid flooding my hot throat as I caught my reflection in the mirror wall. Sweaty skin, red face, hair in a now messy knot on the top of my head, bright white sneakers, and sweaty workout gear. My heart thudded in my chest as I wiped at my mouth. I was working, I was dancing, creating sequences for others to enjoy.

But the best part?

The beaming smiles on these rosy, sweaty faces told me *yes, yes. Give us more.* I was helping women enjoy themselves, feel good about themselves in a new way, in a fun way. Push themselves to get stronger. And they valued what I offered. They appreciated it. I twisted the cap back on the water bottle.

No more hiding, no more worrying, no more giving in. I'd cut that damned zip tie for good. I raised my water bottle to my reflection. *Go get it, girl.*

CHAPTER 38
NICOLE

I WAS in my second week of teaching, and it was going better than I'd hoped.

The big clock on the studio wall told me it was noon exactly. Time to clean up and head over to Tania's antique shop, The Rusted Heart, where Jill was working today. I looked forward to hanging out with her and finally seeing the antique store and art gallery I'd heard so much about.

I got dressed, said goodbye to Craig, and headed down Clay Street to the shop. Pushing open the door, a small brass bell rang out above me. Linda Ronstadt's voice singing "Blue Bayou" filled the shop. "Hey, you!" Jill greeted me as she helped a lady choose a necklace in a display case.

"Hi, Jill." I strolled around the gallery, admiring all the funky pieces of found art and and novelties Tania had collected to re-sell in her store—from ordinary household items from the turn of the century to handmade crafts from another age, and a wide variety of curiosities along with contemporary works of art of all kinds. I wandered in between paintings and watercolors, small sculptures, a few vintage photographs of cowboys, and one of a tiny Dakota Territory train station from the nineteenth century.

My phone rang. Trick. "Hey."

"Hey. Done with class? How'd it go?"

I grinned to myself. It was a simple thing, Trick asking me how my day was going, knowing that I had just taught a class, knowing how much I enjoyed it, that it was important to me. His expressing interest in what I was doing was incredibly special. For Trick, it seemed natural, a simple thing, but this thoughtfulness was something that I'd never had from the man in my life. For me, now, this "simple thing" was a huge thrill.

"Class was a lot of fun. There were even more people there today."

"Terrific. You at The Rusted Heart?"

"Yep. Jill's with a customer right now, and I'm giving myself the tour. It's incredible."

"Sure is. Wanted to let you know, everyone's going over to Pete's tonight for drinks. Lock came home and things went real well. He got us two new jobs, including one for one of the cars I found in Kansas City."

"Trick, that's fantastic."

"I'm psyched. You up for going out with everyone tonight to celebrate?"

"To the famous Pete's Tavern at long last? You bet I am."

He chuckled. "Thought you'd like that. I'll see you back at the apartment later. Got to run."

"Okay, bye."

A night out with everyone at their favorite watering hole here in town? Yes, please. It would be my first night out on the town with everyone and there was plenty to celebrate.

As I tucked my phone back in my bag, my gaze snagged on a painting hanging on the wall before me. An ethereal fairy who wore a long shimmering metallic gossamer dress, with silvery purple hair and pale lilac eyes cavorting elegantly in the night sky with shooting stars dancing around her. I moved closer, transfixed. This enchanting spirit was painted on a block of irregularly cut stripped wood that was obviously many, many decades old.

"What do you think?" Jill came up next to me. "You like it?"

"I love it. She's beautiful. And painted on that rough, raw wood…makes her even more magical."

"Tania brought it in yesterday. The artist was an elderly woman with no formal training from back in the Great Depression. Her family found a stash of her stuff in their attic and this was there. Seems she painted on anything she could get her hands on, like this piece of wood from a barn."

"Her imagination and creativity knew no bounds."

"No matter the circumstances."

"That's a hell of an inspiration." An innocent, playful spirit. light on her feet and filled with light, her vibrant colors shimmering over the harsh worn texture of the old wood. I swallowed hard against the rising emotions clogging my throat. "Is this piece for sale?"

"It is. Are you interested? I can offer you a sweeter price—"

"Not necessary, but thank you. I have to have it."

"Okay, great. Let's take care of that for you." Jill went to the front desk and brought up her invoicing on her computer screen. I made the purchase, a huge smile on my face.

I used to enjoy shopping, it was my distraction. Often, a careless habit. But since I'd been here, I hadn't given one thought to any of that, and I hadn't missed it with everything going on and keeping busy. To find this beautiful painting that sang to me, had me mesmerized here in Meager, now? A sign. A true, right purchase of the heart that was worth every penny of my own money.

I leaned on the reception desk as Jill finished with the sale. "Trick just called me about everyone going out tonight to Pete's."

She grinned. "Yes. I just lined up my babysitter. Thank goodness she's free tonight. I'm so looking forward to a night out."

"Me too." I glanced back at my starlit nymph. "But I don't have anything to wear. And I think I'd like to change it up a little bit for tonight."

Jill's eyes widened. "A little bit or makeover?"

"Makeover."

Her face lit up. "The whole nine yards—hair and clothes and shoes, jewelry?"

"Yes to all."

"Haircut only? Or color change too?"

"Both."

"Excellent. I'm on it." She grabbed her phone and made a call. Suddenly, she was making an appointment for me. "We are so in luck. Our local salon has an opening in an hour and a half for you. That gives us a good chunk of time to shop for clothes, which we can do right down the street. Let's do this."

"Can you take off right now?"

"It's fine. I'll come back once I get you to the hair salon." She locked up The Rusted Heart, and we went down two blocks to "Veronica's Vintage," a vintage clothing boutique.

"Hey, Veronica!" exclaimed Jill as we entered the shop. "This is my friend Nicole."

"I know Nicole. My thighs are still screaming from taking your class the other day. Job well done, bitch."

I laughed. "Good to see you again, Veronica. Sorry, but not sorry about your legs. Coming back for more, I hope?"

"You bet I am." She laughed. "How can I help you guys?" She ran a hand through her sleekly bobbed reddish brown hair.

"We're going out to Pete's tonight with our menfolk, and Nicole wanted to wear something a little edgier than her usual…" Jill glanced at me in my sweatpants and fitted T-shirt. "…comfy casual."

"Too much comfy casual," I affirmed. "Not enough biker old lady."

"Yeah." Jill's eyebrows jumped up, a grin slicing over her lips.

"I didn't know you were with the club. Cool." Veronica grinned. "Which hunk of man is yours?"

I blushed. "I'm with Trick."

Veronica's grin froze, her eyes popping wider for a split second. "No kidding." Her voice had gone flat. She cast a glance at Jill who pressed her lips together. Veronica took in a breath as she scanned my body. "All righty, let's see…I'll go pull a bunch of things to start with as a baseline, and I'll meet you guys in the fitting room in the back, okay?"

"Great, thanks."

"This is going to be so much fun." Jill clapped her hands together. "Veronica always has interesting pieces, and she's very good at mixing and matching."

"Thank you for taking time off to do this with me."

"My pleasure, truly." Jill slid her arm through mine as she led me to the dressing room. "I'm guessing things with Trick are good?"

"Well…" We entered the dressing room, and I lowered my voice. "I don't know if this fake relationship is going to turn into something more or how long it will last, but the right now feels real good."

"That's great. You don't have to think about tomorrow."

How I wished that were true, but I had a stubborn ego-driven husband back in Oklahoma, who refused to sign our divorce papers.

Jill squeezed my arm. "As you know, my big true love began with a fake relationship so I'm a huge supporter."

"By the way, does Veronica not like Trick? When I mentioned him, she seemed to be taken aback, or was that my imagination?"

Jill dropped her bright yellow vinyl tote bag on the stool in the corner. "A while back, Tania and I set her and Trick up on a date," she whispered. "He'd had this bad breakup and had sworn off women. It took forever to convince him to just meet her for a damn drink. They finally went on the date, but he wasn't interested. But after, she kept trying to get him interested. It was a major no-go."

"Ohhhhh."

Veronica burst into the dressing area, a mound of clothes in her arms. "I pulled some good stuff." She hung up the clothing on the hooks along one wall. "Let's start with these and figure out what fits you best and how it fits the vibe you're after."

I tried on an endless number of jeans, leather and pleather pants, blouses, and printed T-shirts. Through different combinations, we figured out my vibe. Chic biker old lady.

Over an hour later, I'd chosen a whole new wardrobe for myself. Pieces that I never would have considered while shopping back in Oklahoma in my former life. Darker, richer colors, a tighter fit. Gone were the natural tones, the airy pastels, simple skirts, and pretty blouses. Black, purple, burgundy, a slash of fuchsia or silver. Irregular outlines, off-the-shoulder pieces. Fabrics that hugged my curves. Even a bit of fringe detailing.

Jill and Veronica styled me up every which way, showing me how I could use certain pieces in formal or casual looks. "You've got an amazing body and you've got to show it off." Veronica turned me to the mirror where a new Nicole stared back in black tight pants with fringe down the outside of the legs, a low-cut, V-neck blouse that was gossamer with a see-through black bralette underneath. The blouse had cuts in the fabric down the front showing my skin. On my feet were platform sandals with criss-cross leather straps studded with metal. On my shoulder was a black suede bucket bag with silver chain detailing.

"I have the perfect necklace for this outfit back at the shop," said Jill. "I'll go grab it. Be right back."

Veronica and I confirmed our final choices, and as she rang up the pile of clothes, Jill returned with a silver double chained necklace with small medallions hanging from it as well as a long black leather cord with silver beads knotted at the ends.

"Jill, these are beautiful! You made them?"

"I started taking silver metallurgy classes last year, and this is one of my first designs. Wrap this leather cord around your neck and the beaded ends fall down your chest. Perfect." She adjusted it on me. "This is my gift to you for your new beginning here in

Meager. I know if it wasn't for the men and the women of the One-Eyed Jacks, I don't know what would have happened to me."

My eyes blurred, and I hugged her. Jill's genuine wishes filled me to bursting. Knowing that she'd survived such a trauma and had the support of everyone and was now living a beautiful life with a man who deeply loved her and their family was a true inspiration.

"We've got to get you to the salon," said Jill.

I paid the bill, and Veronica handed me the four shopping bags. "Have fun, you two."

"Thank you for everything."

Jill and I dashed over to the beauty salon up the main road two blocks, and once I got brought to a chair, Jill went back to the shop to take care of business. I texted Trick that I was getting my hair done at the salon and would be here for a couple of hours at least.

Livie, the colorist, inspected my hair. "What color were you thinking today?"

I told her.

"Perfect choice," she said. "Should be easy since you're a natural blonde. Let's do this."

Two hours later, my hair colored and trimmed into a waterfall of long layers, Jill flew through the doors of the salon and came to a halt in front of me. "Holy. Shit."

"No shit." Livie nodded her head at Jill as she hung her blowdryer back on its wall hook. "What do you think?"

"Be honest, Jill," I said.

"You look fucking amazing. Purple and pink are definitely your colors."

CHAPTER 39
TRICK

MY FINGERS CURLED TIGHTLY over my bike keys.

"Do you like it?" Nicole stood in the middle of the living room, in tight black pants with fringe on the sides of her long legs, the sexiest sandals I'd ever seen, and a see-through blouse with cut openings down her front showing skin and a black cropped camisole underneath. Sexy silver and leather jewelry draped down her chest and dangled from her ears. Her makeup was different too. Bolder, darker. She'd lined her eyes with some kind of metallic blue and black. Smudged and smoky, just-outta-bed-but-still-hungry-for-it sexy.

Fuck. Me.

But it was her hair that had my attention from the moment I saw her when she came home. Mostly purple, edged with pink. It made her blue eyes pop, and her pale skin glow even more. My old lady was a rocking dream.

"I thought, since we were going out with everyone, I wanted….um…" She shifted her weight. "Trick?"

I charged over to her and took her mouth, my hands digging into that silky hair, my tongue ravaging her. So fucking beautiful. She always was to me, from moment one. Out of breath, I kissed her forehead. "I am really, really digging this look on you." I ran my hands over the smooth leather, palming the curves of her ass. "Kinda like Sandy at the end of *Grease*, huh?" Chuckling, I gripped her ass cheeks and brought her up against my hard-on.

"I like it too. A lot." Her fingers squeezed my shoulders. "I feel beautiful, the kind of beautiful you make me feel." She licked her bottom lip, and I almost lost the last shred of my control.

I twisted her around to face the mirror on the back of the front door. "Fucking beautiful, Zip. Inside and out." I pressed my hands down her sides, over her hips, and back up across her tits and she let out a tiny gasp that had my dick twitching. I pulled her hair back over a shoulder. Soft waves of purple-pink silk. My teeth nipped at the side of her neck, and a shiver raced over her. "Say it, Nic." I palmed her tits.

"I'm beautiful." A shy smile enflamed her lips into a grin.

"Yeah. Sexy as fuck." Pressing my hips against her ass, I closed my eyes as my face sank into her scented hair.

"I'm sexy as fuck." Her body straightened in my grip, and I met her bright gaze in the mirror as she swept her arm up, a hand digging into my hair.

"You're my sexy as fuck." I slid my hand under her see-through blouse to that scrap of a bra and tweaked a nipple.

Letting out a sharp cry, she lifted her chin. "I'm your sexy as fuck."

My hand went between her legs and stroked. "I want to bury my face in your pussy so fucking bad, eat you 'til you scream, but we got to get to Pete's." Turning her around in my hold, I licked her lips. "You want my mouth on your sweet pussy tonight, Zip?"

"I want your mouth everywhere on me tonight." She brushed my lips with hers. "You want my mouth on your cock tonight, babe?"

A low chuckle rumbled in my chest, burning there. "You're killing me."

"See? You're such a good teacher."

"Teaching you how to talk dirty? What a gift."

"You have many, many gifts." She planted a kiss on my lips as her hand cupped my dick, and I sucked in air to get a hold of myself.

We locked up, got on my bike, and sped through the neighborhood to Clay Street. Nicole's arms were tight around my waist, and her body slammed against mine as we dove through the crisp night air. She felt solid on my bike and around my body. My pulse echoed the roar of my Harley's engine—thundering, loud, wild.

I parked in the back lot of Pete's alongside my brothers' bikes in our well-lit section of the lot, as we always did. Shoving my keys in my pocket, I wiped my hair back from my face, and Nicole slid her hand into mine. Our fingers threaded together, and I pressed our hands against my thigh as we made our way around the building to the front door.

I opened the door for her, and my pulse ticked up. Were we walking the red carpet, for fuck's sake? Hardly. We were in Pete's Tavern, the old bar in Meager that I'd been going to since forever. The same bar that my parents once hung out in.

But tonight it looked different, felt different.

"There they are!" shouted Jill.

"Woo! Look at you, Nicole. Fuck, you look fantastic!" Tania hooted.

Grace fluffed Nicole's hair on her shoulders. "Stunning. Gorgeous."

Laughing, I let go of Nicole's hand as the old ladies encircled her. Nicole laughed and blushed under their shower of compliments.

Why did I love it so much when she blushed? It turned me on, but it also did something to me deep inside. There was still innocence in this world, genuine emotion. And seeing her happy with the other women made my heart fucking bounce.

"Hey, man," Dawes and Dready greeted me with a cold beer bottle. Butler and Boner were here. As usual, Uncle Willy was at his favorite perch at the bar, flirting with Sara, the pretty young bartender.

A big hand gripped my shoulder, and I swiveled around. I knew that grip. "Hey."

"Bro." Lock and I shook hands, bumped fists, and hugged the way we had since we were teenagers. Lock was only a handful of years older than me, and he was the one whom I'd made friends with first at the club when Willy had brought me here. Willy even had him babysit me a couple of times when he'd go on runs with the club, or the club would have a big party.

Big mistake.

Lock had shown me the finer points of riding and had even let me ride one of his and Wreck's many bikes, which often didn't end well. I drank my first whiskey with him. Learned how to pick up girls with him. I'd always been tall for my age, so we'd passed as the same age and he'd get me into bars. We'd go to concerts together. Steal cars and bikes for joyrides together.

"Could you two stick to fixing cars and bikes instead of stealing 'em?" Willy had fumed at us after we'd caught the attention of local law enforcement. Wreck had given us his harshest silent stare. Their disappointment in us had burned deep. We stopped the illegal antics after that. Well, sort of.

After he graduated high school, Lock had gone off to serve in the army, and I finished high school and learned everything about cars and bikes from Wreck. But just before the end of Lock's second and final tour of duty, Wreck had gotten killed. Lock came back a different man and joined the club right off.

I was still in school, and we didn't hang out the way we used to anymore. Even though I worked at the repair shop on the weekends and we'd see each other frequently around the club, Lock was in another zone.

Working with him now, not only as a brother in the club, but as part of his professional team, collaborating on projects, was gratifying to me, and I know it was for him too.

A hand slid around my arm. Nicole, eyes bright, cheeks pink. Happy to be here, with me. I slung my arm around her shoulders. "Nic, this is Lock." She looked up, and her face froze for a split second into something more like shock. "Lock, this is Nicole, my old lady—"

"Miller—" Grace bulldozed into Lock. She always used his real name. Laughing, he grabbed his wife and kissed her. "Nicole, did you finally meet my old man?" said Grace, a hand at Lock's chest.

A grin pushing at her lips, Nicole only nodded, still not speaking. She was stunned. Some kind of jolt of shock and awe. "Good to meet you, Lock." Her voice was low and breathy.

"You too, Nicole. Heard a lot about you." Lock extended his hand to her, and she took it and they shook.

"I've heard a lot about you too." Nicole let out a sharp laugh. "So great to finally meet you." She let go of his hand with an uneasy laugh. Her face was flush again.

The four of us talked over the music, Nicole's gaze remaining on Lock. Boner and Jill joined us.

Nicole leaned into me. "So Lock's a member of the club, right?"

"Yeah, of course. You remember the guy I told you about who used to run the repair shop, the one who gave me my road name?"

She nodded. "Wreck."

"Lock is Wreck's little brother."

Her hand gripped my arm. "Lock is Wreck's little brother?"

"They had different dads. Their mom was this bitch who dumped Wreck's dad and then a little while later ditched Lock's dad when Lock was just a baby. She took off with another guy and left town. How do you do that? What a piece of work. Blows my mind."

"Uh-huh." Her eyes wide, she hung on my every word, working hard to listen in the crowded and very loud bar. "Did Lock grow up with Wreck?"

"No. Lock grew up on the Pine Ridge Reservation with his dad and grandma, but then she died and his dad was going through a lot of shit. Things got real tough for him. Things are real tough in general over there, but…well, anyhow." I rubbed a hand across my chin. I didn't want to tell her Lock had tried to kill himself. That was incredibly personal, and back in the day, he'd shared that with me in the strictest of confidence. I cleared my throat. "So Wreck managed to find Lock through someone he knew at the reservation, and he fucking went over there and got him. Didn't even know him, but he brought him to Meager and raised him himself."

"Wreck just went to Pine Ridge and…"

"Yeah. He had to. That was Wreck."

Her brow furrowed, and her teeth scraped her lip. "How old was Lock when Wreck brought him to Meager?"

I shrugged. "He was in high school. And fun fact: that's when he and Grace first met too."

"In high school?"

"Yep. Goes to show you, you never know where and how the twisting roads of life will lead you."

"They lead you back to Meager." The tone of her voice was spooked, and my insides tightened.

"Ladies and gentlemen!" declared the bar's manager over the speakers. "Let's give a big warm welcome to one of our favorite bands, Meager's very own, Thorns & Roses!" The whole bar burst into applause and hoots, but Nicole remained perfectly still in the frenzy bubbling around us.

My hand went to her back and I leaned into her. "Zip? Something wrong? You okay?"

Nicole's body stiffened at my question. Silence settled in the bar as the first notes of an acoustic guitar filled the space. "Everything's great," she whispered, flashing me a quick smile.

Taking a long swig from her beer bottle, her attention settled on the band.

An icy electric prickle raced over my skull and down my spine as my hand dropped from her body.

She was lying.

CHAPTER 40
NICOLE

I'D FOUND my missing brother.

It was Lock. Lock, Trick's good friend and boss, Lock, the head of Wreck's Eagle Wings. Lock, Grace's husband.

His real name was Miller. Miller.

My brother's name is Miller.

That wild ocean storm in my soul had eased. My brother was alive, he was healthy, happy, he had a family, his own business—Richie's business. He was a One-Eyed Jack. He was here in Meager.

"Nicole, have some buffalo wings, so we can start on the nachos." My heart jolted at the sound of Miller's deep voice, at the warm gleam of his big dark eyes as he pushed the basket of buffalo wings toward me.

"Thanks." Grinning, I grabbed the basket of wings, even though I didn't think I could eat to save my life right now. Trick only glanced at the basket and went back to keeping his attention on the bluesy country rock band playing. Our waitress loaded our table with two more pitchers of beer and four baskets piled high with gooey spicy nachos and everyone dug in.

"You want the Ruby Red or the regular?" asked Miller, holding a massive pitcher of the red beer.

"The Ruby Red, please."

"You got it." Lock glanced at his wife and grinned as he refilled my glass as well as hers.

"Is this a special beer for the festival?" I asked Grace.

"Yep. This is a new red ale that Pete's just debuted in honor of the Ruby Red Festival," she said. "Ruby worked here for a bit, and she got me a job here too."

"That's so cool."

"Ruby was the coolest chick ever," said Tania.

Grace laughed. "She sure was."

"Here's to Ruby!" I raised my glass.

Giving his wife a quick kiss on the cheek, Lock raised his glass of red ale, and everyone at our table did the same. "To Ruby!"

A giggle escaped my throat as I brought my beer to my mouth. His rich voice had my pulse racing. I wanted to listen to my brother's voice and learn its every nuance, every shade of meaning, to take in his gestures, his body language, learn as much as possible about him. He was a part of Richie. A part of our mother. And I wanted to be a part of him. A part of his world.

The band finished their set and the lights in the bar brightened a notch. My gaze darted around the crowded tavern. At the bar sat Lenore with Alicia. I turned to Trick. "I'm going to go say hi to Lenore and Alicia, they're sitting at the bar."

"Okay." He barely looked at me.

Something was wrong, but there would be no way to discuss it here in a loud bar with live music playing and all our friends seated around us. Pushing through the crowd, I made it to the bar. Lenore and Alicia paid their bill to the bartender, empty dishes between them.

"Hi, Lenore. Alicia."

"Nicole?" Lenore did a double-take as she put her debit card back in her wallet. "Look at you, you look amazing! I love your hair. I'm loving all of it."

"Thank you."

Alicia tilted her head. "Love what you did with your hair, babe. Suits you."

"Thanks, Alicia."

"You here with Trick and everyone?" asked Lenore

"Why don't y'all come join us at our table?"

"I can't. Got to run," said Alicia. "I'm off to meet my man at our favorite casino hotel in Deadwood."

"And I need to get going too. Finger's on his way home after a few days away, so I want to be at the house when he gets in."

"Special night planned?" I said.

"You bet. Although, every night is special." Lenore grinned. "You having fun tonight?"

"It's so great to be able to come out with everyone after being holed up at the club."

"I'll bet," murmured Alicia.

"Well, well, knock me the hell over."

The three of us turned toward the acidic voice on my side. Veronica, the owner of the clothing store where I'd shopped earlier today, gawked at us.

"Hi, Veronica. Veronica helped me pick this outfit out at her store."

"You guys made amazing choices," said Lenore.

Veronica's eyes narrowed at us, a lopsided grin slashing her face. "What's really amazing is that you two are buddies, huh?"

"Why is that?" Lenore's voice got pointed. Alicia's back straightened.

Veronica shrugged her shoulders, her eyebrows quirking as she let out a long, lazy laugh. She'd had too much to drink. "So civilized of you, Lenore, to be pals with your ex-lover's new woman. Is that a club thing?"

"W-what?" Ice razored over my skin, my insides clamped.

Lenore's eyes were steely. She didn't move a muscle. Alicia lifted her chin.

Veronica gestured at me. "You giving Cinderella here pointers?"

"Move the fuck on," Alicia hissed at her, and Veronica flinched.

The bartender placed a cocktail on the bar in front of Veronica and she gave him money and grabbed her drink. "Have a good evening, ladies." She stalked back into the crowd.

Alicia shot Lenore a look as she put her handbag strap over her shoulder. "I have to get going. Bye, my loves." Squeezing my arm, Alicia left the bar.

"Bye." My insides kept flip-flopping as my mouth attempted to release words. "You and Trick? You were together?"

"It was a long time ago. And it wasn't a relationship. We hung out."

The pieces began to fit. Trick's uncomfortableness in Nebraska when he had to ask Lenore's husband, Finger, for help. I'd realized it was some sort of personal drama, but not this. His sudden tension when he'd laid eyes on her that night.

I shifted my weight. "You're the tragic ex?"

"The *what*?"

"The ex he felt so burnt by that he hasn't wanted to consider another relationship since."

"He did take it hard, but I didn't think it was about me essentially."

"Essentially?"

"Trick wanted things I'd told him from the very beginning, I didn't have in me to give, things I wasn't interested in whatsoever. But then suddenly he had all kinds of expectations. He wanted to turn it into a committed relationship, and I didn't. He insisted, so I checked out."

My knees got wobbly. Where was I? On shaky, rocky ground. Ground I foolishly thought was filled with sweet-smelling flowers. *Fool.* "He'd told me there was someone he'd liked a lot who'd broken up with him, that it had upset him. And after that, he was done with relationships. I had no idea it was you."

"Nicole, does it matter? It's in the past. and I'm finally married to the only man I've ever loved."

"I realize that. It's not that, it's not a jealousy thing…It's…"

"Mmm." She sipped at the last of the iced water in her glass, her gaze hanging on mine. "It's a why-didn't-he-tell-me thing?"

"Yeah, that."

"Only he can answer that question." She put her empty glass on the bar top. "I know I don't want this to shadow our friendship."

"I don't either." I touched her arm. "Truly, I don't. It won't."

She covered my hand with hers. "Good, I'm glad."

"Me too." Then why was I crumpling inside?

I knew why.

If Lenore was Trick's ultimate dream woman, how could I measure up to all that she was? A woman that he'd put on a pedestal? A woman he hadn't wanted to let go of? Whose rejection still burned?

Lenore was sophisticated, edgy, assertive and self-assured, and incredibly sexy. I was nothing like her. Plus she was older, she'd probably taught him a thing or two or more, and surely, he'd found it addictive. What man wouldn't?

She was a strong, confident woman, a businesswoman, well-versed in club life, whereas I was not those things. She fit in his life. I didn't. My gut twisted. Since I'd met him, Trick had to tutor me in almost everything. Lord, how tedious it must have been for him.

The polar differences between me and Trick now seemed stark, exposed in the harsh sun. I'd never considered them much of an issue before.

And since he hadn't told me from the beginning, from that first night when we'd met up with Finger and Lenore in Nebraska, before the fake relationship even began, that could only mean he was still carrying that Lenore wound. That torch. He wasn't over her, and who could possibly compete with that? Nobody.

Right, Veronica?

Trick might be attracted to me, enjoy my company, enjoy the sex, but at the end of the day I was a temporary gig, and that made it no-strings-easy and convenient for him. Furthermore, I was still a legally married woman. Hell, I was the perfect short-term fake girlfriend with benefits for a man completely uninterested in anything more. And all that no-strings-easy sexploration had been my idea, hadn't it?

That sting in my gut rekindled and flared again. Had I been hoping for more from him? Did I want more?

Dammit, I do.

Well, too damn bad!

After all this time together, after all the good sex—at least, I thought it was good—I supposed he didn't feel that pull between us that I did?

I did feel it, didn't I? I'd been attempting to blithely ignore it all this time, but it was there. A force of nature between us, there in the laughter, riding on his bike, the deepest of hugs, the smallest of touches. The way he took my hand in his, held open a door for me. Every kiss, the gentle ones, the deep raw ones. The fierce way he looked at me when he moved inside me.

STOP.

Maybe he was only being nice to me because he had to be, was told to be, because he felt sorry for me. Me, the trapped bird he'd rescued because he was a good guy. Because our lives and his club depended on it.

Lenore squeezed my arm snapping me out of my daze. "Nicole, I'm sorry you found out like this. That was real Mean Girl of Veronica."

"I picked up on something earlier today when Jill and I were at her shop. She had a definite reaction when I mentioned that I was Trick's old lady. Jill told me they'd gone out once, but he wasn't interested."

An eyebrow perked on her forehead. "Since the tragic ex had shot him down?"

I winced. "Sorry."

She let out a soft laugh. "You have nothing to be sorry about. I have to get going. You're swinging by my store tomorrow morning so we can go over everything for the festival, right?"

"I'll be there."

She got up from her stool, adjusting her handbag on her shoulder. "Talk to him."

"It's fine. He doesn't owe me any explanations."

"Honey, you like him, and that's a good thing. He's a good person as are all the men and women of the Jacks. But Nicole—" She gripped my arm again, tighter this time, and my gaze jumped to meet her suddenly hard one. "—no matter what the circumstances are, you always owe yourself first."

CHAPTER 41
NICOLE

WHEN WE GOT HOME from Pete's, Trick headed to the
fridge and grabbed a bottle of beer. "I'm going to catch this Moto
race I taped and didn't get a chance to see yet." His tone was
brusque, and he barely glanced at me. Sucking on the bottle, he
grabbed the remote control and threw himself on the sofa.

Something was off, wrong. Had to be.

This was the first time that I felt a wall between us. And the
first night that Trick had not come to bed with me when he was
home. Every night we'd chat and spoon to fall asleep, or get
naked and fool around. Usually both. Something was up, and I
had no idea what that could be.

He'd been quiet at the bar the latter half of the night as well.
At least with me. I raced through what I might have said or done
that could have possibly upset him or made him mad. I hung my
bag and jacket on a chair. Maybe he just wanted to see the race.

I used to do this with Logan too—try to guess why he was in
a mood, why he might be annoyed with me. A foolish, draining
exercise that would leave me riddled with anxiety at the end of
it. Once I left him, it had been a huge relief to not live like that
any longer, not fear his moods with apprehension as I did almost

every morning and every night when he'd come home. It had taken a physical toll on me as well as an emotional one.

I was done with that.

"Okay. Good night." I left the living room. Even though it bothered me, now was not the time to pick at this. It was after one in the morning, he was in a mood, and I was exhausted in more ways than one. Tomorrow was another day.

In the bedroom, I took off my new clothes. The heap of them on the bed mocked me as I got into my jammies. Veronica was right. Tonight, I'd dressed up like some kind of bright-eyed Cinderella, and now it was way past midnight and the glorious magic spell was over.

The race announcer's excited voice rose from the living room. I stuffed the clothes in the dirty laundry basket and washed up.

The next morning, I woke up and Trick was gone. That was a first, too.

Letting out a heavy breath, I showered and got ready to go into town. I had a very full day and I was looking forward to it. This morning I had appointments with seven store owners, including Lenore, to confirm their preparations for the Ruby Red Festival, and then I had two classes to teach. After that, Grace and I would go over festival details at her house, and then we'd go to Eagle Wings to work at the office. And then Shannon was going to take me to The Tingle so I could lead my first stretching class for the dancers and get my first pole dancing class in. Yep, big, big day. I swallowed down the last of my coffee.

The center of town was only a ten-minute walk away from the apartment, and I looked forward to getting fresh air and sun on my way to a long, busy day. Grabbing my two backpacks, I locked the front door behind me.

Four hours later, after a morning teeming with checklists, phone calls, confirmations, re-ordering a variety of items, and so much lively conversation at over ten shops in town, I left Lenore's store with her and headed to the Meager Grand for a much-needed coffee break before my first class.

"Two tall cold brews with frothy coconut milk, please." Lenore placed our order at the front counter as I was begoggled by today's incredible variety of sweet and savory baked goods lined up row after row in the display case before us. Colorful frosted cupcakes, enormous chewy-looking cookies bursting with chocolate pieces, others with raisins, walnuts, and pistachios. Flaky small and jumbo croissants, lemon scones, and fat blueberry bran muffins. Oh my.

"Thanks for helping me out with my festival table. I knew I'd left a few things to the last minute." Lenore went down the counter to where we'd pick up our coffees.

"I'm glad I could be helpful at crunch time. Everyone's tables are going to look so good with the red banners and those table runners."

"You're enjoying your job, aren't you?"

"I am. I've gotten to meet every store owner in town. It's been loads of fun."

"Obviously, you're not the introverted type." Lenore laughed as she grabbed a bunch of napkins.

"I grew up in a small-town environment, so I like this. It feels good."

"There you go, ladies." Shelby, the barista, slid our iced coffees over the counter.

"Thanks, Shelby." I handed Lenore her coffee.

Lenore took a long sip. "Just what I needed."

"Oh yesssss," I agreed as I drank. We made our way through the crowded coffee shop toward the exit.

"Lenore, honey—" An elderly woman at a table with her friends had reached out her hand and touched Lenore's arm, stopping her. I recognized Mrs. Camden, who was seated next to her, and said hello.

Lenore put her hand on the woman's arm. "Hey, Gigi."

"How's my nightie doing?"

"It's turning out beautifully. I'm doing the final trim work now, and it will be finished the week after the festival."

"Thank you, my love."

"Of course, darling. Have you met Nicole? She's new to Meager. Nicole this is Gigi. Gigi's daughter Erica owns the Meager Grand, and one of her granddaughters, Violet, is my daughter-in-law."

"Great to meet you, Gigi." I held out my hand.

"You too, Nicole." She squeezed my hand in her strong one, her eyes squinting for a moment. "Are you the dance cardio queen? Erica and Jessa told me all about the class. They love it."

"Yes, that would be me. Next week I'll be starting a low-impact version of the class. You should join us. Starts next Thursday."

"That's the class I told you about, Gigi," said Mrs. Camden. "Nicole's very good. Come with me."

"I just might."

We chatted, and Mrs. Camden introduced me to the other ladies at her table before we left the Grand.

I slid my sunglasses back on under the glare of the afternoon light. "You have a son who's married?"

"I do. From my first marriage."

"Wonderful."

"He is wonderful," Lenore murmured.

"So you do custom pieces for clients too?"

"All the time now. When I first opened my store in Meager, it was met with a good deal of wariness and suspicion. But over time, they stopped gawking and started buying. Then a lot of ladies would come to me and ask if I could make them custom pieces of all kinds from simple to complex. Gigi wanted a simple but elegant nightgown with a matching robe in a high-quality fabric, and another customer I have wants a Victorian-style corset with all the frills."

"They're treating themselves to something they truly want."

"Exactly, and I enjoy making that wish come true for them."

"Hey, Nicole!" shouted out a familiar voice from above us.

Tim, a high schooler on the Festival team was on a tall ladder hanging banners and bunting.

"Hey Tim!" I waved up at him. "Looks great! Be careful up there." I turned to Lenore. "I've worked on a bunch of charity events before, but I've never been as excited as I am for the Ruby Red. This event is meaningful and important to the whole town, and that makes it so special. I truly felt that today."

"It is special. Every year it raises more and more money and more awareness. And it's not only a lot of fun, but brings people to Meager, and this town deserves the attention and the income. When I first moved here, it was tired and worn at the edges. Slowly but surely, it's been having a renaissance, and it's been so great to be a part of it.

"And with events like the Ruby Red and the Founders Festival and summer concerts that are now annual recurring events attracting attention, more and more people make it a point to ride through here on their tour of the Black Hills. We've gotten noticed." She sipped on her coffee, a smile forming on her lips. "You like it here in Meager a lot, don't you?"

"I do. I certainly appreciate it after my lockdown experience. Sure, it got built up in my head as the days went by, but it did not disappoint. It's more than another quaint small town. There's lots of colorful history, but most of all it's the people. Everyone is working hard together to make the festival a success. I heard so many stories about Ruby today from the people who remember her. It was very touching."

We walked another block, and Lenore stopped at the window of the pottery store. "I love Stella's work. I can't stop collecting her ceramic coffee cups and dessert dishes. The patterns she comes up with are so intriguing, and I love the way she uses color. What do you think of that green bowl in the back to the right?"

"Very bold, with that black and purple trim." I shot Lenore a grin, but my lips froze. Someone familiar caught my gaze over her shoulder. Down the block on the corner of a side street was a man in a rust-colored pickup truck. Long, black beard, that heavy round face. I'd never forget that face. My breath cut as he stared at me. Stiffening, I forced my attention back to the store window.

"What is it?" Lenore moved closer to me.

My chest caved in. "It's um…"

"Keep your eyes on the store window and find something you like." Lenore's tone was instantly firm yet hypnotically calm. "Relax your shoulders. Take a sip of your coffee. Good. What's caught your eye here in the store?"

"The..the pink vase with the blue striped handle."

"Pastel girl." She let out a laugh. "Now tell me what you saw over my shoulder."

"There's a man in a truck parked down the block behind you. I recognize him. He's a Smoking Gun."

"Look at me and give me a smile now."

I did as she told me.

"That's it, you got this." Lenore pointed at the window again. "I like that set of gold-striped teacups to the left. What do you think of them?"

I forced myself to admire the tea cups. "Cute."

"Maybe too cute for me. Look at that polka dot milk jug."

"I don't like polka dots," I breathed.

"Neither do I. Keep looking at it and describe the guy."

"Long black beard, round, heavyset face, big stomach." My mouth dried but I pushed through.

"Excellent." She tapped on the window. "Do you like that yellow teapot?"

"I'm not one for yellow as much as lilac. That one." I pointed to the lilac teapot, my hand shaking.

"That's it, Nicole. You got this. Tell me one more thing, how do you know this guy? Did he talk to you? Did he do something to you?"

"He was at the raid on my mother's house in Oklahoma. He

tortured my brother in my mother's bathroom. Cut him with this big, long knife. Dog made me look."

"Did he do anything to you?"

"No."

Lenore slung her arm around my shoulders and held me tight. We both kept our gaze on the store window, looking at nothing, seeing everything. She licked at her lip as if she were trying to figure out if the teapot would go with her decor. She was so natural and relaxed, while we were putting on a show for the man who was probably keeping tabs on me for Dog. I could only imagine what Lenore had been through as a biker wife all these years.

"Look at those turquoise dessert dishes with the dragonflies on them. Now those I love." Letting go of me, Lenore fished out her phone from her bag and with a slight smile on her face, tapped it and brought it to her ear. "Do you like them?"

"Love the colors." I cleared my throat. "Gives me those spring-summer vibes."

"Me too—keep looking at the window." She brought the phone to her ear. "Hey. Down the block toward Pete's from where I'm standing." Her voice was pure military precision. "Rust-colored truck. Heavyset man with a long black beard inside. May be a Smoking Gun, and he is checking us out. Watch him, get an ID, and get that information to the One-Eyed Jacks as soon as possible. We're heading back to my store." Tucking her phone away, she remarked with a smile, "I adore that blue glaze on the matching cups, don't you?"

"Love it." I grinned like an idiot as we both faced the store window. "Who was that on the phone?"

"I always have a Flame's prospect who keeps an eye on me here in Meager. I told him to tail our new friend and ID him with the help of our security specialist and to let the Jacks know."

"Right. Good. Should we go in the store now and pretend to shop?"

"No." She shot me another improbable grin. "We want this

guy to keep watching us and stay out in the open. Let's leisurely walk back to my store and keep window shopping as we go." She slid her arm in mine and we began our stroll.

"I have a class to teach in twenty minutes."

"I'll drop you off at FitSmash, and I'll have my prospect keep his eyes on the studio until the Jacks send someone."

"Thank you."

"Hey, Lenore. Hi, Nicole, how are you guys doing?" A woman stood in front of us on the sidewalk, and I blinked, my fingers digging into Lenore's arm.

It was Carol Anne Woodruff, who owned a small knitting shop a block down from Lenore's store. I'd conferred with her earlier today. My lips tipped up. "Hey, Carol Anne. Good to see you again."

"You too. You ready for the Ruby Red, Lenore?"

"I am now after Nicole came to my rescue," said Lenore with a grin.

"Same here. So great to have you on board this year, Nicole."

"I'm so glad." I put on my best smile, but this one was genuine. "Lenore, you have to see all the red hearts Carol Anne crocheted as a special souvenir item for the festival. They're amazing."

"Hearts, huh?" said Lenore.

"I even put them on a few mini tote bags I made. I'm addicted to hearts, always have been. I am that woman. I am not ashamed."

"Those tote bags are so cute," I said. "I need one in my life."

Carol Anne smiled at me. "Not to worry. I'll make you one after the festival."

"You're so sweet, thank you."

"Carol Anne, I did want to stop by after the Ruby Red and ask you if you'd be interested in a collaboration," Lenore said.

"With Lenore's Lace? Are you kidding me? It would be an honor." Carol Anne's back straightened. "What are you thinking of? Give me a hint."

"A crocheted halter top for the summer. Just a few unique pieces. Now that you said hearts, I'm seeing a big red heart over each boob. What do you think?"

Carol Anne's eyes popped open. "Love it. Are you free around closing today? Come over to the shop, and I'll show you what I have so you can get a better idea."

"I'll be there."

"Terrific. Girls, I have a thousand things to do before the festival, and luckily the husbot is cooking his burger casserole extraordinaire for us tonight." She let out a laugh.

"Good for you," said Lenore.

"Bye now!"

We continued our stroll down Clay Street. "Carol Anne does beautiful work," I said.

"She does. I'm so happy her store is doing well. For years, she wanted to turn her hobby into a business, and now that her husband retired and is home all day, she wanted to get out of the house."

"Mighty inspiration right there." I let out a laugh.

"And she achieved the dream."

"It's never too late to start over, is it?" I murmured.

"No, not in my book. Not ever. Speaking of which, how are things with Trick?"

"Things are…okay."

"Oh. Okay, huh?"

"Mhmm."

"Did you get a chance to talk to him about…"

"No, not yet. We got home real late, and I didn't see him this morning when I woke up."

We came to a stop at the door of FitSmash. "Here you are. You have a good class, Nicole."

"I will. Thanks for everything."

We hugged. "My prospect is down the block, and like I said, I'm sure that any moment now the Jacks will show up or be in touch at the very least. When you're done here, don't leave alone. Do. Not. You got that?"

"Got it."

"And if you need to talk, you need anything, call me. Anytime. Okay?" She smiled on purpose once more. "I'm sure it's just assholes wanting to intimidate a woman."

I smiled back, my cheeks aching. "I'm glad we were together."

"Me too."

I dashed inside of FitSmash, my entire system jammed with caffeine and adrenaline. What better way to teach two forty-minute cardio classes?

CHAPTER 42
NICOLE

"GREAT JOB, EVERYONE!" I swiveled around, faced my class, and applauded them as they applauded too.

"Thank you, Nicole."

"That was fun and kick ass at the same time."

"I didn't think I'd make it through!"

"You did great, Erica. You're getting stronger with each class." I grabbed my bottle of water from the floor and glanced at my phone screen. Five missed calls from Trick. Dang.

"Nicole? Your man is waiting for you outside," said Jessa.

"Excuse me?" My gaze shot to the studio's big front window facing Clay Street. There stood Trick, a surly Trick, his cut jaw tight, two of his fingers motioning for me to come outside. My breath cut, and, dropping my phone and water bottle at the reception desk, I darted outside. "Hey."

"Get over here," his voice growled.

As if pulled by the power of a magnet, I went to him. He grabbed me, roughly pulling me into his embrace, and took my mouth in the deepest, raunchiest kiss. Well, almost all of Trick's kisses were deep and raunchy. If not, they were gentle and sensual. He was a thorough, intense kisser, and it gave me a deep, dark thrill each and every damn time. Like right now.

My body surged against his as my arms swept up his back. I was surrounded by firm muscles. "Wow," I breathed against his lips. "Lucky me."

"I heard what happened. Had to come see you."

"Glad you did."

His warm hand caressed the side of my face. "You okay?"

"Right this very second, I'm kinda dazed and giddy, but yes, I'm okay. I was with Lenore, and she picked up on my having noticed him right off and helped me stay calm and describe him. She called her Prospect bodyguard and let him know then brought me back here. I'm so grateful I was with her and not alone."

His features remained drawn, his jaw tense as he listened.

"And the Flame stayed across the street the whole time during my class, and well, now here you are."

His hands slid to my waist. "You were okay to teach?"

"It did me good, and it went great. Everyone enjoyed it, and so did I. That playlist Shannon helped me with is top-notch."

"So you know, the Gun took off, but the Flames ID'd him. We expected them to check up on us, and it happened."

"Like you said, it was expected. We're good now." I supposed that kiss here on the street for all to see was for the benefit of the public. My hands fell away from his body.

He released his hold on me. "I got to get back to work. You have another class, right?"

"I do. Then Grace is picking me up to go to her house to go over things one last time for the festival then we're going to Eagle Wings. So, I'll see you there."

"Dready's here across the street. He'll be watching you, and he'll tail you up to her house and stay. Unless you want to cancel everything and I'll take you to the club?"

"No. I'm good."

"Okay."

"Okay."

We stood there, staring at each other for an awkward,

charged moment. He put his sunglasses on. "I got to get back to work." His voice had a crisp edge to it. He was back to that moodiness again.

"Me too. I'll see you later."

"Yep." He stalked off down Clay Street.

My heart banged against my ribs. He'd come right over to make sure I was okay, even though he was still in a mood. He'd needed to see me. To touch me. And I knew that high-octane kiss was more than a show.

I opened the door of FitSmash. That was something. That was a lot of something.

I'd take it.

CHAPTER 43
TRICK

I PUSHED OPEN the purple and black door of Lenore's Lace and spotted her at the counter by her cash register. "Hey, Lenore, you got a minute?"

She raised her head from a box she was opening. "Trick. Sure. What's up?" She took off her reading glasses and put down the box cutter. "Is Nicole okay?" She moved toward me.

"She's good. I just came from seeing her at FitSmash. I wanted to pop in and say thanks for being there for her today. I'm glad she wasn't alone."

"I'm glad she wasn't either. You don't have to thank me. She handled herself well. She's tough."

"She is. More than she thinks."

"She kept her cool and described the Gun spot on, and I called my guy and let him know right then and there. I'm assuming you got word from the Flames? They found out who he is?"

"It was Blub, Dog's Sergeant at Arms."

"Did you guys send someone to keep watch?"

"Dready's here. She has another class to teach, so he'll be on the street." I glanced out out the window to where Dready stood.

"Good. I told her to call me anytime if she—"

"Uh-huh."

"I'm glad you came over to see her. I'm sure it did her good."

"Yeah." I took a step back toward the door. "I gotta get back to work. Thanks again."

"I want to say one thing."

I stopped moving, my head slanting. "Which is?"

"It can't be easy for her to be thrown into all this. Not only being forced into the life but being in danger, especially now that she was starting to feel comfortable."

"I'm very aware."

"It's just that, I know what it's like to be taken and be thrown into a totally different and very brutal world without wanting it."

My spine straightened. "Lenore…" I'd never heard how she'd gotten into club life. It was all a blurry secret.

She continued. "I also know what it's like to lose the most important people in your life, the people you love. Don't let that happen to you, Trick. Don't let it happen to Nicole. If today has taught you anything, don't take any chances. Don't take it for granted."

My chest tightened. "What's all this about? She say something to you about us?"

"We don't talk about that. But all this time, she seemed real happy, the two of you did. I get that this situation was forced on you by extreme circumstances, but to me, the two of you seemed connected from the beginning. Today I got the impression that things are not so smooth, and it's a shame."

I blew out a breath. "We've just been having a … thing."

"A thing?"

I dragged a hand through my hair, my gaze darting to the door. "Look, I got to go."

"Trick."

"What?"

"Un-thing the thing. She's a good woman."

"You think I don't know that?"

"This is what you've always wanted, and it's what you deserve."

I grit my teeth. "Jesus, you're gonna tell me what I deserve?"

"And you know what else?"

"You're going to tell me anyway."

"She likes you, cares about you, and I can tell you're into her too. We all can."

"Terrific. All you ladies yapping about my personal life again?"

"For fuck's sake, we care about you. And you wouldn't be here right now if you didn't care about her." She remained still, calm, but her eyes blazed, pinning me there in the middle of her store. "You've never had issues with feeling your emotions, with showing them, so if you're blocking them now, stop. Don't block the very thing you've always wanted, and don't use what went down with us as an excuse to do it."

My head jerked back, and my neck tightened. "We really going to have this conversation now?"

"I wanted to hit a nerve, and I did. I like her and I like you. You're good people, and you both deserve the best. You have that in each other. Don't let it go." Her voice was firm yet full of emotion—an emotion I didn't recognize in her.

An electric current jagged through my veins. I only nodded, pressing my lips together.

She went to the door and held it open. "Thanks for coming by. Take care."

"You too." I tracked outside to my bike, the sun's harsh rays needling my eyes.

CHAPTER 44
NICOLE

GRACE HAD PICKED me up after my second class, and now in her SUV, we flew over the road leaving town and ascended a hill into the woods. Suddenly a clearing broke and the asphalt led to gravel led to a big log cabin with a newly built garage on the other side of the drive. A renovated log cabin in a secluded area of town.

I got out of the car. "Wow, what a great location, in the quiet of the big woods. This is fantastic."

"Our closest neighbor is further up the hill and his property is even bigger than ours. We're very lucky we have all this magnificent quiet to ourselves. We love it."

"I love it, too."

Shoving Trick's mood shifts and that Smoking Gun having made an appearance in Meager out of my mind, I focused instead on stirring brownie batter in a huge bowl in Grace's kitchen, which now resembled more of a chocolate battlefield than the sleek and modern kitchen that it was.

Grace stirred a second batch of brownie batter. "Thanks for helping me get all these brownies done. I completely forgot about the bake sale at Thunder's school. So much going on before the festival."

"I'm glad to help."

I asked her about Ruby, and she told me all sorts of stories about her bold sister from their childhood through their twenties. Ruby's wild times, her addictions, her determination. How she'd turned her life around and fell in love with a good man and had a son. Finally, her battle with lung cancer.

"A bone marrow donor was never found for Ruby?"

"No, and by then it was too late for her. She'd accomplished so much good in her life and was so happy and fulfilled when she got sick. Made the whole situation even worse. I would think over and over: Why is this happening to her? Why now?"

"There are never answers to those questions."

"No, there aren't. And that sort of thinking only sinks you deeper into the quicksand. The clock was ticking, and I had to do something, which is how the fundraiser started. None of us had matched for Ruby, so I wanted to widen the reach and ask the public to get tested to see if they could be possible donors, not only for Ruby but for anyone who was in need."

"This festival and all the good it does for families and for Meager is her legacy now."

"It is. I know she would have been thrilled to see how that one thing we did for her has turned into a yearly street fair in our town that not only helps medical miracles happen for families in need but is a lot of fun and does so much good for our hometown." She wiped her hands on a towel. "That's a damn fine legacy."

"And it's yours and the club's too."

We filled the two prepared pans with batter and brought them over to the large oven. Grace set the timer. "Her being sick got me to find our father who we hadn't seen in years. We reunited with him before she left us. He met her son for the first time then, and was there for him like a grandpa should. They're very close now."

"That's wonderful."

"It is." Grace took a sponge and wiped down the counter

next to me. "After my first husband got killed, I left South Dakota, and Ruby getting sick is what brought me back. Otherwise, I don't know that I would have ever come back to Meager. And where would I be now? Nowhere good, that I know for sure."

My eyes filled with water and I lowered my head over the sink, washing the bowls and spoons.

Grace put the egg carton back in the refrigerator. "Ruby's son, Jake, is coming for the festival. We're all so excited to see him again. Then he'll come back to spend most of the summer with us like he does every year. He's five years older than Thunder, so it's a lot of fun for the boys and for us."

"And loud?"

"Very loud." She laughed. "Jake's dad travels for work more often than not, so it's great to have him whenever we can. He also stays with my dad for a couple of weeks. They go fishing and camping. Sometimes Miller's dad joins them too."

I stacked the last washed mixing bowl on the rack. "Could I ask you a question?"

"Sure. Go ahead."

"Trick told me how he used to work for Wreck back in the day when Wreck ran the repair shop, so I assumed the repair shop was owned by the club, but you and Lock own it as well, right? I was wondering how it all works."

"After Wreck died, all the men pitched in and ran the shop. But when Miller and I got married, we had this idea to create a customs detailing enterprise. Miller had always done custom paint jobs for clients' motorcycles, so this was a great opportunity to level up for everyone.

"He brought our idea to the club to ramp up the repair shop and modernize it as a joint venture. The club approved it, and we and the club invested money to upgrade the facility and branch out from just auto and bike repair to custom detailing. So the club owns a stake in the business and we do too."

"I see."

"My man is a talented artist and it's fantastic to see him use that talent on all sorts of projects now and get the recognition he deserves. It's so thrilling to me to see his visions come to life."

"He's combined his talents with Wreck's. Taken his legacy somewhere new."

"He has, yes. I'm so proud of him. Wreck sure would have been."

"I'm sure he is," I murmured, as I loaded the dishwasher with the leftover odds and ends.

Would my mother be proud of her forgotten sons and all that they had accomplished? They weren't wealthy or college-educated suit-and-tie corporate types, but they had made their marks. They had achieved and improved not only their own lives but the lives of those around them for years to come. And more importantly, the people around them loved and respected them. Certainly, that was priceless. That's what family was all about.

I put the canisters of sugar and cocoa back in the pantry. "Trick loves his job. He's always telling me how happy the customers are with the results and how exciting that is for everybody."

"I get such a kick out of every reveal. Even years later, it's so satisfying each time. And for the cash register." She let out a laugh.

"My dad built up a business with a friend of his, which became very successful, but I think over time, those sorts of thrills wore off for them and for our families and turned into… something else."

"What kind of business?"

"Parts for oil pipelines."

"Oh. Big, big business."

I threw away the empty butter wrappers. "I really admire you and Lock for building a business together as well as a family."

"We love it, and we love doing it within the club. There's always been a lot of support there."

Support from your club family. Even Dog had remarked as such. I dug the toe of my boot into the floor. How unlike my experience of family. "I see that."

A car pulled up in the driveway. The kitchen screen door popped open. "Mommy!" came a shout and pounding feet. Little feet. A small boy bounced into the kitchen. Long black hair, big dark eyes. Just like his dad's. A big genuine smile. Just like his mom's.

"Whoa there!" Grace swooped him up in a hug. "You home from school already, honey?"

A teenage girl with a high ponytail and a nose ring, carrying a small Batman backpack came into the kitchen. "Hey, Mrs. Lebeau. He couldn't wait to get home today."

"Because he knows I'm baking brownies for the school bake sale, that's why."

Thunder giggled. "I want to taste, Mommy, can I?"

Grace put him down and handed him a spoon coated with melted chocolate. "I saved this for you." The little boy's face lit up as he took it.

"Thank you so much for picking him up and bringing him home, Angel."

"No problem, glad I could help. Bye, Thunder."

"Bye," Thunder said between massive licks.

My heart pounded furiously. I knew Grace had a child, but to see him now, now that I knew that he was my brother's child. My mother's grandson. My nephew. What would Cindy think if she could see me now with the grandson she didn't know she had? Would her heart melt like mine?

Speechless, I was glued to the spot as my nephew licked at the drippy chocolate spoon, his face smudged with it. He laughed as his mother ruffled his long shiny black hair. His father's hair.

"Nicole—" Grace's voice brought me back to the kitchen.

"This is my son, Thunder." The boy's dark gaze landed on me. "Honey, this is Mommy and Daddy's new friend, Nicole."

He waved at me along with a garbled, "Hi."

"Hi," I said, waving back. "Grace, when Thunder smiles, he's all you."

"Right?" She giggled, taking the spoon from him and leaving it in the sink. "But when he's serious, he's all daddy."

"I'm just like Daddy!" Thunder raised his arms and flexed them.

"Wow, look at those muscles!" I clapped my hands in applause, and he pressed his lips together on a slight grin, his face blushing.

"You keep getting bigger every day. What am I going to do with you?" Grace planted a kiss on his cheek. "Go wash up now, baby." Thunder kissed his mommy back, and stealing a glance at me, sped out of the kitchen and down the hallway.

"He's wonderful, Grace."

"He's my miracle. I lost my first baby with my first husband and had to have surgery, which left me unable to get pregnant again. But with the help of a surrogate, Miller and I had Thunder. Jill was our surrogate."

"Jill? How wonderful. That's a true blessing for all of you."

"It was. It is. Do you want kids one day?"

"I do. I…had a miscarriage last year."

"Oh, I'm so sorry."

"Thank you. I found out that I'd been pregnant after a car accident I'd been in, which had led to losing the baby. I was just over a month along, but it was through that experience and other events that I realized I couldn't be married to my husband anymore."

"You had said that you were separated. Does he know that you're here?"

"I haven't talked to him, but my mother and brother know that I'm in South Dakota, so I'm sure they've told him."

"Maybe he'd agree to the divorce if he found out about you

and Trick living together." She popped a new filter into her coffee machine and measured out ground coffee.

"There's an idea."

Grace set the buttons on the machine and it came to life. "I hope it all works out the way you want it to."

"Me too."

She took out two mugs from the cabinet. "You and Trick seem good."

I shifted my weight, my gaze going to the coffee machine. "We get along fine."

"I'm glad." She poured the coffee and handed me a mug with the Rusted Heart logo on it. "I thought we could do our festival work out on the front porch."

"Sounds great." I followed her toward the front door. Earlier we'd come in through the kitchen door so I hadn't seen the rest of the house yet.

Wood accents paired with industrial metals and neutral tones. A big sectional sofa with thick pillows sat before a stone fireplace. Green plants and original artwork accented the great room. "Your house is so cozy and uncomplicated, Grace, I love it."

"Thank you. We spent a while renovating it and enlarging it. Originally, this was Miller's brother's house."

I stopped in my tracks. "This was Wreck's house?"

"Back in the day, it was smaller, darker, piled high with all kinds of stuff. Miller did a ton of work on it over the years, and then I came along and we added a room and all sorts of goodies like the porch." Grace opened her front door and the sun poured through the house, the glare making me turn away. My breath cut at the sight of the framed poster on the wall in the entryway.

A black and white photograph, a kind of collage. Wreck on his bike, zooming on a road, and yet that road was inside a woman's chest. A woman with long hair, holding an old-fash-ioned microphone as she belted out a song on a stage. A rock singer from the early 70s?

"You like it?"

I only nodded, my lips parted. No sound came out.

"That's Wreck, and that was his woman, Isi. She was a rock singer back in the day."

"What an incredible photo."

"It was created by a local photographer who's a big deal now. Violet Lanier. She's a family friend. Her mom, Erica, owns the Meager Grand."

"Right, Jessa's sister."

"Violet's married to a rockstar you might have heard of. Beck Lanier?"

I blinked. "The guitarist for Freefall?"

"He's the one. By the way, Beck is Lenore's son from her first marriage."

"She'd mentioned her son, but I—No way!"

Grace laughed. "Yes, way."

"I met Gigi recently, Erica's mother, and Lenore mentioned… oh gosh." My eyes remained glued to the photo, the dynamism of it. Both Wreck and Isi had determined looks on their faces doing what they loved, yet connected. "Did Wreck and Isi get married? Did they live here?"

"He did buy this house for her. But unfortunately, Isi and her brother were killed in a holdup at a mini-market. It was a real tragedy for Meager. Their family owned the original general store in town for generations. In fact, Isi was Gigi's cousin."

My lower lip trembled. The newspaper article I'd found in my mother's jewelry box flashed in front of my eyes. "Did Wreck ever fall in love again?"

"Nope. Isi was it for him. He ended up getting killed a few years later."

"His one and only…" I whispered, taking in the image of the two of them, their unique energies forever joined in the photo by Violet.

"Forever and ever." Grace pointed to another black and white poster-sized photo over the fireplace in the living room. This one was splashed with dashes of red paint. "Violet did this one for us too."

It was a younger Miller, a teenager, sullen but sporting a flicker of a smile with Wreck's arm thrown over his shoulder, an old damaged motorcycle at their side. Wreck grinning, beaming at the camera. The two of them pleased and defiant all at once. Brothers. My mouth dried. *My brothers.*

Superimposed around that image from the past was a recent picture of Miller with Thunder on what was probably the same bike, only now the bike was restored.

"Both pics were taken right out front here," said Grace. "Same spot."

"Same bike?"

"That's right. Wreck had found that old Indian motorcycle, which was badly damaged, and the two of them worked on it together as their project. They never got to finish it though because, after high school, Miller went into the army and Wreck got killed before he came home. But Miller finished it with help from the guys at the shop. Willy found a lot of parts that were so hard to find. One day it'll be Thunder's bike." She took in a breath. "We named Thunder for Wreck—Richard Thunder LeBeau."

"That's beautiful." My heart twisted in my chest. "These collages are a kind of family history in vibrant images aren't they?"

"That's how I see them, and that's why I wanted them here in our home."

These photographs were so unlike our family photograph in the fussy gold frame, where we all stood in our "proper" places as commanded by the photographer. Frozen smiles, frozen poses. The happy family.

"They're remarkable, Grace. A real treasure. Violet's very talented." I finally tore my gaze away from the photograph, gritting my teeth against the cauldron of emotions simmering inside me.

I'd lost something, missed out on something, something that I'd never had in the first place. How could that be? I'd grown up with every advantage, everything a child could ever need or want, all my family intact.

And Miller? Abandoned, found, abandoned, found. But now he had his own family within a greater family. Beloved and cherished. And together they were building on their inheritance. Building on all that love.

Grace led me outside to her porch where a pillowed sofa with a quilt on one end awaited us. "You okay?"

I forced my lips into a breezy grin as I sat down next to her. "I was thinking how the power of family is truly amazing."

"It sure is. You sure you're okay?"

"I am. Better than okay." I sipped my coffee.

Grace opened her festival file folder and took out her checklist. "Let's get cracking."

I had to tell Grace and Lock and Trick and Willy the truth. How? Would I invite them over and make my announcement over cocktails and appetizers? My stomach flip-flopped at the thought of organizing a get-together for the sole purpose of presenting my true identity to them. They obviously hated my mother, a legendary villain in their story, so would they hate me too? Be suspicious of me?

No matter what, I couldn't keep it to myself any longer. Firstly, I would burst from the emotions, but secondly, they deserved to know.

Could I ever truly belong to this family? I wanted to, more than anything. Would they accept me?

Thunder appeared on the porch barefoot, holding a toy train, a shy smile forming on his lips as he caught my gaze.

Lord, I hoped so.

CHAPTER 45
NICOLE

AN HOUR LATER, Grace's father came over to play with his grandson, and Grace and I hit the Meager Grand to bring everyone at Eagle Wings a round of iced coffees and a variety of snacks.

We got to the club, and I busied myself distributing the goodies to everyone. Trick was in the middle of a major engine overhaul, and I got a quick smile and a *hey* when he came up for air from under the car.

"I got you an iced latte. There are cookies and muffins too."

"Great. Thanks." He slid back under the car.

In the office, I dealt with organizing the files Grace had left for me in a pile while she returned endless phone calls and replied to emails. Time flew by.

A dark blue pickup truck with beautiful galloping horses painted on the sides parked out front, and an older Native American man got out. A baseball cap on his head, wearing a plaid shirt, faded jeans, and cowboy boots, he moved slowly and carefully, yet he wasn't frail. There was something robust about him. Once upon a time, he'd been an active man.

Dropping the invoices on top of the filing cabinet, I went to the front window. I knew who he was. It was him, my mother's once-upon-a-time great passion, the rodeo star. Miller's father.

My pulse thumped in my neck. Grace was on the phone, explaining an order to a client. All the guys were working. Taking in a breath, I opened the door and went out toward him. "Good afternoon, sir. How can I help you today?"

He stopped and squinted at me, his face crinkling, a smirky smile slashing his weathered features. "And who are you? I'd remember you, pretty lady."

"I'm Nicole. I'm helping Grace in the office today. And your name?" I asked shamelessly.

"I'm Jason."

My heart thudded in my chest. *Jason, his name is Jason.*

"Nice to meet you, Jason. Are you Miller's dad?"

"I am." His chin lifted a degree. He was a proud dad, as he should be.

"What kind of accent is that? You're not from our parts."

"Oklahoma."

"Ah." We entered the courtyard. "I'm here to see Trick. He ordered a part for me, and I told him I'd stop by to pick it up. It's for a friend's truck."

"Great. Trick's inside. How about I take you through to him?"

"I know the way, but, heck, I'd be a fool to turn down such agreeable company."

"Well, thank you, sir." I twanged my accent up a notch. "So would I."

He chuckled, a rumbling, rough sound, which shattered into a cough. We entered the bay.

"Watch your step here—" We weaved through plastic curtains, free-standing tool kits, and old ripped-up car seats that had just been removed. On the other side of a Ford Mustang with red stripes freshly painted on her stood Trick in an old tee with cut-off sleeves, his bulky arm muscles tightening as he handled a heavy-duty tire. I'd missed those arms wrapped around me last night. I'd missed him.

"There he is—hey there, Trick!" Jason's voice boomed through the workroom.

Trick's gaze landed on us, and his jaw tightened. "Hey, Jason. How you doing?"

"Good. Stopped by to pick up that part on the way to visit with my grandson."

"Hang on, be right with you." Trick wiped his hands on a cloth.

"I met your grandson earlier today," I said.

Jason's eyes widened, a grin slashing his face, his chest puffing up. "Ah, that boy."

Trick came over to us with a package wrapped in heavy plastic. "Any problems with it, you give me a call."

"Thanks, son. I'll let you know how it goes."

Trick waved at him, his hard gaze shooting at me, pricking my chest like a pointy dart. I walked with Jason out of the bay to the courtyard. "Nice to have met you, Jason."

"You too, Nicole." He tipped a hand to his hat. Old cowboy cool.

A rumble exploded. Miller zoomed in on his motorcycle, parking next to his dad's truck. "You flirting again, Dad? Watch out, Nicole. He's a lady magnet."

"He is, huh?"

"It's my natural charm. If you got it, you got it." Jason chuckled, but a serious look remained on his face as he strode over to his son. There was something about his bearing, his gate that had me grinning. Jason had rodeo hotshot forever ingrained in his body and his spirit.

Miller slapped an arm over his dad's shoulder, and the two of them spoke as they walked toward Jason's truck. Willy arrived on his bike and he and Jason, shook hands in that biker bro way, the three of them talking.

A wall of warmth came up behind me. "You want to tell me what the hell is going on?"

I spun around. Trick towered over me, his features drawn tight, hands planted on his waist. Eyes blazing. He was angry.

"What are you talking about?"

"Since last night at Pete's when you met Lock, something's been up with you. Like you're in this daze. Blushing, tripping over yourself."

My face stung. "I'm not blushing or tripping over myself."

"Hell yeah, you are. Now you're doing the same with his dad. You trying to impress Lock? What the fuck?"

"W-what?" I stammered.

"And then you get yourself invited over to their house today. How'd that go?" He leaned in closer to me, lips snarling. "You pulling some kind of act on us all? Maybe you're as much a piece of work as you say your husband and your family are. Or maybe that's some lie you told to get us to—"

"Trick—No!"

He crossed his arms across his chest. "You saw something tastier come along, that it? Doesn't matter that he's married with a kid and his wife is your friend?" He got in my face once more, and my heart pounded in my chest up my throat.

I blinked. "No, of course not. How could you—"

"Or maybe you're just a bored rich housewife who wanted a cheap thrill ride, and I'm the sucker who believed you and helped you—in more ways than one."

"Trick, hey! Cool it." Boner grabbed his arm

Trick pulled away from him and lunged at me. "Which is it, huh?"

"I haven't lied to you. I just—"

His eyes flashed at me. "Just what? Just hot for Lock?"

"My God, no. That's not—"

"It's not WHAT?"

"It's not THAT!"

"What is it then?"

"He's…"

"He's what?"

"He's my brother!" My heart stopped as the words left my lips.

The world stopped.

Everyone froze. Everyone stared. The oxygen got sapped from the courtyard as if we were in the eye of a tornado. The glare of the sun dimmed.

Trick stumbled back as if he'd been punched. "What the hell are you talking about? That's fucking crazy."

I struggled for air, teetering. "We…"

"Jesus, it's you?" Lock's loud voice shuddered through me, and my gaze lifted to meet his stony one, his father and Willy standing behind him.

"What the hell is going on?" Trick gritted out.

"We have the same mother," muttered Lock, his eyes boring a hole through me.

"Cindy," murmured Jason.

"Yes. Cindy," my voice apologized.

"Shit, you do look like her," said Jason.

"Guymon, Oklahoma. I fucking knew it," Willy spit out.

"Willy?" Trick turned to his uncle, a plea.

"Guymon is where Wreck and Lock's mother ran off with some other guy," said Willy.

"My father." I swallowed hard past the dust clumped in my throat.

Slowly, Lock strode toward me, his gaze drilling over me from head to toe as if seeing me for the first time. "I was fifteen years old when Wreck brought me here from the rez. And I looked into his eyes…eyes the color of yours and wanted to know who our mother was. Had to know. Now that I was off the rez, I figured I could find her easy. Wreck knew where she was, he'd mentioned it—emphasis on mention—because he never talked about her.

"The idea of going to Oklahoma, seeing her for myself, had

sunk its teeth into me like a poisonous snake and wouldn't let go. I stole a car from one of the guys, didn't have a license or even a permit, and I headed out to Oklahoma to find her myself.

"The police stopped me, and Wreck tracked me down and got me out of trouble, but he didn't talk me out of seeing her. He knew I had to see for myself. So he took me to Guymon to get that poison out of my veins for good."

His cold voice seeped through my bones, and my insides shuddered. "You came? You came to Guymon?"

"We got to your house in the afternoon. Parked across the street. Cindy drove up the driveway in a red minivan. Two little blond kids hopped out."

"I was in elementary school when we had that car."

"Bright pink Barbie backpack, your pretty blond hair in a long braid. As you all headed to the front door. You and your brother in a rush to get into your nice house after a long day at school. Your brother said he was hungry and wanted pizza, and you, *Buttercup*, you were hopping on your feet and shouted out you had to pee."

Icy prickles raced over my skin, my body swayed, breath cut. "You and Richie saw us? You saw us?"

His eyes narrowed. "I saw. I saw her in a brand new life with her brand new kids in a brand new world that had nothing to do with me and Wreck, but especially me. I sure didn't fit in that pretty picture and never would."

"Son." Jason put a hand on Miller's shoulder.

My skin burned under his scorching gaze, my chest heaving for air.

"That day, I stopped dreaming of coulda-beens. That day, after seeing it with my own eyes, I finally understood what Wreck meant when he told me I had to *not* care about her anymore. And that's what I did then and there. I cut her snake poison right out of me."

"Honey?" Grace stepped outside and rushing past me, went to her husband.

"How did you find out about me?" Miller said. "She tell you?"

"She never said a word. A few weeks ago I found—I've got it inside, hold on—" I ran through the open door of the office, and in my backpack I grabbed the small cosmetic bag I carried with me everywhere and darted back outside, opening it. I handed Lock the tiny beaded bracelet, and his eyes narrowed at it. He didn't recognize it.

"I gave you that bracelet." Jason's mouth dropped open as he fingered the small beads. "Your grandma made it for you." Lock's chest expanded with a deep breath.

"Years ago I'd found it in her jewelry box and I asked her about it, and she told me it was a souvenir from South Dakota. But, now, the day I left home, I found this photo and that told me the truth. That's when I found out she had another son." I handed Jason and Lock the photo of them with Mom. "You're wearing the bracelet."

Lock's eyes widened, his jaw clenched, his knuckles whitening as he gripped the photo.

"That was my mother with another family I knew nothing about," I said. "I asked her about the two of you, but she only told me the barest of facts."

"I'll just bet." Lock's lips snarled. "We're her dirty little secret."

"You are, yes."

"Nicole!" Grace's eyes flared.

"No, baby, it's the truth." Lock lifted his chin. "And it's a relief to finally hear it said by someone who's been living that truth."

"She told me you'd gone to live with your dad at Pine Ridge. She didn't get a chance to tell me your name or anything else, because just then the Smoking Guns raided our house."

"How do you know she would have told you more?"

"I don't. She didn't want to. We knew about Richie, and that he'd gotten killed in a bar fight, but I only found out he was a

One-Eyed Jack when I discovered this that same day—" I handed him the newspaper article with Richie's photo. "She'd never told us he was a member of a motorcycle club."

Willy pointed to the picture on the yellow paper. "That was when Isi and her brother got killed."

"And all this brought you to Meager?" Lock asked.

"I wanted to find you. I needed to find you. I needed to know what happened to you. I needed to know that you were okay."

A thick eyebrow pitched on his forehead. "A fuck of a lot happened to me."

"That's why you wanted to come to South Dakota?" Trick said. "That's why you stayed?"

"I wanted Jackson out of debt to Dog, and my mother safe, but I also saw the opportunity to come here without anyone stopping me, not my husband, and especially not my mother, because she would have stopped me." I shifted my weight. "But most of all, most of all, I wanted to find my brother."

"He's buried at Rock Hills Cemetery," gritted out Lock, eyes seething.

My head slanted under the force of his cold voice, his withering look. But I clung to that gleaming gaze of his. "I wanted to find you, Miller. You. Alive or dead, I had to know. I'd missed out on Richie, she'd kept us apart on purpose. I didn't want to miss out on you too. The moment I found out about you, I had to find you."

Lock winced, the muscle along his jaw pulsing. "What do you want from us?"

"You're not my dirty little secret. You're my phenomenal surprise. A gift. And I want to get to know you and your family. Have some kind of relationship with you if you want that too." I sucked in air, and my shoulders sank. My insides sank. "But why would you? Stupid of me."

"Does she know you're here?" Jason asked.

"Yes." I wiped at my nose, at my water-filled eyes. "She's not happy about it. Not happy with me."

"She know you found me?" said Lock.

"No."

"You lying?" Trick said.

"Trick, man—" Boner clamped a hand on his shoulder.

"I'm not lying. And I'm sorry, Trick. Forgive me. I should have told you sooner, once we got to Meager, but I was being cautious. I didn't know what each day would bring, and I was afraid. Then when you made that comment about my mother—"

"Oh, that offended you, did it?"

"No. It's the truth."

His eyes widened. He didn't expect that.

"That's when I realized that things were much more complicated, more loaded than I'd expected…and that you all knew what had happened."

"Everyone in the club knows the story. We're a family," said Willy.

"Yes, you are a family, and I felt that you'd be suspicious of me, of my motives. You'd hate me too. I figured being cautious was a good idea. But mostly, I wasn't brave enough to take that chance."

"Jesus, Nicole. All this time you could've said something," Trick let out a breath, his head shaking. He was disappointed in me, and my heart sank.

"I knew Wreck had been a Jack from that newspaper clipping, so after you cut me free at the the Smoking Guns' party and you walked away, I saw the back of your jacket with the club's name…I couldn't believe my luck. Sheer, dumb, divine luck. And then you helped me, you lied for me, and put yourself and your club in danger for me. And after the longest night of my life, suddenly we were in Meager, exactly where I'd wanted to be.

"I was so excited, but I was really scared too. I'd been from one bike club to another. One lockdown to another. And then after all that, I had to pretend to be your old lady to keep us safe.

"I didn't know my brother would be in Meager, or that he

would be a One-Eyed Jack. I didn't know if he even knew Richie. I figured once our lockdown situation was over, once things settled down, I could try and find out some information on my own in Rapid or at the reservation somehow, and then I'd tell you, ask for your help."

"And this whole time, from when you came until the other day, Miller was out of town," said Grace.

"Right," I said. "I had no idea he was the man I was hoping to find." My gaze snagged on Lock's once again. "When I met you at Pete's, and then Trick told me you were Wreck's little brother, my brain exploded. I was so excited, but at the same time, I got anxious in a whole new way. Suddenly, you weren't a dream anymore, a hope. You were real. It was all real."

"I don't think about her ever." His leaden words were bullets blasting through my flesh, ripping through me. "But just looking at you now…" Lock turned his head away, and my heart lurched against my ribs. I sickened him.

"I'm sorry for the pain she caused you, and you, Jason. I'm sorry for the pain I'm causing you right now. I want you to know from the bottom of my heart, that I'm so glad that you had Richie and he had you. I'm so glad that you're happy and have a beautiful family of your own." My eyes spilled with tears, and I wiped at them. "That you are loved so well by so many."

"You didn't expect that, huh?" Lock gritted out.

"Oh, I prayed for it. I hoped."

Jason moved toward me, his face stern, and my insides tightened. He took my cold hands in his warm ones, and relief flooded through me, my shoulders sinking. "You do look like her, you know. Tall, same hair. Those eyes, just like Richie's. It's a jolt for us because you are what came after."

"Oh, Jason." More tears spilled down my face. "What came after was not necessarily better."

His forehead furrowed as his hand went to my cheek, and I leaned into his touch. "Thank you for the bracelet and the picture, Nicole. They are precious to me. Thank you for bringing them back to us. That was very thoughtful and brave."

My heart thudded in my chest and a small cry escaped my lips at his warmth, at his grace. Both his hands took mine again, his mouth lifting into a small grin, his gaze remaining on me. "Miller—" His clear and strong voice rang out like a church bell. "Isn't this remarkable? You have a sister."

CHAPTER 46
TRICK

MY MIND BLANKED. Nicole was Lock's sister?

She stood there talking with Jason, her eyes filled with tears, lips parted, trembling. I swallowed hard at the sight of her so vulnerable. Butterflied and splayed open. She and Jason hugged and he went to Lock and Grace. I moved toward Nicole.

"Nicole?" Shannon jogged up to her. "We got to get to The Tingle. You've got a class to teach…" Shannon's voice trailed off as her gaze darted around at all of us. "You okay? What the hell's going on?"

"Nothing. Let's go. I don't want to be late." Nicole wiped at her face and charged out of the courtyard toward Shannon's car.

Shannon swiveled around and shot me a glare of the what-the-fuck-did-you-do-to-her-asshole? variety, and jogged off after Nicole. The two of them zoomed off the property in Shannon's pickup truck at top speed, Nicole's purple-pink hair flying out the window.

"You okay?" Uncle Willy thumped my back.

"Nope."

"Didn't think so."

I took in a breath. "Got work to finish."

"Trick!" he called after me, but I only tracked off back to the car I'd been working on.

I spent the next hour getting everything on my to-do list done, even shit for tomorrow morning. I glanced at the clock.

My insides wrenched and twisted replaying her explanation, her confession, her discovery of Lock's existence. Lock and Jason's emotions rolled through me over and over again. A video on loop. A sting of anger whipped through my veins like a fireball. Was I angry because I thought she'd wanted to stay for me?

I'd been an obligation. I'd been fun and games. I'd been a way for her to get to Meager in the first place. And all along she'd only wanted to stay to find her brother. Now she found him. She didn't need me anymore, except for the aforementioned fun and games, of course. I slammed my tool drawer shut.

Nicole hadn't only been running away from her overbearing family but running toward the hope of a brother she'd never known even existed before that day; the day Dog and his men had invaded her life.

When she'd finally met Lock at Pete's, she'd known. I could tell something had happened for her that she wasn't sharing, but suspicious me—yeah, jealous me—had assumed she'd had the hots for the man.

And instead of trusting this woman who had become my lover, instead of attempting to be cool and put my shit aside, and asking her straight out once we got home from the bar, I'd flipped my fucking switch and gone into pissed-off mode. Here-we-go-again mode.

Idiot.

I slammed down the hood of the Mustang.

Un-thing the thing.

Lenore's words marched through my brain. In past relationships with women, I'd been emotional, open, hopeful, and that had gotten me sliced open and burned. With Nicole, I'd been doing my no-emotions-not-open-to-anything-more routine, and yet, I felt burned. What the fucking FUCK?

I liked Nicole. A hell of a lot. Dammit, who was I kidding? It was more than "like." She'd blown everything wide open. And my clinging to my idea of what I should do to protect myself was desperate bullshit.

Un-thing the thing.

Charging into the bathroom, I washed my hands and face, went to my locker, and changed. "I'm heading out!" I announced as I stalked out of Eagle Wings.

Boner lifted his chin at me. "You going to find—"

"That's right."

"Good."

I got on my bike and took off for The Tingle.

————

Ten minutes later I pulled into the parking lot of the club's strip club and went in through the back door, where one of our prospects stood guard. He stood. "Hey, Trick."

"All good?"

"Yep."

"Trick?" Cassandra, the glamorous nightclub manager, stood in the hallway in a yoga outfit.

"Hey, Cassandra."

"Kicker just left. I didn't expect to see you here today. Everything okay?"

"I came by to pick up Nicole. She done with class?"

"With her stretch class, yes. But she's taking another class right now."

"What do you mean?"

"Shannon is teaching her to use the pole."

Fuck me. "Ah. Yeah. Right."

"They're on the main stage."

"Thanks."

"You bet."

I headed down the dark hallway, past the dressing rooms and

the stock area for the bar. Music blared, a steady beat thumping through the walls and the floor as I made my way toward the doorway to the nightclub.

"You got it, that's it," shouted out Shannon, spotting Nicole on the pole centerstage. "Keep going."

My blood pumped fiercely through my veins. I slid back against the wall and watched Nicole in stripper heels, a halter top, and skimpy boy shorts slide around that pole, her innocent ponytail whipping around. One bare, long, sexy leg twisting around the other, her abs tight, her arms taut as she twirled.

My jaw tightened painfully. Hot as fuck, strong, and graceful as all hell.

If her fucking husband could see her now.

My back straightened. But there was no husband, not anymore, and I didn't give a shit that they were still legally tied to each other. This glorious woman right here, exploring a form of dance she'd always wanted to, exploring sensation and pleasure and her freedom of choice, functioning in a new-to-her world, was my fucking woman.

Mine.

And now she was connected to my family in a way that was wholly unexpected and flipping insane. A way I loved. A way that hit me so fucking deep.

Nicole was a gift. A fucking glorious gift.

Nicole landed on the stage floor and stumbled back a step. "That was crazy." She and Shannon laughed and talked.

"You did great."

Un-thing the thing.

Pushing off the wall, I charged toward the stage. My boots made a loud thudding noise on the floor, and both women's gazes shot up and landed on me.

"Hey, Trick," said Shannon, an eyebrow raised, a hand going to her hip. "What do you think? First time on the pole and she's got the basics down already."

"She looked amazing. Fucking awesome."

Shannon shifted her weight, her eyes narrowing at me, at Nicole. "Totally awesome. Um...I have to go talk to Cassandra. I'll be back in five."

Nicole's breathing remained heavy from the exercise and she only stared at me as she wiped at the sweat on her forehead. "That's okay, Shannon. I'm going to go home with Trick. Right, Trick?"

My chest swelling, I only nodded.

"You sure, Nic?" Shannon picked up her hoodie from the floor, wrapping it around her waist.

"I'm sure. Thank you, and thanks for the lesson." She gave Shannon a quick smile.

"'Kay..." Shannon eyed me and left the stage, closing the heavy stage door behind her.

"Hi," Nicole said, her voice soft.

"Hi, Zip. You looked amazing up there. Did you like it?"

"I liked it. It's real tough, but I'm going to keep practicing when I can."

"You should."

She came toward me, hips swaying in those heels, her skin shiny with sweat, her erect nipples visible in that cropped tank, and she sat down on the edge of the stage. I moved in closer to her. "Nic, I wanted to tell you that I'm sorry about the things I said to you back at the club. I was a dick, and I didn't have to be that dick."

"You were upset."

"I was upset that you'd been keeping some kind of secret from me. But you don't owe me your deep secrets."

"Trick—"

"That night at Pete's I knew something happened, something changed, I could tell, and I flat out asked you, but you denied it. So my brain went into overdrive coming up with reasons, and I got stuck in that tunnel until I exploded today."

"I'm sorry I didn't tell you I was Richie's sister." Her fingers tightened around the edge of the stage. "Do you hate me now? Does everyone hate me?"

"They don't hate you. Right now everyone's in shock. Jesus, Nic—" I said loudly, and my voice echoed through the big space. "You could have said something a zillion times over. Even from the very beginning when you said you wanted to come to South Dakota, you didn't. When you found out I was a One-Eyed Jack, you—"

"I know, but I was afraid Trick. I wasn't sure about how you or any of you would take it, and I let those moments go. Then I realized that if I found my other brother, he probably wouldn't want anything to do with me, because, like Jason said, I was what came after. After his mother abandoned him. I was the product of her new life far far away. Would he be happy to meet me? I wasn't so sure anymore.

"When I was little, I had a fantasy about meeting Richie and what that would be like, then he was gone and that was over. And then I found out there's another brother out there somewhere? I had to find him. But once I got here, all those starry-eyed expectations I had suddenly stewed into a panic in the face of reality."

"I get that. But I'd offered to help you find your mother's family in Rapid, remember that?"

"I remember, and that meant a lot to me. I'd wanted to tell you then, but then the highjacking happened, and…anyway, yes, I could have said something much sooner."

"I thought you trusted me is all. I don't want you to be afraid ever again. Not anymore. Not with me, Zip. No doubts, not ever, you hear?" My hands went to her thighs, and just touching her skin had my fingers burning, my pulse racing. My breathing ticked up as I stroked her smooth skin. "Zip…I wanna kiss you so bad."

Her back straightened, her tits jutting out. "You're just hot for what I did on the pole."

"I'm hot for *you*. Always have been."

"How about for Lenore?"

I slanted my head, my fingers stopped their stroking. "What?"

"Lenore is your tragic ex, isn't she?"

I stilled. "She told you?"

"No, Veronica told me. Last night at Pete's she saw me and Lenore together and made a snide comment about us and you."

I blew out a breath. *Motherfuck.* "Okay. It didn't seem to bother you to know that I've slept with Shannon and Lucy, so how is that different?"

"What you had with Lenore was different. She affected you down deep," said Nicole. "That night when we stopped in Nebraska, you were freaking out about having to talk to Finger. You and Dawes had a big discussion about it before we went into that bar. It sounded like there was some kind of past drama involved. And then when we went into the bar, and you saw Lenore standing there with him—"

I shrugged. "I was surprised, that's all."

"All the times we talked about your ex, you could have said it was Lenore since I knew who she was. But something stopped you. She and I have become friends, and it would have been nice to know the whole story. You obviously still have feelings for her."

"No, I don't."

"You feel something, though. Every time you talk about her, every time you see her, like when we went to her store—"

"It's not about her, dammit!"

"Then what's it about?"

"It's about me!" I wiped a hand down my mouth. "She and I were just a hookup that kept on hooking up. From the beginning, she was completely honest with me that that was all she wanted from me. But I liked us together, and I became convinced we were something more. So convinced that I knew I could change her mind, she was just lying to herself, to me. Hell, I was on top of my man game with her, doing all the things. She was just in denial.

"I was the one in denial. She kept reminding me, but I kept on keeping on. Kept believing for both of us. I thought that would be enough to get her to see it my way. To feel it the way I thought felt it. The worst part was I kept making plans in my head. For sure, she'd come around soon enough. But she never did.

"At one point, she even told me I needed to find someone my own age, someone who I could have a family with because I'd want that. But I was all nah, I don't care about that. But she was right. I did care. I've always cared because I've always wanted that. That was my dream, and fuck me, I was willing to give it up because I was so convinced she was IT.

"She didn't want my enthusiasm or my feelings, so I pretended to be cool with it, but it was a lie. I lied to myself over and over again. You think I didn't notice all the old ladies high-fiving her because she'd scored the young stud on call? You think I got off on my brothers high-fiving me because I'd scored the older woman on call? Down deep I felt pathetic."

"That's not pathetic, Trick. That's a deep desire to want something so much that you're willing to ignore anything and everything that doesn't give you the outcome you want so badly. You believe in your perfect dream so hard that—"

"It was plain stupid of me. And in the end, I became this pushy, demanding jerk. The kind of jerk that I'd never been before and never wanted to be. And she didn't deserve that. Like how I acted with you today. That was a fail, and I hate that."

"You were hurt."

I let out a dry laugh. "Finger beating me down hurt and it hammered all that pathetic right here into the core of me where it's festered." I tapped my chest, and her eyes followed the movement. "The cherry on that cake? Finger turned out to be her long-lost love of a lifetime, and right after all that shit went down, they got back together and got married. Turns out they even had a kid together years ago that he never knew about. A girl who lives nearby with her adoptive parents, and they get to see her now."

"Holy shit. You must be glad they found each other again and are happy, right?"

"I am. From what little I know it was a long, hard road for them. So hell yeah." I leaned back against the edge of the stage next to her. "One could say I was Finger's come to Jesus, and then they lived happily ever after. You're fucking welcome."

Nicole let out a snort. "I love that. For them and for you."

I dug a hand through my hair. "When I had his boot on my back, my face pressed against Lenore's living room carpet, that's when I decided I was done. I couldn't let another woman in. Fucked with me every time."

"I don't want to fuck with you, Trick."

"Oh but you want to fuck me, don't you? I am good for that. That's what it comes down to with me. Trick—good for a hot fuck. Trick—perfect filler material. Empty calories."

"That's not how I see you. Not at all."

I turned and faced her. "Oh come on, sweetheart." I grinned hard, crossing my arms. "*I'll be your special project*, remember?"

"Yeah, but—"

"I taught you loads of shit, didn't I? Got you coming every night? Coming back for more?"

Her face flushed. "But that's not—"

I raised my hand in the air to stop her. "Let me tell you a story, so you get how experienced I am in epic stupidity fails with women. My first girlfriend, back when I was around seventeen and working at the club for Wreck?"

"When you lost your family?"

"Yep, right after. She got pregnant. Did she tell me, the guy she said she loved, about it? Nope. She went and got rid of it right away, and over a month later, a whole fucking month, she happened to mention it as she was getting on my cock. She thought I'd be relieved to hear the news. I wasn't relieved, I was shocked as hell. Upset. And she got mad at me. *She got mad at me, you believe that?*

"I didn't know if I would have wanted to keep the baby. We were real young, and I barely had cash in my pocket for a night out, let alone diapers and doctors, and rent and food for three. Same for her. But we weren't some hook-up. I loved her. That was my kid too. We made him together. Shouldn't we have made that decision together? Gone through all that together? She didn't want that. She didn't need me. I didn't fucking matter."

"Trick…"

My vision blurred. My throat burned. Sailing back over my dark sea of sewage did not agree with me. "I'm just a sucker for punishment. Can't learn my goddamn lesson. Even with you, my fake old lady. Why can't I ever learn to not dive in headfirst? To not give a damn?"

She raised her chin, eyes gleaming. "But you did dive in—you cut the zip tie, didn't you? You do give a damn now, don't you?"

My lips pressed together, and my muscles shook with the effort to tamp down my goddamn emotions. "I fucking do, and that pisses me off."

Nicole launched at me, digging her fingers in my hair. The scent of her that I'd come to know so damn well, that I'd come to crave surged through me as she pressed her body against me. "I piss you off?" she whispered against my lips.

"No. You make me crazy." I crashed my mouth on hers, my tongue invading, my teeth nipping, my fingers digging into her hips, keeping her close. I wanted her closer and closer.

Her hands shoved against my chest. "But I'm temporary for you, right? I'm your filler material, your empty calories? You're no messy complications? So you being mad is an ego thing? A he-man thing?"

"What?"

Her fingertips dug into my shoulders. "This is how I see it: if Lenore is your dream woman, how can you want me?"

"There's no comparison."

"My point exactly!" She pushed at me again.

I pulled her back. "That's not what I meant!"

"What did you mean?"

"This." I took her mouth, kissing her slower, deeper, swallowing her moans. I gripped her head in my hands, keeping her close. "You are my dream woman, Zip. You. You dropped into my life and made me feel again, made me give a damn, made me high." My forehead sank against hers. "You showed me how good it could be. How real. You made me want again. Want so damn much. Want that dream again."

Her hands slid up my back. "I want that dream too, Trick."

"That's just the orgasms I give you talking."

She let out a small laugh. "Oh, those orgasms are spectacular—but I feel things with you I've never felt before, which only makes the orgasms even more spectacular." She stroked the side of my face. "I used to think all this would never come true for me, but you made it come true. You did that. You like me as I am, for who I am. That's everything to me."

My pulse thudded in my veins, and I cupped her face. "Nic, you're a fantastic woman inside and out."

A wobbly grin lifted her lips. "You respect me and you support me, and that's given me this sense of freedom, a freedom to grow, to be more me. Nothing holding me back, pinning me down, and I love it. I didn't know it could be this way."

"You deserve all that and more. "

"So do you, Trick. Can't you see that? I want to be that for you too. That trust, that support. That freedom." Her hand went to my chest and rubbed, rubbed where I'd tapped it earlier. "I want to take away that hurt and fill you up with that enthusiasm of yours."

My heart swelled at her words, at the determined look on her flushed face. I tugged on her hair, her head pulling back, and she let out a gasp. "But now you found what you came here for, you don't need me no more."

Her fingers dug into my sides. "I need you."

I rocked against her. "You need my cock."

"I do, but I feel things for you."

"You're fucking married."

"I don't care!"

"Neither do I." My lips smashed hers.

Our bodies surged against each other, furious for more. She wrapped those legs of hers around my waist and pulled me in, the hooker heels digging into my ass. My jaw tightened, my dick hardened like a rock. I slid my hand under that damned tank top and found her naked tit and squeezed. "Don't start something you can't finish, baby, because the way I'm feeling right now…"

Her tongue dove into my mouth, demanding, hunting. "Fuck me, Trick. Fuck me now."

"Here? You sure?"

She pushed me, and I stumbled back. Getting on all fours on the stage, her ass in the air, those heels catching the light, she moved like a cat in heat, humping the stage like a pro.

"What are you….what are you doing to me?"

"Showing you that I'm sure. No shame, no fear." Sitting up on her knees, she arched her back, hands in her hair, hips grinding, my dick pounding in my jeans. "You watched me dance before right?" Her pelvis rolled again as she licked her lips real slow, and a sting blew through my balls at the sight.

My mouth dried. "Yeah?" my voice croaked.

"So…" Turning around, she flicked her ponytail over her shoulder as she wiggled that perfect ass at me. "You need to tip me for having watched, don't you?"

"Tip you?" I breathed.

"Mmm." She crawled over to me on all fours. "With your cock."

The blood backed up in my veins. "Zip…"

Getting up on her knees again, she ripped off her tank top

and squeezed her bare tits together. "Fuck me, Trick. I want you to fuck me."

"Get over here," I said through gritted teeth, my pulse jamming in my veins.

Her eyes flared and, back down on her knees, tits swaying, she crawled slowly to the edge of the stage in front of me as my fingers fumbled with my damn belt, my zipper. She yanked the boy shorts down her legs, over the shoes, and spread her legs wide for me, a hand on each knee, her pink pussy glistening with juice. The sharp scent of her arousal filled my senses. "Goddamn, woman. Every time I see that pussy dripping for me, I got to eat it before I bang it."

"Do it."

Grabbing her legs, I shoved her back onto the stage as my tongue finally dipped in her wet heat. She cried out as I lashed at her plump clit, as I sucked on her. Moaning, she raised her hips, her legs now dangling over my shoulders. "Come on my tongue, Zip. Want to feel that clit throb on me." My lips suckled her clit as two of my fingers curled into her cunt and stroked. Her body shuddered and twisted. On a long loud moan, she came. Her juices flowed over my lips, my hand, down her thighs.

Undoing my jeans, I let out a grunt as my rock-hard cock finally gained its freedom. Panting, Nicole flushed and gleaming with sweat, lips swollen, propped herself up on her elbows, her legs circling my middle.

Steadying my hands on the stage on either side of her, I slammed into her and she cried out. Thrusting fast and hard, I pounded that pussy. Pounded as Nicole's heels dug into my lower back, my insides roaring, her tits bouncing.

"This fucking perfect cock..." Her fingernails dug into my shoulders.

"Fuck, I love it when you talk dirty and demanding to me." In one long, slower thrust, I drove deeper, my balls slamming against her pussy. Her head rocked back as she gasped. I pulled out long and slow, our harsh breaths mingling, our sweaty skin sliding. Her body desperately ground on mine as I slowly inched back inside her. Her cunt tightened around my shaft, and my entire body throbbed. "You fucking know what I need, don't you, Zip?"

"I know, babe, I fucking know." The gleam in her eyes, the confidence and heat in her tone, her heels scraping my flesh, and those killer legs squeezing around my middle made my heartbeat speed up even more. No doubts, no questions, only us lost in our need for each other. Nothing but sensation inside and out.

I thrust all the way. Our skin steaming, my muscles burning, my heart exploding, Nicole clawed at me, and I bit the side of her gorgeous tit.

"Trick!"

The sweetest, wildest sound I'd ever heard.

CHAPTER 47
NICOLE

"ALL DONE." The health worker at the bone marrow donor registration booth sealed the baggie with my tester swab sample inside. "Thanks for registering."

"Thank you for being here."

He picked up his tablet. "Let's hope we can save a life."

"I know we will." I put my sunglasses back on, fixed my Ruby Red Team lanyard on my chest, and took a slow walk by the tables. We were three hours into the festival and it was already crowded.

Carol Anne had a crowd of ladies around her small crocheted tote bags and change purses that had cute red hearts on them. She'd stuck to her theme of red hearts for her entire booth, which was fitting. Her husband stood at her side, packaging peoples' purchases.

Two tables down, Lenore was doing big business with her perfumed oils and body sprays as well as her new line of tobacco and rose-scented candles had made their debut at the Ruby Red. Naturally, she had a glorious display of red lingerie on display as well.

The Meager Grand Café booth, manned by Erica and her team along with her mom, Gigi, and her daughter, Jessa, were selling red cupcakes and red cookies, as well as thick slices of the most rich red velvet cake I'd ever tasted in my life. I'd tried a piece of that splendiferous cake a few days ago when I'd popped by the Grand to check on Erica's preparations for the festival.

"Well, well, well, look at you. Slumming, huh?"

My heartbeat jammed at the sound of that voice. I swiveled around, my lungs fisting in my chest. "Jackson?"

"Jesus, what the hell did you do to your hair? Is this your underground look?" He let out a bitter laugh.

"What are you doing here?"

His head jerked back. "Is that how you greet your brother who you abandoned weeks ago?"

"I didn't abandon you."

"If you were going to run away I had you pegged for L.A. or Dallas even. Not…here." He made a face. Disapproval, distaste. "Mom told me you were here."

"Did she tell you how I got here? After I paid that bounty hunter biker president all the money you owed, he wouldn't let me walk away. He took me to his club in Kansas City to keep me there, but I managed to escape."

"What I know for a fact is that you took off with those lowlifes, and Mom's diamond necklace disappeared."

"I told you, they must have taken it. They went through the house, didn't they? The necklace was thrown on the bed after you emptied the jewelry box. Remember that?"

"I want that necklace back, Nicole. I need it."

"I don't have it."

"I don't fucking believe you."

"That's too bad because that's the truth. I'm not interested in the necklace or anything of yours or Mom's."

"I was bleeding, and you took off with them. Not a word from you after."

"I'm sorry you suffered, Jackson, I am."

His lips twisted. "I need you to pay Jolene. She's been waiting, and you promised. I need you to do it right away, because—"

"I'm not paying off your little mistress. I paid off your debt to Mr. Rooney and those bikers. I saved your life and stopped them from going back to the house and hurting you and Mom again—because they threatened me with that if I didn't pay them. And I think they killed Mr. Rooney too, so they could keep all the money for themselves."

"The cops are all over that one. They found paperwork with my name on it. This is getting out, and I'm fucked."

"You involved yourself in this world, and this is how they operate. They don't make appointments through secretaries or file documents on deadline through lawyers. Or say please and thank you. People like Mr. Rooney and those bikers threaten and terrorize you until they get what they want out of you."

"That turned you on, huh?"

"What are you getting at?"

"Your husband thinks you ran off with those criminals on purpose."

"Is that what you told him?"

"Basically, it's the truth. And that's what he's telling everyone. It's bad enough you took off but like that? We can't even show our faces at the golf club."

"You can still afford the membership?"

Jackson leaned into me, his lips a snarl. "Listen to me, you spoiled brat. You are coming home with me, you hear? You're going to go back to your husband where you belong and you're going to give me that money to pay Jolene—

"And the board meeting is next week."

"Yes, it is. We need you there to vote in our favor. To show that the family is a united front."

"But we're not a united front. Have we ever been? Really?"

"Get off your high horse already. There's no time to waste."

"I'm not coming back."

"We're your family!"

I knew what family felt like now, and it wasn't what Jackson was offering.

"You're being ridiculous, Nicole. What's going on? You fucking some guy here, is that it?"

"Instead of being relieved and grateful that we survived that house raid alive and your debt was paid for you in full, you're whining. Go back to Oklahoma."

"All right, all right." Jackson shifted his weight, wiping a hand down his face. He was working hard at this. He was desperate. "I get it, Nicole. I do. You had yourself a little delayed teen rebellion, and you enjoyed it. That's great. Terrific. But now it's time for you to come home and be a grownup again."

"Listen to me, Jackson. For once, listen to what I have to say and take it seriously. I'm staying in South Dakota. I don't want to be married to Logan anymore. I barely like him, and he barely tolerates me. There's nothing there. And I am not giving you any more money. Daddy left me that money for me. If you already ate yours up, that's on you, but what's left of mine is mine. And if you and Logan don't run the company into the ground, there should be plenty more for all of us for years to come."

His jawline tightened, and his hand rubbed at the back of his neck. Was he tamping down his urge to yell and curse at me or trying to figure out what else to say to convince me?

"I've been real generous with you over the years, you know I have, and I don't expect you to pay me back for any of it. I don't. What I want is for you to leave me be and for Logan to sign off on the divorce."

"I'm in a real pickle here, Nicole. You have to come back with me." He smashed his lips together. "If you don't, I'm going to tell the police you stole Mom's necklace, you hear?" His finger pointed at me. "You up and left your family in the dust. A family who always took care of you. You took off with those bikers like some whore."

"Impressive. The minute I decide to do what I want I'm a

whore. But you and Logan? Partying, gambling, vacations with women on the sly, the drugs. That's just boys being boys, right?"

He averted his gaze. "You've broken her heart, you know that? Does that even matter to you?"

"Because she thinks I took the necklace?"

"That's one reason. But you coming out here has got her in knots, fuck knows why. She won't tell me, but she's real upset."

I lifted my chin. "I needed a big change, and the scenery here appeals to me. The evergreens, the mountains—they fill my soul."

"Seriously? You came out here for the fucking trees?"

"If Mom didn't tell you why I came out here, she's the one lying to you. It's her story to tell, not mine."

"What are you talking about? Goddammit, Nicole. I didn't come all the way out here to play guessing games with you."

"Good, because I'm done playing games and pitching in and patching up for everyone. You need to leave because I'm not going back to Oklahoma with you."

"You're abandoning us? At a time like this?"

"That's just it, Jackson. I'm not abandoning my family."

"I don't get you at all." Jackson shook his head, his lips pressed together. I'd confused him.

"That's okay. What matters is that I'm not coming with you. I'm staying here. And that's my decision to make."

He slid his sunglasses back down. "I tried, but you leave me no choice."

"What does that mean?"

Spinning on his heel, he charged away from me, bringing his phone to his ear as he stalked down a side street off Clay.

A rush of adrenaline washed through me, and I took in a breath and exhaled. Face to face, eye to eye. I hadn't folded, bowled over, or felt bad. I'd pushed off the destructive pressure Jackson had dished out and stood firm. Firm, knowing that what I wanted, what I was doing, was good for me and true to me, and what he required of me was so damn wrong.

I returned my attention to the festival, Clay Street teeming with even more people. Up ahead at Mr. Patrick's fried doughnut stall, I spotted Jill, her hands full with her baby boy, and her daughter Becca, who held Thunder's hand as they waited in line. I darted over, eager to see them. "Hey, Jill, need some backup?"

"Nicole! Thank God, yes, please."

"Hey, Thunder." I took his hand in mine. "Those doughnuts sure do look good."

"I love doughnuts," he said.

"The fresh kind, right? Not the ones wrapped in plastic in the supermarket."

"Only fresh!" he shouted out loud, and we all laughed.

Jill ordered the doughnuts, and I paid Mr. Patrick. "My treat," I insisted when Jill tried to protest.

"Everyone, say thank you to Nicole," said Jill.

"Thank you, Nicole!" Becca and Thunder's voices rang out.

"You're very welcome." I squeezed Thunder's hand in mine, and he swung our arms between us. We got the doughnuts, and I gave him his, his eyes flaring.

"Nicole, could you take Thunder back to Grace? I promised Becca we'd find her best friend, who's waiting for her up the block in the other direction."

"You bet." I turned to my nephew. "Let's go find Mommy, Thunder."

Thunder's only response was to take a monster bite of his doughnut. His face and hair were streaked with sugar, his fingers working hard to hold onto his precious sweet treat. I grabbed napkins from the dispenser in front of me and squatting down in front of him, wiped his hands and his cheeks.

This is my family now. They may never understand and that doesn't even matter. What matters is this. This.

Thunder's sugary finger poked at the side of my mouth. "That's a big smile."

"It is, huh?" I laughed. Taking his clean hand in mine, we

headed in the direction of the main Ruby Red Festival booth where Grace was working.

I kept my eye on Thunder at my side as we weaved through the thick crowd on Clay Street, around the booths selling leather accessories. I came to a halt before a breathtaking stall. My personal wonderland. "Wow, look at that." Pepper's Boot Shop's booth displayed the most colorful and dazzling array of cowboy boots I'd ever seen.

I'd been to the shop a couple of days ago and had been mesmerized by the selection. Seeing the wild variety of colors, textures, and designs out here in the sunlight made my heart sing. My fingers traced over the red flowers embroidered on the smooth leather of a chocolate brown boot.

"Mommy's favorite store," said Thunder through a mouthful of doughnut.

"Oh, honey, mine too. I have to come back here later and do some serious shopping."

Joining the flow of the crowd once again, I spotted Grace's booth up ahead. "Almost there, Thunder."

"'K."

A hand grabbed my upper arm and pulled. "Hey! What the —" My heart boomed in my chest. I stared into the dark eyes of the Smoking Gun biker who had tortured Jackson. The one I'd seen right here on Clay Street the other day. Blub.

"No!" My grip on Thunder's hand tightened, pulling him close to me.

"Don't say another word, bitch."

CHAPTER 48
NICOLE

"LET THE BOY GO."

"Shut your mouth." Blub pulled on me, dragging me with him down a side street.

I pulled back hard. "No!"

He clamped a fat hand over my mouth, his thick mustache bunching up over his mostly hidden mouth. "I swear I'll cut you and have him watch."

I nodded, and he slowly peeled his hand off my mouth. "He's just a little boy. Let him go, and I'll come with you. I won't yell. Please. He's an innocent child. Okay?"

Scowling, Blub grabbed Thunder by the arm and hauled him over to the wall of the building next to us. "Hey!" I darted over to them. "What are you doing?"

He shoved Thunder against the old brick facade, the boy shuddering like a rag doll in his grip. "You stay right here, kid. Close your eyes. Count to ten. Then you go. And you forget all about me or I'll come visit you at night, you got that?"

Thunder only stared at him, eyes wide, body frozen.

"Shut up!" I crouched before my nephew, cradling his cold face in my hands. "Thunder, look at me." His breaths came in hard and fast, the doughnut falling from his little hand, the wrapper fluttering at his side. "Look at me, honey." Finally, his gaze locked on mine, and I grinned, trying to act normal. "I have to go with this man. I know him, it's okay. But you are going to stay here and play that game first. You play it for me, okay?" The boy nodded. "Good. All you have to do is close your eyes and count to ten, and when you get to ten, you open your eyes and run back to the festival. Everyone who loves you is there, right?"

He nodded, his parted lips pale.

"Remember, Mommy's waiting for you." I swept the sugar-coated strands of dark hair back from his face. "Close your eyes now. That's it. Start counting." My voice got shaky. I brushed his forehead with a kiss. "I love you, Thunder."

My insides screwed into a tight ball as Thunder closed his eyes, his little body shaking. "One. Two..."

Blub pulled me down the street toward a pickup truck. The same truck I'd seen him in the other day.

"Why are you doing this? Where are we going?"

He checked my jeans pockets, found my cell phone and tossed it. He opened the back of the truck bed. "Get in."

One final time, I quickly glanced down the street. Thunder ran, and a piece of me ripped from my chest and flew with him. Steeling myself, I climbed into the darkness. A big hand shoved me, and my body smashed against the metal bed of the truck. He rolled the top down. "Wait!" Darkness. The stink of old plastic and dirty metal. Struggling for air, I rolled up into a ball as the truck blared to life and charged forward into the unknown.

Was he taking me to Dog? To Kansas City? I comforted myself with the knowledge that Thunder was free. Terrified, in shock, but physically unharmed and free. Would he be able to tell what happened?

Not too much later, the truck slowed down, leaving smooth asphalt and jerking and bouncing over rocky terrain. My body slammed into the left, the right. Finally, the truck came to an abrupt stop. The top rolled back, and my eyes blinked in the glare of the hard sun. "Where are we?" I blinked, shielding my eyes.

"Move." Blub pulled me out of the truck and pushed me ahead of him through trees to a clearing where there was a motorcycle parked as well as a blacked-out SUV. A familiar man stood waiting for us.

"There she is," said Dog, his arms folded across his chest. "My little runaway."

"What's going on?"

"What the fuck do you think is going on?" snarled Dog. "You got to pay for shooting Lex. You got to pay for taking off."

"I don't belong to you, Dog."

"But you belong to me, sweetheart." The blood backed up in my veins at the sound of that voice. Staring at me, that familiar smirk on his face, was my husband slamming shut the door of the SUV.

"Logan?" Icy needles razored around my heart. "What are you doing here? What the hell is going on?"

"Dog informed me you were playing house with another man. What a naughty girl you've turned out to be, Mrs. Jameson."

"Informed you? Y'all know each other?"

Logan turned to Dog. "What's his name again?"

"Trick," muttered Dog.

"Right. Trick." He let out a sharp laugh.

"What's going on? Why are you and Dog—"

"Shh." His lips a sneer as he leaned into me. "You don't get to talk."

Dog gestured at Blub, and my arms were pulled tightly behind me.

I winced at the pain. "Why are we here, like this?"

"I came all the way out to this shithole to make sure you understand what's at stake for you. I'm not playing games here. You say yes and things go smoothly for everyone. You say no, not so fun times ahead for you."

My chest tightened. "You and Jackson came here together, didn't you? He's in on this with y'all?"

"Honey, you know your brother. He didn't want to be here for the messy part. I always have to take care of the details. He insisted on talking to you first, try the nice way. Which he did, right? But you wouldn't budge, so he called in the cavalry."

"I'm not—"

"This isn't about what you want." His hand gripped tightly around my neck, and I struggled for air. "You have a vote to make, papers to sign, and my cock to suck."

"I'm not signing anything or voting your way. And your cock, as we both know, doesn't need me."

"No, it sure doesn't, but you're my wife, and you need to get back in line."

"I've been in that line for what feels like my whole damn life. I'm done."

"You're done?" His eyes flashed. "Is that what you said? Aw honey, so am I. You and your brother put me here, in this position!" He got in closer to me. "Dog and his crew raiding your house? I set that up. Your brother telling Dog you had the money to pay? I counted on him doing that, and he did, because…Jackson. Dog doing whatever it took, touching you, cutting Jackson, stealing from mommy to force you to pay up? I gave him the green light."

"You?" My brain whirled like a top spinning out of control. "How could you put our lives in danger like that? Why?"

"You were about to pay off Jackson's Lolita, right? I had to stop you. I wanted her to tell her sad story to the town and humiliate Jackson, have him investigated for taking a minor out of state to have sex with her. I even threw cash her way and she was all ready to share her sob story including photos from that trip they went on to Vegas—and they are damn good pics. The board wouldn't be able to ignore that. But if you handed her that money, I couldn't be sure she'd bend my way."

"And you'd get voted as CEO instead?"

"With you at my side, Mrs. Jameson. All the votes right there. Why should I be playing second fiddle to such a fuck up? Your father knew it too. It was a good plan, but you went and fucked it."

"I ruined your big plan?"

"You took off with the goddamn bikers who raided your house, who threatened you and your family. Who the fuck does that?" Logan bit out. "Never in a million years did I think that you, of all people, would do something insane like that."

"What a shock it must have been for you."

"You better wipe that grin off your face, sweetheart, or I'll—"

"What about Mr. Rooney? Did you have Dog kill him?"

"Someone had to take out the trash. Rooney had run out of patience and was making threats. Couldn't have that. Dog was more than happy to keep the full payout for himself. Made sense to both of us."

"Did Dog tell you he tried to keep me at his clubhouse for his personal use?"

Logan scoffed. "Come on now. You ran off with the President of the Smoking Guns. Comes with the territory, don't you think?"

My back straightened. "So I was supposed to shatter into a million pieces and be grateful my life was spared by the big bad biker over here, is that it? Then post-trauma, I'd come running back to you, and you'd be all sweet and caring and attentive—at least until the board vote, right?"

"But you fucked it up. And Dog here couldn't believe his luck that you actually paid him the full amount *and* jumped in his lap. I can't blame the man for wanting to keep you for himself, at least for a little while."

"You don't give a shit, do you?" I asked.

"I figured once he got tired of you he'd send you back to me, and then you'd be even more grateful to be home safe where you belong after such a dirty, awful escapade. You'd probably never leave the house again. But you ruined that too by taking off for

South Dakota with yet another biker. What the fuck is it with you and bikers?"

"Hey!" Dog's sharp voice cut the air between me and Logan like a knife. "This is real entertaining and all, but we don't got time for this shit."

My heart pounded up my throat at the thought of what else they might have planned. "And Jackson knew about this plan? He agreed to it?"

"Jackson had no choice. I told him I'd take care of it, and he agreed. He'd fucked up royally in more ways than one, and once again, I had to come up with a solution to clean it up or it wasn't ever going to happen. But I was done. There was no more time to waste on his promises and his bullshit. The board meeting is around the fucking corner. I need to get rid of him and you need to come to heel."

"Wow. Now I'm impressed."

"I'm so fucking over this shit. Your mother and brother freaked out that you'd taken off with Dog, and I had to hold their hands and play the pained, jilted husband. Finally, you called Mommy, and they begged you to come home because they needed you, but no, you refused. Appalling behavior." He barked out a laugh. "Then Dog tells me that you're living with this Trick, so I figured you must have been having too good of a time with him, is that it?"

"In fact, yes, I have."

He slapped me, and I stumbled, my cheek blazing with fire, throbbing with pain. Blub shoved me back in Logan's direction. Glaring at me, Logan rubbed his hands together. "This is the plan: Dog and I are taking you back to Oklahoma, where you'll be the repentant wife for the public and vote the way I need you to at the board meeting. Also, you're going to pay Dog a fat sum of cash as an apology for shooting his guy, and then you'll be all squared with him."

"Fuck that. It was self-defense."

"Oh, mouth." Logan's hand slid back up my throat once

more. "If you don't agree to that, I'm going to let him take you and do whatever he wants with you. Outlaw justice sort of thing. Sound good to you?"

My stomach flipped over, sour swirling up my throat. "That's quite a deal coming from my husband."

"I figure if anyone can liven you up, my bet's on Dog. And this handsome devil here—" he gestured at Blub "—seems like the enthusiastic type."

"I am, I really fucking am," Blub grunted.

Logan gripped my chin. "Darlin', I can't get it up for you anymore, but I'd sure be up to watch all that. *That* would fucking do it for me."

"Jesus." Dog scowled at Logan. "You two are worse than me and my ol' lady. We'll send you a video, how's that?"

"Fuck off," Logan bit out, his eyes hanging on mine. "How does that sound, honey? Next stop, Kansas City? And as a bonus, Dog will go after your Trick dick, won't you, Dog?"

"That Jack is gonna eat my shit and die," muttered Dog as Logan chuckled.

A hand from behind me dug into my shoulder. "That little boy? I don't forget a face," Blurb's voice seethed in my ear.

I twisted in his grip. "Gentlemen, that's quite a menu to choose from."

Logan's tongue swiped at his lip. "What's it going to be, Mrs. Jameson?"

"Fuck you, Mr. Jameson."

CHAPTER 49

TRICK

WHERE THE HELL WAS NICOLE?

I'd marched up and down Clay Street. We were supposed to meet here at some point today, and like an idiot, I hadn't been specific. I knew she'd be busy and on the move, so I figured I'd catch her wherever and whenever. We wouldn't miss each other on Clay Street, no matter how crowded the Ruby Red Festival became.

Something was wrong. She wasn't here.

"Hey, Trick."

"Jill, hey. You seen Nicole anywhere?"

"She was just helping me with the kids. She treated us to doughnuts at Mr. Patrick's stall."

"Where did she go?"

"She took Thunder to bring him back to Grace at the main booth up front. Everything okay?"

"Yeah, fine. I'll go meet up with her there."

She put a hand on my arm. "Can I just say something?"

"Sure."

"I think you two are great together."

"Jill—"

"I didn't say you should put a ring on it. All I said was you seem to enjoy each other, and I'm glad for you. For both of you."

My shoulders dropped, my lips curving into a grin. "Thanks."

She batted her eyelashes on a giggle. "You're welcome. Now go find your old lady."

Bumping into people as I headed down Clay to get to the first stall where Grace was, I moved to the right to let a man pushing a young woman in a wheelchair down the crowded sidewalk. Glancing down the empty street as I crossed, my feet stalled and my heart dropped a thousand feet without a parachute. A little boy with long dark hair ran toward Clay, toward me.

"Thunder?" My pulse jammed, and adrenaline heaved through me. I ran, and he flew into my arms. I lifted him, holding him tight, my hand on his chest. "You okay, buddy? You okay? What's wrong? What happened?"

"9-1-1!" he said, gulping for air, his fingers pulling on my hair. "9-1-1!" That was the emergency code his parents had taught him in case anything ever happened. Something simple and neutral that he could say without having to form words, explain, or get frustrated.

"I gotcha. You're good. You're safe." I stroked his cold face, my heart galloping in my chest. "Have you seen Nicole, bud? Where's Nicole?"

Thunder raised a shaky arm, a finger pointing down the block from where he'd come running. "9-1-1!"

Whipping out my phone, I called Lock and told him to meet me at Grace's booth ASAP, and I ran with Thunder in my arms. Up ahead Grace stood at her stall, laughing with Lenore whose stall was next to hers. Grace did a double take, her gaze snagging on us. Her head tilted, her eyes narrowed. She knew. She charged toward us and took her son from my arms without a word.

"M-Mommy." Thunder touched his mother's face. "Mommy, 9-1-1."

"Trick?" She shot me a look.

"He was with Nicole. She's gone missing. I found him running toward Clay."

"In my store, now." Lenore ushered us to her boutique which was right behind her stall.

On the small sofa, in his mother's lap, in the safety of her embrace, drinking from a water bottle Lenore put in his hands, Thunder described the guy. Big black beard and mustache, overweight.

Lenore smashed her lips together, her gaze shooting to me. She pulled me to the side, out of earshot. "This sounds like the Smoking Gun Nicole and I saw in town."

"It's Blub, their Sergeant at Arms. He wasn't just gawking the other day. They've been planning something more."

The door slammed open, ending our conversation. Finger and Lock filled the small shop.

"Daddy!"

Lock swooped up Thunder in his arms and held him hard, his face sinking in his son's neck, his back heaving. "What a brave boy you are, Thunder. My brave boy." Grace's eyes filled with tears for the very first time as she put a hand on her husband's back.

Lenore reached out for her old man, and he hooked his arm around her neck. "I got a lead on him," Finger eyed me, lifting his chin. "Let's roll."

"Go get our girl." Lenore kissed her husband and went to Grace, who fell into her arms.

I went to Thunder and rubbed his back, and he met my gaze, his head leaning on his dad's massive shoulder. Poor kid was wiped out. I brushed his hair back from his watery eyes. "Thank you, little man. You helped us so much. We're going to go bring Nicole home now."

He chewed on his lip the same way Nicole always did, and my heart screwed tight. The heart I thought would never function again. The heart I'd tried so hard to shut down. Nicole had filled it with her generosity and kindness, her genuine joy.

Her trust in me.

I couldn't lose her, not now, not like this.

Not ever.

Finger and I charged out the door.

"Hang on—" Lock handed Grace their son. "I'm coming with you."

CHAPTER 50
TRICK

LOCK and I rode alongside Finger. I'd alerted Boner, who got the rest of our brothers on their bikes, heading to the same location that Finger had outlined for me. He already had his men on their way.

We rode past the turn for our clubhouse, where the prospects stood guard, and outside the Meager town limits, past the land that I knew belonged to the Hildebrand Ranch, and finally into the Black Hills. Finger motioned for us to pull off the road at a turn at the side of the woods. Parking our bikes in a granite overhang surrounded by rock formations and a dense cluster of pine trees, we left them with Dawes and Dready and two Flames.

Finger gestured silently. He and Boner and Catch would head in one direction. Butler and Pick in another, and me and Lock to the left. The rest of our men were coming up on a hiking path on the other end of the clearing we knew was at the center. We all set our phones to vibrate only, and went off, navigating through the woods, moving quickly, watching where we stepped. My hand slid over my gun in its leather holster.

I was fucking ready.

My mind raced with the twist of possibilities. Dog wanting her back, demanding more money? Lex wanting revenge for her shooting him? Wanting to kill me? Was all this an excuse to lure the Jacks and the Flames into a war? To squash us and bring down Finger? My gut churned with liquid fire.

The whole reason she and I were together was to protect her from any Dog blowback, for fuck's sake. I'd given her my word, I'd promised her she'd be safe. My pulse hammered in my veins as we hiked through the woods. The rustle of leaves and branches in the wind overhead made a chill razor through my insides. *She has to be okay* kept looping through my brain. Okay and untouched.

I'm coming, Zip. Hang on.

The memory of her soft whispers against my skin last night after she'd come on me seared through my veins. *"Trick, Trick…."* Her fingers stroking my chest as we fell asleep wrapped around each other. Her small smile when she watched me get dressed this morning.

I blew out a huff of air. *Let her be safe.*

The growly low tones of Dog's voice had me stop in my tracks. *"Jesus, you two are worse than me and my ol' lady!"*

"Fuck off!" another man yelled. He had a Southern type of accent. Or was it Oklahoman?

Lock gestured for me to go left while he went right, both of us readying our weapons. Grabbing my phone, I messaged Boner that we could hear them. Crouching, Lock and I proceeded carefully, a clearing visible through the thinning trees ahead of us. A big SUV with tinted windows was parked next to what had to be Dog's chopper, and the truck Blub had been seen in was behind it.

There was more talk from the unknown male, and I strained to make it out, but it was barely discernible. He must have been in her face, the fuck.

"That Jack is gonna eat my shit and die," boomed Dog's voice.

Ah, was the fucker talking about me? Gritting my jaw, I pulled the safety on my gun. My phone vibrated, and meeting my gaze Lock lifted his chin. We proceeded slowly, carefully through the brush. My pulse pounded. In the distance, a guy in a navy blue polo shirt, dark jeans, and a leather jacket had his hand at Nicole's throat. Blub was behind her, holding her arms at her back. My straining muscles coiled.

"What's it going to be, Mrs. Jameson?" taunted the guy with the accent.

"Fuck you, Mr. Jameson!" Nicole's voice boomed out clear and strong.

My heart flew out of my chest at her defiance. *That's my Zip. My woman.* My phone vibrated a second time, the signal to go.

"Stop it! Stop it, Logan!" Another man jumped out of the SUV and into the fray, and I stopped in my tracks. "It doesn't have to be this way! Nicole, come on, don't make this any worse."

Logan? The fuck with his hands on her was her husband. And this one? Was he her brother, Jackson?

"Jackson! How could this get any worse?" Nicole sputtered. "The two of you colluding to kill, steal, kidnap."

"I didn't mean for it to go this far. Can't you just come home with us and do as Logan says, please, Nicole? And then this will all be over, I promise. We can all go back to the way things were."

"Fuck this!" I growled. Signaling Lock, I charged through the trees, my gun at my side, ready.

Dog's mouth dropped open at the sight of me zooming toward him. "What the—" Scowling, he drew his gun, but I fired and his gun flew out of his hand. I fired again and his shoulder jerked back.

"No!" Jackson shouted out. Another shot was fired, and his body seized and dropped to the ground. Jackson clutched at his chest, blood streaming over his hands. He'd been shot. Stumbling, Dog took off.

Logan held a gun. "So sick and tired of your fucking whining!" The fucker had shot his best friend.

"No!" Nicole's head knocked back as she was twisted around.

A long, wide silver blade glinted in the sunlight. "Move and I cut her!" shouted Blub, holding the knife at her neck.

"Trick!" Nicole cried out.

My heart leaped out of my chest, my every muscle burning at the sight of her being held. "Nic!"

Like a silent panther, Boner came up behind Blub and threw a small chain over his head. Blub jerked back, eyes wide, choking as Boner kept the pressure up. "Drop the knife!"

Flames and Jacks appeared all around us, weapons drawn. I held my arm out so they wouldn't fire.

Logan gripped his gun with both hands. "Is this your boy toy, sweetheart?" A mixture of contempt and enthusiasm was stamped on his cold, hard features.

"You the husband?" I shot him in the arm, the thigh. His body popped and jerked with each shot. I shot him in the foot. Wailing, he went flying back, and I stood over him. "Are you the husband? Answer me, dammit."

A bloodied, shaky hand lifted toward me. "I-I'm the husband."

"Not anymore." My boot stomped on his knee, and he screamed. I stomped on his thigh. "Not anymore, you piece of shit!" I kicked him, punched him, the coppery taste of blood filling my mouth. Triumph. Justice. "Piece of shit!" Smashing the barrel of my gun in the side of his face, I ground it into his cheek. "This is what you deserve, motherfucker. This! For everything you've done to her. What the fuck did you kill her brother for?"

Lock twisted around, his eyes narrowing on Jackson's crumpled body just beyond us.

"Isn't he your buddy?" I pushed.

"He's a jackass," Logan spit out blood, gasping.

"I got him. Go." Lock's voice boomed behind me and he shoved at Logan, kicking his gun away, making him turn over, face down on the ground.

Gagging and gurgling filled the air as Boner applied more pressure. Blub's head had jerked back, the chain tight around his neck. He struggled but still held onto Nicole, holding onto the knife at her throat. Jamming a booted foot on top of Blub's, Nicole twisted away from him with a roar.

She ran.

She ran to me.

I ran to her.

And our bodies crashed into each other. Like that first time. But this time, I knew down deep in my bones, in my fucking soul. I knew.

I loved her and she was mine.

"Zip. Get behind me."

Blub collapsed to the ground, and Pick and a bunch of Flames dragged him away.

A shot blasted by my side and with Nicole in my grip, I hit the ground, my body covering hers, dust filling my mouth.

"You think you're gonna put me down?" Dog's voice boomed as he charged forward, a gun in each hand, the doomed lone survivor. "You're wrong, motherfuckers!"

"Jackson!" Her voice screeched through my heart, her arm reaching out toward Jackson. We'd landed a few feet away from her brother. More shots rang in the air. She tried to get up, I pushed her back down.

"Zip, no!" I gritted out.

We had to take Dog and Blub alive. We'd all agreed earlier. Finger wanted Dog for himself, and we all needed vital information from the two of them. Another bullet rang out. Dog's body jerked to the side. Another shot, and, howling, he collapsed to his knees.

Guns raised, Catch and Finger approached him as he squirmed and twisted on the ground. Finger buried his boot into Dog's chest. "You don't get to die today, asshole. You get to pay."

I eased my grip on Nicole and she scrambled to her brother's side. "Jackson? Jackson, I'm here. I'm right here." She grabbed his bloodied hand as I pressed on the gunshot wound on his chest. Fucking blood everywhere.

"S-sorry. I'm sorry," said Jackson between shallow breaths, his glazed eyes hanging on hers. "I didn't want to hurt you. I just wanted to….to…" He stilled. He stilled in that silent way dead people do.

"Jackson!"

"Ah fuck." I sank back on my knees and wiped my face with my arm. Something flashed by. Nicole. Running, a gun in her hand. "Nic!"

"Logan!" she yelled.

Logan attempted to crawl away, but I'd left him bloodied and wounded and in a fuck of a lot of pain. He only moaned, a bloodied hand raised in the air.

Standing over him, she aimed the gun. "How could you kill Jackson? How could you? Lying piece of shit." Her body shook. "I hate you, I hate you for everything. For what you did to me when I didn't know any better. For all the years you screwed with me, for all the years….I hate you." She had to have this moment. Her words were flames from her heart.

"Don't shoot me, please, please don't. Nicole, wait. I'm sorry I—"

"You don't deserve to breathe the same air I do." She wasn't shaking or trembling now. She was cold hard steel with a purpose. She raised the gun.

I darted forward, but Lock was there before me. Slinging his left arm around her chest, his other hand around hers on the gun, he smoothly pulled her back. "Don't do it, Nic. He's not worth the bullet. Don't let him stain you forever. Let it go. Let him rot in jail." He kept moving her back inch by inch as he spoke and she finally released the gun into his hand and turned in his hold, burying her face in his chest. I took the gun from him, and his other arm wrapped around her.

A heap in the wild grasses, Logan struggled to raise his head, his face dirty and bloodied. One swollen eye lifted at me. "What are you going to do with me? Kill me? Where's Dog?" Catch kicked at him. "Shut the fuck up. It's over. You're over."

Dropping Logan's gun, I pointed to the side pocket of Catch's pants. "Gimme one, man."

Grinning, Catch handed me one of the zip ties he had sticking out of his pocket. Kicking Logan over onto his chest, Catch taunted him some more, as I crouched down and fastened a tie around Logan's wrists, pulling tight. Grunting, the fucker muttered curses and threats.

"You like that? Get used to it." My hand fisted in his hair and yanked his head up. "You're not worth the fucking bullet is right. You're nothing but dirt." I leaned down into his bloodied face. "You tried to break Nicole, but she's smarter and stronger than you ever fucking imagined." I smashed his face into the dirt.

My gaze landed on Nicole in Lock's arms, clinging to him, nodding as her brother spoke to her, a hand in her hair. He held her, reassuring her amidst the ruin and the rubble.

A smile broke over my lips, shining its warmth on my racing heart.

Family.

CHAPTER 51

TRICK

BONER, Butler, and Dawes took care of Dog's bike and Blub's truck. Finger and Kick had Dog and Blub tied up and on their knees. Time for a chit-chat.

"Don't fucking touch me, you animal! Nicole!" Blood was caked on Logan's nice clothes, in his hair, across his jaw.

"Shut the fuck up." Lock shoved at Logan, who had his hands tied behind his back, and ground his gun into the back of his head. "The police will be here in less than an hour to pick you up. Until then, you don't talk, you don't whine, you don't move."

We had an hour before Kicker would personally contact our local sheriff and let him know what happened and our location. Until then, it was time for the Jacks and the Flames to extract information from the President and Sergeant at Arms of the Smoking Guns.

Twilight had crept over the sky. Grunting and shouting, terse words, cursing filled the air. Jackson's body lay still where he'd fallen.

In the darkness, Nicole and I sat together on a boulder at the edge of the small field. Our hands were bloodied. Her tears were no more. "It breaks my heart that Jackson had agreed to go in on this horrible plot of Logan's to manipulate me. He gave him carte blanche to get the job done. He was that desperate. And he had no idea that Logan was planning his downfall the whole time."

"I'm sorry they did this to you, Zip. I'm sorry, he died. But, bottom line, they're both fuckers."

She glanced over at Lock. "The worst thing of all is that Thunder had this awful, traumatic experience because of me."

My lips brushed the side of her face. "He's okay. I'm the one who found him running down the street."

"You did?"

"Yeah. He's okay. He'll get through it. He will. Especially when he sees you're okay." I grit my teeth against the memory of finding Thunder on the street.

Bolts of lightning cracked bright chasms in the night sky, and she visibly flinched at the shocking, momentary display. "I've never seen anything like this," she murmured, taking in the dark sky continuously chiseled with light.

"Dakota storms are real unique this way. This could go on for a while with no rain or anything." Taking her hand in mine, I brought her to an overhang of rock, safe from the open field.

Thunder cracked in the distance, rumbling in the earth beneath us and she let out a small gasp. Just like the storm that hovered over Meager that morning Dawes and I left for Kansas City. Only now, rain fell, and the sound of the drops on the rock, the blades of grass, and the brush, almost seemed too loud.

She let out a small sigh. "My mother is going to be devastated."

"Of course she is. Losing a kid, no matter what age, is horrifying for a parent."

Laughter bubbled from her mouth as more thunder boomed. A burst of light jagged over her face. Ghostly bright light, harsh. We were plunged into the shadows again, and that dull throb in my chest was now more bittersweet than bitter.

Once the police arrived, once her brother's body was taken

away, once Nicole told her mother what happened, everything would change.

Would she leave Meager? Leave me? Why wouldn't she? She'd been hunted here, her brother had been killed here. Being in Meager had unleashed more pain and horror for her than one person should experience in a lifetime.

Thunder rumbled. Another boom and crack filled the air. That bittersweet sting rippled through my chest. I had to tell her. I had to. It was now or never. And never was too fucking real. Never I knew all too well.

"Nic," my voice whispered roughly. "Before I met you I was stuck somewhere I didn't want to be, but I did it to myself to stay uncomplicated and safe. And suddenly there you were, zip-tied to a fence. There you were, running for your life. You were a loud shock to my system, a jolt right through me, just like this thunder. And everything changed forever."

I touched a lock of her hair, sliding it between my fingers. "I didn't want to like you, but that was impossible. You were a force of nature by my side and in my bed. A true friend, a true lover."

Thunder boomed, and the ground beneath us vibrated. It was over us now. Her hand tightened in mine.

"You feel that, Zip? That raw and incomprehensible force of nature that reveals all the truths in its sharp cold light? In that split second fear clutches at you, and you feel it. That moment, all that might and magnificence. Baby, without you, I can't think straight. With you, I can't breathe right, my insides get all twisted up. Doesn't make any sense, but nothing's normal anymore, not that normal I thought I needed."

Thunder crackled. White bolts of light flashed, flaring over us, illuminating trees, the field. Her brother's lifeless body. Illuminating the truth. She didn't flinch, she kept her gaze on me.

"Zip, all these years I've been bumping into shit in the dark. And you were this sudden flare of light that showed the cracks in my tight little life. A light that filled the empty I kept denying, kept ignoring, and kept feeding. Storms roll through and fade away, and then everybody goes back to their lives. But I don't want us to fade, I don't want us to stop. I don't want to go back—"

"Neither do I," said Nicole. "And after today, after everything I found out, I don't know what normal is any more. It's all been ripped away. From the beginning of this crazy road I've been on, you were there to tell me it was okay. That no matter what, I was whole, I was brave. You helped me see all the awful for what it was and all the good in me. You did that."

I held her tight, burying my face in her neck. "God, I love you, Nic. I love you."

"I love you too, Trick. I love you." Crackles and loud pops exploded around us and she pulled back and smiled at me. "You saw me, you heard me, and you gave and you held me. I've never had that. I found strength in me because of you. This is my home, right here with you, Trick. I don't want to leave Meager. I don't want to leave you. Not ever." A grin lit up her face. "Kiss me. Kiss me while all this crazy whirls around us and sets itself on fire."

We kissed, we exploded, we flew. Thunder cracked and boomed, and we clung to each other, claimed each other with that kiss.

The sounds of engines filled our ears, and blue and red lights flashed over the rocks, the field. The police had arrived along with an ambulance. Sheriff Trey Owens got out of his cruiser and walked toward the dead body at the edge of the field followed by other officers and paramedics.

I pressed Nic's hand in mine and let it go. We would have to go to the station to be questioned. And then? Then we'd be free, free in a whole new way.

We'd be together.

At least, I hoped we would.

CHAPTER 52
NICOLE

AT THE MEAGER POLICE DEPARTMENT, Sheriff Owens inspected me for every flicker of emotion. For any lies I may be telling. Exhaustion had set in, but I plowed forward.

"Logan Jameson and I have been legally separated for over a year. He was furious with me for leaving him, and more recently, for refusing to go back to the marriage. Subsequently, I'd left Oklahoma without letting him know."

The club had decided that we shouldn't tell them that Trick and I were in a relationship, fake or not. It would fuel a potential theory that what went down had occurred because of some sordid love triangle and, by extension, the One-Eyed Jacks would be implicated.

"My ex-husband-to-be and my brother, Jackson Dumont, needed my signature on corporate documents and my vote in their favor at the next company board meeting, two things I was not willing to give them."

"Why's that?"

"We had differences of opinion. Ethically and business-wise. My brother was heavily in debt to several people and twice I had taken care of his debts—most recently to Dog, the president of the Smoking Guns, who was acting as a bounty hunter hired by a Mr. Rooney in Guymon to whom Jackson was in debt. Dog was so impressed by my being able to pay such a large amount of cash that he wanted more. In return for not attacking my mother or her house again, he insisted I help him bring the cash I gave him to Kansas City, but then he decided to keep me at his clubhouse, and I ran away. He'd contacted my brother after I'd paid him and told him that I hadn't paid and that he was still owed money. But that was a lie."

Something eased in my chest. It was good to tell my truth. Tell it out loud. To know that I was doing the right thing and standing up for myself. "Mr. Jameson today told me that he had arranged for the Smoking Guns to threaten my family so that I would relieve them of Mr. Rooney's debt that I had not wanted to take care of on my brother's behalf. Which would, in turn, make me grateful to Mr. Jameson and sway my vote and keep me in the marriage."

"And how and why did you end up here in Meager? Just luck of the draw hiding out in our neck of the woods?"

"My mother is from Rapid City originally, and her first son from a prior marriage had lived in this area. I've always wanted to see Meager and the Black Hills. I thought it would be a good place to lay low."

"Uh-huh." He twisted his lips as he studied me.

My pulse ticked up under his inspection, an inspection that was meant to make me uncomfortable. "This has been extremely upsetting to me, Sheriff. For the past month, I've been hounded by each of these men, and now I've learned they've all been working together to make me do what they wanted—for me to go back to being Mr. Jameson's wife, to sign, to vote, and of course, to pay more. In the end, it exploded in their faces, and my brother is dead."

Owens leaned over his desk, his hands folding. "Mr. Jameson is waiting to have a lawyer present before he shares his version of events."

"Of course."

"Will you be pressing charges against him for assault and kidnapping?"

"If he signs my divorce papers, then I might be inclined not to pursue these charges against him. I'll have to confer with my lawyer first."

He glanced at one of the many documents littering his desk. "Ah, this came in earlier today, I was going to contact you. Your diamond bracelet was recovered in Kansas City."

"Was it? Where was it found?"

"In the possession of a Mrs. Carrie Randolph. The wife of said Dog. Local law enforcement had gone over to her home to question her with a warrant to search the premises. But there it was on her wrist when she answered the door. They arrested her."

"I see."

"Will you be pressing charges for the theft?"

My mind raced with the idea that the Jacks and the Flames might want to use the threat of Carrie being sent to prison for some kind of leverage with Dog. "That's great news about my bracelet's recovery, but, again, I'd like to confer with my lawyer first."

"All righty—" The Sheriff pushed back from his desk and stood up. "If anything else comes up, I'll be in touch. Are you leaving our parts or staying? Because—"

"I'm living in Meager now."

Smirking, he led me outside his office into the front hall of the small police department. Lock, Trick, Grace, and Tania were there. Sheriff Owens's eyes narrowed at them all. "I gotta say, there is something that is sticking for me."

"What's that?" I let out a small breath and gave him my most ladylike and patient smile.

"Why would the Smoking Guns invade Meager? The One-Eyed Jacks must be the reason. Don't tell me that the Jacks weren't playing footsie with Dog's crew." He cast a dark glance at everyone.

"I wouldn't call it an invasion. It was only their President and his henchman. Dog had had an agenda where I was concerned and my husband had hired him to terrorize me and bring me back to Oklahoma."

"Be that as it may, this is the kind of shit that happens when an outlaw element thrives like a fungus in your hometown." His smirk turned deeper, sharper. His caustic statement and matching sneer were only met with silence. No one as much as let out a huff of air or rolled their eyes or shook their head or crossed their arms. Even a simmering Trick, a stony Lock, remained still. Obviously, the Sheriff enjoyed slamming the club, and they were all used to his crap and did not give in to his baiting.

"Sheriff, the One-Eyed Jacks are not responsible for bringing Dog to Meager. They have nothing to do with all of this terrible drama. This is all because of my brother, my estranged husband, and me. The One-Eyed Jacks only tried to help me and protect me."

"See, that's the thing. Why would they do that? You promise them cash too? Or maybe you asked them to get rid of your husband for you, and your brother just got in the way? I mean, why not, huh? Let the bikers do your dirty work?"

"That's not true, sir. I left Oklahoma because I wanted to be free of my husband and brother's constant manipulation and pressure. To be free of it at last. Do you know what that's like?"

"That's all fine and good, sweetheart, but—"

"Ms. Dumont."

His back stiffened. "Ms. Dumont, in my experience, outlaw motorcycle clubs only do things when it directly benefits them or for one of their own. Not just for some pretty face with a hot bod attached to it. Unless, of course, you—"

My eyes flared. "With all due respect, Sheriff, you need to watch your choice of words."

His eyes narrowed, his jaw tightened. He was done with our little dance. "Why would the One-Eyed Jacks come to your rescue?"

"Because she's my sister." Lock got in the Sheriff's face. "Nicole is family."

CHAPTER 53
NICOLE

BACK AT THE CLUBHOUSE, Tania, Lenore, and I sat together, waiting for the men to come out of the meeting room. Tania had made us coffee, and we drank silently.

Finally, they came into the central lounge where Lucy and Shannon had bottles of beer, shots of liquor, and sandwiches waiting for them. Trick came and sat on the arm of the sofa next to me, his hand cuffing the back of my neck, rubbing. Lenore handed her old man a shot of whiskey. He downed it and planted a kiss on her forehead.

"Anything you can tell us?" Lenore took the empty glass from his hand and Shannon refilled it.

"We got some information from Dog about his connection with what's left of the Calderas Group. He admitted to working one-on-one with Raptor. Raptor acted as an agent for Dog to make a business connection with Calderas so he could make extra cash that he never reported to his National. He refused to give any specifics about their bromance, but once I brought up kidnapping and human trafficking as a way to not only make cash but create a profitable underground pipeline between a cartel in El Salvador and the Smoking Guns in our country, in our territory, he blinked. Thanks to you, Nicole, I knew what to ask for."

"Good. I'm glad."

"But the fucker won't give up Raptor," Finger continued. "Won't tell us where he is. But his old lady getting arrested for stealing your bracelet has brought lots of unwanted heat and attention to his club. We can hold your pressing charges against her over his head, but either way, her arrest has blown open wide the front fucking door to his club to the law and he ain't happy. He's already feeling the squeeze. To top it off, he's under investigation for the murder of that loan shark in Oklahoma. Who knows, he'll probably point the finger at your ex for that one."

"Fun times ahead," I said. "I should have mentioned this earlier, especially as the whole Carrie thing went down with my bracelet, but that night at the Guns party, Raptor stole something from me, something he seemed enthused by, and something Carrie wanted too."

"What was it?"

"My mother's diamond necklace. I'd grabbed it before Dog got me out of my mother's house. It was a total impulse, but after he told my brother he was taking me with him to Kansas City, I thought I might be able to use it as insurance or some kind of bribe. That night at their party, Raptor found it in my bag. He could tell it was real right off. He inspected it like he knew what to look for."

Finger let out a dark laugh. "He knows his stones. Robbery was always his specialty. Jewelry was his favorite."

"But now he's stealing women," said Lenore.

"He saw it was a Tiffany necklace and he got all excited. Dog's wife wanted it, but he only laughed at her and put it in his jacket, and it was right after that she noticed the bracelet on my wrist and took it. Anyhow, that's when he stopped caring that I was older than their usual girls, and he told that tattooed gang member he was with to drug me and get me in their van."

"My God, Nicole…" murmured Tania.

"Would you be able to describe that necklace?" Finger asked.

"Sure, I would. I used to play with it when I was a little girl, pretend I was a princess." A rueful laugh escaped my lips, and Trick's hand stroked my back.

Young Nicole had sparkling, glittering hopes for her bright future.

My hand went to Trick's thigh and squeezed the hard muscle. Where I was right this minute was the complete opposite of all those girlish diamond dreams, yet I was now living the essential truth of them. Good friends, a man who was true, who truly loved me. Who respected and honored me. A man I trusted with my life and my heart. A home.

"Tania, you got a paper and pen we could use?" said Finger.

"You bet." Tania got up and went to the bar and came back with the materials requested.

Finger slid me the paper and the pen. "Write down a description of the necklace. Style type, number of stones, the type of cut, any other gems, colors, the type of clasp. Antique or new. All of it. And sketch it too."

"I'm no artist, but I'll do my best." I took the paper and pen and got to work. Who knew my impulse snatching of my mother's most precious treasure, the sparkly emblem of her success, might bring down a wanted outlaw and destroy his reign of terror?

"Whatever you can give me will be good. I'm going to get this info to a contact of mine in Chicago who I know will be able to track it. He's got reach in all sorts of very low and very high places." Lenore's hand slid around her husband's forearm and squeezed. "We'll find the necklace, and we'll find that bastard."

"Could I ask, why you want to find Raptor?" I said.

"A while back Raptor belonged to another club in Nebraska, the Broken Blades."

"You remember Pick when we got to Nebraska?" said Trick.

"Sure."

"He and Raptor were in that club together. Good friends, too," said Butler. "Then that club fell apart, and Finger made a play to patch their members into his club."

"You mean, to take them over?"

"Yeah." Finger slid his arm around Lenore, who was in his lap. "But, the Broken Blades refused and instead partnered with a Salvadoran crime group who were looking to spread their business through our territories."

"The people who Boner knew from a long time ago?"

"Right," said Butler. "And together they'd wipe us all off the map."

"Raptor is the one who'd initially brought the Calderas Group to the Blades table," said Finger. "And then he brokered a collaboration with them and the Blades with the Smoking Guns. All that to spite me, because everyone knew the Smoking Guns were not my favorite people."

"And to weaken us and make all our lives hell," said Trick.

Finger swallowed down his whiskey. "But push came to shove, and we took them all down, the Broken Blades and the Calderas Group, and we kicked the Smoking Guns back to Kansas City. We got whoever was left of the Blades to join my club, like Pick. But not Raptor. Raptor was in a rage. He didn't want any part of us and took off to parts unknown, and has been under the radar for the past couple of years since all that went down. I figured he'd partner up with the Smoking Guns eventually.

"And he did, as a nomad. I had no idea what nomad meant when I met him."

"Being a nomad kept him underground and fluid. Seems he started working with whatever was left of the Calderas group to help them revive their brand after the feds got through with them. Only this time their contraband was different than before." The muscle along his jaw tensed. Disgust and fury were obvious in the ugly curl of his lips. "Dog hasn't been the most commercially successful President of the Guns, unlike his former Prez, so working with Raptor was real important to him. By providing women and even children to this cartel, Raptor and Dog and the Calderas people were making serious bank and gearing up for their resurrection."

I shuddered, and Trick brushed his lips on my head.

Finger lifted his chin. "Thanks to you, Nicole, we learned what exactly their dirty business is, and now we might finally get our hands on that fucker and stop them. Stop it all."

CHAPTER 54
TRICK

LAST NIGHT, when we got home, she'd called her mother and told her that another of her sons had been killed. It was a mess.

After the initial shock of the news had worn off, her mother had started blaming Nicole for the chaos wrought by Logan and Jackson. I'd heard her scream phrases over the phone like, *"If only…"* and *"Why didn't you…"*

That's when I signaled Nicole to cut the call. I wasn't going to stand by and let that nasty poison flow and do its damage. No way, no more. She got off the phone, and without another word, I took her to our bed, undressed her, and held her in my arms as she cried softly and finally drifted to sleep.

This morning she'd woken up pale and exhausted and queasy. Nothing like emotional torment and ugly reality. I kissed her shoulder when she got back into bed after a trip to the bathroom. "Want me to make you feel better?" She only giggled softly. Spooning in bed, I'd stroked her clit and once she started moaning, I slid my cock inside her, making love to her, whispering how good she felt, how much she meant to me in time with my long slow strokes, and we came together.

We'd drifted off to sleep again, but fifteen minutes ago she'd woken up and called the funeral home in Oklahoma. She put her phone back down on the night table.

My arms slid around her waist from behind once more, and she let out a sigh, leaning back against me. A rush filled my veins, and my eyes closed. I liked this, feeling her weight against me, her need for me, her trust in me. The two of us united, dealing with shit together. "You're going to bring him back to Oklahoma?"

"Once his body gets released in a few days. They'll let me know." An ache spiraled in my gut. The thought of her leaving and going back to her mother. Would she try to convince her to stay? Of course, she would. Try to make her feel guilty? Absolutely. Her mother would be alone, now. Alone and bitter and sad. She might play Nicole for all it was worth. After all, Nicole was all she had left.

And hopefully, that motherfucker Logan would immediately agree to the divorce and that would happen as soon as possible.

I kissed the side of her face, as my arms tightened around her middle. "Zip, you must be exhausted. You didn't get a good night's sleep and we haven't eaten anything yet. Why don't I make us some eggs and—"

She turned in my embrace, facing me. "Babe, I want you inside me."

A short laugh burst from my mouth. "My girl is hungry for my cock, huh?"

She kissed me. "No one's ever defended me the way you did last night. Protected me. They'd only tell me to calm down, that I was imagining things."

"You deserve so much more than you ever got from any of them. Especially that husband of yours. When I saw him handling you, talking shit to you, I fucking lost it."

"You did." She licked her lips as her fingertips brushed over mine, sending a spike of electricity straight between my legs. "I liked it."

"I'm not sorry for any of it, Zip."

"I don't want you to be."

"Good. He deserves to be in the ground."

"It made me high to see you go apeshit on Dog, on Logan. To hear what you said to them."

"I meant every fucking word."

"That's the thing, Trick. I knew you meant it, and that made me love you even more." "Huge thrill." Her lips pressed against mine, her tongue invaded, claimed. Her teeth nipped at my lip.

My chest tightened. "A thrill, huh?"

"Mmm. I want to show you how much you mean to me. I need to show you." Her warm hand slid down my abs and cupped my balls. I winced, a grunt escaping my throat. I was so hard for her, so hungry for her touch that it was fucking painful. So hard for the words coming out of her sweet mouth. "Ah, shit," I groaned.

She stroked my rock-hard length. "Nothing and no one is hanging over us. Not anymore." Her hand tightened over my hard shaft and stroked, and pulled. Everything pulsated, everything went blurry. Pushing away the bedcovers, she got between my legs, and her lips found my dick. "You're so hard for me."

A guttural sound escaped my throat at the sight of her licking me, hair hanging, tits swaying. "I'm always fucking hard for you, Zip."

My cock slid out of her mouth. "I want to fuck you to celebrate us."

I let out a groan. "Say that again."

Her cheeks reddened as her tongue padded my engorged tip. "I want to fuck you to celebrate. We're alive, we're together."

"Fuck me, Zip."

With a grin on her face, she sat up over me and guided my wet, throbbing cock inside her slick cunt. My fingers dug into her hips, my every muscle straining. "Ah, shit..." She rocked her pelvis and I thrust inside her, filling her completely. "Jesus, Nic." Her head knocked back and I filled my hand with a tit and kneaded, twisted. "You feel it?" I thrust again.

"I feel you, Trick." Her hands covering mine on her breasts, she ground down on me, taking over and bringing us into a quicker rhythm. Needy, hungry. Intent. Gone was the unsure and insecure woman. Gone were the doubts and second-guessing.

Our bodies slapped together, her hips rolling, our flesh slick with sweat, heavy with need. Nicole was chasing me, chasing with me.

"Zip…" I groaned, my fingers rubbing her swollen clit.

She cried out loudly, her gorgeous tits jiggling. Flipping her on her back, my grip burning into her flesh, I pounded into her. My woman chanted my name as our backboard banged against the wall.

Nicole was mine, all mine. Always.

"I fucking love you, Zip. Love you."

"Trick…" She let out a long loud cry as she came.

CHAPTER 55
NICOLE

ROCK HILLS CEMETERY was a beautiful graveyard on a gently sloping hill at the edge of Meager.

A black iron gate towered at the entrance, and surrounding the cemetery was an old stone wall that looked as if it had been built by hand, a piece from another age.

I got off the back of Trick's bike, handed him my helmet, put on my sunglasses, and took in a deep breath. The air was cooler today, and that unique fragrance of the Ponderosa pine and the wild grasses…even the clover seemed sweeter up here. If I could bottle that scent, I would. It was a homecoming to me, a new, gleaming world. My world,

My man slung an arm around my neck, pulling me close, his lips brushing my cheek. "You okay?"

"I am." I rested a hand on his chest.

He took the flowers we'd bought and handed them to me.

I was set to leave for Oklahoma tomorrow morning. All the arrangements had been confirmed with the funeral home in Guymon to pick up the coffin from the airport. The funeral would be in three days. The thought of the viewing, all the people, the service, the burial. All the condolences and sentiments. My mother…But I wouldn't think of all that now. Tomorrow was another day for other sorrows.

Today was the date stamped on Trick's chest, and together with our family, we would make this day a celebration and remembrance, and, most of all, healing.

Trick led me up the hill, over a narrow pathway which brought us to a field of tombstones. I wrapped my free hand around his arm.

He let out a long sigh. "I haven't been here in a long, long time. It was just too hard. I liked knowing they were here, close by, but it's good to come."

"Yes, baby, it is."

He brought us to a stop in front of a simple tombstone.

WATTS

Terrence & Delilah & Brie
Beloved Parents & Sister

"So Watts is your last name?"

"Yes, ma'am."

"Holy cow, I don't even know your first name! That's nuts."

He chuckled. "Cooper Watts, pleased to meet you, Nicole Dumont." He bent down and brushed my lips with a kiss as we laughed.

I cupped the side of his face. "Hi Cooper, my love."

Uncle Willy arrived. He and Trick hugged, and he hugged me too. I laid half of the white roses on the grass before the stone marker.

"I used to tell my sister she talked too much," muttered Willy.

"Ma did love to talk and discuss. She never told you a simple story about who she saw at the market, let's say. She'd always tell it like it was the most intriguing tale. She'd fill you in on every detail—how they looked, what they were wearing, their facial expressions, even the weather."

"Exactly." Willy cleared his throat. "You have no idea how much I fucking miss the way she'd tell a story."

"I do, Willy, I do," murmured Trick as I slid my arm through Willy's, his hand covering mine.

I said a prayer for the souls of Terrence, Delilah, and Brie. For the ones they'd left behind, my new family. *I promise I will do everything to care for Trick and Willy, to love them both.*

Leaning over, Trick touched the engraving of his family's name in the granite. Willy turned to the left. "They're here."

Down another path stood Lock, Jason, holding Thunder's hand, and Grace, holding her nephew Jake's. They stopped at a tombstone a few yards away.

Trick reached out his hand for me, and I took it. With Willy leading the way, we went over to the LeBeaus. We greeted each other with hugs.

"We stopped at Ruby's, and Jake brought his mom flowers," Grace squeezed Jake's shoulder.

"Red roses," said the boy.

"Beautiful," I murmured.

"Hi, Aunt Nicole."

I crouched down and Thunder gave me a tight hug, and I hugged him right back and gave him a kiss on the cheek. "Hi, Thunder," I whispered back. The boy moved, and my breath cut.

Richard "WRECK" Tallin
Ride Hard & Ride Free Forever

Finally.

My heart pounded in my chest as I placed the white roses in the grass. My fingers traced over my eldest brother's name.

I'm sorry we missed out on each other, Richie.

I wanted to meet you so much, to get to know you, to laugh with you. To understand you. You saw me, though, didn't you? You came to Oklahoma. I'm so sorry I never came to you.

I'm here now, and I'm staying. I love Trick. Miller is beautiful.

Grace and Thunder are beautiful. You made our family possible. And our family is growing.

I love you, Richie. Can you hear me? I hope you can hear me. Can you?

A small hand slid over my shoulder, and I glanced over. Lock's beaded baby bracelet was on his little wrist. Thunder smiled at me. I hugged him, nestling my face in his neck, and he giggled, and I giggled too. *I love you, Richie. I love you.*

Rustling and movement rose behind us, murmurs. Jason grabbed Thunder, his hands over the boy's chest as he pressed him back against his body. He was protecting him. Something in my chest pinched and standing up, I turned around.

"Nicole."

It can't be. "Mom?"

Cindy stood in the distance, her short blonde hair freshly blown out, wearing one of her favorite pantsuits with a thin beige overcoat.

"You're fucking kidding me," muttered Willy.

Grace slid a hand around her husband's arm as she pressed against his body. Lock was a stone, his brow furrowed, jaw tight.

Holding her stern gaze, I walked toward her. "Why are you here?"

She visibly stiffened. "I wasn't sure you'd come back with Jackson, so I came to bring my son home. And I came here to see —" Her cool gaze darted to everyone around me. Her eyes widened.

"Who's that, Grandpa?" Thunder's voice rose behind me, and her eyebrows shot up.

"Mom."

She blinked, her attention thankfully returning to me. "Is that…that's…"

"You need to go."

"I want to see Richie."

"You can't be here now." I remained calm on the outside as I winced inside. Two sons gone violently, and one other son whom she could never have, would never know. And a grandson.

"Nicole?" Her voice had gone fragile.

"Mom, please."

"You're taking their side against me?"

"There are no sides here. There is, however, a divide, and I'm respecting it. You have to respect it too. You, above all."

Her shoulders stiffened. Oh, she was strong, she was tough, no matter the circumstances, and I had to admire her for it. "You're coming home with me and Jackson, aren't you? I'll be alone now. I…I…"

"I'm bringing Jackson to Oklahoma, and after the funeral, I'm coming back to Meager. This is my home now."

Her lips tightened. "No."

"Yes. I came here to find Richie, and I found him. I found him in all these people here in Meager and at his club. Most of all, I came to find Miller, and I found him. I found him with a family of his own. That's what I've always wanted. To find them. To know them."

"Why do you have to stay here? You have a life in Guymon."

"No, Mom, I don't. I don't. Meager is where I belong. This is where my heart is, and I'm in love with a man here, and I'm staying with him."

Her eyes flared. "With some biker?"

"Yes." I held out my hand to Trick, and he took it and joined me. "This is Trick and we're together."

She cast Trick a swift, cold glance, her eyes narrowing at me. "You're already married."

"That's been over for a very long time." Adrenaline rushed through my system. I had to do it now. Now, here, was perfect. "What I am now is very much in love with Trick and pregnant with our baby."

"Zip?" Trick sputtered.

"It's true. I found out this morning. I wanted to tell you

another way, but I'm glad it's here, all of us gathered together, here with Richie. With our family."

"Yes," said Grace. "Yes!"

"All right!" Willy said loudly.

Trick only stared at me. Numb. Frozen.

I put his hand on my middle. "Babe, you're going to be a daddy. This is happening."

His beautiful face was drawn tightly. "I'm going to be a daddy?"

"The best daddy." I grinned.

Hooting, he grabbed me in an embrace, lifting me up, whirling me around. "I love you, Nic."

"I love you too." I planted a kiss on his lips. A kiss full of promise and delight, of deep, hot joy. Everyone around us cheered and applauded.

"Nicole!"

Trick put me back down on the earth as I met my mother's annoyed gaze. "After we bury Jackson, I'm coming home to South Dakota to be with Trick and raise our child together." A smile formed on my heart the second the words left my lips. I went to her. "You'll always be my mother, and I will always love you."

Her shoulders dropped. "Honey…please."

"You're not losing me."

"I already have!"

"This is my choice, and you need to respect that."

"You don't know what you're doing. You're going backwards."

"No, that's just it. I'm moving forward because this is where my heart is."

Her head jerked back. "Are you trying to make some kind of point here? Trying to punish me?" Her voice was hushed yet harsh. "You think I abandoned my boys without a second thought? Leaving them behind hurt. It stung, but I did what I had to do."

"You did, yes. For yourself." I took her hands in mine. "I know this must be difficult for you, being here, seeing them, I realize that. And I'm sorry you can't be a part of this right now. I truly hope one day, maybe. Maybe. But now, it's impossible."

"How can you abandon me at a time like this?" she bit out.

"I'm not abandoning you. I've always been there for you, for Daddy, for Jackson. Always. This, now is my time, my desire."

Her features twisted into a harsh scowl. Anguish buried in indignation. I knew the varied catalog of her tight expressions so well. But there were no forced smiles from her today, no ignoring the facts and pushing her agenda forward with indirection and distracting suggestions. I'd made my intentions clear. She would retreat, there was no alternative.

Mom pushed my hands away as a strangled cry escaped her lips. My heart twisted in my chest. The loss of a husband, two sons, and yet a third son and grandchild whom she would never know. "I don't understand you at all."

"I know you don't, Mom. But that's okay. We're different."

"Yes. We are. Very, very different." Turning, she charged down the hill. The cool breeze whipped around me, bracing me, and something inside my chest loosened and surged. I took in a long breath of the sweet, fresh air. Trick's arm slid solidly around me. "You okay, Nic?"

"I'm more than okay."

Trick led me back to our family.

Willy had the biggest grin on his face as he talked with Jake. Grace held Thunder in her arms as Jason whispered to him, the two of them chuckling. My gaze settled on Miller, a smile flickering across his austere features. A smile that filled the depths of my soul. A blessing.

My brother lifted his chin at me, and I smiled back.

CHAPTER 56
TRICK

NICOLE WAS LEAVING for Oklahoma today.

I'd woken her up early this morning with my mouth between her legs. I took her there slow and gentle, prolonging her orgasm until she could barely breathe, then I rocked inside her and made love to my woman, slow and steady, tears spilling down the side of her face, as she moaned softly.

I increased the pace of my thrusts. "I want to memorize the feel of you in my arms, around my cock. Memorize the taste of your tongue, your tang. Those lips. Your cries. Mine, all of it mine forever."

"Yes, forever," she breathed.

In the shower I washed her, rubbing her shoulders, rinsing her hair.

Turning around in my arms, she wiped the wet hair back from my face. "Are you worried, babe?"

Emotions had glutted my chest, my throat. I couldn't speak. I busied myself with rinsing her off, my hands skimming over her silky, wet curves. Over her tummy where our baby was growing. I didn't reply. I only slid my hand over her pussy.

"I'll be home in a week." She panted, planting her hands on the tile wall. I bit her shoulder and she came again.

A part of me fully expected to get a phone call in a few days that she'd have to stay just a bit longer. Then that bit longer would turn into another week, another two weeks, until—

Stop it.

We toweled off and got dressed. I admired her tits now firmly encapsulated in the lacy bra she'd just fastened around herself. The urge to bite into her flesh overwhelmed me.

"Are you staring at my boobs?"

"Yup." I grinned, and she laughed as she wiggled her panties on. "They're going to get bigger, aren't they?"

"Oh yeah." I wagged my tongue at her. Grabbing her, my towel fell from my waist as I put my arms around her, pulling her back against me as we both took in our reflection in the mirror. I put my hands on her belly, and we both stared at the mirror in silence.

"I have a little something for you." She moved to the dresser and took out two small wrapped boxes from the top drawer. Two gift boxes wrapped in gold and blue paper. "I wanted to get you something special before I left."

"Uh-huh. To remember you by because you're—"

Warm fingers brushed my lips. "Stop. Because I wanted to mark this occasion—the occasion of us, of our baby."

I broke out into a huge grin and kissed her.

"Open it." She handed me the blue box.

I ripped open the paper and tore off the small lid. A silver necklace lay inside. Hanging at the base was a kind of medallion —three silver lightning bolts melded together. "Zip…"

"It's us, Trick. You, me, and our baby." Her eyes gleamed as she tore open the gold box. "And this is mine. Put it on me." She held a similar necklace, just smaller in size. She moved her hair out of the way and I put it on her. "Jill made them for us. Luckily she had the thunderbolt charms and could do it right away." She immediately took the other necklace, and putting it around my neck, fastened it there.

Her hand stroked the triple bolts over my chest, over my

tattoo. Life and death together. Gain and loss, joy and hurt. "We found each other in a storm of crazy. We crashed into each other by the force of our having dared to take a risk. Like you said. A flare of lighting, the boom of thunder."

"It's beautiful. Fucking perfect."

"I read that in many mythologies, thunder and lightning were considered divine weapons, and I think they're our weapons too. They're our strength, that collision of circumstance and boldness."

"And bravery." He cradled my face with his hands.

"In all that, we created our baby, Trick. We did that."

"We did."

"You're my dream come true, Cooper Watts. You are. From the moment I laid eyes on you, I could feel it. You excited me, you scared me." Tears filled her eyes as she smiled. "You're my home, and I am coming back to you. And it's going to be you, me, our baby, and all our family together here in Meager. And we're never going to be apart again."

"Never." My voice came out rough.

Her hand embraced my neck. "Believe it." Her whisper was rough, heavy.

My forehead slid against hers, my overflowing heart pounding in my chest. "I believe in us, Zip. I believe."

CHAPTER 57

NICOLE

"YOU'RE BACK ALREADY? Both appointments, done?" My mother brushed her hair at her dresser mirror in her bedroom.

"I filed my vote with the board, which went smoothly and quickly. Logan was removed unanimously. And my lawyer is filing the signed divorce papers as we speak."

She put her brush on the dresser. "Congratulations."

"Thank you."

"I made us appointments later this afternoon with Janie."

"I don't need a blowout or a haircut."

"You could use a refresher, that's all. She's been doing your hair for years. Who better to touch it up?" She gave me a pointed look.

"Mom."

"I need a trim, so I thought we could go together. Do a little shopping, have dinner—"

"Mom. I'm leaving tomorrow morning."

"Oh, come on, Buttercup. Stay. Stay for me. Please. It'll be the two of us. We'll have fun."

"You don't need me."

"What a thing to say. Of course, I need you. You're my daughter."

My hand went to my belly. "I have a child that needs me and her daddy. And I need him."

Her face tightened. The past week that I'd been here for Jackson's funeral, my divorce finalization, and the board vote, she hadn't mentioned my pregnancy once. Not once. As if she could will it away with denial.

"I'm going home to Meager tomorrow. And you'll go back to your busy life. You have Melissa and the kids to help out. And a trip to Palm Beach to reschedule."

"That's in two weeks."

"Ah. Nice. Good for you."

"Honey—"

I threw my arms around her. Could I stop her with love? Unconditional daughter love? I hoped so. I hoped it would make a dent. "I love you, Mom."

She wrapped her arms around me and squeezed. "I love you too."

Since I'd been in Oklahoma, Logan was about to be indicted for Jackson's death. Dog had been arrested for the murder of Mr. Rooney, our local loan shark and underworld liaison. And Dog's chapter paid back the Flames and the Jacks what they owed them from that heist of their property.

I'd dropped the charges against Carrie, but before I did, she'd gotten into a violent fight in jail and severely injured the other inmate and a security guard and would be doing a few years of time on that score. My diamond bracelet would be on its way back to me shortly.

Law enforcement was dismantling Raptor's chain of human smuggling, but unfortunately, Raptor hadn't been found yet, which made me uneasy. But I knew the Flames and the Jacks were working hard to find him, and it would only be a matter of time.

A loud rumble filled the air. That sounded like a vintage

muscle car kind of engine that Trick would work on. My heart bolted in my chest, and I darted to the window.

A sleek and shiny black vintage Camaro stood in our driveway. The car door opened and there he was, my man in jeans and a sexy V-neck T-shirt and boots. The silver of his triple bolt necklace against that gorgeous firm chest caught the glare of the sun. Swiping a hand through his thick hair, he slammed the car door shut, and my heart exploded.

"Trick!" I leaned out the window, my hand waving.

His gaze shot up at me, and he grinned. A wide, deep sexy grin. My grin. The sun had risen for me.

"He's here! Trick's here!" I charged through the house and down the stairs.

"Why did he come here? Did you tell him to come? What's going on?" Mom said from behind me.

And there it struck me in the middle of the staircase.

I swiveled around and faced her. "Mom—remember, when I'd found the photo of you and Jason and Miller and you said to me that obviously I'd never been swept away by a passion greater than myself? I have. It's Trick. He's it. And now I know. I've been swept away, but I'm holding on. Trick is the man of my dreams, the dreams I never knew I had."

Her face fell. "Nicole—"

I turned and flew down the stairs. I ran out the door and Trick grabbed me, lifting me up.

"You're here!" I soaked in his hard hug, in his thick muscles holding me tight, in his scent of fresh wood and gasoline and metal.

"I couldn't stay away. Couldn't. Came to bring you home, Zip. Had to come." His voice was full of emotion, and my heart leaped.

"I'm glad you did."

Putting me down, his hands cradled my face. "Are you? You're not mad?"

Trick was here. For me. For us. He'd come all this way.

"I'm thrilled!" I hopped up on my toes and kissed him, diving into his taste that I'd missed so much, that had me soaring. He released me, and I wiped at the edge of my mouth. "You remember my mother?"

"Of course. Ma'am—" He held out his hand to her.

Pursing her lips, she took his hand for the shortest shake I'd ever seen. That didn't matter. It was fine, okay for now or for always. I'd accepted it and I was moving on. "I'll leave you two." She went back into her house.

"I got everything done."

"Everything?"

"The vote, the divorce. Done."

"Terrific, Zip."

"I can't wait to go home."

"See, I was thinking…" That sly grin curled his lips. "When you left here the last time, it was on a wing and a prayer. A jump off a nasty cliff. I thought this time around, you might want to undo that nasty juju and leave with your old man."

"Absolutely, but where's my old man's bike?" I gestured at the car.

"Well, seeing as to how you're pregnant, I didn't think you being on the back of my bike all the way to South Dakota was a smart idea. So I brought this special ride instead."

"Is it yours?"

"No. It's Boner's car, but he lent it to me to bring you home. It was his and Lock's idea. You remember Lock telling you how when Wreck first brought him to Meager, he stole a car from the club and tried to come out here to Oklahoma to find your mom?"

I froze. "This is that car?"

His eyes lit up. "Yep. Back then it belonged to Dig, Grace's first husband, and after, Boner inherited it."

I touched the glossy hood of the car. "Oh my God. She's gorgeous."

"She sure is. I got to work on her a few years ago when Lock refurbished her from top to bottom as a wedding gift to Boner and Jill."

"Wow."

"You remember, Lock got stopped by the police on his way here, so he and the Camaro didn't make it to Oklahoma. But he dared, he risked in this car."

"Yes, he did."

"So, Lock thought you'd want to leave Oklahoma and come home to Meager in this car."

Tears filled my eyes and Trick leaned into me as my fingers stroked the racing stripe detailing. "And I thought maybe—if you're up for it—you could get behind the wheel at some point and drive her. If you want."

My pulse jolted. "I...oh my gosh." My hands flew to my mouth. My heart squeezed. "I want to."

"I knew you'd love it. I love it, too."

I flung myself at him and he lifted me up, my legs wrapping around his middle. "I love you," I whispered. I shouted. I hugged him, my fingers brushing through his thick hair. "Let's go home, babe."

He grinned. "Just what I wanted to hear coming from my old lady's mouth." He kissed me. The flick of his insane tongue sent shivers through my flesh, making all sorts of bright and dark promises.

"Ah, Zip..." His eyes gleamed with water in the sunlight. "You got to know, you found me, and you're bringing me home too."

CHAPTER 58
NICOLE

"HERE COMES THE BRIDE, all dressed in white," Thunder beamed at me as he let go of the end of my long, white empire-cut dress beaded with tiny rhinestones, two long slits on either side, which Lenore had designed and made for me. I clapped for Thunder's song, and he bowed his head to me as if I were a queen.

I am a queen.

"Bouquet!" Thunder handed me my cluster of white peonies tied together with a thick shimmery silver ribbon, and I gave him a kiss on the cheek. "You're so pretty, Aunt Nicole."

"Thank you, my love. And you're super duper handsome today."

He giggled. "Yep."

Jill held a mirror up. "What do you think?"

The hair jewelry she'd made for me as a wedding gift was gorgeous. A bright silver chain twisted into a thin glittery tiara dripping with tiny rhinestones all along my hair.

"It's starlight in my hair. Thank you so much. It's beyond."

"It turned out perfect! Just like I wanted it too."

Jill's handmade treasure matched the diamond droplet earrings I wore, earrings my mother had sent me as a wedding gift. She wasn't here, but she'd sent me a gift, and I valued it knowing that for my mother it was meaningful, it was a step.

"Hey, beautiful bride, you ready?" Lock stood before me in a black dress shirt and black jeans and shiny black boots, his One-Eyed Jacks cut over his shirt.

I stretched out my hand to him. "So ready."

He took my hand in his. My other hand went to my baby bump. "Let's do this."

Grace handed Thunder a small crocheted box with crocheted red hearts all around it, a gift from Carol Anne to hold our wedding rings. My ring bearer, in the same outfit as his dad, complete with a leather vest but without the Jacks logo, straightened his back and took his place in front of me and Lock.

"Everyone set?" Alicia shouted out. She had been the club's "event planner" for years, and even though she was no longer a formal part of the club, she was part of the family and always would be. After talking with Grace, I'd asked Alicia to help me organize our club wedding, and she'd been so touched, so moved, and had done a fantastic job.

"We're all set," replied Tania as she, Grace, Mary Lynn, Jill, and little Becca along with Mary Lynn's two daughters holding baskets of rose petals, took their places in front of Thunder.

Together, we walked through the clubhouse doorway, which was festooned with pink and purple flowers. The heels of my new cowboy boots from Pepper's—black with pink and lilac embroidered vines and flowers that the old ladies had given me as a shower gift—made clacking noises on the cement. Solid and firm footsteps over the earth as I made my way to my happy ever after.

All the men's bikes were lined up in the field behind the clubhouse. So many bikers on either side of us, each engine revving and rumbling, the men shouting and hooting.

A biker wedding.

In Oklahoma, I'd had the huge church wedding and gala reception to end all weddings with each and every glittering detail. This family-only wedding at the clubhouse? Absolutely perfect.

The local pastor, whom I'd met with last month, stood at the head of the line, waiting for us. Before him stood my old man with Dawes, his best man. The two of them smartly dressed in black dress shirts and black jeans, polished boots, and their cuts.

The procession began. Becca and Mary Lynn's girls took the lead, laughing and throwing flowers in the air, the ladies sashaying before us, and Thunder, holding the ring box with great solemnity, ceremoniously stepping down the aisle toward my waiting groom. I caught Lenore's gaze in the crowd. She and Finger were whistling and cheering along with everyone else.

Lock squeezed my hand in his. We'd arrived. He leaned into me and kissed my left cheek and my right. I touched the side of his face. "Thank you. This means the world to me."

He hugged me. "Me too, Nic." He brought my hand to Trick. "Be good to my sister, asshole."

"Way fucking better than good, asshole," Trick said, laughing as he took my hand in his, kissing it. He whispered in my ear. "My gorgeous, gorgeous angel." We took our place in front of the pastor. Grace, my maid of honor, at my side, and Dawes at Trick's side.

The pastor moved forward and welcomed our guests. He recited words about faith and trust, about building a family. About the power of love. Cleansing, redeeming, forgiving, unconditional.

He invited Grace to share a blessing with us. I had no idea what it was—a passage from the Bible or an excerpt from a favorite book or song? She'd been quite mysterious about it too. The pastor moved to the side and Grace took his place.

"For Nicole and Trick, I wanted to offer a breath of good wishes from her brother Wreck, who had offered these very words to me a long time ago in this very spot. I'd written them down back then because they were that special to me. A simple gift from a wise and loving man who touched all our lives. I can now pass them on to you today as you exchange your rings with Willy's help."

My heart drummed in my chest, and Trick and I exchanged glances as he squeezed my hand.

Go ahead, son," Lock urged Thunder forward, a hand on his back.

Thunder came forward bearing his ring box. He held it high as Willy also moved forward. Willy reached into the box and took out a black band and gave it to Trick.

"Trick," said Grace. "Please repeat after me as you put the ring on your old lady's finger. Nicole is your woman." Trick held my hand in his suddenly shaky one and slid the ring on my finger, holding it there against the diamond solitaire ring he'd given me a few weeks back. "Shield her heart and soul with your own."

"Nicole," breathed Trick. "You're my woman. And I will shield your heart and soul with my own."

You did from the very first, my love. You do every day.

"Nicole," Grace said as Willy took the other black band from Thunder's pillowed box and gave it to me. "Trick is your man." I slid the ring on my old man's finger. "He's yours to support and keep strong when he's not able and when he doesn't know how."

"Trick, you are my man. And you're mine to support and keep strong when you're not able and when you don't know how."

"Bring it home, Willy," said Grace with a smile.

Willy put a hand over our clasped hands, a firm grasp, and my gaze fell to the matching tattoos around my and Trick's wrists, mine in henna until after I'd had the baby—a zip tie to always remember, to always celebrate how far we'd come.

I'd taken a risk and gotten tied to a fence, and against all the rules and reasons not to, Trick had clipped that harsh bind from my wrist and set us both free.

That was our love. Sordid beginnings, epic evolution. Love required a bold risk, didn't it?

"Trick and Nicole," Willy's strong voice rang out. "You take care of each other, and you do it right. Do it well. Real well," he chuckled and the guests broke out into hoots and cheers, and we laughed. "All right, settle down!" He cleared his throat. "And always, but always—" his voice became serious, a touch rough. "Always be fair." Releasing our hands, he whooped and clapped and whistled loudly, and everyone joined in, cheering and hooting and whistling.

"Can I kiss my old lady now?" shouted out Trick, and I threw back my head and laughed.

"Hold on!" said the pastor. "By the power vested in me by the state of South Dakota, I now declare you husband and wife. Kiss your wife, Trick!"

Trick lifted me up and kissed me and kissed me and kissed me, our heartbeats colliding with the exploding roar of the motorcycles, the shouts and cheers of the Jacks.

All the Jacks. A swell of pride and passion that knew no bounds. One-Eyed Jacks past and present, here at the clubhouse in Meager, our patch of the glorious Blacks Hills of South Dakota where my and Trick's roads had led us.

Later, as I danced with my husband, his body curled around mine, his mellow gaze promising me the world, I knew.

This is where I was always meant to be.

Somehow in this convergence of extreme circumstances, in my risk-laden choices I knew that I had a small hand in bringing to light the shards of our lives, the jagged sharper blood-laden ones we'd kept hidden under our hearts and denied for so very long. That hunger, that age-old need.

Now they are mending, rearranging in a new, unexpected way. A glorious way. I knew that diamonds were not as precious as the stars you savored in the sky, not as precious as a worn leather bracelet with a few colored glass beads, that tiny souvenir of a haunted past that thrust me into my brighter future.

That I was finally part of that rhythm, that beat, that vibration that was created decades before my birth, that was jolted and torn asunder. And yet through my firm belief that there was hope for us all, together we have mended and sealed its shorn and ravaged edges and healed so many bruises.

That rhythm is alive.

I feel it on the road on the back of Trick's bike, I feel it in the warm press of my husband's hand, of his chest against mine in the quiet of the night, in the eager hug of my nephew, in the dark gleaming eyes of my brother. In the leap of our child inside me.

Oh, what a blessed gift.

That is the gift I was given and pass on through my laughter, through our love, through my blood. *His* from a generation ago, it is mine, it is ours. Grows and grows.

Endures, always.

BOOKS BY CAT PORTER

- Lock & Key MC Romance Series -

Reading Order

1 - Lock & Key - Lock & Grace

2 - Random & Rare - Dig | Lock & Grace

3 - Iron & Bone - Boner & Jill

4 - Blood & Rust - Butler & Tania

5 - Fury - Finger & Lenore

6 - Lock & Key Christmas - Lock & Grace

7 - The Dust and the Roar - Wreck & Isi

8 - The Fire and the Roar - more Wreck & Isi

9 - The Year of Everything - everyone in High School

10- Thunder & Flare - Trick & Nicole

The Lock & Key MC Romance series - The Boxed Set - books 1-4

Boxed Set of books 1-4

- The Wind & the Roar Duet -

Beck & Violet - Friends-to-Lovers Rockstar Romance

*(*Same small town as Lock & Key series*)*

1- Whirlwind

2 - Whisperwind

Dagger in the Sea - Turo & Adri

Mediterranean Romantic Suspense Adventure

- Unraveled Destiny Series -

Steamy Arranged Marriage Historical Romance

ABOUT THE AUTHOR

CAT PORTER was born and raised in New York City, but also spent a few years in Europe and Texas along the way, which made her as wanderlusty as her parents. As an introverted, only child, she loved reading and going to the movies, and had very big, but very secret dreams for herself.

She graduated from Vassar College, was a struggling actress, an art gallery girl, special events planner, freelance writer, restaurant hostess, and had all sorts of other crazy jobs all hours of the day and night in New York to help make her dreams come true.

She has two children's books traditionally published under her maiden name.

She now lives on a beach outside of Athens, Greece with her husband, three children, and four huge Cane Corsos, freaks out regularly, still daydreams way too much, and now truly doesn't give AF.

She is addicted to reading, classic films, cafe bars on the beach, the Greek islands, Instagram, Pearl Jam and U2, bourbon she brought home from Nashville and whiskey she brought home from Dublin, and realllllly good coffee.

Writing has always kept her somewhat sane, extremely happy, and a productive member of society.

www.catporter.com

Email - catporter103@gmail.com

Sign up for my CatList to receive Trick & Nicole's bonus
epilogue: https://www.subscribepage.com/tf_epilog

amazon.com/author/catporter

bookbub.com/authors/cat-porter

instagram.com/catporter.writer

twitter.com/catporter103

pinterest.com/catporter103

tiktok.com/@catporter_writer

facebook.com/CatPorterWriter

www.ingramcontent.com/pod-product-compliance
Lightning Source LLC
Chambersburg PA
CBHW030951190726
48285CB00004BB/1305